Droplets

MEAGHAN RAUSCHER

Droplets

For my sister, Lauren, without your encouragement and patience this story would not exist.

ACKNOWLEDGEMENTS

《》

Enormous thanks to CreateSpace for giving me the ability to publish my work and share it with the world. To Kasey Kavanaugh, for her enthusiasm and generosity that has helped this series become what it is and for heading social media outreach. To Kjersten Johnson, for her wonderful and witty editing and funny comments in the margins. To Laura Gordon at Book Cover Machine, for the wonderful cover design. To Kayla Sanner, for her constant support and work.

To my parents, grandparents and many siblings; thank you for your love and encouragement over the last few years. Thank you for being my first readers and critics. Your opinions matter the most.

And to Lauren, words cannot express how much it means to me that over the past few years you listened and helped this story come to life. Thank you for talking about these characters as though they are real people and for providing suggestions that keep my mind working. You were there from day one on this story, and I could not ask for a better person to be Lissie's number one fan.

Droplets

MEAGHAN RAUSCHER

Contents

《》

Prologue

Finally, it was all falling into place. How long had he waited for this moment to feel accepted and acknowledged as a man? His father may be a lord of great recognition throughout all of England, but he was nothing compared to his first born son. He knew he would be the greatest of the Walsh family to have ever lived.

Looking up at the stormy sky he turned and moved along the beach. His dark, heavy cloak tugged at his strong frame while the waves crashed severely upon the sandy shore. Droplets of rain created little divots on the grainy ground. With each thud of the rain he felt his heart skip a beat. His future was bright and clear. *Much clearer than this sky.*

Curling his lip, he whistled and Hector bounded towards him. The old hunting hound had found something interesting to smell a ways back and came prancing over to his master with a lopsided, panting grin. The dog knew he was supposed to stay by his master's side, but what did it hurt to let the hound have some leniency in his old age?

"Come on," he spoke softly, running his hand over the boney head of the grey dog who'd been his companion for the last eight years.

Sensing a change in the wind, Hector raised his nose in the air. Tail poised behind him, the dog pointed his snout down the beach, eyes fixed upon something in the distance.

"What are you looking at old boy?" the young man laughed, and rubbed the dog's head once more. Nothing could keep his spirits down. Not tonight.

Turning on his heel, the sand scrunched beneath his boot and lifting his eyes forward he froze. *There she is.*

The picture of incarnate beauty perched upon a rock with the sea lapping up against its base. Her pale white skin shone brightly beside the dark dress that covered her slim frame. Long, dark tresses cascaded over her shoulders grazing the boulder upon which she sat. Her face was turned away from him, but he knew she was aware of his presence. She had been so acute the last time they met. At his side, Hector growled, his fur standing on end.

Her head turned slowly, the black hair rippling in the wind with perfect ease. Once her eyes met his own he felt drawn to her, just like last time. *No, this is different. I don't need her anymore and she never came back for me.*

"I am happy to see you again," her voice was like honey sucking him in. Everything about her enticed him and yet every part of his body wanted to flee. She looked the same as before, but something was different. An urgency coursed through her, some excitement that he didn't want to name.

"I know, I promised you last time," he said confidently, trying to override the mounting fear in his chest. "But I cannot help you anymore."

Her lips curled back in a grin and she ran her tongue over her lower lip. "I was hoping that wouldn't be the case. It's time for us to go. I offered you a long life, and a place to conquer the world while ruling by my side. You agreed."

Begrudging his foolish judgment from two years prior, he took a step back and shook his head. "Whether or not I agreed, I cannot fulfill your obligations anymore, my lady."

A soft laugh escaped her lips and she brightened in complexion. A burning filled her eyes and swallowing hard he stepped back. *She looks at me as though she owns me, as though I belong to her.*

"You have a choice. You can come willingly or" she tilted her head to the side, "I can force you."

On any other day he would have laughed if a woman had ever dared to threaten him. He was the most skilled swordsman in the county, upheld by all with knighthood in his future. But here and now he felt the weight of her words. The gleam in her eyes told him that there was more to her than what met his eye.

"I will not go." He said with more force this time even though his insides were shaking with fear. Her responding laughter irked his pride and made him angry. Once more he stepped back, Hector followed his lead. The way the dog's fur ruffled warned him further of what kind of danger this woman withheld.

Looking down, the darkly clad woman reached out her hand and touched something behind the rock. Obscured by her body for only a moment, a child stepped out into the open. The boy's face was pale, as pale as the skin of the woman sitting in black. He watched as the young boy's hair rippled slowly and noticed how the sharp, grey eyes of the child were aged with time. Stepping forward, the boy came closer.

Pulling out his sword, the young man waited, unsure of what to do. Hector growled loudly, lips curling back over his teeth and nose twitching in anticipation.

He stood resolute, waiting. The boy walked close ignoring Hector and strode around them in a circle. *Who is this child? Certainly not hers.*

In response to his thoughts, the boy looked back at the woman and she nodded her head in approval. Still holding the sword tight in his hand, the young man shifted closer to Hector. But the boy reached out and snatched the dagger from the belt at the young man's own waist. Before he could move, the boy plunged the sharp medal into Hector's chest. With a howl of piercing pain, the dog crippled to the sandy shore.

A silent scream issued from his mouth. The hand that held his sword shook violently as the little boy yanked the bloodied dagger from the old dog's body. Still frozen, he watched the young boy and then the dagger was in his own flesh. It sliced deeply across his thigh, crippling him to the ground. With a cry of pain, he held his hand over the wound as oozing blood pulsed through his fingers.

The woman was suddenly standing above him. She reached for the dagger in the boy's hand and replaced it in its sheath. Her pale fingers moved swiftly as she grasped him underneath the shoulders. He struggled, but as if from nowhere a blade appeared at his throat. He froze.

"It's time to go." She said into his hair and dragged him heavily toward the ocean.

His mind clouded. Eyes taking in everything, the shore, the boy, the woman, his leg, and his dog lying dead upon the ground next to his fallen sword. The waves crashed louder, pounding in his ears until they ran over his legs. He bit back a shameful cry of pain as the icy water flooded into his open wound.

"It is time," the smooth voice spoke gently above him, the urgency evident. "The future waits."

A wave smashed over his head and took his breath away. He felt himself being pulled into the depths of the water, moving faster than he could have ever believed possible.

But his only thought was for the dagger in his belt.

He would wait for the right moment.

1. Murmur

It was my favorite time to be on the ocean. The sun was just meeting the horizon and bright brushes of rosy oranges and pinks splattered across the sky.

Ever since I was a little girl I had thought it was the most beautiful thing anyone could witness. I liked to watch the colors unfold across the sky as the sun sank lower and lower— eventually completely hidden from view.

"Still watching the sunset I see." The familiar voice came from behind me.

I knew what would come next: it would either be an annoying hug, a pinch on the shoulder, a smack on the back, or a knuckle to the head. These sorts of "greetings" were passed out by my nineteen year old twin brothers who continued to greet me this way even though I had turned seventeen last month. For some reason they refused to see me as anything but a little girl and I had long since given up trying to understand it; it must have something to do with their older brother instincts.

A pair of muscular arms came and rested along the railing beside mine. "It's always amazed me how you can look at the sunset for so long." Derek, who was older than his twin Sean by two minutes, waved his hand toward the skyline. "I just don't have your patience."

"Like I didn't know that," I said sarcastically and rolled my eyes.

We both laughed. It was common knowledge that Derek didn't have much patience for anything; he took after our father in that way. They were both always on the go, never stopping.

Sean, the other twin, was different. He was more like me: able to slow down and take in the world without worrying about what needed to be done next.

We continued to stare out across the open sea, each lost in our own thoughts in the companionable silence.

We were on the deck of my father's yacht which was only used on rare occasions because vacation was not a word that often fit into Dad's vocabulary. The yacht was named after my great-great-grandmother: the *Lady Marie*. She was the wife of my great-great-grandpa, the founder of the Darrow family fishing business. The boat, which was fairly new, had four bedrooms and a small kitchen. Over the past few years, the Darrow fishing business had exploded into a company which contained ten lobster boats and a large crew of men, along with a restaurant in town. With the business growing, my dad was able to purchase the yacht to use for family use.

For the men in my family, lobster fishing ran in their blood. My father had lived in Coveside, Maine for his entire life and was a lobsterman just like my grandfather, great-grandfather, and great-great-grandfather. My dad carried on many great family traditions including running the family restaurant the "Darrow's Catch." This business was his pride and joy, and both would pass onto my twin brothers someday.

The Darrow family followed old customs. Being a female I had never worked on one of the fishing boats. Instead, I was a waitress on the weekends at the restaurant. In the restaurant, everything on the menu was made from scratch and only the women, who had been born and raised a Darrow, knew the recipes. These recipes had been passed down from generation to generation. You could ask me about any appetizer, soup, entrée, or dessert and I would be able to spout off all of the ingredients from memory.

I could even recall my aunts teaching me how to make the lobster chowder, our specialty, when I was barely able to talk. *They* taught me because my mother had died in a car accident when I was five years old. At the time, Dad was unsure of what to do with me and my brothers. For the most part we lived with our relatives while he was gone on extended fishing trips, but this came to an end when I was seven and he married my stepmom Jillian. She was as much a part of our family as the rest of us, and through her our family grew. There have been five additions to our family, ranging from eight to two years old, with one more on the way. We make a large group, but it works; the love I feel at home is unlike any other feeling in the world.

Startling out of my thoughts, I scanned the horizon and noticed that the sun was only half visible: just a soft orange arch gently grazing the ocean surface. I couldn't believe how fast it had set, much like how quickly the past three days had flown by.

Each year as a tradition, my brothers, father, and I would go on a one week getaway aboard the *Lady Marie* just before school started. I always treasured these moments I had with just my brothers and Dad, for they were the most important people in my life.

There were too many memories tied to the ocean, weeks spent in the sun, fishing, talking, and laughing. I remembered playing cards, jumping on the bunks below, helping steer one of the lobster boats through the waves, listening to Dad tell his tales of the sea—and the memories kept coming, each one precious in its own way.

"What are you smiling at, Lissie?" It was Sean who spoke.

I had been so lost in my thoughts that I hadn't seen him join us at the railing. His eyes searched mine curiously.

"Nothing," I shrugged, "Just thinking about how nice it is to finally spend some time with you guys. It's been forever since we've been able to do something like this." I waved my hand as if the movement described the past week.

"That's true, we don't see each other as often anymore," Sean said as a sly grin crept across his face. "Especially now that you have dates every weekend with—"

He broke off in a grunt when I elbowed him in the ribs.

Both Derek and Sean knew I had no romantic life. Aside from Jonathan, who I sat next to in most of my classes, I had never really been involved with the other sex. Sure I had had my crushes, but what girl hasn't? But they had never really amounted to anything. I decided that when I fell in love I wanted it to be special, and with someone who would love me unconditionally. My hopes were a bit above par for being in high school, and so I chose not to worry about it and instead kept my head focused on more important things.

"Whoa, I think someone just got touchy! Don't you think, Derek?"

"You know what? You couldn't be more right!"

I opened my mouth to protest, but Derek grabbed me about the waist and I shrieked instead. He held his fingers in midair above my ribs, taunting me with the fear that he would get me in my ticklish spot. I started to laugh despite the indignity of it all.

"Now come on, Lissie. Tell us who the handsome devil is," Sean prodded jokingly.

He leaned over and squeezed my leg right above the knee; I yelped. It was another one of my very ticklish spots.

"Hey! That's no fair!" I said, laughing so hard I could scarcely breathe, "You know that spots just as bad as my ribs!"

"Oh! Really?" I shrieked again and ducked beneath Derek's arms, laughing as I stumbled away from them on the deck.

"What is going on out here?" Dad spoke from behind me with a soft chuckle in his voice.

"The usual," I shrugged, "I was being tormented."

Dad smiled, "Well remind me to beat them up later."

The twins grinned at one another. Dad's challenge was exactly what they wanted. They believed they could beat him in a wrestling match, but I knew better.

"Please do," I waved towards them and was rewarded with identical devilish smiles, which made me giggle. My brothers couldn't look evil even if they tried.

With dimples in their right cheeks, light blonde hair, and blue eyes, they looked more angelic than devilish. They had inherited these looks from Dad, and even had his stature along with similar mannerisms. Aside from Dad's rough blonde beard, they looked like younger versions of him.

I, on the other hand, was sort of unique.

I shared their golden blonde hair, but my eyes were a mystery. No one related to me had my color eyes; they were a sort of greenish-blue—almost a turquoise. Dad liked to call them sea-green because I loved the ocean so much, and he told me that when I was younger the water had changed my eyes because I swam as much as a mermaid.

"Alright, kids, I'm starving. Let's go eat some dinner." Dad placed a protective arm around my shoulders and pulled me toward the cabin that would lead us to the kitchen below.

Later that night, after throwing a gray sweatshirt over my head, I paused to look in the little mirror hanging on the wall of my bedroom. My suitcase was open on the floor, its contents spread out in a great radius. I had to balance myself while putting up my ponytail as the gentle swaying of the boat rocked the mirror from side to side.

The girl looking back at me was the same as she had always been: plain. I had never found myself to be pretty, only decent-looking. There really was nothing special about me; my hair was simply golden blonde, and it fell about my shoulders in wavy ringlets.

My sea-green eyes stood out from the rest of me if I wore certain colors, especially lavender, but I normally avoided these because they would attract attention. Maybe it was because when I was young Derek and Sean had made fun of me, saying I looked more like a fairy than a human. Whatever the reason, I tried to blend in with everyone else wherever I went—never doing or wearing anything to make myself stand out.

Shaking my head from my thoughts, I hurried out of the room and climbed up towards the deck. Stepping into the night air I smiled to myself: it was a perfect night. The stars were shining brilliantly without any man-made light to pale their existence, and a soft breeze blew gently, lifting strands of my hair over my face. Shaking them out of the way, I walked to the bow of the *Lady Marie*, my favorite spot.

I sat down with my back to the point of the boat, forearms resting on my knees, and breathed in the fresh smell of the ocean. My eyes flickered up to the stars once more and gazed at their beautiful patterns and shapes. I began to hum a soft tune to myself and before long was singing out loud.

It was almost eerie to hear my voice mix with the rhythm of the waves hitting the *Lady Marie*. Its rhythm changed the tune of the songs, and I found myself making up simple rhymes to go along with the slap-slapping of the waves. Time passed as I sat there at the front of the boat singing to myself; I was in a world of my own.

Gradually as I sang a sound reached my ears. It was different from the sounds of the thudding water, or the soft wind as it whispered by. It was strange and beautiful, a soft murmur, just barely noticeable.

I continued to sing but a little bit softer trying to figure out where the noise was coming from. My ears told me it came from over the edge of the boat, but my mind wouldn't let such a crazy thought take root.

The soft murmur moved in and out, and up and down with my voice. A sense of foreboding began to pound in my veins. I felt as though I was not the only one breathing in the silence; as though *someone* rather than something was singing along with me. Though I was petrified with fear, I couldn't stop. There was a deep curiosity that made me want to continue this strange duet.

Cautiously, I began to sing louder—coaxing the murmur to join me. When my voice reached a new pitch the murmur joined in, and yet I still couldn't tell what it was exactly. It was beautiful and hardly above a softly spoken conversation.

The murmur spoke no words; its voice mumbled softly as it danced in intricate patterns around the lyrics. Sometimes it would match my tune and follow along, other times it would go off into its own rhythm.

I moved from one song to the next, hardly speaking the words, voicing both jaunty melodies and mournful ballads. The slow songs caused the murmur to join in with a stronger voice. In a way I felt that it enjoyed these slow and beautiful tunes more than the fast, upbeat songs. I don't know how long I sang, but eventually I couldn't think of any more songs. My voice stopped abruptly, as did the murmur's.

The peace that had come while I was singing with the murmur disappeared. I had a strange feeling that whatever had been singing with me was not natural or safe. My ears strained for any noise that would give whoever or whatever it was away.

I could hardly hear anything above the loud, quick beat of my heart. My hands were cold as if no blood was reaching them. I didn't want to move a muscle for fear of missing a sound; for a long time I sat barely breathing above a whisper.

With the fear came logic; I must have been kidding myself. Common sense told me I was just imagining the murmur and it had not been there, but the other part of me knew I was lying.

It was probably just an echo, or it could be my brothers pulling a prank on me. They were probably watching my horrified face and about to yell, "Got you!" This was an assumption that I could live with. I was satisfied with it and stood to make my way back inside.

Trying to act casual, to show Derek and Sean I was unafraid, I paused to look out across the sea. Then, because my mind had to know, I leaned over the side of the boat just to prove there was nothing there.

A loud splash resonated from the water right beneath me. I strained my eyes, seeing large ripples in the water. My eyes scanned the black liquid frantically, trying to find where the thing that had been the murmur went.

Finally I saw something. Out in the distance, there was a bright and shiny rippling pillar in the water. It continued to move back and forth, as if in perfect rhythm with the waves. It was a strip, no longer than a human body but, it undulated as if it had no distinct form.

I was captivated by it and could not pull my eyes away.

The shiny form stayed there in the same spot, just below the surface, tempting, and captivating me. Though I saw no eyes, I felt it watching me. The form continued to ripple in the water looking at me with that invisible stare and I gazed back. I was drawn in by it with acute curiosity.

Not thinking, I stuck my hand out as if to beckon the peculiar form back to me. Quick as a blink, the glowing form turned around, plunged into the depths of the ocean, and was gone.

Stunned for a moment, my hand froze in midair while my mind raced. What could that have been? What sort of *thing* shined silver like the moon, but within the ocean?

A shiver ran down my spine. My palms grew sweaty and my legs wobbly. I had no idea what I had just seen. I knew I was clearly awake, everything felt too real and alive to be a dream. For a moment I stood not knowing what to do or where to go. It was strange to stay out here by myself, yet I could not calm down.

The minutes passed and my mind slowly began to regain control. I told myself to settle down, knowing I wouldn't be able to show my face to my father or brothers if I was this wired.

After what seemed like days, my heart returned to its normal rhythm. I took a steadying breath and made my way along the length of the deck to the cabin.

I didn't know what I had seen in the water, but I wouldn't think about it until later. I had to get inside and act normal; the weird murmur would just have to wait to consume my thoughts completely.

2. Storm

Glaring at the horrid red clock across the room, my eyes tried to focus. The numbers on it continued to disappoint me. It was two o'clock in the morning and I was still unable to fall asleep.

I needed to calm down, but I couldn't. Every time I closed my eyes I saw the odd shiny form in the water. It flickered behind my eyelids, taunting my existence. The very presence of the fantastical murmur threw everything I thought to be real into doubt and I would go crazy tossing and turning the thoughts over in my mind. Quickly, the fear of the unknown would take hold and I would open my eyes once more.

Nothing I could think of described what I had seen and heard. There was no concrete answer for the combination of the two. I had never heard anything make a sound so pure, and yet so chilling; nor had I ever seen a form that was so beautiful. The only thing that compared to it was the reflection of a full moon glinting off a slowly moving river. Yet, there was something more to it. The feeling of being watched had been too real for me to now disregard. It had felt conscious and calculating, as though it followed my every move. It had felt *human*.

The thought sent a sudden shiver of fear down my spine and I pulled the comforter on my bed up to my chin, while curling into a tight ball. I tried to get rid of the eerie thoughts.

I jumped from subject to subject, trying to think of anything to make myself fall asleep. My brain would not cooperate, however.

Frustrated I rolled onto my stomach and tried to place my limbs in a comfortable position that would tempt them into sleep. It didn't work. Both my brain and body were far from rest. Yet, sometime in the night, my exhausted mind finally drifted off.

I was outside. A cold wind hit my face, chilling me to the bone. Across the air, a sound rose above the wind. I wanted it to stop, but it only pressed harder against my ears. It was coming from right behind me, getting closer and closer. I could feel its breath on my neck as it continued to move in a tune, unaware of my stiffness. Slowly, the murmur began to change. It gradually became a voice that sang words rather than notes. It was breathtakingly beautiful and yet part of me was more scared than I had ever been before. Tears sprung to my eyes at its beauty, and I knew that if it asked me to do anything, I would. I was its prisoner, stuck in a web of lyric and melody. But then, just as I was about to surrender everything I knew to it, the words drifted away and a loud whirring took its place. The murmur sounded angry, whereas before it had been calming and peaceful. It was loud, desperate, and almost violent. I wanted to run but couldn't. I looked down at my feet on the deck and urged them, willed them, to move, but my body wouldn't respond. Then the deck began to tip, and the sound that had once been a murmur grew louder. It was almost deafening. I looked into the water and saw the silver form waiting for me. A loud scream escaped my throat as I hit the icy water....

My head smacked something hard and I opened my eyes to a soft blur. Confused, I sat up and waited for my eyes to adjust. I groaned, realizing my forehead had smashed into the wall beside my bed. I rubbed the spot on my head that had been hit; and hoped it wouldn't bruise.

A loud droning buzzed in my ear: a continuous, deafening roar. It grew louder, filling me with fear as I remembered my dream. Goosebumps rose on my flesh and I rubbed my arms to ward off the cold. Fear filled me as I thought about having to relive the nightmare.

The *Lady Marie* was tipping from side to side. The tremendous roar was coming from outside, and the soft rain from earlier had turned into thundering pellets. We must have hit a rough patch of weather; it wasn't the first time this had happened.

With an exhausted yawn, I looked at the clock across the room, which dictated it was five in the morning. I had been asleep much longer than I thought. Shivering, I pulled my comforter up to my chin and again drifted off to sleep.

It seemed mere minutes before I woke again. Frustrated, I looked across the room to see what time it was, but my clock was not on the dresser. I searched the room, but could not focus because the room was moving, as though jumping up and down. The walls swayed about making my eyes dizzy and my head spin. I tried to search the room for the missing clock, but it was moving and swaying and I was too dizzy to see it.

The wind outside screamed in cacophony with the constant thud of the waves hitting the side of the boat. The gray, dull light seeping in through the window seemed to squeeze me, trapping me alone in my bed as I was jostled about by the continuous rocking.

Trying not to panic, I forced my mind to stay calm even though my heart was racing within my chest. If I let myself, I could conjure up millions of visions of us drowning at sea. My hands felt like ice and I tried not to give into the visions wracking my mind.

Not wanting to be alone, I jumped out of bed, changed into a pair of jeans, threw on a coat, and hurried out of the room. Staying calm while being by myself would be an impossible task, I needed others to distract my fears.

"…and now I don't know what to do. I've never been in a situation like this." Dad sounded worried.

"Ah, come on we've been through worse than this." Derek assertively said. Though he sounded confident, there was an edge to his voice as though he, too, was nervous.

"No," Dad grumbled. "All we can do is wait it out. That rock took off the whole rudder, we are at the mercy of the storm now."

Took off the rudder. I stood in the hallway bracing myself against the rocking of the ship. Did that mean we could no longer steer? How would we get home? Panic threatened to take hold, but I pushed it back knowing it would do no good. I had to trust my father, the seasoned sailor.

"Once the storm is over we can fix it, we just have to wait for it to finish." Sean's voice was low, but his words rang with optimism. Of course he would be the one to find the silver lining in all of this. Dad grunted in agreement.

In the silence, I decided it was time to make my presence known. Acting like I had just walked down the hall and hadn't heard everything they had been saying, I stepped into the room.

In unison they turned and smiled at me, attempting to hide the truth. But I could see the stress in the worried lines on each forehead.

"Good morning," Derek greeted kindly. His twin sat beside him holding a thermos, and he smiled softly at me; with effort I smiled back.

"Don't worry about the storm, everything is going to be fine," Dad reassured as he reached for my hand and pulled me towards the table.

I nodded, knowing my voice would betray how scared I really was. I took a seat at the table across from my brothers. Both of them were eyeing me with careful expressions. Suddenly a great crack of thunder split the steady thrum of the rain. We all jumped in our seats, and I bit my lip, a nervous habit. Sean grasped my hand under the table and gave it a gentle reassuring squeeze.

"Sheesh! Your hand is freezing! Is there any circulation going on in that little body of yours?"

I shrugged, "I'm just a little nervous is all."

Dad cleared his throat, "Everything is going to be fine. In fact I wouldn't be surprised if it is over in a couple hours. It came in so fast; it will probably leave even faster."

The storm did not leave quickly. It wasn't gone in a couple hours; in fact it had yet to leave when eight hours had passed.

My nerves were shot and my muscles incredibly stiff from being flexed and stressed for so long. I really tried to relax and pay attention to the card games we played, but I could never get rid of the nagging fright. It was impossible to settle down and not worry.

Dad, Derek, and Sean were beginning to get as nervous as I was. They couldn't believe the storm had gone on for this long. They knew we were being blown far off course and charting into unknown areas.

The card game we had been playing for the past three hours had practically become unmanageable. The *Lady Marie* was now rocking so much that the cards were sliding right off the table. As though the sea had heard my thoughts, it began to toss the ship even more than before. Dad threw down his cards with a sigh and we all followed suit, watching them slip onto the floor. We swayed with the motions of the boat, rocking backwards as the *Lady Marie* climbed a wave, crested, and then in a breathtaking moment plunged back to the water below. Each wave knocked the air from my lungs, jolting all thought, aside from survival, from my mind.

Unexpectedly, a huge jolt hit the front of the ship. Dad was sent sideways out of his chair onto the floor and Derek tumbled backwards while Sean grabbed the table and held onto it in order to stay up right. I was thrown forward, my mid-section hitting the edge of the bolted-down table and I let out a large yelp of pain.

I looked about and saw that I was on a slope above Dad and my brothers. I waited for the *Lady Marie* to go crashing back down into the waves, but it didn't move. She stayed tilted up and motionless. Creaks and groans resonated throughout the cabin while waves hit the outside of her with throbbing pounds.

Dad was still lying on the floor, a mask of horror upon his face. He looked at the boys.

"She's been hit," tumbled out of his mouth before he could stop them.

My frantic voice filled the strained moment. "What do you mean she's been hit?"

Dad would not meet my eyes. He seemed to be trying to communicate something secret with my brothers.

"What's going on?" I pleaded, "Dad, look at me, please tell me what is going on!" He still had not turned.

"Dad!" I shouted. Finally he looked at me. What I saw in his face frightened me even more.

"Lissie, I need you to go into your room and stay there," Dad held up a hand as I began to protest. "Derek, Sean, and I are going to go up on deck to check the damage."

"Damage! What damage? How do you know there's damage?"

"I think," the words came from Derek, his voice strangled as if he couldn't believe he was saying this, "I think we have run aground."

I tried to wrap my brain around the words. He couldn't possibly mean them *for real*. He had to have been joking. But the waves were there as proof, pounding the side but no longer moving the *Lady Marie*. Choking on my own words, I spoke.

"Do you think she will go down?" The answer I received was a shrug from one brother, and a bewildered shake of the head from his twin.

Struggling to do as Dad said, I braved the thought of sitting by myself in my room, and began to walk down the now sloping hall. I could hear the others following me, though they turned and climbed the stairs that would lead them to the deck, rather than go to my room. I stumbled on through the darkness, jumping every time a wave hammered the *Lady Marie*'s side.

Sitting on the floor with my back against the wall, I began to worry. I had no idea if anything was going to happen to them while they were up there. The minutes ticked by slowly and I rocked myself back and forth.

I was past frightened now: I was terrified. I couldn't wait to be back home on solid ground. If only this storm would stop, then we could just relax and fix the problem.

My body continued to shake; I could hardly take the stress of being by myself anymore. With shaking hands, I crawled under my bed to pull out the clock that glared brightly in the room. I determined that I would wait five more minutes before going up.

I watched the clock as it slowly ticked off the minutes. Finally, the five minutes were up; I dashed to the door and ran for the stairs.

The great spattering of the rain swept over me as I stepped out on deck. I pulled the hood of my jacket over my head as the water began to forcefully pelt my face from every direction. I had hardly been on deck for more than a few seconds, yet was drenched from head to toe.

My eyes searched the deck through the sheet of rain and found Dad and Derek leaning over the edge and Sean nowhere to be seen.

They were yelling at one another over the rain. I slowly walked towards them, slipping slightly with each step. I was able to hear over the rushing storm what they were saying.

"We can't reverse her off the rocks. She's stuck." Dad's voice was furious and frustrated.

"We've got to do something! Every minute she's getting weaker. She's not going to be able to stand these waves much longer. Eventually they're going to crush her!"

"What do you want me to do, Derek? We can't back her up or we might lose the motor as well. If we get in a lifeboat we'll drown for sure. We can't call for help because there's no signal. So what do you want me to do?" He was beyond frustrated, "All we can do is sit and hope she holds."

Fear gripped my body as I listened to them. Wanting to find solace, I looked for Sean. As I searched the deck I turned about to look for him and a massive gray shape in the distance caught my attention. I stood transfixed, peering through the rain at the large form which stretched across the horizon. It looked like an enormous cloud that was moving ever closer. I strained my eyes even more to see what it was exactly. Slowly, chills spread over my wet skin and my eyes widened as understanding hit me: a massive wave was headed straight for the *Lady Marie*.

My mind racing, I whipped around. Dad and Derek were still arguing over what to do, completely unaware of the wave. Thinking quickly, I rushed towards them. This was a killer wave and it was going to strike the *Lady Marie* and strike her hard.

My boots slipped on the slick deck and I smacked into Derek's side as he turned, catching me.

"Are you all right? What are you doing up here?"

Thinking my voice wouldn't work, I turned and pointed to the huge wave, that was getting closer every second, while my hand shook in the pelting rain. I watched as their faces changed from confusion to realization and then to horror. Dad yelled, "Hurry, get inside! Sean, get over here!"

I looked to the left and saw Sean bounding up the sloped deck. Derek grabbed my hand and tugged me hard towards the cabin. Dad was just in front of us and Sean, being the faster runner, joined him.

The wave came ever closer. It was coming faster and faster; I pumped my legs, desperate to make it inside.

Dad and Sean were in and moved to make room for us. All of a sudden my boots slid out from under me on the slippery deck. I let go of Derek's hand to brace my fall. I hit the deck with a groan, and Derek was a few steps in front of me before he realized what had happened and turned around.

"No, run!" I yelled desperately and jumped to my feet. He saw me get up and continued the mad dash for the cabin door.

The wave was almost upon us. We had no more than a few seconds to make it inside. Derek jumped inside the cabin, and Sean and Dad stood on either side of the door frame, their hands outstretched to pull me in.

I reached out for them, but for that one second time seemed to stand still. Out of the corner of my eye, I could see the wave coming. It had already hit the side and would soon hit me. A look of gut-wrenching terror was upon Dad's face and the horror in my own eyes reflected the twins'. With one final lunge, I jumped for my father's hands, knowing they were all that could save me from impending death. For a split second, our slippery fingers met and grasped for the others. And then the wave hit me.

3. Request

My feet were thrown from the deck as the sheer power of the wave took over. I was hit so hard I couldn't breathe and ice cold water stung my skin. It surrounded me on all sides, taking me in its vast current and ignored my struggling, flailing limbs. I tumbled around, searching for some way to escape, but I had no idea which way to go. Up and down no longer existed; the water pushed me in all directions and never paused for a moment. A burning built within my lungs, a choking need for air. Frantically, I struggled for the surface even though I didn't know which direction the surface was. I could see nothing—the shadowy water swirled and smashed and fell in every direction.

I was suddenly hauled by a current and my head broke the surface. I choked and gagged the water out of my lungs. Short gasps brought slight relief as the oxygen subdued my body's strangled desire.

A large wave rose before me and took me under. Again I fought for control, though pushed about against my will, and then the surface reappeared. I struggled for it and broke through, gasping as another wave pulled me under. Over and over it happened, the constant tugging on my body as though it were a rag doll in a hurricane. There was never enough air to satisfy my lungs, only enough to keep breathing.

I resurfaced and waited for the next wave by taking full advantage of the break, but the next wave did not come. My stinging lungs throbbed as I searched through the rain. The waves were no longer as high as they had been before, and I was able to keep my head above the surface. The overwhelming iciness of the water engulfed me, and my teeth chattered as the terror of what had happened set in. Shivering, I saw my frosty breath in the torrential rain.

I searched for the *Lady Marie*, but she was nowhere to be found. I yelled, but my voice was barely audible over the storm. In desperation I continued to scream, my raspy throat cracking out gargled calls for help.

The seconds ticked by as if in slow motion. I turned around desperately hoping for a glimpse of the boat, but nothing came. Panic seized my heart, plunging my mind into the worst of fears. Logical thoughts fled and I could think of nothing to do but to stay afloat. That's all my mind could process: *stay afloat Lissie, stay afloat.*

As I turned in the water, something dark began to form on the horizon. Hope rekindled within me. Thinking it was the *Lady*

Marie, I struggled through the waves toward it. Hardly progressing, the currents suddenly began to push me towards the shape that had seemed so far away. With everything I had left, I used the current to muster my strength as I swam harder. Lifting my head out of the water, my hopes drowned to the bottom of the ocean. The form was not the boat, but an island. It stretched for a great distance on either side, spanning what had to be a mile long coast. Relief flooded my veins replacing the disappointment and I began to swim toward it.

My limbs felt like lead as I let the waves drag me toward shore. For a second, I was thrust under and my boot grazed the bottom. I realized then that my other foot was sheathed only in a sock and the roaring sea was now home to my other shoe.

I cried out in relief when I saw how close I was to solid land. I could just make out a sandy beach through the rain and continued to struggle forward. The desire to get out of the water made me press on despite the overwhelming exhaustion.

Out of the corner of my right eye something flashed. Perplexed, I pushed my hair from my eyes. The water level was just beneath my shoulders, but I was still being tossed about by the waves. A sense of foreboding pressed upon me as I looked to see what had flashed. I gasped.

The strange, shiny form I had seen the night before was in the water. Intense fear froze my body and mind. It was one thing to look at a strange creature while you were on a boat, but quite another when you were in the water along with it.

The shiny form floated not even twenty yards from me. I wondered if I would be able to make it to shore before it came any closer. Then, in the blink of an eye, it rushed straight past me. I screamed, and my throat burned from the salt coating it. I spun around, and the form was closer than last time. Once again it whizzed right past me; I screamed and moved out of the way, closer to the island.

My body was paralyzed with fright—I had no idea what to do. I tried to find the form again, but could not see it. I desperately tried to locate it, and turned to see if it was behind me. A strangled shriek of terror escaped my lips scarcely heard above the storm.

A shirtless man was in the water, directly in front of me. Dark hair blew about his face and there was a beast-like focus in his curious dangerous eyes as he stared at me with a gaze that pierced my soul. I averted my eyes from his quickly, and looked down into the water.

Once again I gasped, my eyes widening in horror. The shiny form was floating directly below the man, moving slowly back and forth counter to the rhythm of the waves. I looked back up at him to see if he realized this: it seemed that he was unaware.

There was something strange about him. He did not look like a normal human. His dark, long hair moved about his head and face as though he were still underwater. The wind moved it in a soft wave rather than whipping it around in the frigid air as mine did.

His skin was mesmerizing, shimmering as the rain splattered against it harshly. But the water did not seem to soak into his flesh; instead, it ran down his face and shoulders without the slightest glitch as though he was marble. His face was strong and beautiful, yet there was danger and boldness written in every feature. The eyes were a hard, deep gray as they stared at me in curious wonder. As he puckered his lips slightly and furrowed his brow, I realized that he seemed to be debating something.

Without warning, he reached a hand to my face. His skin was slippery as though he was covered in grease. My body immediately pulled away from his touch, my instincts telling me to flee. My moving had angered him and fury creased the creature's face. I tried not to let him see me move back even farther, but his eyes flickered toward my feet in the water. His face hardened even more and he shifted closer to me. With a strong hand he grasped my chin while turning my face from side to side. My breath came in short gasps, every nerve screaming at me to swim away before he got closer. I knew he was not human. He couldn't be—he was too different.

The creature continued to look at me, his judgmental gaze sliding over me. Grasping a strand of my hair, he fingered it, and then nodded his head. He pulled back slightly and I shrank away in fear, glad to be out of his reach. The waves picked up their strength again and I was taken under. A firm hand grabbed me under the arm and pulled me to the surface. I choked on the water and blinked to clear the salt from my eyes. With both hands, the creature reached out to me and I inhaled sharply. He paused. Again he stared at me curiously, and then all of a sudden he pulled me up against his chest. Like lightning we shot across the water far, away from the island.

The wind whipped around my face and I couldn't see anything around me. I held on to him tightly, hoping he wouldn't let go. Rain pelted against my face, stinging my frozen cheeks. My hands were shaking and kept slipping off the creature's slick shoulders, but he continued to crush me against his body.

Confused, my mind tried to catch up with what was happening. Everything around us was a blur as I attempted to open my eyes through the thundering rain. The speed at which we moved was incredible; we were flying over the water with the greatest of ease. I tried to grasp how we were moving so fast when a bright flicker caught my attention. I looked down to see what it was—the shiny form was right beneath us and was keeping up. It was waving beneath us, so close that my legs were almost touching it. I peered at it trying to figure out what it was.

It was long and shiny, reaching a few feet longer than my own legs. I had to lean to see the end of it and realized it slowly tapered at the end and split into a sort of "y" shape. All of a sudden it dawned on me. This was no separate form; this shiny thing was the bottom half of the man holding me. Shock consumed me. I could think of only one word for the creature that now held me against his chest; a creature that only existed in fairytales and myths. A merman.

I peered back up at the merman and found him looking at me. He seemed to be aware that I had just figured out what he was. It did not stop him. He continued to use his powerful dolphin-like fins to propel us through the waves, his back taking the blunt of the oncoming water while keeping me stable.

I tried to gather my thoughts, ignoring the increasing speed of the merman. Where was he taking me? I didn't know what to do. I couldn't stop him. From the size of his arms and the firmness of his grasp I could tell he was incredibly strong. And escaping him by swimming was pointless because he moved faster in the water than anything I had ever seen.

Then, out of the shadows, a shape appeared. The merman headed straight toward it. I wanted to scream, but I couldn't. He sped up and I was able to make out the shape of a boat. My heart leapt. Had he really brought me back to the *Lady Marie*? I couldn't believe it. Sure enough, her gold lettering identified her, and flashlights shimmered from her deck onto the crashing black waves.

Without warning, the merman jerked us underwater and a small scream escaped my mouth while salt clogged my throat and nose. We plunged into the depths, with him grasping tighter when I squirmed. Panic constricted my throat, but he changed course and shot toward the surface, a great choke broke from my mouth once air reached my lungs.

Gathering myself, I glared at him for not giving me a warning, but he did not seem concerned with my disapproval. Instead, he slipped one arm from around me and raised a hand in the air. I flinched hoping it would not come near me, making his jaw tighten at my reaction, but he did not bring it any closer. He placed his large hand on what looked like a wall. Confused, it took my mind a few moments to realize he was touching the side of the *Lady Marie*.

Gratefulness consumed me as I looked at the boat in relief. Trying to escape his arms, I pushed against him but he held me forcefully. Cocking my head to the side, I tried to understand what he wanted.

A wave crashed over us and hit the boat with a resounding thud, but I did not go under. The merman held me up as though the water had no power over him. A shiver ran through my spine as I realized the amount of strength he had. In a jerky movement, he flicked his head toward the boat, his hair rippling in a dazzling wave. I had no idea what he wanted.

"Lissie! Lissie!" the desperately pleading voice belonged to one of my brothers, but I couldn't tell which one. "Lissie!"

"I'm down here!" All the salt water had made my throat dry and scratchy and I was certain my yell wouldn't be heard.

Within a second, the arms that had held me so tightly disappeared. I fell beneath the surface but kicked back up again. The merman was gone.

Two beams of light found me and flashed over my face. I could see two figures on deck, but one quickly disappeared.

"Lissie?! Oh, thank goodness!" Derek's usually strong voice was stressed even through the pouring rain. "Just hold on!"

The second figure returned and yelled, "Catch!" I caught the rough rope and held on to it with the little strength left in me. I was pulled up out of the water and before long a strong pair of arms reached out and yanked me into a desperate hug. I tucked my face into the wet jacket and shivered, the tears stinging my eyes.

"Thank goodness you're alive," Dad choked. Bright lightning flashed and a crack of thunder exploded across the sky.

"Are you okay?" Sean asked, his hand rubbing my back. I had no idea if my voice would actually work and didn't want to pull my face away from Dad's chest. I nodded.

"Let's get you inside."

I felt a soft tug and my feet began to move, but I kept my face hidden. I didn't want to see any more of this dreadful storm. All of a sudden Dad stopped, and his body stiffened.

Reluctantly, I lifted my head. Five men clothed in black pants stood before us, their arms crossed over their broad naked chests. The rain filtered down their smooth bodies without a pause, their eyes peered at us with cold hatred. Yet I recognized the man at the front of the pack immediately. He was the merman who had saved my life, yet he stood on legs. *How was that possible?* My mind tried to grasp what I was seeing. I was sure that I had seen him with fins, yet here he was before me with two legs.

The merman was still naked on the upper half of his body, and the cold pounding rain seemed to not faze him. A pair of modern, black board shorts rested low on his hips. Like a mighty ocean god out of an ancient story, with his hair floating in the wind, and his arms hanging loosely at his sides, he stared at me like he had before.

The men behind him all glared, their eyes as dark as their leader's—it was obvious that the merman who had saved me was in charge. Their folded muscular arms bulged against their broad chests, presenting a daunting sight. They were all various heights, but one stood out on his long lean legs and reminded me of a runner. Each of them had dark hair like their leader except for the one who stood toward the front of the group. His hair was a light blonde and cropped shorter than the others. It hung just long enough to touch his eyes. But out of all the baleful glares I received, his was the worst.

"Who are you?" Dad shouted above the rain.

The merman did not answer but continued to look at me with those eyes that pierced my soul; I shuttered in my father's arms. After not being answered Dad tried again, "Who are you? What do you want?"

For a while, the merman continued to stare, but then he unlocked his gaze from mine and looked at my father. The rain rushed like a river down his chest as he spoke in a powerful and dangerous voice.

"I want her."

4. Change

Time stood still. No one spoke. No one moved. The seconds ticked by.

"*I said*, I want her." The merman spoke slowly as if we could not understand him.

"No," was the firm reply from Dad. His voice was calm, but a deep anger was hidden beneath it.

Silently, he unwrapped his arms from around my body and stepped in front of me, never taking his eyes off the merman. Afraid of what would happen, I peeked around his back.

The merman's gaze was still upon me. His eyes were intense, the cool grey reflecting the dark clouded sky above. They seemed to have no depth, like the vast ocean surrounding us.

He spoke again, "No matter what you do, you cannot take her from me. I want her and she will be mine."

To emphasize his words, the merman crossed his large arms over his chest. The overall size of him was incredible. He was taller than my brothers, and his arms were swollen with toned, powerful muscles.

"What do you want with her?" Sean asked protectively.

"She will be mine." The merman repeated this phrase again causing a shiver of cold fear to trickle down my spine. He meant what he said and a feeling of doom hung over me.

My mind could not grasp his meaning. *What could he want me for?* I was human and he was this mystical creature who lived in the ocean, yet here he miraculously stood before me. *Why would he pick me?* He had never met nor seen me before today, but then... I gasped, as realization hit me.

He was the murmuring noise last night. He was the one who had heard me singing, and had sung along. I suddenly remembered the odd feeling I'd had when it seemed as though eyes were watching me. I stared back at the merman, the silent wonder burning in my gaze.

His cold dark eyes answered my question. I was right. He had been there last night listening to me sing; he had watched me as I stood looking out over the ocean.

"You can't be serious!" My father's voice was beyond outrage as he shouted above the pouring rain. "I don't even know who you are," he looked the merman up and down, "or what you are."

"I am a merman." The statement was short and to the point. Dad stared at him in disbelief, his eyes blinking rapidly.

"If you're what you say, how can you expect my sister to live with you? She is human," Derek laughed in disbelief.

A slow smile crept over the merman's face and those behind him joined in on what must have been an inside joke. The blonde one flexed his jaw and licked his lips as though anticipating what was to come. With a shudder I looked away from him.

With a chuckle the merman spoke, "There are ways of changing that little detail." A great crash of thunder struck, placing emphasis on his words. "She will not remain human after this night. Tonight I will change her. In fact in a matter of minutes we can both leave."

I hardly heard what else was said. A great whirling rush filled my head and clogged my ears. Everything went fuzzy. *What did he mean? That I would become a mermaid?* I didn't want to be one, I wanted to go home and get away from all of this danger and fear.

Dad couldn't find his voice. He continued to open his mouth to try and say something, but nothing came out. It was Sean who spoke above the sharp whipping wind.

"You won't take her! You will have to kill me before you ever get the chance to take her." His voice was filled with disgust.

"Maybe we can just count on that happening," the merman said as he finally took his eyes off of me and turned his piercing gaze onto Sean. The other mermen straightened their posture; the evil blonde one dropped his arms to his sides, his muscles flexing as though he was ready to attack at any moment.

"Believe me: you, your brother, and father would be no match for me. I would hardly even call it a *scuffle*." The merman spoke these words with a defiant sneer on his face. It was obvious he liked the idea of a fight, and that he wanted one. Regardless of the four mermen behind the leader, however, Derek was about to challenge him.

My brothers had always protected me, but they had never come to blows over my safety. But even if they had fought, those fights would have been different than this; they would have been against other humans. There was no telling what kind of strength or power this merman and his group could display. Remembering the incredible speed the merman had had in the water suddenly filled me with fear. This could not turn into a fight, or else my brothers' lives would be taken. I was pulled from my thoughts by Derek's voice.

"We won't give her to you freely. You'll have to kill us before you get to her." As he said this, he balled his hands into tight fists at his sides.

"As I already said, that would be no problem. But please, do hurry up and make your decision. This ship will not hold against these waves much longer, and then we will all go down. Or at least you will." A hardness spread over his lips, "Marina and I will be perfectly safe."

Marina? Who was she? He had looked at me when he said the strange name, but why had he meant to call me that? It made me feel like an object rather than a person who could hear and feel.

"So that's it then," Dad had finally found his voice. "We're just supposed to hand her over to you and then drown."

My breath caught at the look on Dad's face. He appeared ten years older than what he had been yesterday. I knew I had to figure out some way to get us out of this, but I didn't know what to do.

"No, that is not what will happen," the merman's harsh voice rose above the roar of the storm. I could tell that he was used to ordering others around.

"I can see your sons, easy match that they would be for me, are not going to give up the idea of a fight. So I will give you three options. Either you die trying to fight me and I take Marina; you drown and I take Marina; or you give her to me and try to survive after we leave." His voice was calm and smooth as he proposed the death of my family.

Dad did not reply, but instead pushed me farther behind his body as though he was ready for an attack. Derek and Sean moved to place themselves between the assembly of mermen and me. They were going to try and protect me even if it meant certain death.

My mind began to spin; I could not let this happen. Not while there was still breath in my body. The merman had given three options, two of which resulted in the deaths of my brothers and father. But the last one had not.

I gazed back at the merman. His eyes were focused on Derek with a merciless black look of hatred—his deadly thoughts were written upon his face. I watched as his muscles twitched, waiting for Derek to make the first move. The mermen before me widened their stances, their faces filled with anticipation. Disgusted, I knew they were going to kill the people I loved most and they would do it before my very eyes.

"Stop!" I shouted at them. Quick as a flash the leader's gaze snapped to mine. I stepped out from behind Dad; he laid a restraining hand on my shoulder and shook his head.

For a moment I looked at his face and saw the sadness there. Yet I could not let it stop me. I reached up and pulled his hand away from my shoulder. Giving it a slight squeeze, I let it go and turned back to the ever-staring mermen.

"I will go with you, but only if you let my brothers and father live." My family protested, but I ignored them.

"I already said that was an option," the leader retorted back at me.

"No, you said you would let them *try* and survive on their own. I want you to make sure they live." I watched his features, waiting for him to consent. "I know you have the strength and power to keep them alive. Please do this, please, and I will go with you freely." Tears filled my eyes as I begged, "Please, it's all that I ask."

My voice grew strangled, as it reached a higher pitch. His eyes glazed for a moment and he blinked. Shaking his head, he peered even harder at me through the rain, his head cocked to the side. There was a confirmation in his eyes as though he had finally found what he was searching for.

Finally he spoke, "Very well. I will see it done." His eyes lifted from mine and found Dad. "I will keep you and your sons alive as long as you never speak a word of this to any human or try to search for us. After this night she will be mine and no longer your concern. Understood?" He didn't wait for an answer. "Come."

The merman spun around and walked to the door that led below deck, but not before he raised a stilling hand to the other mermen, commanding them to stay. Afraid, we followed, passing the mermen who glared at us. My one boot clunked on the deck as I gripped Dad's coat desperately.

Inside, we walked down the hall toward the kitchen and found the merman waiting for us. He looked entirely out of place, a mystical being in this ordinary room. I stopped walking and stood across the room from him. My brothers and father followed suit, sticking close to my sides.

The merman's arms were folded across his chest once again, and the rain water from outside slipped off his body into a puddle on the floor. He seemed to dry so quickly; as soon as the water left his flesh it was as though he had never been wet. The water did not penetrate his skin the way it did for us. We were soaked to the bone, our clothes dripping all over the floor. The only hints of him having been wet were his pants and hair. His dark shoulder length hair was only slightly damp and the black pants were just as wet as the clothes that stuck to my body.

I glanced up and saw his gaze was fastened on me once more. I moved uncomfortably, fidgeting with my soaked jacket. The very thought of him taking me away tonight was so repulsive and unreal that I could not believe it. Yet, there he was right in front of me with a look of impatience on his face.

He spoke and the words were heavy upon my ears, "I have to make sure before this is done. You are eighteen, are you not?" I became curious, but didn't dare to voice my wonderment.

"No," I shook my head. "Seventeen," I said in a barely audible voice as I looked at the floor.

A deep silence stretched after my softly spoken words, the only sound being the pounding waves and pouring rain. Gathering my courage, I looked up at him. A look of stunned surprise was upon his face, but it turned to anger quickly.

"That cannot be true! You look at least nineteen." The merman gave me an accusing glare, "You're lying."

"She's seventeen." Derek spoke so harshly I barely recognized his voice.

"Are you really?" The merman raised an eyebrow, and looked at me so violently that I almost lied just to please him.

"Yes," I said trying to show him it was the truth with one simple word.

A frustrated sigh escaped his lips and he raised a large hand to rub the side of his face. He mumbled under his breath but I could not make out the words. The hand came down and his head rose. He took a steadying breath and spoke, "that changes things."

"How so?" I could hear the same little glimmer of hope, which was beginning to build inside me, in my father's voice.

"She will not go with me tonight," he sighed again in frustration. "It appears I was mistaken about her age."

"So you will not take her?" Sean blurted.

"Not yet, if that's what you mean." The tiny bubble of hope which had been building within me shattered. My fate lay before me, forever tied to this dangerous creature.

"Her age does not cancel her fate, it merely prolongs it. She will be mine, eventually." The merman gave me a questioning look. "When is your eighteenth birthday?"

"August third," I spoke quietly. This made his scowl deepen as he comprehended how long it would be until I turned eighteen.

"Until then I will allow you to live with your family. After that day you will be mine." The words seemed to form chains around my wrists, binding me to an unavoidable doom. "However, even now when you go home you will not be the same."

Of course I wouldn't be the same. How could he think I would be? Before this I'd had no knowledge of fairytale creatures existing, and now I was being thrust into their world.

"What do you mean?" Dad asked, trying to contain his anger.

"There will be a change within her. A change she can either except or hate, it does not matter to me for it will happen regardless." As he spoke, he took a step closer to me. He beckoned me with his hand to cover the rest of the space between us.

Dad sucked in his breath. I pitied him along with my brothers. They were as powerless in this situation as I was. There was nothing we could do to change the odds in our favor. The merman had complete and total control over us.

Gathering the rest of my strength, I obediently stepped as close to him as I dared. He was now an arm's length away from me. My body shivered, whether from fear or the cold I did not know. With a graceful move he stepped forward, bringing us closer.

Involuntarily; I shifted to the side and then moved back a few paces. My racing heart escalated as he followed, I could not look at this creature without complete fear filling my body. My subconscious picked up on the loud voices of my family, but I was too focused on the merman to understand them. The creature paid the words no mind, until he jerked and with a sharp movement held his hand up in a warning. Derek was caught in mid-step, his eyes on fire as he glared. Again, pity for my family washed over me.

Refocused, the creature looked at me and once more I stepped backwards. My back hit the wall cutting off my escape, as though I'd had a chance to get away from him.

The merman reached out his hand and grasped my chin softly. Every one of my nerves stood on edge, urging me to flee despite the fact that I couldn't. I was trapped.

It was strange to be touched again by him and I forced myself to not pull away. His skin had an odd feeling to it. It was neither hard nor soft, neither rough nor smooth. It felt human, yet there was something alien about it and it made goosebumps crawl over my flesh.

I held perfectly still while his eyes roved over my face. He seemed to be mentally tabulating, checking for something. The crease in his brow suddenly cleared and he moved his hand back to rest at his side. Slowly, his gaze moved from my face and all the way down my body.

I did not like the way he looked at me; it made me feel like an animal being inspected before purchase. I fidgeted only slightly as he moved his eyes back up to mine. A cold, terrible smile spread across his face. It made me think he liked what he saw and fear gripped my stomach.

Once again his hand moved. This time it did not reach for my face, but instead toward the waistband of my soggy pants. Not knowing what would happen, my breath became ragged and my eyes widened.

Slowly, the merman slid my jeans off my right hip. I held my breath. I wanted to slap his hand away, but knew I couldn't. He stopped moving the waistband; my jeans were now a few inches lower than they had been seconds before.

Without a word, the merman took a small step back and bent his left arm away from me. Suddenly, five sharp knifelike objects, which were no more than four inches long, protruded from the back of his forearm. They were all jagged and pointed upward toward his elbow. They glinted in the dim light of the kitchen, the pointed edges proclaiming the power and life-threatening skill this creature had.

For a moment I had a quick vision of him using those blades to kill. I could see the way that he would lift his arm and use the blades to slice through flesh. The realization churned my stomach.

I shook my head slightly, watching the merman as he held his right arm out directly in front of him. He took his left arm, the one with the protruding blades, and grazed it across his right forearm. I looked away not wanting to see what this strange creature was going to do to himself.

When I looked back at the merman he held a small piece of flesh in his left palm. My stomach lurched; with deep, heavy breaths and an ever-pounding heart, I glanced back at the small piece in his palm. It did not look soft, but rather, hard and no larger than my thumb.

I glimpsed the arm that he had cut and was surprised to see a small gash in the same shape of the piece in his hand. Blood slowly oozed over the wound, slipping easily over his arm, but he did not seem to notice. I would've thought that anything as otherworldly as him would not bleed, but it appeared I was wrong.

The merman focused his eyes upon me again and my heart accelerated once more under his defiant stare. I could feel the blood rushing through my veins, the fear in my fingertips.

I had known this merman withheld strength when he stood before me earlier, but now that I had seen the sharp blades come out of the back of his forearms I was petrified with fright. I shrank as far into the wall as I could, trying to stay away from him.

My worst fears were realized when the merman all of a sudden placed his weapon against my hip. I caught my breath and sucked in my belly, even though I knew it would not help.

"What are you doing?" Dad yelled and stepped toward the merman from behind.

But it was too late. I had already felt the small slice across my flesh. It stung and, if I had been breathing, I would have lost my breath in that instant. I felt a tiny trickle of blood make its way down to the top of my pants. I glanced down quickly and saw a cut, no more than three inches in length, angled slightly across my hip.

The merman bent over as if he were going to study the wound he had just made. Then, with lightning quick speed, he took the tiny, hard piece of flesh that had been in his hand and thrust it into the small cut. A minute cry escaped my lips as pain seized my hip, and then spread throughout my whole body with tight cramps.

Derek threw himself on top of the merman, knocking him to the ground. Without a moment's hesitation the merman pulled Derek from his back and threw him to the floor as easily as if he were wrestling a child. He then stood in front of me.

"You cannot remove what I put within you," he said, the look he gave me was so honest I had to believe him. "You will only cause yourself harm if you *dare* try and remove it."

I turned from his penetrating gaze and looked about the room. Dad, Sean, and Derek glared at the merman with such hatred that even I was scared. The merman did not notice, it seemed, since he turned toward me unafraid to leave his back open to attack.

The burning in my hip increased. At first it started in a small spot, but then continued to grow. My breath caught as I placed my hand over the tiny cut, trying to keep it from stinging. A small hiss escaped my mouth.

"Lissie?" Dad ran over to me. "What is it?" he asked me and then, "What did you do to her?!" he shouted.

This was directed at the creature standing before us, who had a look of pleasure on his face. I tried to concentrate on what his response would be, but my ears were throbbing. My vision blurred and I could feel myself moving, but I didn't know where. The last thing I saw was the blood on my fingers and the floor moving toward my face. Then darkness took me.

5. Home

"I just don't understand. What's wrong with her?"

The soft-spoken words penetrated my sluggish mind and prodded me awake. They sat, barely reachable, outside my grasp. I recognized the voice, but could not place it with a face that I knew I should know. A veil had been drawn over my inner eye, making a barrier between what I knew and the imaginative world in my mind. It was all too confusing.

A deep sigh resounded in the room. "I don't know." This voice was more concerned; a deep love filtering through its resignation.

I wonder what they are talking about. The thought ran through my mind and since I could not seem to correctly command my body to move, I waited. I decided to listen to the conversation and see if I could figure out what they were speaking about.

The deeper voice spoke, "What time is it?" I missed the response, but the man with the deep voice sighed heavily as though it was a bad omen.

"33 hours," he mumbled audible enough for me to hear. He must have been closer to me than the other voice.

"Any sign of movement?" The younger voice spoke again, optimism saturating his tone. There was no response, and I wondered what was supposed to be moving. *An animal maybe?*

Another sigh exhaled in the room; the person closest to me seemed to be under a great amount of stress.

"Don't worry, Dad," the younger voice said, trying to sound chipper. "She'll wake up soon." His words triggered a spark in my brain. It was like I was trying to swim through molasses, each thought clinging to another and not letting me move forward. With all the brain strength I could muster, I surged away from the blank expanse and toward the veil—I felt it would give me the answer I needed.

In that instant it was as though my brain reconnected with my body: I was whole once more. Satisfied, I opened my eyes while exhaling loudly in relief. A pale light angled across the ceiling from the small window on the wall, and dark shadows standing beside the walls created odd, boxy shapes. Feeling lost and alone, I turned my head to figure out what was really going on when a hand suddenly grasped mine. Gasping in surprise, I looked up.

Blue eyes filled with fatherly love and concern washed over my face, taking in every inch. A small smile pulled at his lips as one of his large palms came to rest upon my cheek. Within an instant, it all flooded back into my mind. Everything: who I was, where I had been, and what had happened. The memories flashed dramatically in my head: the pounding rain, the glare of the merman, and slice of his blade across my hip. An imperceptible shiver rolled down my spine.

"Honey, are you okay?" Lifting my eyes to his, I noted the care and worry in his gaze. He sat on a chair next to my bed. The room was familiar now that I had my memories and I recognized the surroundings of my bedroom on the *Lady Marie*. There was a slight rocking, a gentle swaying, that revealed the instability of a boat at sea.

With a squeeze of my hand against his palm, I whispered, "I think so." Relief healed the few wrinkles around his eyes.

"Good to have you back," the younger voice said and I knew it was Sean's. Turning my head, I saw him leaning against the doorway with a smile. "You had us worried for a little while."

"Sorry," I said again in a whisper, not sure why I was speaking so quietly. Glancing down at Dad's large hand surrounding my own I bit my lip. I knew what I needed to ask, but couldn't quite figure out how to ask it. My eyes flickered up.

"Dad," my throat croaked, "what happened?"

Sean cleared his throat loudly, "Umm, I'll go help Derek. He'll be happy to know you're awake." Without another word he left the room, closing the door behind him.

Looking up at my father, I waited. I expected him to begin explaining, but he said nothing. He continued to gaze around the room, all the while avoiding eye contact. He knew what I wanted to know, but seemed to not want to tell me. But I had to know, *needed to know.*

"Dad." I squeezed his hand again, and he closed his eyes while sighing heavily.

"All I remember is what he put in me." I struggled to speak, "and then darkness."

Finally, he turned his face to mine. "I will tell you, just give me some time." He took a deep breath, "After you fell to the floor and were unconscious, I didn't know what to do." He rubbed his forehead with his hand and his voice broke off as if it wouldn't work. I squeezed his arm, trying to tell him that he should continue.

"The twins brought you in here while that monster spoke with me." He spit the words in disgust, as though he hated having to say them. Then his tone became calmer, "I asked him what exactly he had done to you, and he told me he had placed a part of himself inside you." I remembered the strange hard piece of flesh the creature had sliced off his forearm and put within my skin. Involuntarily, I moved my hand to my right hip.

"He told me his flesh is very different from a human's. He said it is made up of tiny little scales which are hard to penetrate. The piece of flesh that he put inside you is made up of these very same scales." Giving a distressed sigh, he looked across the room at the wall. "Lissie, I'm sorry, I hardly understand any of this myself."

"It's okay." My voice was soft, "all I want is to know."

"Well, he said that piece," he nodded towards my hip, "of flesh, or scales, would eventually change you into a mermaid." He paused to gauge my reaction. Controlling my face, I made sure my expression did not reflect the fear flooding, pulsing through my veins. His words had been expected, I knew they would come, but somehow the happenings of last night felt like a dream. To hear them from my own father's mouth was to declare their testimony and press upon me the reality of their existence.

"I asked him what this meant and he said that little by little you would obtain the abilities of a mermaid." Shock absorbed me and this time I was unable to keep my emotions from my face. Dad held up his hands in an attempt to explain his lack of knowledge. "He didn't go into detail about what these abilities would be, so I'm as clueless as you are. But he did say you would be able to live at home without anyone noticing a difference. His only warning was to not get wet in front of anyone."

If it is possible to feel both relief and fear at the same time, then I was experiencing it. Relief for being able to go home, but fear in the knowledge that I was now different from those around me. It was too much for my mind to grasp.

"When you blacked out, I asked him what was wrong with you. He said it was the change taking place and that you would regain consciousness within a day." At this point he stopped speaking and placed his hand along my face. "You gave us quite a scare for a while." He tried to smile, but the false happiness didn't reach his eyes.

"How are you guys alive?" My throat closed with emotion, but I tried to keep speaking. "I remember him saying something about how he was going to leave you to fend for yourselves." My voice was shaky, but I tried to conceal it. I don't think I fooled him.

"Well, what I think it boils down to is that he was too quick to guess your age." A sad look came into my sweet father's eyes, and I yearned to comfort him even though I knew there was nothing I could do. "Because he couldn't take you himself, he had to save us."

"He saved you?" I butted in with a fierce intensity. He nodded.

"He said, 'take care of her until I return.'" His hand closed tighter around mine. "He left the room to go out on deck, and I was debating following him, when the *Lady Marie* shook and groaned so loudly I thought for sure she was breaking apart." His eyes were blank as if seeing the memories before him, "Then all of a sudden she was free on the ocean. When I reached the deck all the men had disappeared." He shrugged his shoulders, signifying the end of his tale.

Silence fell between us. I didn't know what to say. What do you say to your own Dad after you have been told your destiny is to live with a terrifying merman? A merman who isn't even supposed to exist? No social skills could ever prepare you for a situation like this.

Instead of saying anything, I just looked at my father. He had always been there for me and I couldn't imagine my life without him. He was the silent comforter I knew rested at home whenever I had had a rough day. I never dreamt there might come a day when I would be so far away from him.

"Thank you," I said, not really sure what I was thanking him for. He bobbed his head up and down, obviously feeling awkward. "Umm, I'll just get cleaned up." Again he bobbed his head, and while moving to stand up his large body filled what little space I could see. Placing a gentle hand on my cheek, he leaned in to kiss my forehead and quietly left the room.

The kiss left a cold mark on my skin as though it was part of my past and would not belong in my future. Pressure built behind my eyes while I pinched the bridge of my nose. Thinking of my future was too much at the moment, but it bombarded me relentlessly. My plans were gone, washed away before my eyes like debris after a hurricane. There was nothing I could do to stop the merman from coming back for me; I was at his mercy for the rest of my life. Claustrophobia pressed upon my chest and threw me into a panic. My heart raced, sporadically skipping beats. By breathing slowly and deeply, I was able to subdue its stutters.

Then, with more strength than I had ever had I sat up. Determination filled my mind; I would not let this merman get the best of me.

When sunrise broke across the sky the next morning, it brought with it the sight of Coveside. The town was tucked into the rocky shore, with houses and small businesses lining the beach. Waves broke gently on the sand, and crashed in tremendous white splashes over the boulder-filled cliffs.

The sight was familiar and brought some stability to the reckless emotions I had been feeling for the past twenty-four hours. Trying to keep my thoughts in check, I avoided thinking about what had happened to me. It was difficult enough to act as though I was the same, but when my brothers and father acted as though at any moment I would sprout fins and flop around on the deck, the task seemed impossible.

Hurrying through the motions silently, I helped the twins tie the *Lady Marie* to the dock and gather all of our belongings. They carried the large duffel bags to Dad's truck and threw them in the bed, moments later clambering in themselves. I climbed into the cab and buckled quickly, making sure to look out the window and avoid their gazes. The pity in their eyes was not something I wanted to see.

Dad finished on the boat and hopped into the driver seat trying to act as normal as possible. I appreciated his attempts; they were helpful, but only reminded me of what had happened. There was really no solution to the problem.

We pulled out of the parking lot and onto the small road which lead to Main Street. Upon reaching the intersection; my eyes immediately flickered to the Darrow's Catch, the sight sending warmth into my heart. Here was something familiar that could not change. The old truck idled past while I stared at the building until it was beyond my range of vision.

Rumbling along the road slowly, the truck was at a casual speed in regards to the many pedestrians walking along the sidewalks window shopping. Some well-known family friends raised their hands in greeting. Others ignored us, their clothing displaying that they were tourists. I suspected I might see them in the restaurant later—Darrow's Catch was the most popular restaurant in Coveside and attracted many tourists.

Lost in my thoughts, the rest of the drive seemed to take mere seconds. It had always amused me that walking to the restaurant was quicker than driving to it, due to the short pathway that cut through the woods and down the hill our house rested on. When we drove we had to take roads that led us in a wide circle much farther out of the way. The restaurant was really only a quarter of a mile from our home.

Pulling into the driveway, Dad tooted the loud horn without warning, making me jump. He mumbled an apology and unbuckled. I followed his example and jumped out of the cab, hitting the pavement with a jolt. The solid ground felt wonderful, much more stable than the way my life felt.

The side door to the light blue house I called home opened, and my half-siblings came running toward us. Smiling, I opened my arms as Caitlin and Sara ran in my direction. At five and six years old they idolized me, whereas their eight year old brother Aaron prized Derek and Sean. Sara slammed into my chest, declaring in a loud voice that she had missed me so much she thought she was going to die. Caitlin bobbed her head in obvious agreement, and I laughed.

Kissing Sara on the head, I let her slide to the ground and I gave Caitlin a huge hug. "Did you have fun?" Caitlin grasped my hand.

I nodded once more, "Yes, lots of fun and I will have to tell you all about it."

"Mamma was worried about the storm," Sara chirped in.

Grabbing her hand I swung our arms back and forth, "Well we are all safe and sound, aren't we?" I smiled at her and she giggled with glee. Out of the corner of my eye I saw Dad looking at me, but I trained my eyes ahead. Now was not the time.

"Finally, you're back!" My step-mom called from the door, her eyes kindled with the excitement she had passed onto each of her children. Her hand rested on her increasingly large belly, which had grown even more since we had been away.

We all took turns greeting her and paraded into the house, Aaron grunting as he stumbled and dragged my bag across the ground. His face was a mask of determination, refusing help from anyone who offered.

Entering the house, I scanned the kitchen; everything in the wide white-cabinet room was in place. The blinds of all the windows were open, revealing a vast view of the ocean and its rolling waves. Sunlight spilled through the windows onto the seashell-filled jars, which were out of reach from the younger children.

The large space opened up into a living room with cream couches, and wooden furniture in a distressed turquoise. Books were stacked on old bookcases, creating a studious and yet comfortable environment. Dominating the room was a stone hearth fireplace, where we often gathered in the winter with hot chocolate. Along the back wall of the living room rose a staircase which led to a small balcony and the many bedrooms up above.

"Withie!" A loud screech came from the kitchen table, coming from a curly-haired little boy in a booster chair clapping his hands together. Justin, as always, was bouncing up and down with excitement to see me. For some reason I was his favorite, and I knew he had his own special place above everyone else in my heart. At three years old, he loved to follow me anywhere in the house, always accompanying me while I read, finished homework, or simply listened to music.

Letting go of the girls' hands I walked over to the table to give him a hug and kiss. I then kissed his younger brother Kaleb on the cheek. Kaleb was the youngest at fifteen-months old. The youngest until the new baby arrived, anyway. And by the looks of Jillian's belly that might come sooner rather than later.

"Here, go ahead and sit," Jillian gestured to the table while tucking her dark brown hair behind her ear, a habit she was unaware of. "I'll whip up a batch of pancakes for all of you." She waddled her way to the stove while Dad protested, saying she should rest and get off her feet. I knew how that conversation would go.

On the table were the beginnings of breakfast, half cut pancakes and syrupy plates were scattered all over the place. It was Saturday morning and this was home, for the first time since I had been thrown overboard I truly felt myself relax.

After a long breakfast, we retired to the living room to watch a movie. I plopped on the couch, letting Justin totter toward me and scramble onto my lap. He fit comfortably against my body, and his small weight was reassuring.

Placing a tiny, sticky hand upon mine, he looked up at me. I glanced down into his sunshiny face knowing what he wanted. With a quick move I placed my mouth against his neck and blew, giving him a raspberry and making an unpleasant sound against his skin. He laughed with glee, clapping his chubby little hands together.

Caitlin nudged my side, "Can we watch a movie now?" Her gaze was pleading, something she was able to do quite easily with her large brown eyes.

"Sure," I said, shrugging in acceptance. She darted away with Sara in tow to the movie cabinet. Aaron walked over with them bickering, about the movie they were choosing.

"Did you pick a good one?" I asked jokingly, when they rushed back to the couch with dazzlingly bright smiles on their young faces. Caitlin nodded, causing her curly-pony tail to bounce up and down, while Sara giggled. Aaron frowned even more, and I waited for the girls to reveal which movie was chosen. If I had a guess it would be one with a princess.

"Well, let me see it." I stuck my hand out, but being dramatic as always, Caitlin made a show of sliding the movie out slowly from behind her back. With a sudden burst of uncontainable excitement her partner in crime yelled, "It's *The Little Mermaid*!"

Behind me in the kitchen something, heavy hit the floor, while Caitlin berated Sara for ruining the surprise. I glanced over the couch, noting how Dad stood frozen in the kitchen, his eyes fixated upon me. The word that had slipped so loudly from Sara's mouth affected him more than it had me.

"Randall, are you okay? You look really pale." Jillian walked over to him and rubbed his back. Derek and Sean both stood like statues, their hands frozen in mid-air with dirty plates and syrup-covered silverware. For a half second more they stood transfixed, and then, as though the frozen-flash mob was over, they moved in unison.

"Whoops, I have such butterfingers." Dad said in a normal and calm voice. Without another moment's hesitation he scooped the pieces of the broken platter off the ground and placed them on the counter. The twins slipped to the sink and rinsed the plates without a glance toward me or Dad.

I was impressed by their antics—their actions didn't cause the ever-aware Jillian to suspect anything. All three of them were able to hide their feelings better than I was. The mistakenly dropped word had thrust me back into the fear of my unknown future. It was my new reality and one I did not want to face, especially in this home where so many happy memories rested in the light-colored walls.

"Hey! Can we watch the movie now?" Sara looked at me, tugging on my sleeve. I tried to get rid of the lump that was lodged in my throat as I realized I would not be there to watch her grow up. The thought made me want to lock myself in my room and cry. I took a steadying breath.

"Sara, use your manners." She mumbled please and waited for my answer. "How about we watch something else," no matter how hard I tried I knew I wouldn't be able to say the word mermaid. "It's a good one, but what about Aaron? He wants to watch too and that's kind of a girly movie. So why don't we watch something everyone will be happy with?"

Mumbled "okays" were the response to my request, but I didn't care. There was no way I was going to make it through watching *The Little Mermaid* without pulling my hair out.

After much debate, *Toy Story* was decided and before long the familiar jokes and scenes played before my eyes. Midway through, Derek and Sean joined us acting as normal as possible. They laughed, looked surprised, and got scared in all the right parts. This was all for the amusement of the younger ones. At one point Sean was hiding behind a pillow as though scared of the evil child Sid, who switched the heads of a pterodactyl dinosaur toy and a doll.

When the movie finally came to an end, I stood very carefully with a sleeping Justin on my shoulder. Jillian entered from the kitchen shaking her head.

"That boy just goes and goes until he wears himself out." She smiled, "Would you do me a favor and put him in his crib? Kaleb is already up there."

When I nodded my reply she said thanks, and I headed for the stairs. I could feel Derek's and Sean's eyes boring into my back. I climbed the stairs with care and was half way up when I heard the following footsteps of the twins. Carrying the sleeping toddler into the room he shared with Kaleb, I placed him in his bed.

After giving him a kiss on the forehead, I walked to my room and found both twins waiting for me. Sean sat on the edge of my large bed, forearms resting on legs, and Derek leaned against the window ledge with his hands in his pockets.

Taking a deep breath I looked at both of them, the water filling my eyes quickly. I shut my door softly and headed for a seat next to Sean on the bed. It was time to get all this pain and frustration out into the open.

———————————

I lay in bed that night thinking of the things Derek and Sean had said. Staring up at the ceiling I secretly hoped it would swallow me whole and take me away from the fate that awaited me; the very fate I never wanted to meet.

The conversation with Derek and Sean had been awkward. None of us knew how to address the situation, and I was hard pressed to try to act as though nothing had changed. The problem was everything had changed. I was no longer the same; the sister they had grown up with was no longer me.

When Sean finally breached the silence and tried to be serious about what had happened, something snapped and I could not stop myself from laughing. The situation was so absurd and we felt silly speaking of creatures which used to only exist in our childhood imaginations. Somehow the laughter eased the tension, bringing us back together to how we used to be. For just a moment in time I was able to forget about the fate awaiting me. I was able to just laugh with my brothers, giving me some peace of mind and helping me feel as though I was still the same person inside, no matter what would end up happening to me.

I rolled onto my side annoyed that I couldn't fall asleep. My mind was buzzing with different ideas. I had to admit that even though I was disgusted with the idea of becoming a mermaid, I was also curious. I wondered if I would be able to move as fast in the water as the merman had. The speed he had moved at was incredible, no motor boat would have been able to keep up. *Would I be able to do that?* And what about the blades in his arms, would those come out of my arms too? It was all so scary and yet amusing at the same time. I rolled over to my back and giggled.

The image in my mind of me being a mermaid was too funny. I conjured up a mixed picture between Ariel, from *The Little Mermaid* with puffy, red hair and bright purple seashells, and a half naked woman with fins, sprawled across a rock with long hair covering her breasts.

My mind surged with curiosity, refusing to calm itself. I wondered whether my body would look entirely different, but I remembered the merman had stood and then had sprouted fins in the water. The anticipation was too much.

With a sudden surge of excitement, fear, and curiosity I made my way to the bathroom. The faucet squeaked as I turned the knob to the bathtub, and I cringed at the sound. As I watched the water fill the tub, a nervous bubble built in my stomach.

When the water was high enough, I leaned over and turned the faucet off. It became incredibly silent and eerie. The water was placid, unmoving and yellow-tinged from the color of the ivory tub. I bit my lip in worry about what was going to happen. Part of me wanted to drain the water and go back to bed; but the other part knew I would never fall asleep until my curiosity had been quenched.

I glanced over my shoulder to make sure I had locked the door to the bathroom. Cautiously, I slipped out of my clothes, not sure why I was doing this in the middle of the night. Inching my way closer and closer to the tub, as though it was going to bite me, I lifted one leg, and quickly placed it in the water, to get it over with.

It was the strangest feeling I had ever experienced. The water was around my leg, pressing up against it, but there was a barrier between my skin and the water. It was as though the liquid could not really touch me, as if I was covered in water repellent. I could feel the water around my leg, but it didn't soak into my skin.

Again testing the new abilities of my body, I pulled my foot back out. The water rushed down my leg with speed, as though nothing got in its way as it slipped down to the rug on the floor. I leaned over to touch my skin and feel if it was wet. I was pretty sure that it wouldn't be, but logic told me it had to be wet. My fingers brushed against perfectly dry, smooth skin. Shock surged through me, as the weight of what I had become sank in.

I stepped into the tub with the same leg I had used before. The rest of my body followed and I sank down into the water until the surface reached my shoulders.

I waited, expecting something to happen. Maybe for my legs to become glued together and sprout fins. Nothing changed. I decided maybe I needed to be entirely wet. I slid down into the tub and went all the way under. Again I waited, and again nothing happened. I came up for air.

Oddly, disappointment flushed my soul. Up until this moment I had not realized how much I desired my transformation. It had only been three days since I was changed but the merman had said I would be different immediately. A lump wedged its way into my throat while I tried to laugh away my embarrassment and frustration.

I sunk into the water again, this time keeping my head above the surface. I was in total comfort in the water, as though I was one with it. The water was neither hot nor cold, but rather a comfortable warm, even though I knew I filled the tub with hot water. I wondered if this was how the merman had withstood the cold water of the ocean so well.

My mind was filled with visions of what the merman had looked like. I didn't think of him because I was attracted to him, but because I was attracted to the idea of what he was. I longed to be like him, out in the ocean just swimming. The feelings were so desperate; I had such a pressing need to swim. It was a primal urge like I had never known before that took over my thoughts. My body responded, my fingers tingling, my legs pressing tightly together even though nothing changed. My lungs strained to take a breath underwater, but the logical part of my mind refused to believe that I wouldn't choke.

Resurfacing with a gasping breath, a flicker of light caught my attention. Looking down into the water I gasped at the sight on my skin. The cut, which the merman had placed on my hip, was shimmering with a soft, almost transparent, lavender glow. Like a stained-glass window, it refracted any light that touched it into lavender shimmers.

Moving to get a closer look, I gasped once more. The ripples upon the surface from my movement caused the lavender scar to dance with flashes of twinkling colors. I was transfixed in watching the small cut rippling beneath the surface. It reminded me of the merman's fins, the odd shape I had seen the night I was out singing. They had always been constantly changing even though the merman himself hadn't looked like he was moving. Now I knew why. The water was what caused the fins to look like they were in constant motion.

Time slipped by as I watched the shimmering of my little cut. Finally, I ducked under the water one more time and then stood. The water rushed down my smooth skin like a river. I reached for a towel and then remembered there was hardly any need for one. Once all of the water ran down my body I would be perfectly dry. I waited a few seconds and then stepped from the tub, just as dry as I had been before getting in the water. I quickly pulled on my pajamas and was just about to head back to my room when I saw my reflection in the mirror.

The girl standing opposite me looked very different from the one I usually saw. I was used to seeing an average girl, with soft golden curls, and a calm face. Now the reflection had eyes wide and open with curiosity. Mischief and excitement were bubbling below the surface of every feature. This girl was more aware of the world, or more ready for the world. She was ready to do new things and live differently. I placed my hands along the counter to support myself as I looked at my reflection.

I turned my head from side to side to get a better look at this new me. My hair caught my attention. It had changed not in color, length, or style, but rather in its movement. It lay on my shoulders as normal hair would, but if I whipped my head around it did not follow quickly. Instead it floated along and settled on my shoulders once I was still. It reminded me of the hair I had seen upon the merman.

It was like I was underwater, and my hair had a hard time moving through the air. I moved my head from side to side and watched as the hair rippled in slow motion. It was beautiful to watch, mesmerizing to look at, just like the shimmering cut on my hip.

Uncertainty of what I was becoming trickled into my mind. I just hoped that I would not inherit the cold dead look in the merman's eyes. Although, if I had to spend the rest of my life with him, and who knew how long that life could be, I would not be surprised if I looked as evil as he did.

A soft shudder ran down my spine and goose bumps rose on my skin. Ignoring the reaction, I turned and walked back to my room, with the merman's dark gaze engraved in my thoughts.

6. Visitor

A month passed, allowing me to settle into my normal routine. The jumpy nervousness of being found out slowly dissipated as the days went by. If it wasn't for the lavender scar on my hip, I would have thought the encounter with the merman was all a dream.

I worked every weekend at Darrow's Catch from noon till close. I liked being a waitress, especially for people that I knew. It was one of the neat aspects of our town. There was a large group of residents who, like my father, had lived in Coveside their whole lives. These people were long-term family friends and usually visited the restaurant every Saturday or Sunday night, making my job more fun than usual.

I had another all day shift today which I knew would be hectic. Saturday nights always were, what with the regulars coming out, and the many tourists who had heard from locals that Darrow's Catch was the best place to eat seafood. It would be busy, but busy was good. It kept me from dwelling on thoughts (thoughts which would send me to an asylum if I ever voiced them).

The restaurant was within walking distance from our house. Originally, the Darrows had lived above the restaurant. But a while back, Dad had decided to use the whole building for business. We were then able to serve twice the amount of people, and eventually Dad bought the old house next door and joined it to the main building. He and my uncles knocked out the side walls of the houses and joined them together to look like one large structure. We used both of the first floors and one of the second floors of the houses for the restaurant. The other second story was a gift shop. The expansive kitchen stretched across the back of both buildings.

My feet trudged up the back steps, which led directly into the spacious kitchen. I glanced around and saw I was first to arrive, but knew the others would be here soon. In preparation I began to pull out the cooking ingredients. Not long after I had accomplished this task, my cousin, Chelsea, walked through the door. She was short and trimmed; her body built like a gymnast, and had an easy smile that spread wide across her face.

I smiled and greeted her, "Hey, girl!"

"Hey, nice shirt," she laughed. Our uniform was casual: jeans or khakis with a Darrow's Catch t-shirt. Sean had designed the shirts about five years ago, and we now sold them as souvenirs in our little gift shop. The front of the shirt was plain with the words Darrow's Catch up in the top left corner, and a small lobster hung off of the capital "D". The back of the shirt had a drawing of the restaurant on it. The traditional Darrow's Catch sign could even be seen hanging over the front porch.

Of all the different colored shirts we owned, Chelsea and I were wearing the same one. I laughed along with her as she came and stood beside me, tying a small waitress apron around her tiny waist.

"You ready to get started? Laura won't be here for another hour or so," she said through gritted teeth. "She refuses to get out of bed before ten, and Mom says it's fine! I mean really!"

I nodded my head in agreement, knowing it was not a smart idea to take either of my cousin's sides. Usually they got along, but when they did not it was best to stay out of their way. I praised my aunt for not letting them both come in at the same time; hopefully being apart would give them time to cool off.

The day passed in a blur. Laura eventually arrived, along with Jessie and Hannah, two of my other cousins both from different families. Their mothers were right behind them. These three women were the reason why the restaurant was packed every weekend. People said they had never tasted better food than the food they ate at Darrow's Catch. I was dubious of this, but knew that all of the credit went to my aunts, who were magicians in the kitchen.

Laura, Chelsea, Jessie, Hannah, and I worked the restaurant with ease. We had faced many a packed house and had no worries or problems with it. Each of us was able to fly around the tables with incredible speed. We dodged and ducked, carried and served. We had worked together like this for a good three years and could almost read one another's thoughts.

My head jerked up as the bell above the door jingled, announcing the entrance of another customer. I glanced over my shoulder to see who it was.

Four teenage boys from my high school trudged through the front door and were speaking to Laura, who was playing hostess tonight. Laura had never met a stranger, and we often had to remind her to seat people at tables when she got too carried away in her greeting duties. It looked as though I was going to have to remind her again. When it came to teenage boys, Laura never knew when to stop talking.

I made my way over to the hostess stand. As I walked up, one of the boys named Trey smiled at me. He was tall and stood with his hands in the pockets of his Northface jacket and wore a baseball cap on his head. I inwardly groaned, because I'd seen that look on his face before. Why was it that some boys couldn't take a hint? Trey was a nice guy, but I wasn't interested.

"Hey, what's up Lissie?" This came from a guy named Jonathan who was standing next to Trey.

Jonathan had short red hair, and freckles splattered all over his face and arms. Out of the group I knew him best, but I still didn't know him all that well. He had simply been in multiple classes of mine and we had gotten to know each other through school over the years.

I recognized the other two boys, but I had no idea what their names were.

"I'm doing great thanks," I lied. "Umm... we're pretty busy right now but I'm sure Laura can find you a table."

I smiled, and gave Laura a solid nudge when I said this to remind her of her job. Laura quickly turned to grab some menus and silverware. With a polite voice that had suddenly become business-like, she said, "Follow me please."

She whipped around on her heel to lead the gangly boys to their table. Jonathan spoke up before he followed her.

"Just know I'm only going to pay if you are the one serving us," he said with a friendly grin. "We haven't talked in a while."

"Oh, and because we aren't busy at all, I'll be able to sit down and chat," I responded sarcastically.

This got a soft chuckle out of him and he turned to follow his friends. I watched to see what table Laura put them at, and then headed back to the kitchen to fetch some previous orders. When I finally got the chance I weaved my way through the chairs over to the circle table the boys sat at. I put on a smile and pretended to be formal because I knew it would make Jonathan laugh, "Hello, my name is Lissie and I will be your server tonight."

A wide grin split across Jonathan's face, and I was quick to notice that one had crept across Trey's as well. "Is there anything I can get you for starters? What would you like to drink?"

I whipped out my notepad and pen, then turned to Jonathan who sat just to my right. He was grinning from ear to ear.

"First of all, my dear lady," he spoke in a mock British accent, exaggerating his words to sounds proper. "I must introduce myself and these fine gentlemen who accompany me this evening. My name is Jonathan, Sir Jonathan Bates. I am here tonight on a sort of outing with my dear friends. This here is Trey Watts," he nodded toward Trey. I glanced at him and he smiled. "Over here on my left is Ethan Daniels," I quickly looked at the dark haired boy; he had a crooked smile and looked like a good time. "And this fellow right here is Adam Robinson." I looked over at the tow head that sat straight across the table from me. Jonathan gazed up at me with bright eyes and grinned even wider now that he had finished his speech.

"How do you do?" I asked with an even better British accent than Jonathan's. This was met with laughter from all four boys. I then transitioned back to normal speech, "Now how about I take your order?" A few minutes later I walked away from the table with drink and entrée orders.

I couldn't help but over-hear Jonathan say, "Told you she was awesome."

The night continued with me rushing around. I moved with more grace and speed than ever before. When their orders were ready, I walked into the kitchen to grab the food for my faux-British customer. I chuckled to myself as I thought of Jonathan's silly attempt to sound British. Once I had placed the four entrees on the large plastic carrying tray, I headed out to the dining area.

I was standing right beside Jonathan when I heard the bell above the restaurant door jingle again. It was amazing that over the constant hum of voices I was still able to hear the noise. I guessed it was my constant awareness of who I had to serve next. I reached for a large bowl of lobster chowder and as I leaned forward to set it in front of Jonathan, I glanced up to see who had come into the restaurant.

Both bowl and tray fell from my hands. Jonathan yelped loudly as the hot chowder landed on his lap, his friends howled with laughter, and my tray crashed to the floor with a loud clatter. Soup sprayed and covered the floor, and everyone fell silent and looked at me, but I hardly noticed.

It was *him*.

7. Him

There he was. The merman. His broad stature took over the doorway, and his stance demanded attention.

His legs spread in a powerful stance and his hands were casually tucked into the pockets of his jeans. A dark black shirt with long sleeves covered his arms, hiding the incredible muscles which I knew lay beneath the thin fabric.

My eyes widened in disbelief and fear. All of the dread and horror I had tried to overcome in the past month crept back into my veins. Blood pumped hard within my chest while I tried to concentrate on breathing.

"Are you alright?" Trey had stood up beside me and placed his hand on my arm which had frozen in midair. His head kept swinging between me and the merman.

I began to gather my bearings. My mind searched desperately for an explanation as the merman strode across the room toward me. There was power in every stride he took, yet to me each step seemed like an unwanted calling to the fate that awaited me. My breath caught in my throat.

He stopped right in front of me. I couldn't speak. I wanted to say something to make the strange scene appear normal, but my voice was suddenly gone. There was nothing I could think to say and his dark eyes bored into my own, chilling my spine with the same fear and dread I had experienced on the *Lady Marie*.

As I gazed at him, he surprised me with a warm, friendly smile. The merman reached out and calmly took me by the wrist. His grip was strong and firm, a silent demand that I do as he requested. With a soft jerk he led me toward the front door.

Glancing back at the table, I saw Trey's face filled with concern. The others looked stunned as well. They seemed frozen in the moment—as unsure as I about what to do. You could have heard a needle drop it was so quiet in the restaurant. Everyone had stopped for the moment. They could feel the otherworldliness, uniqueness, of the merman. With each step we took I hoped someone would stop him from leading me out the door, but knew no one would. I was his.

He didn't let go of my hand once we left the restaurant. Instead he turned left and began to walk down the street with a brisk stride. Pulsating fear throbbed inside my heart. *Was he taking me away for good?*

He was no longer as gentle with me as he had been in the restaurant. His grip tightened around my wrist, forcing me to fight the urge to wince. Shoppers lined the streets, and couples meandered hand in hand along the sidewalks, but no one gave us a second glance. They seemed to be avoiding eye contact, actually.

He led me down Main Street, weaving past people as though they were not worth acknowledging. The ocean loomed before us at the end of the road; its white caps a beckoning call to the creature inside of me. A desperate struggle began in my mind: the desire to stay and the instinct to swim. But the forceful, dangerous grasp revealed what would happen if I followed my instinct, and everything inside of me yearned to be away from him. I tried to pull back, but he only tugged me along behind him with more force.

The sand crunched beneath our feet once we reached the shore, but the merman still held fast to my wrist. I expected him to lead us straight into the water, but instead he turned and tugged me to the left where he continued to lead us along the shore. Up ahead were the rocky boulders and stony walls I had played on so much as a child. At high tide the water crashed against the rocks, spraying whoever was nearby. The water was visibly creeping closer and closer to the rocks as the sun sank lower and lower in the sky.

Without hesitation, the merman led us toward them. He walked past the first set, which reached high above our heads, and then stopped on the other side. With a tremble, I realized we were hidden from view. No one would be able to see us from the main port, and the many lights which I knew glowed in Coveside were completely concealed from us.

The ocean wind whipped around us, my hair lifting gently in the wind as I watched the merman's move in a similar manner. His hair was as dark as I remembered, still hanging loose to where it touched the tips of his collar bone.

With a jerk he released my hand, allowing me to feel free for a moment, until he turned back around to face me. His jaw was clenched tightly; all traces of his fake smile had long since disappeared. In its place, his eyes held the deep anger I had seen in them over a month ago. His very gaze was like a hand closing around my throat, a closeness making me struggle for breath.

Adrenaline pumped through my veins as I thought of what he could do to me. I had no defense. I was his victim in every definition of the word. He could do whatever he wanted.

He saw the fear in my eyes and smiled in response, but it was not like the one he had given before. This one made my blood turn cold and I fought the urge to flee.

Finally he spoke, his voice as deep and dark as I remembered. "Are you well?" I was taken aback by the question. *Why did he care?* I struggled to find my voice, but couldn't quite reach it.

"You look fine," he said as his eyes slid up and down, analyzing my body. They were filled with hunger, a deep desire of something long sought for.

Looking back at him, my stomach tightened as I guessed what sensual thoughts ran through his mind. It made me squirm under his bold gaze and again the cruel smirk crept across his handsome, but evil face.

"So, Marina, due to your untimely blackout, I was unable to explain things. Is there anything you would like to ask me?" His tone was monotonous as though he could care less. When I didn't speak, he prodded further with another question. "How has your transition been?"

My head whipped up in response.

"What do you mean, exactly?" There was a slight tremor in my voice, but I tried to hide it.

"Haven't you noticed anything different about yourself?" The words were straightforward and unfriendly, the sneer still in place.

"Yes, I have," I said just as coldly. "If you are referring to the fact that my skin doesn't get wet and my hair dries incredibly fast, then yes, I have noticed a difference." The merman looked like he wanted to laugh at my attempt to sound rude.

"Have you used your fins yet?" He asked, taking me by surprise.

"F-f-fins," I stuttered, my mind trying to catch up with the picture in my imagination. "You mean, I could actually have fins like, like, well... like... yours?" My voice trembled.

He spoke to me as though I were a child, "It's been about a month, has it not?" When I nodded he continued, "If you fully submerge yourself in a natural body of water, then yes, you would have fins similar to mine."

I couldn't help but notice the bit of pride in his voice when he spoke of his own fins. I let the information sink in.

To think, if I entered the ocean I would have fins instead of legs! Why, it seemed impossible. Again I looked out at the ocean with disbelief, and once more the strong surge rose within my chest—deep desire to immerse myself in the watery splashes and twirling currents. A world of curiosity and endless possibilities opened before me like the pages of a book.

A sudden thought occurred to me and I asked it aloud, "What's your name?"

I blurted it out so quickly before thinking of what I was saying and instantly regretted asking. I glanced up to catch his reaction. His lips pursed slightly and his eyes narrowed marginally while scrutinizing my face. He paused, his features hesitating about whether he should tell me.

"Morven." The word slipped from his lips sounding harsh, cruel, and powerful. I nodded my head as though this were a completely normal conversation we were having.

Feeling more confident now that I knew his name, I asked another question that had been bothering me. "Why do you call me Marina? My name is Lissie."

A furious look crept across Morven's face and I took a step backward. He followed me. I continued to move back, but he matched me step for step. His eyes were deadly and filled with anger.

My back hit the rock wall behind us. The cold stone poked and pricked me along my back. Petrified, I looked at the ground with wide eyes and watched as Morven's feet stopped within an inch of mine. He was breathing heavily, his body close to mine. Summoning my courage I forced myself to look up.

He stood above me, hovering. The sight of him was incredible. His broad and expansive shoulders took up all my vision. With a quick movement he placed both of his arms to either side of my body, thereby cutting off my potential, but unlikely, escape. My breath shortened as I looked into his cold, dead eyes. When he spoke, it was with a more fearsome tone than I'd ever heard him use, "Your name is Marina because I say it is."

The finality in his voice was chilling. I managed to nod even though the back of my head was crushed against the rock wall.

Again I looked down at the ground. Panic was rushing through my body. His strong form proclaimed the power he had over me, and even though everything within my being screamed for me to flee, I couldn't. I was completely at his mercy. I had never felt so helpless.

I could still hear his steady breathing and was aware of his chest moving up and down in a steady rhythm. A soft chuckle escaped his lips, and I looked up to find an icy smile on his lips. My heart thundered within my chest while my body trembled in fear. Shrinking into the wall even more, I cringed. I hoped he would pull away and release me from this trap.

Without warning, Morven leaned his head toward mine. I reacted instinctively and turned my face to the side, gasping when his cool dry lips touched me on the cheek. I held perfectly still, frozen with fear, staring at the ground which was barely visible under Morven's muscular arm. His lips moved persistently across my cheek and grazed along my jaw. There was a rigid fierceness in each kiss that prickled my stomach into a tight knot of disgust. My chest heaved as I tried to think of some way to stop him.

I had thought that the lips would stop when they reached the bottom of my jaw, but again I was wrong. They continued to move down my neck to the base of my throat. A small cry of fear escaped from my lips unintentionally and I pressed them back together quickly.

At the sound of my whimper, Morven raised his head. Out of the corner of my eye I could see his amusement; he was smiling again and his shoulders shook slightly, which angered me further. He stood, patiently waiting for me to look at him, but I wouldn't give him that pleasure.

A tear slipped down my cheek and fell to the ground. I fought with all the strength I had to hold back the pressure behind my eyes and maintain my composure, but he saw straight through my façade.

Again a short laugh escaped Morven's lips. He muttered something softly to himself and then spoke loud enough for me to hear.

"Aren't we innocent?" My fear turned to burning anger at his mocking. How could he mock me after what he had just done, or what he had suggested he could and would eventually do to me?

I whipped my head up to meet his gaze with a furious glare of my own. I would not reply to his rude comment. I would not give him the satisfaction. He became cross, his eyes lighting with anger and a deep frown pulling at the corners of his stern lips. A small feeling of bravado surged within me and I gained some courage. There were ways I could fight against him and not go quietly. I would fight him every step of the way.

"You would do well to reply in the future." The ferocity in his voice made the fear return, but this time I hid my fear and instead prodded him further.

"Why were you there, that night, when I was out on the boat by myself?" If I hadn't been watching him so closely I would not have noticed the slight movement he made: an uncomfortable gesture which pulled him slightly away from me. "I remember seeing you. I know you were there, you sang along with me."

My voice rang with clarity and I could not help the pride which filled my soul as I realized I had him flustered. "Why were you there?" I again badgered. "Tell me."

Once more his stormy eyes met mine, but they were clear of all thought or expression. For just a moment he gazed in my direction as though he could not see me, and then a fraction of a second later the sharpness returned and he shook his head slightly. I held my breath, unsure of what had just transpired, while he looked at me with a sly and somehow satisfied grin. There was something about my voice that had hypnotized him, if only for a moment.

Then, with a sudden movement, he stepped back from me. I took a huge breath of air as if I had just come up from underwater. The wind whipped around us, tossing loose strands of my hair into my eyes. I watched Morven cautiously to see what he would do next.

He was standing a few feet away from me gazing out over the ocean, his eyes slipping back and forth across the horizon as though he were searching for something. He turned back to me and I could see this was it. He was going to leave me now, at least for some time.

"Until next time, Marina." He nodded in my direction and whipped around, running straight toward the ocean.

The speed with which he moved was faster than a human, but not so fast that I couldn't see him. The water reached his knees and yet he still ran with power and grace. The waves crashed up against his waist and then with rapid athleticism he sprang into an arched dive over a wave and slipped into the water. A gray shimmer of light shone in the water for a brief moment and then disappeared in an instant.

A relief like I had never known before flooded me. My muscles relaxed as I sank to the ground. My back was still pressed against the solid rocks. A sudden, pitiful cry escaped my lips and the tears began. I couldn't stop them from coming.

Something had changed in that brief moment when I had found the courage to ask him why he had been near the boat the night I was singing. For just a moment he had been entranced, something about my voice made him fall under a spell. Maybe I did have a way of protecting myself against him after all.

As I stood to walk back to the restaurant I recalled the look he had given me when he realized that I had momentarily mesmerized him. For in that moment I knew it was true. I was his. And I was just what he had been searching for.

For the rest of my walk only one word hung in the air, swimming through my mind, dancing on the waves of thought.

Marina.

8. Unknown

Upon reaching the restaurant, I took a large breath and prepared myself for the scene awaiting me inside. I opened the door cautiously and the scene was so normal it was as though I had stepped back onto my home planet. When I had been with Morven, my whole world had been filled with fear, desperation, and anguish. It was as though the earth had stopped moving, each second had worn on my nerves and self-control just too much.

The welcoming chatter and buzz of voices pulled me from my thoughts. No one noticed my presence at first, luckily, because I had been standing with my mouth hanging open.

With all the confidence I could muster, I crossed the room to where Laura was still playing hostess. As I walked, the restaurant slowly quieted and the weight of wondering eyes pressed upon my shoulders. I ignored it, trying to act as though what just happened was a typical, daily occurrence.

Laura spotted me and her body went rigid with excitement. It was like watching a puppy try to contain itself from jumping on those around it when its owner had told it to sit.

Thankfully, she waited until I reached the hostess stand to loudly whisper what she could no longer restrain. "Oh. My. Goodness. Who the heck was that guy?!"

She was so loud I cringed. "You have to tell me everything right now!" She started to tug me back toward the exit, but I dug my heels into the wooden floor and stopped her from moving me any farther. Confused, she glanced back at me. From the corner of my eye I saw three figures approaching. Internally, I groaned. How was I going to get through this without looking like I was lying?

"Who was that, Lissie?" Chelsea asked. She looked a little unhappy about what happened—I assumed she was the one who had to clean up the mess I had made. The four girls, who now stood before me, held their breath for my answer. I tried to find my voice.

"He's just this guy." I knew my answer wouldn't satisfy, and it sounded weak even to me, but I shrugged my shoulders and tried to play it off as nonchalantly as possible.

"Well, does he have a brother or cousin? Cause," Laura fanned herself with her hand, "I mean whoa, he was hot!"

Chelsea rolled her eyes. I glanced at Jessie and Hannah to see how they were taking this. Jessie was laughing at Laura's joke, but Hannah seemed to be studying me with concern. I cringed, not wanting her to see what I was hiding.

"Shut up, Laura." All three girls stopped laughing and stared at Hannah like she was from a different planet. "Can't you see that she doesn't want to talk about it?" Hannah continued. I struggled not to fidget under their concerned glances and pitying expressions.

"Oh, Lissie!" Jessie apologized. "I'm sorry we didn't mean to be rude, we just wanted to know who—"

"Hey," Hannah said and then glared at Jessie. "Just leave her alone and get back to work. We'll get fired with all five of us talking when we're supposed to be working."

My disappointed cousins dispersed among the sea of tables, heading back to their individual jobs. I couldn't have been more grateful for Hannah. She watched them leave and then turned back to me.

"Umm....," she hesitated as she nervously wiped her forehead. "You were only gone like thirty minutes, so some of your tables are still here. Jessie and I split them between us, while Chelsea cleaned up the mess you made. She loved every minute of it," Hannah said sarcastically. Her smile was contagious.

"Why don't you get back to the tables you were working? You look like you could use a distraction right now." I nodded and placed my hand on her arm.

"Thanks," I said quietly. She shrugged and headed back to the kitchen. I stared after her, not sure of where to start. My eyes grazed the room for an unrecognizable customer who wouldn't bother me with too many personal questions. In other words, I was looking for tourists who had never met me.

Someone was waving his arms at me and caught my attention. I looked to see who it was. There at the same table as before sat Jonathan with a big happy grin on his face. He waved for me to come over to him. Reluctantly I did.

"Hey there, girl!" Jonathan's friendly smile spread across his face. "What was that all about? Hmm?" He raised an eyebrow making a joke of what had happened. "Who the hell was that guy?" I swallowed the hard lump lodged in my throat, and tried to shrug it off with a laugh.

"He's just this guy I know."

"Course he is," Jonathan said and winked knowingly. "But the question, Lissie, is," he looked at me with happy eyes, "how *well* do you know him?" The other guys at the table giggled while I blushed at his insinuation. Trey, however, looked particularly irritated by Jonathan's question.

"Jonathan," I said, trying to sound normal and relying on my flirting skills to get through the awkward moment. I lightly smacked him on the shoulder. "Do you really think so little of me to sleep with a guy like that?" I hooked my thumb over my shoulder as though Morven was still standing in the doorway behind me.

I had never tried my hand at acting, but I knew I had to pull this one off. I couldn't let a rumor like this be spread around, even if it was probably better than the actual truth.

"I know, I know, Lissie," Jonathan said, still all smiles. "I've never thought that little of you. I mean you've never been that sort of girl, if you catch my drift." I nodded and rolled my eyes at him thankful he had dropped the subject. Even though Jonathan and I were really only friends at school from all the classes we had taken together, I still had a sweet spot for him.

"I see you've had your soup," I gestured towards the empty bowls, trying to change the topic.

"Not to mention all over him, too," Ethan said, reminding me of my blunder when Morven had arrived. The other boys started to laugh rambunctiously and I took my leave, all the while aware of how Trey's eyes followed every move I made. Pushing the idea from my mind, I got back to work. I tried to clear my head of all thoughts—especially those which revolved around a certain pair of stormy gray eyes.

———————

I heard the waves crashing on the shore, smelled the salty wind, and felt the cool sand beneath my fingers. I exhaled and opened my eyes to look around me. My breath hung in the air. I started to shiver and became aware of a loud noise that sounded like a storm. The pouring rain hit the sand, creating dents in the grainy substance. I sat up confused. I did not know where I was.

Getting to my feet, I trudged along the shore calling out for help, hoping someone I knew would hear me. I said each of their names over and over again, but nothing happened. Nothing changed. I was all alone on some beach. I continued to walk, my clothes drenched and sticky against my wet skin. I didn't know where I was going, I was just walking. The rain poured, thundering from the sky in torrents. I continued to walk because it was all I knew to do, yet I soon realized someone was walking beside me, matching me step for step. I stopped, he stopped. Part of me wondered if it was him. I began to panic. I turned and looked up, but I could not see him. He was a silhouette, a blurred image, but enough for me to realize that it was not him. This person did not walk with power and malice. I became happy knowing he was not the one who I feared, and continued to walk. I wanted to say something to this stranger, but didn't know what. All of a sudden the person beside me stopped. This time I stopped, too. I turned to see what was wrong, but he disappeared. Just like that he wasn't there anymore. And then, without warning, an excruciating agony and sorrow filled my chest. Crippling in pain I fell to the sand and cried out in horror.

My eyes flashed open and took a moment to focus. When they finally did, I saw my bedroom ceiling above me. I was breathing hard. Looking around, I saw that everything in my room was still in its proper place. A shaky breath escaped my lips.

"It was just a dream," I mumbled to myself. Even though I knew it had been a dream, I couldn't shake the strange feeling off.

I had never been one to have nightmares. Sure, I had vivid dreams where I was scared or hurt, but not like this. I had never felt such terrible pain, sadness, and anguish in a dream. Maybe that was why it bothered me. Instead of experiencing fear like a usual nightmare, I had felt the pain of losing someone I loved.

I had only felt it when I lost my mother, but even this didn't compare to the strong emotions that had grasped and pierced my heart to the point of crying out as though I were being tortured. I could still feel the throbbing spot where my heart had felt like it was going to burst into a million pieces.

I shook the thoughts from my head and got up to go to the bathroom, thinking that a splash of cold water on my face might do me some good. When I reached the bathroom, I opened the door to find Jillian sitting in the dark on the edge of the bathtub.

"Hey," she said softly and I could hear the smile in her voice. "Couldn't sleep either?"

"Nope," I said and took a seat beside her. We sat in silence for a bit, and just when I was about to speak Jillian cleared her throat.

"Oh, boy," she exhaled. I looked at her in an odd way. "I was hoping to save this until morning. I hadn't really figured out what to say to you yet, but we're ahead of schedule and I'm just gonna have to wing it." She glanced at me to see if I followed along. I didn't, but I let her talk anyway. With Jillian it was better to just let her talk and eventually everything would make sense.

"Your Aunt Sue called after you were in bed," she said. Still confused, I waited. "She told me…." Jillian drifted off. She took a big breath, "She said some guy came to the restaurant and took you outside for a while."

I froze, I hadn't expected Morven to show up in this conversation. I wanted to smack myself for thinking Laura would keep her big mouth shut.

Jillian looked at me, visibly concerned. I could see her in the mirror, but couldn't bring myself to look directly at her. I was such a coward.

"Lissie, honey, please look at me," she asked. I did so cautiously. "I know you're young and all, believe me I've been there before, but just be smart okay? There's a lot of stuff I did when I was your age that I regret."

Her face was so serious and caring that I almost broke down and told her the truth, but I didn't, I couldn't. I remembered the threat Morven had made the night he changed me.

"I know," I muttered. I looked guilty, for not being able to tell her the truth. My toes played with the fuzzy bathroom rug under my feet and I stared at them as though they were the most interesting things I'd ever seen.

"It's not what it looks like. He's just some guy and I would never…" I waved my hand, "do stuff with a guy before I was married." Jillian let out a sigh of relief.

"I'll hold you to that. I knew you were smart, I just wanted to make sure." She smiled, "Besides, it's good for a girl to have standards. Guys respect that." She put her arm around me, "And don't you worry, I won't tell your father. There's no reason for him to know anyway—this is girl stuff."

She laughed and was back to her cheerful self. I wished I could let her know how thankful I was for not telling Dad. She had no idea what she was really keeping from him.

"Thanks," I said with more gratitude than she knew.

"Whoops! Do you have to pee? I'm just sitting here jabbering away in the bathroom and you've probably got to go." Jillian chuckled to herself. "You've got to love pregnant women."

I laughed as she stood up with a sigh and said goodnight, while proceeding to waddle out of the bathroom with her hands pressed to her lower back. A moment later I heard her groan and then softly swear. I opened the door to find her standing in the hall with her back facing me. I saw the water on the floor and realized what was happening.

"You okay?" I said, still in a whisper.

"Wonderful," she said, excited for the arrival of the long-awaited baby.

"I'll go wake up Dad."

———————

Five hours later we were at the hospital and Jillian was in full-fledged labor. The baby was coming early, but the doctor said it wouldn't be a problem. All of Jillian's kids had come early, why would this little girl be any different?

I sat in the waiting room twiddling my thumbs. I was nervous, as I always was in this situation. The idea of meeting a new sibling had always been nerve wracking and rewarding. I bounced my legs up and down and checked my phone again for the time; it had been five hours since Jillian's water broke.

Derek and Sean were still at home. They were supposed to keep an eye on the others while we took care of Jillian. Of course, it was only six in the morning, so they probably weren't even awake yet. My job was to call them when our new sister was born and then they would all come and see her.

The minutes ticked by slowly and finally Dad came out smiling brilliantly to tell me my new sister had arrived. I called the twins and with the little ones they made it to the hospital in record time. When they arrived, we all followed Dad to Jillian's room.

We peeked around the entrance to the room. There lay Jillian holding a small bundle in her arms. She looked up peacefully.

"Come meet your new sister," she invited. We all crept forward, afraid to make too much noise.

Kaleb, who was in Derek's arms, gave an excited gurgle and kick. It broke the silence and Caitlin and Sara rushed to the bed. They crooned over her, calling her sweet names and introducing themselves in a formidable fashion. I stayed back, not wanting to bother their happiness.

"What's her name?" Sean looked at Dad. Jillian gazed up at Dad and together they said with smiles, "Emly." Emly, I thought. Emly is my new baby sister. I watched as the scene before me unfolded.

Jillian sat there on the hospital bed, letting each of her children see Emly. Justin was on his knees beside his mother, while Aaron stood right beside her. Caitlin lay at the bottom of the bed trying to hold Kaleb, who kept crawling around. Derek was craning his neck to see Emly and Sean stood beside him with Sara propped up on his knee. Dad was leaning on the bed with his arm around his wife.

It was like watching a scene from a movie, or looking at a picture that I was not part of. Somehow I knew I was not meant to be there. I no longer fit in. Ever since I had been changed, I was not who I used to be. A new world had been opened before my unwilling eyes, and I now knew it was where I belonged. This scene was not part of me anymore.

I had known for quite some time this moment would arrive, and tears threatened to spill over my eyes. I had been waiting for it, anxious and unsure of where I would be. Simplicity had told me to try and be my old self, but reality had just shown me the truth. I was of a different world and it was time to leave the old world in the past.

Before, I had been too afraid to leave. Too afraid to face this new phenomenon on my own. But that had all changed last night when I had seen Morven. For some reason, that small moment had given me the push I needed to take my future into my own hands. I could not let him control my fate.

Instead, I would face the new path before me, a path of my own creation. Without knowing it, Morven awoke a burning courage and desire to survive within me. I would do all I could to keep myself from whatever he had planned. I was not Marina, nor would I ever become her.

Tears welled up in my eyes, but I blinked them back and hoped no one would notice. I looked again at my family, all huddled around the hospital bed, and wondered if it would be my last and only memory of them all together.

Derek and Sean,

I know one of you will find this when I'm missing. I'm gone. I'm sorry, but I had to go. He came here and I didn't want that fate. If I went with him, I would be trapped in a cage for the rest of my life.

Give everyone my love, especially Dad and Jillian. I'm sorry, but I had to do this. I had to get out while I still had the chance.

All my love,

Lissie

The tears were pouring down my cheeks as I wrote it, my nose running like a small child's. I didn't know where I was going to go, or live, or how I was going to survive. My family was all I knew, yet I had to leave. With a heaving heart I read over the words, making sure they were enough. But I knew nothing would satisfy my family.

I glanced at the small bag I packed which lay on the bed. I had fashioned a waterproof bag that I could strap to my stomach. It looked like a flat fanny pack. A set of clothes was tucked tightly inside it, which would be of use whenever I reached land somewhere. The thought of being naked in a strange place was not one I appreciated.

Strapping the bag tightly against my stomach, I glanced at the clock. It was time to go.

I inhaled deeply and looked out the window of my room. I couldn't see the ocean, but knew it was there. I felt its pull to join the waves—a part of me wanted to be out there in the water. The desire was stronger than I had ever felt before. Maybe it was because I had finally made up my mind, or because I knew I would be in the water soon. I didn't know what it was, but the anticipation was strong and it was time to leave.

I lay my scribbled note on my pillow and crept across the room out into the hall. Everyone was quiet and asleep. Jillian was still in the hospital with Emly. They would be coming home in a day or two. My throat tightened knowing I would not be there to see them.

I shook the thoughts from my mind. I could think about all of that later, right now I needed my wits about me. I tiptoed down the stairs, praying I wouldn't make a noise. Reaching the side door of the house, I let out a sigh of relief, unlocked it, and pushed it slowly open.

A loud squeak resounded throughout the house. I cringed and paused. My ears strained for any noise that would tell me someone was awake. A light thump sounded above my head. I heard a soft groan and swore under my breath. Of all the people in this house to wake up, it had to be one of the twins. I followed the noise of the footsteps as they padded toward the bathroom. I didn't dare to move the door another inch, in fear that it would squeak again.

Suddenly, the padding feet stopped. They stayed in one place for a moment, and then headed back to the twins' room. I held my breath and waited to hear the creak of a bed. It never came. Instead I heard mumbling voices. My mind was on alert, *what had they noticed?*

My blood pounded faster as I heard two sets of feet make their way down the hall. I waited, hoping they were doing something out of the ordinary. What exactly I didn't know.

My hopes were dashed when I saw a foot and part of a flannelled leg appear on the stairs. That was it.

I shoved the door open, a loud squeal emitted throughout the house.

"Lissie?!" I heard from behind me, but didn't look back.

I jumped the four stairs that led to the driveway and sprinted for the path leading to town. I ran faster than I ever had before, the anticipation of hitting the water pumping through me. My ears strained to hear if anyone was following me. I heard the squeal of the side door open and I internally cursed myself for not climbing out my window.

Pounding down the path, my bare feet hardly touched the soft dirt. I could hear my brothers behind me and I knew they could see me. Their loud grunts were getting closer. I pumped my legs faster; one of the boys groaned.

I continued to run with speed that I had never had before. My brothers neither gained distance nor let up. I knew that if I made it to the water I would be safe. After that, they would not be able to follow me.

I saw the restaurant up ahead, which meant my goal was getting ever closer and closer. I whizzed past Darrow's Catch, heading straight for the ocean. The wind was cold and whipped against my face. Sean finally caught on to my plan.

"LISSIE, NO!" he yelled, but I couldn't let him stop me.

I ran as fast as I could. My feet reached the pier and I sprinted across the wooden planks. The end of the chase was in sight. I could see it, taste it, feel it. The pull from the ocean was so strong I wouldn't have been able to resist it even if I tried. The feet that pounded on the boards behind me picked up speed. They were determined to catch me, but I wouldn't let it happen.

I reached the end of the pier and made an inhuman leap onto the railing. Quickly I dove into the water and a ripple ran down my spine. My clothes ripped and where my legs had been there were now fins.

With an instinctive movement I shot forward from the pier into the unknown.

9. Refuge

I swam and swam for two days without stopping. There was no telling where I was; for all I knew I could have been swimming in circles. My body was exhausted and I was tired of trying to figure out what I should do next.

Where was I going to go? This question had been running around in my mind ever since I had left home. There was no place for me to hide from Morven, but I was going to do everything within my power to stay away from him.

These thoughts only made me feel more desperate and worn out. I needed somewhere to sleep, somewhere to eat—really just some place to be. In the back of my mind I knew what I really needed was home, but I couldn't go back now.

I paused. The feeling of the refreshing salt water was all around me, and it felt so *normal*. To think of being on land and breathing air seemed strange and foreign. I looked around me at the vast ocean floor. The sand rippled in soft identical mounds that went on and on for miles. The emptiness of the water made me feel lonely and desperate; I sank to the ocean floor and lost sight of the surface up above.

I dropped my hands to my lap and stared at my fins. Though it had been two days and they felt just as normal as legs, I couldn't help but be mesmerized by them. In reality it was one big tail that began just below the lavender cut on my hip. It was as solid and thick as my two legs put together. From its starting point at my hips, it tapered down to about two feet past where my toes should have been. At this point it split off into an elongated v-shaped fin. The tail's color was dazzling; each individual scale, when in the sun, shined different shades of lavender. They even shimmered and danced with color when it was dark, though the colors were much paler than when in sunlight.

The very bottom of my tail, my fins, the part which split into the v-shape, was different. It was made up of partially transparent flesh that was a paler lavender than the scales. It was lucent, sheer and appeared slightly weak. In reality it was firm and powerful, making swimming an easy task.

I wore nothing on my upper half. Instead my chest was covered by a smooth band of lavender scales that reminded me of kelp. The faded color matched my fins perfectly and spread from under one arm to the other.

Aside from the pack I had strapped across my stomach, my skin was completely open and free to the water pressing against it. Somehow it all felt natural, as though I was meant to be this way. The feeling both frightened and excited me at the same time.

I floated and pondered, the events of the past two days swam through my mind. It was like an aquarium at the bottom of the ocean, one where I was allowed to get as close to marine-life as I wanted. The only problem was their fear of me. I quickly noted that I could move quicker than any of them, and I succumbed to the idea of being a predator—though I had yet to hunt. Even the one shark I had happened upon had been afraid of me; but I was scared enough for the both of us while I watched the large fish swim away in panic. It had taken a long time for my heart to return to its normal rhythm after such an encounter.

With a loud sigh, I looked around me and returned to the present moment. I knew what I *had* to do, but I was afraid to do it. Since submerging myself in the water, I had yet to break the surface. I was too afraid I would be spotted by someone and what the consequence would be if such a thing happened. But there was nothing else I could do: I needed to figure out if there was land anywhere nearby.

Glancing up above me, I could just barely see the sun shining down into the water, creating a dazzling image of light. I was mesmerized for a moment, but then began to move cautiously toward the surface high above me. As I got closer, the sun reached me and the lavender from my fins shone with spectacular beauty. My stomach tightened in a knot, when with one timid, final kick, I pushed myself to the surface.

My head broke through the water and I took my first breath of air in two days. It felt the same as breathing underwater, except it was thinner and not as fulfilling. The sun shined brightly, making it difficult for my eyes to adjust, and the waves gently churned the ocean around me. With little movement from my strong fins I was able to keep my head above the water and ignore the strong undercurrent that latched at my flesh threatening to pull me into its grasp.

I looked around and realized I was entirely alone in the middle of the ocean; there was nothing but water for miles and miles. Being underwater had felt foreign originally, but coming back to this and finding myself still alone was like a knife to my heart. I was truly on my own.

Pressing on, I swam closer to the surface in what I hoped was the direction of land. My stomach began to grumble loudly and the thought of raw fish was beginning to sound appetizing. The only problem was every fish I came upon was already well hidden or too far away for me to find the will to chase down. My energy was dropping quickly and I knew I needed to find land as soon as possible; the idea of sleeping in the water sent chills of fear and dread down my spine.

Coming up to the surface to check my whereabouts, I scanned the horizon in a routine manner. It took a moment for my brain to realize what the dark shadow stretching across the horizon actually was. I moved forward, disbelieving. I squinted in the light. *Could that really be land?* I was too exhausted to think otherwise, and a tired smile spread across my face as I dove beneath the surface with renewed energy.

I reached the island in mere minutes. My head was above the water and my fins now touched the bottom.

The island was massive, stretching out across the horizon as far as I could see on either side. There was a beautiful beach tucked into a pocket of surrounding trees gently blowing in the sea air. Behind there, appeared to be a thick forest of trees full of green leaves and branches reaching up toward the blue sky. The sand was perfectly white and the waves touched it softly. Farther down the shore there were rocks and cliffs, their gray structures protruding boldly from the ground and standing resilient to the water smashing hard against their sides. This place had a mystical feeling to it.

Nervously biting my lip, I moved closer to the shore. I felt my legs reappear and my feet squishing into the ocean floor as I walked toward the beach. I paused, thinking how neat it was that my body could change its own constitution, when I stumbled over a rock and plunged head first into the water. Coming back up, I tried to stable myself. My legs felt wobbly and uncertain, as if they were unsure of whether they could hold me up. Looking down at my shaky knees I gasped. I had forgotten I would be naked. My arms immediately covered my chest and I sank to my knees with waves slapping against my hips.

For a moment I knelt there too stunned to move, and then I broke into laughter. It may have been the exhaustion that caused me to laugh so hard, but I couldn't stop for a long time. The situation was just too comical and the desperation and hilarity of it all only made me more aware of how strange a thing I had become.

Finally reality set in and I made up my mind. The small pack on my stomach contained a dry set of clothes I could change into. The problem was actually getting into the cover of the trees to change into them. Everything about this island suggested it was deserted, but I was too self-conscious to believe it. With a deep breath I worked up enough courage and made a mad dash out of the water, through the sand, and into the shady cover of the large-leafed trees.

Feeling more like myself once my clothes were on, I began to trudge my way along the outer rim of the island. I was afraid to go too far into the trees, not knowing what I would find there. The ocean was my shelter and comfort; it provided an escape from any walking creature, and I wanted to keep it in my sight at all times.

As I walked around the large piece of land, my stomach grumbled and I searched for food. After hiking for about a mile, I arrived at the large cliff I had seen from the water. Huge, with sharp edges, and points protruding along its enormous gray form, it daunted the eye and made me shiver in amazement.

The spot became my land marker and I used it as I walked around the island looking for food. After passing a slight curve in the land, I came upon small pools filled with all sorts of living creatures. My stomach growled in response to the sight of fish and small crabs sitting just beneath the tantalizing surface.

Feeling like a shipwrecked soul, I found a stick and sharpened it with a rock to make a poorly fashioned spear to catch the fish. After I managed to catch three fish on the stick, and wrap up some of the small crabs in the pack I had, I proceeded back toward the cliff.

Approaching the gargantuan rock from this different angle showed a jagged collection of boulders naturally stacked upon each other. Their existence provided a pathway to the top of the large gray structure. My only thought was for safety from whatever might live on the island; I thought the top of the cliff might give me the reassurance I needed to fall asleep.

The climb was easier than it looked, and I reached the top with fish and crabs in hand. My stomach clenched in anticipation as I set my raw dinner down and went to find sticks to make a fire. My heart went out to my father, thanking him for training me and my brothers in survival, "just in case." At the time it had seemed silly, but now I was glad for having paid attention to everything he had taught me.

Walking back through the trees with a pile of sticks in my arms, I spotted something I had not seen before. There in the rock wall was a small opening, a cave of sorts, but not so small that a person couldn't fit inside. I bit my lip, wondering if I dared to enter. For a fraction of a second I wondered if a human could live inside and decided to check it out later, but not at the moment. Right then my stomach was controlling my mind and its insistence was all I would listen to.

It took some time to get a good fire started to roast the fish and crabs, but the wait was worth it. Finally, with a satisfied stomach, I lay down to rest my tired eyes.

The top of the cliff was unbelievably large and flat, creating an excellent viewpoint of the ocean and horizon. Soft grass covered the surface and blew in the sea air as though trying to imitate the crashing waves below. I lay down in the grass with nothing but the darkening sky for shelter. Somehow I felt lucky, and slowly closed my eyes, drifting off into a much desired sleep.

————————

The smell of charred wood reached my nose and tickled my brain awake. I pulled my eyelids open lazily and blinked at the bright red sky. My mind moved slowly as I tried to figure out where I was. Turning my head to the side, I saw the small extinguished pile of burned wood that had cooked the delicious meal the night before.

Looking up at the light sky, I wondered what time it was. I sat up with a soft groan. The sight which met my eyes was unbelievable. Bright streaks of pink were jumbled with blurs of deep red and swirling orange clouds grazed the horizon. The breathtaking canvas of colors was reflected perfectly in the churning waves, making the sight transcendent. It was a moment before I realized that the sun was resting on the horizon in the same place as the night before. It was sunset again. I had slept the day away.

Casting my thoughts aside, I deeply breathed the crisp ocean air. The sight and the smell reminded me so much of home. Pressure built behind my eyes, but I pushed it back. I knew there was nothing that could be done about it.

Determination penetrated my soul. I slowly unfolded my legs to stand, and grimaced at the aches and pains along my spine that came from sleeping on the unforgiving ground. I took one last look at the sky, which was slowly deepening in color and leading to another night of darkness, and turned around.

Alarm shot straight through every nerve in my body. There was a man facing me not even ten feet away. I had obviously caught him in mid-movement since he stood frozen, with one foot stepping toward me and a look of utter surprise on his face. His face was calm, but in one hand he held a knife, the large blade glinting in the setting sun. My eyes widened at the sight of the object, and, thinking quickly, I whipped around intending to jump off the cliff. I sprinted for the edge knowing it was my only refuge. A sound escaped the man behind me, and I heard something fall to the ground, but I did not turn back to look. Safety was only a few more steps away—if I could only reach it.

A strong hand clasped around my wrist with a firm grasp, ruining my escape.

10. Wondering

A small squeal left my lips and I struggled to pull free. The vice-like grip only tightened more, but I pulled harder, not caring. The man's grip only grew tighter. With my other hand I reached around and tried to pry his fingers from my wrist, still ignoring the pain. I strained for the edge of the cliff, but I could not get any closer.

The man's deep voice reached my ears, but in my fright I could not hear what he was saying. Petrified I continued to strain for the water. The man's other hand wrapped around my wrist that was attempting to pry his fingers. Realizing he had both my wrists and I was trapped, sheer panic reigned through my veins. Away I scrambled, my feet clawing at the ground and my eyes never leaving the sight of the water.

With a sharp tug he stopped my progress and I found myself face to face with the man. My chest was heaving from exertion and I trembled with fear. Eyes wide, I tried to calm myself as I looked up into the face of the man who held me captive.

He was young, much younger than I had thought he was. There was something in his eyes, however, that spoke of experience and years beyond what his face showed. He stood taller and broader than my brothers and one glance at his arms revealed large, toned muscle beneath his tanned skin. His chest rose slowly in perfect, rhythm against the white shirt he wore.

My eyes flickered back to his face. They grazed over his strong jaw, looked to his light hair of gold streaked with brown honey. Again I looked back at his face, my perusal taking no more than a second, and met his eyes. The dark brown irises met mine with equal caution and there was something about his gaze that made me think he was as afraid of me as I was of him.

After measuring up one another for what seemed like a lifetime he finally spoke.

"Just stop," he said. His voice was calm and soothing. The baritone words rolled over me, but I had a hard time contemplating what they meant.

"I'm not going to hurt you. I'm sorry I frightened you—it wasn't my intent." His eyes told me more than his words could. I gazed back at him stunned, my breath catching in my throat. A wary confusion began to creep into his face and I felt his grip on my wrists loosen slightly. Embarrassed, I broke away from his eyes.

My gaze fell to his large, tan hands that encircled my wrists with perfect ease. They were powerful and made me fear him.

Cautiously, as though worried about what I might do, he let my wrists go. My arms fell automatically to my sides.

I wouldn't look up. I was too afraid. There was something in his eyes that reminded me of Morven. The seriousness of his gaze penetrated my soul, willing me to give myself over to his control.

"Who are you?" He asked, his deep voice demanding an answer. The abruptness of his question took me off guard and I lifted my eyes to his once more, not sure of how I should answer. *Would he believe the truth?*

"Why are you here?" He questioned even more harshly, making me flinch. I knew I could not answer and once more I remained silent beneath his constant, evaluating eyes.

An irritated sigh escaped his lips, and he looked out over the ocean. His eyes squinted as he stared at the glare coming off the water. Placing his hands along the waistband of his khaki cargo shorts, which were frayed along the edges, he mumbled inaudibly to himself and ran a hand through his golden hair.

I watched him carefully and saw his eyes shift suspiciously. He appeared to be contemplating something, something that included me. I held my breath in anticipation.

"Even if you can't understand me," he said as he backed away from me, his movements cautious, "come." I eyed him, unsure of what he was doing and still pondering his words. Once he was a good distance away from me, he beckoned with his hand.

Did he think I couldn't understand him? Again I continued to stare, wondering why I could not find the courage to speak and partially amused by his lack of perception. He swore under his breath and I hesitated, not sure what he would do.

"Come," he said, as though I were stupid. He repeated the same hand movement. He was half-turned away from me, trying to show that I was to follow him. Giving in to his demands, I spoke, "Okay." He froze and his eyes tightened.

"You can understand me?" he asked. I nodded. He looked at me curiously his hand twitching by his side. Frustration lined his jaw, and I felt guilty.

"Then when I... Why wouldn't you ...?" he was at a loss for words.

"I'm Lissie." I said. My voice was too feeble and quiet.

He straightened his already broad shoulders and crossed his arms over his chest. My eyes flicked away toward the ground and I swallowed loudly. He inhaled deeply and spoke again in that deep voice.

"Well, Lissie, I guess it is," he said forcefully. I could feel his gaze bearing down upon me but couldn't look up. "How did you get here?"

His eyes were intense as he waited for my reply. My mind raced, unsure of how I should answer.

"I'm... not really sure." I said. He looked even fiercer.

"I see," he said disbelievingly. He cleared his throat and opened his mouth to speak, but then closed it again.

I wondered how I could explain myself. I didn't want to cause him any trouble; I had obviously intruded his island. I was sure that I was unwanted company.

I jostled my leg in irritation. Maybe I could make a run for it; I could catch him off guard and be gone in an instant. My plan began to form in my mind. I believed it could work and my heart pounded heavily in anticipation. My right foot moved slightly to get a better stance on the ground. I switched my weight to this foot, but his eyes shifted down as if he saw what I was doing.

"Come on," he jerked his head back towards the trees preventing me from making a dash toward the water. When I didn't move, his face hardened. "You are coming whether you like it or not." His threat hung in the air and we stared at each other, quickly evaluating the other's strengths and weaknesses. His eyes softened slightly.

"Just come on." Again he gestured to the trees behind him and I found my resolve slowly crumbling.

With a renewed sense of courage I stepped toward him. Approval filled his eyes and he made a small nod with his head, as though he was relieved. In a quick move he picked something up off the ground and held it in front of his body out of my sight. Confused I followed him down the slope toward the trees.

Just before stepping into the shadows of the leafy branches from above, he stopped and turned toward me. With an open arm he gestured for me to continue in front of him. I hesitated but the object in his right hand caught the light of the setting sun and sent a sharp thrum of fear through my soul.

I knew I had no choice but to move forward. The dagger in his hand would force me to bend to his will.

Anxiety surged through my veins and pounded in my heart with every step I took. We walked deeper and deeper into the island. There was something about the place that fascinated and frightened me. The grass tickled my bare feet and the air was alive with the movement of the dancing tree branches, but I was constantly aware of the footsteps following my own.

He didn't speak, except to direct me either to the right or left. I jumped every time he broke the silence. Something in his voice made my stomach feel as though it was plummeting to the grass-carpeted ground.

Moving forward, I clumsily stumbled over a pesky root from a tree and staggered to the side. I hastily reached out and caught onto a branch to prevent myself from falling onto the earth. Once steadied, my eyes returned to the young man and widened in surprise. His jaw was clenched tightly, his arms flexed, but what caught my eye the most was the dagger pointing directly at me. For the moment I stood horrified and chills ran down my spine.

Slowly his stance relaxed and the dagger lowered. I hesitated and stepped away from the tree branch.

"Sorry," I said softly. My voice was barely audible.

He nodded, acknowledging my statement, and then spoke, "Before we go any further I need answers." My heart pounded heavily at those words. What could I tell him?

"So," he continued and gave me a questioning look by raising one eyebrow, "who are you?" I swallowed hard, still unprepared to answer.

"Umm, I already told you," I said weakly. I looked at the ground.

I knew what he wanted and when I glanced at his face I could see he expected a full answer. I sighed heavily and looked into the trees while my mouth ran through the quickly constructed story. *At least some of it's true*, I thought.

"A while ago I was on a boat with my father and brothers when we got caught in a huge storm and I was thrown overboard." I took a big breath and carried on, "Since then I'm not really sure what's happened. Being thrown overboard is all I really remember, and I'm not really even sure how I've survived since then. I'm not sure where I am, what I'm doing, or what will happen next, but..." I broke off because I could think of nothing else to say that would enlighten him and at the same time keep me from trouble.

"I see," he said. He rubbed the back of his neck in a distressed manner and looked away for a moment. "Lead on, straight ahead."

"Okay," I nodded, knowing he hadn't bought my story. Without another word I turned around and began to make my way through the trees. The silence behind me was eerie. Like a shadow I knew he was behind me, but I couldn't hear him anymore.

As we got further into the island the trees began to thin out. Between the dark thick trunks of the trees was a brown sea grass that rippled through the air like a sheet rustling in the wind. Up above I heard birds calling to one another, their cheerful voices contrasting with the stretching sunset shadows of the forest.

Further ahead we came upon a wall of greenery that stretched out of sight to either side of where we stood. Immense shrubs grew to the height of a house, the leaves all stretching to the sky as though trying to grasp the last few rays of daylight before the sun hid itself for the night.

Finally making a sound, my captor moved from behind me and walked toward an area in the green wall that I hadn't noticed before. The branches in this spot were worn down, as though from years of use as a gateway to what lay beyond it. I peered into the opening trying to see what lay ahead, but the tunnel was too shadowed to reveal the other side.

Without saying a word, I moved into the hidden opening and passed through the leafy pathway. Ducking under the last branch, I stepped out of the natural wall and straightened up. My eyes widened.

I passed him, went through the vine door, and could not believe my eyes. The natural beauty now surrounding me surpassed the rest of the island entirely. Massive trees with gargantuan trunks stood before me; in between the trees, spanning widely across the ground, were wild flowers of all different colors. The flowers blew softly in the gentle breeze.

Rippling in unison, as though they knew how beautiful they were.

The trees, with thick strong branches, continued so high they looked as if they tickled the now azure clouds. There was something about the branches that were inviting. They whispered on the breeze tempting their onlookers to climb into their grasp. Hidden in the shadows below were the massive roots coming out of the ground and then plunging back into the earth with fervor.

Glancing around, I noticed that the wall of shrubs we had walked through earlier created a large oval surrounding the meadow. The diameter was at least twice as long as a football field and successfully created seclusion from the rest of the island.

Off to one side I noticed a small patch of land containing plants of various shapes, sizes, and colors in neat rows. Before I could even ask what it was, my mind answered the question. It was a garden. Was it really possible that this young man lived here alone?

Flicking my eyes to the side I caught him staring at me. His brow was creased but he looked less tense than before.

"It's beautiful," I said, hoping to distill the silence between us.

Once more he nodded his acceptance. But I couldn't help noticing the pride in his eyes as he glanced over the meadow with a practiced gaze.

I tilted my head to the side. "Do you just live out in the open?" I waved my hand around me. I wondered if this was how his skin was such a golden brown.

"No," he said. One of his eyebrows rose and the creases around his mouth pulled back slightly as though wanting to smile. The change in his face eased some of the tension in my stomach.

He cleared his throat. "*That's* where I live." He pointed up and to the right, and I gasped.

A group of four tall, thick trees stood together, one of which had a rising spiral staircase twisting around its large trunk. At the staircase's end there was a perfectly crafted cabin nestled into the sturdy branches. It stood in the tree with no sign of instability, its two levels reaching high into the treetops. Two small windows were on the front side of the cabin; one near the wooden front door and the other higher up for the second level. The whole cabin was made of wood, but it was not a simple blocked structure standing in the tree. Instead, the cabin was part of the tree as though it had grown from it. The snug wooden structure fit perfectly into the branches, parts of its walls intertwining with thick trunk that stretched toward the sky.

The two-story cabin appeared to be the main structure, but as I looked I noticed there were other cabins in the three surrounding trees. These smaller structures matched the larger one in craftsmanship and design. Completing the house, a series of wooden plank bridges created lofty pathways from tree to tree.

"Did you build that?" I asked with clear astonishment.

He nodded and again I noted the pride in his eyes. He was enjoying my amazement.

"Come on," he said seriously, not letting me gawk at the structure any longer. To my surprise he led the way this time, and I noted that his dagger was no longer in his hand. I spotted the weapon encased in a sheath against his left forearm.

Walking up the sturdy stairs, I had to concentrate in order to keep up with him. My eyes were fixed directly above our heads as we got closer and closer to the looming cabin above.

Our bare feet hit the steps in the same padded rhythm until we reached the top. Leading inside, flat planks of wood created a small deck in front of the door. We were at least four stories off the ground, and I gulped thinking of what would happen if I fell. Glancing upward at the few branches above my head, I saw the sky was getting darker. Soft, tiny stars were just becoming visible on the pale canvas above us.

The creak of wood sounded beside me and I looked at the wooden door that had been pushed open. Inside, I could hear the sounds of feet moving on wood in the night-darkened room. The rough scrape of a match shot through the night air and was followed by the bright flash of fire. Illuminated for just a moment by the lit match, I watched the crouching shadow of the man place the match into a fireplace. Slowly the logs sprang to life and kindled the room with a flickering light. Other patches of light appeared around the room as little lamps were lit by the mysterious man.

Biting my lip nervously I stepped into the warm glowing room.

All the furniture within the confines of the cleverly crafted walls was made of wood. Before the fireplace was an elegant wooden bench, and a matching pair of chairs stood against the far wall. To my left there was an area that served as a kitchen (complete with counters and cabinets), rugs on the floor, and sheer curtains covered the windows. My mind flashed back to the rough hands that had encircled my wrists. Those very hands held more meaning now as I contemplated the skill they had.

The room had a manly feel to it. The rugs and fabric curtains were woodsy, making me feel like I was in a cabin in the mountains, even though I knew I was far from there. In the kitchen was a black wood-burning stove complete with a small chimney leading to the ceiling and through the roof. Off to the corner was a metal basin with a water pump, and across the room a staircase rose to what I assumed would be the second floor.

"You will stay here for the night." The deep voice said. I startled.

"Okay," I said and nodded to confirm that I understood.

He stood across the room with his arms hanging awkwardly by his sides. Once or twice he opened his mouth to say something but then stopped. I waited patiently.

"Sit down here," he said gruffly, his harsh manner returning. "I will get you some food."

Not wanting to give him any more reason to be angry, I quickly obeyed and took a seat on the bench before the fireplace. The wood was smooth and polished, and touched my skin gently. The curve in the seat was welcoming and I found that I would have been comfortable, if not for the male presence that was loudly opening and closing cabinets in the kitchen behind me.

"Here," he said and shoved a wooden bowl and spoon into my hands. Inside it was a thick gravy stew with large chunks of vegetables and greasy, brown meat.

With ease, I watched as he grabbed one of the chairs from across the room and set it next to the bench. He slid into the chair and without a word began to eat the food with relish.

Hesitatingly, I filled the spoon with a chunk of meat and lifted it to my mouth. Surprisingly the gravy was filled with flavor and oozed from the meat as I chewed it. Satisfied, I ate quickly as my stomach woke up and responded to the nutrition hitting its empty confines.

As I ate I could not help but glance at the young man sitting to my left. The same questions ran through my mind. Who was he and why was he here? And why were there more cabins in the adjacent trees? Was it possible that he did not live alone? Looking at the size of the pot on the black-wood stove I knew that it contained a great amount of stew. Were there others who would be eating with us as well? The thought of others made me even more worried.

"You were hungry," the young man said. I jumped and almost dropped my spoon. He put his half-finished bowl on the floor and stood. "Here, I'll get you some more." He stuck his hand out for me to give him the bowl. His manner all of the sudden seemed more hospitable.

"No, its okay, I'm good." He raised an eyebrow.

"You don't want anything more to eat?" He questioned disbelievingly.

"Well," I said. "I wouldn't mind more, but don't we need to save some?" This took him by surprise.

"Why would we need to save some?" He looked totally confused. "I have plenty and it needs to be eaten." He explained this as though I were a child and it made me frustrated. I didn't want him thinking that I was young and immature.

"What I meant was, shouldn't we save some for the others?" Now he really looked at me like I was crazy. But within a moment his eyes flashed and he whipped his dagger out of its sheath, pointing it directly at my chest. Within a moment he became very serious and almost angry.

"What others?" he railed me in a demanding tone. His voice reached new heights of anger. "Are you not alone?"

"No," I said quickly. My eyes were wide and innocent as I pressed into the back of the bench away from the knife. "I am."

"Then who are you talking about?" He bored his eyes into mine. I cowered a little, partially afraid and partially confused by his piercing eyes.

"I assumed there were others who lived in the cabins out there," I said as quickly as possible, and pointed feebly in their direction as if he could see them through the wall. His shoulders relaxed and he sighed with relief. Closing his eyes, he slid a hand across his face and then looked back at me.

"Lissie," he said calmly. It was the first time he had said my name. Somehow the word sounded different when he used it. "I'm the only one who lives here. I'm the only one who has ever lived here." His tone was reassuring and it soothed my nervous thoughts.

He returned the dagger back to the sheath on his arm and ran a large hand through his hair.

"I'm sorry I got so defensive, I just like to know what's going on." He said.

So he would probably like to know that I'm not human, I thought, but I couldn't tell him that.

"What's your name?" I asked, speaking softly. Something about his openness made me want to know, even though my eyes kept flickering to the dagger on his wrist and my heart continued to pound heavily in my chest.

"Patrick," he said. His features had softened and he looked at me with eyes of rich brown. He was still standing and his broad frame seemed to take up the entire room. Something in his gaze made me feel as though I was falling.

"How long have you been here alone?" I asked desperately wanting to know the answer.

Immediately his softened features closed. He tore his eyes from mine and looked at my bowl.

"Here," he said opening his hand to me. "I'll get you some more stew."

11. Company

I woke the next morning with the sun warming my face and a wonderful woodsy smell alerting my senses. It took a moment for my eyes to adjust to the bright light, and I had to wait to sit up and look about the room.

I was in a comfortable double bed with a wooden head and foot board. There was a dresser and bedside table. The rest of the space was filled with half-finished carvings, chairs, tables, and other smaller objects. Woodchips covered the floor and to my left there was a staircase that led downward. I found it funny that I didn't remember walking up them last night.

Wait, I thought. *What happened last night?*

It all came rushing back in an instant. The hill, the sunset, the meadow, the house in the trees, the stew, and then Patrick.

Patrick. Both fear and wonder were bonded together with that name. There was something about him that made me curious, more curious about a person than I had ever been before.

Thinking deeply, I tried to remember what had happened the night before, but the last memory I could recall was falling asleep on the wooden bench. I remembered Patrick sitting in front of the fire lost in his own thoughts, but then nothing after that. *How did I get upstairs?* I blushed when the realization hit me: *he must have carried me up here.* Was this his room and bed? Suddenly everything felt intimate and I was unsure of what to do.

I lay back down in the bed, my heart thudding heavier and heavier. I stared up at the wooden planked ceiling. My thoughts were a mess. There was a manly smell surrounding me and it did nothing to help my thoughts.

After a moment I wondered where he was and sat up again.

Crawling out of his bed I made my way to the stairs. When I reached the edge of them I heard a female voice coming from the first floor. Alarm shot through me. Patrick had said he was the only one who lived on the island. *Had he lied to me?*

Lying down on the dusty floor, I pressed my ear to the wood to try and hear better. Soft voices reached my ears, their words laced with caution.

"I just don't get it," the female voice said, irritated. "How could she have gotten through?"

"I don't know," Patrick said, bewildered. His baritone voice sounded deeper and smoother than I remembered. "She is either more cunning, or *he* has finally figured out how to get through." Patrick emphasized the word 'he' with malice and I wondered at his anger and worried for whoever he was talking about. The small glimpses I had seen of Patrick's protective and cautious nature were enough for me to know he was an excellent fighter.

"Did you find her or did she find you?" The girl's voice cut through the room.

"I found her," Patrick's said in a low voice. After he said this I heard the female sigh in relief. Why would I cause so much distress? I remembered Patrick's tense face last night when he had mistaken my statement about saving food for "others".

"Tell me everything," the female demanded. "I'll need to have the story straight in order to tell Shaylee. You know how she gets." I could almost hear the nod I was sure Patrick gave.

"The night before last I saw smoke above the trees, which led me toward the cave. I hid in the branches of the trees and spotted her eating on the cliff." Abashed, I put a hand over my mouth; I hadn't realized he had been watching. "She looked exhausted, but I waited to see what she would do. I thought it might be a trap."

Trap? For what?

"Of course," the girl seemed to agree.

"Then she fell asleep," Patrick said, mystified. It was as if I confused him.

"Really?" The girl was similarly astounded.

"Yes, she slept the whole night and right through the day. I worried that something was wrong with her, so I climbed the cliff and just as I was getting closer she woke up and saw me."

The girl gasped, "Patrick, you could've been killed!"

Killed? I sat in silence listening to what was going on below, my mind trying to grasp what was being said. *Did they really think I was a threat?*

"I was fine," Patrick spoke quickly as though he did not agree with the woman. "As I was saying, she woke up and when she saw me she turned around and was going to jump off the cliff.

Again the woman gasped but this time she said nothing. There was a long silence in the room below.

"But luckily I was able to catch her before she fled."

"Luckily," the female voice agreed. "Do you think she's with *him*?" Even though I wasn't in the room, I could hear her emphasis on the word. I wondered who this person was and why they refused to say his name.

"That's what I thought at first," Patrick agreed, "but then she told me what had happened to her."

"Don't you think she could have lied?"

"That's just it—I know she lied." I pressed my hand over my mouth, once more while listening intently. "But it's because I knew she was lying that I decided to trust her."

There was some twisted logic, and I could not figure out what he meant. Why trust me when he knew I was lying?

"I know it sounds stupid," Patrick confirmed, "but I figured if she was so obvious in her lie then she could not be working for him. If she was working for him you know she would have had a scripted story to tell and her acting skills would be much better. I think this girl is very genuine actually."

I waited to hear the woman's response. Somehow after Patrick had explained himself, everything made sense. He was right; if I was a threat to him then I would have had a story already planned, a logical alibi. Instead I had stumbled through my excuse which was partially true, and he had been able to see right through it. A new respect for Patrick grew in my mind as I realized how intelligent he was.

"So what exactly did she tell you?" The woman asked, without rebuking his choice of harboring me in his house.

"She told me she had been on a boat with her father and brothers when they got caught in a storm and she fell overboard. She said she doesn't remember anything else." When he retold the story I realized how lame it sounded. No wonder he had seen right through it.

"Patrick, there hasn't been a storm that big in at least a month."

"I know, that's how long she said it'd been since it happened." Patrick lowered his voice and I could just barely hear him say, "It just doesn't seem right though. There's no way she has been living here for over a month. I would have noticed." My heart thudded heavily as they quickly condemned me.

"It's just too coincidental," the female was definitely frustrated now. "The night of that storm was the night we spotted—"

"Shh!" Patrick hushed her, cutting off whatever it was she was going to say. "She might be awake by now."

Realizing they might come and check on me, I hopped up and made my way back to the bed. I slipped in silently, pleased to find the mattress did not squeak. Pulling the covers up to my shoulder I rolled onto my side so my back faced the stairs. Sure enough, a few seconds later I heard a pair of feet ascend the stairs and enter the room softly.

The footsteps came closer to the bed, the sound pricking my memory. I remembered waking up numerous times in the middle of the night and hearing the distant sound of feet walking back and forth across the floor below. The sound had been repetitive and comforting, and each time had lulled me back to sleep. Until now I had thought it a dream.

With a little more drama than necessary, I rolled onto my back and looked up at the ceiling, blinking my eyes rapidly for good measure. A deep polite cough made me aware of who was watching me. My heart sputtered slightly and I internally wondered at this reaction I had to his mere presence.

He stood at the top of the stairs, his hand gently resting on the railing. Something about his expression made my stomach tighten. His eyes were softer this morning, but there was still wariness in his gaze. I noticed that the dagger was still present on his arm.

An uncomfortable silence filled the room and I was all too aware of my presence in what seemed to be his bed. Sitting up, I moved to get out on the side opposite him—I didn't want to come too close to where he stood.

"Breakfast is downstairs," he blurted out as though relieved to have finally come up with something to say. I nodded in response and began to make my way toward him. Something in his expression told me to stop. He ran a hand through his golden hair while quickly speaking.

"A friend of mine is downstairs."

He paused and I widened my eyes to feign surprise, not wanting to explain my earlier eavesdropping. "She wants to meet you."

Again I nodded my head, "Well, okay then." Without another word I passed him and made my way down the small staircase and onto the main floor. Patrick followed right behind me.

Standing next to the empty fireplace was a beautiful girl, her skin golden from the sun and wavy beetle-black hair falling to her waist. Little strands were pulled back in tiny twists to keep the hair away from her dark green eyes. She was slender, with long legs and a toned, muscular body. A pink camisole revealed a bit of her flat belly, and short jean shorts complemented the tan on her lanky legs. Her arms hung at her sides, but they were anything but casual. Something in her stance made the tips of my fingers tingle, and her gaze watched my every move with incredible intensity.

"Lissie," Patrick came up beside me and spoke cautiously. "This is my friend Kryssa." He gestured toward her with his hand and without thinking I moved forward with my hand extended.

"Nice to meet you," my voice said bravely; it sounded braver than I felt. Kryssa stared at my hand for a moment and then took it carefully as though measuring me up. Her touch was cool and soft, yet somehow felt so smooth she almost felt wet. Something about her touch pricked at a memory, but I could not place it.

After shaking my hand Kryssa seemed to relax, but only slightly. Her eyes snapped from mine and clapped onto Patrick's. "My father will want to meet her."

Her words were spoken with finality, as though arguing the point was out of the question.

"I knew you'd say that," Patrick shrugged though his jaw tightened.

"There's no reason to fight it," a softness filtered into Kryssa's voice. "You knew this before I came here this morning."

Patrick nodded while I stood between them feeling self-conscious. *Why were they talking about me as if I wasn't there?*

"Sorry, but why do I have to meet your father exactly?" I asked, turning my gaze on Kryssa. Her green eyes flashed to mine.

"Because he will need to know of your presence here with Patrick." Again the statement was matter of fact, and clearly not to be questioned.

Patrick butted in, "Don't be hard on her, she's not quite aware of what's going on." I felt like a child, but I appreciated his defense as opposed to the anger he showed last night.

"And she will remain unaware until after meeting with my father." Kryssa's eyes were now on Patrick and there was something in her gaze which seemed to be trying to communicate more than was being said.

"At least talk to Shaylee first," Patrick spoke softly, his voice almost inaudible. I could see she was going to disagree, but cut her off.

"Yes, please do," I said, making both Kryssa and Patrick look at me as though I had lost my mind. The wariness returned in Kryssa's eyes. "I wouldn't mind having some time to adjust to things here. I'm not even sure of what happened to me, and from what it sounds like, I would have to answer to your father," I raised an eyebrow in question and when Kryssa did not speak I took it as confirmation to my beliefs. "It just might be better if I have an idea of what happened before I speak to him, don't you think?"

I left the question up to her, but I could tell I had already persuaded her. Her eyes met mine, blank for a moment, and then she shook her head slightly as though to clear a thought.

Slowly she nodded, "Alright I will speak with Shaylee, but it's more than likely she will come here to meet you." Her last words were spoken harshly, but there was something in her eyes which showed respect. Maybe my persuasion had earned her trust.

"Where do you live?" I ventured, wondering if she would tell me.

"Not here," she said softly. Making direct eye contact with me, and this time there was a hint of a smile around her lips. Without further explanation she spun toward the door and strode across the room. Just before she disappeared, she tossed a farewell over her shoulder and the sound of her bare feet on the steps slowly faded away.

An awkward silence fell between us as I struggled to say something. But this silence was different from the previous night. Somehow it was companionable, or at least the hostility was no longer present. Patrick's defense about my experiences made me relax around him. I knew he was wary of me, but I no longer worried that he would hurt me.

For a moment we avoided looking at one another and then I cleared my throat. The sound was much louder than I expected it to be.

"You know, I could've slept on the bench or the floor." My hand gestured feebly while I tried to meet his gaze. "You didn't have to give me your bed."

He smiled, and the difference was amazing. His face lit up and all the tension which had been in his body after Kryssa mentioned her father left his shoulders.

"Yes, I could've done that," his voice ran over me in a smooth wave. "But it wouldn't have been very gentlemanly." *Gentlemanly?*

"Still, I feel bad for taking your bed." Again my voice sounded weak compared to his, but the light in his eyes reassured me.

"I was fine—I slept in the guest room." My eyebrows scrunched and he noticed. "The guest room is in one of the other cabins," he explained for my benefit. But I knew from the sound of his feet pacing, and the dark circles under his eyes, that he hadn't slept all night.

"Oh," was all I could say.

He inhaled deeply and I raised my eyes to his warm brown ones. "I could show you around if you'd like. For the time being you'll stay in the guest room. I would have put you there last night, but I was afraid the night air would wake you if I carried you across the walkway."

A pinch formed in my stomach as he mentioned carrying me, and his eyes moved slightly from mine realizing what he had admitted.

"Yes," I said acting as though I hadn't noticed. "I'd love to see the rest of the house."

He smiled once more and walked toward a side door in the wall that I hadn't seen previously. The sunlight was blinding once he opened the door, and I caught myself staring with my mouth open as he stepped onto the flat wooden walkway that led to the next cabin. He walked smoothly, and the wind lifted his golden brown hair in a gentle flutter.

My heart pumped faster than I wanted to admit, and it took a moment for me to realize he had stopped to turn around and look at me. Heat flooded my cheeks and a smile entered his eyes. The corner of his mouth lifted slightly and then his right eye winked at me quickly.

Wondering at the sudden change in his manner toward me, I hesitated. This was a different person than the one I had met last night, and I found myself all the more curious about him.

"This way," he said, a definite smile in his voice.

12. Water

That night I lay in the guest room, positive that I was never going to fall asleep again. My mind was reeling with all sorts of crazy, and yet in some way believable, ideas.

Rolling onto my side, I stared out the open window. I just couldn't believe what I had seen and heard today. I was now one hundred percent positive that Patrick was not normal. He was different, but I couldn't figure out why. His behavior was both friendly and yet cautious, as though he feared me. But even odder was the life he lived on this island all alone.

Earlier when he led me around the three cabins, I couldn't ignore the facts of how abnormal his life was. The first room he had shown me was the one in which I now lay. The second was a workshop filled with wooden furniture and hand carved wooden animals. The area reminded me of the carvings I had seen in his bedroom earlier in the morning, but this cabin allowed him more space to work.

The third and final room was filled with shelves and stacks upon stacks of books. I spent more time in this space than any of the others. The titles he had were incredible; some dated back to the renaissance while others were more recent. I got lost in a stack of books, feeling as though I was in a different century, and never wanted to resurface. After seeing how much I enjoyed the room, Patrick kindly offered me free reign and allowed me to read whatever I wanted. A stack of books currently rested beside my bed in the guest room waiting to be read.

With an exasperated sigh I went through my thoughts once more. There were only a few options which seemed to make sense, but not one correlated with everything I had witnessed. He could be the grateful subject of a well-endowed relative, but why live alone on an island? There was the possibility of him being a shipwreck victim, but he had friends who visited so why stay here? And who was Kryssa's father? Why did she visit the island instead of living on it? My mind ran in circles, but focused on one pervading thought. What if Patrick was a merman? Although he was different from Morven, the harshness that he showed on the cliff the day I met him reminded me of this new world I was now a part of. But if he was a merman, why would he always have a dagger strapped to his forearm? Wouldn't he have blades like Morven?

Again a sigh of frustration escaped my lips while these thoughts ran around and around in my head. It wasn't until pale morning light began to creep through the window that I finally fell asleep; I dreamt of brown eyes and houses hanging in the trees.

When I awoke the next morning, I felt more tired than when I had gone to sleep. I threw the covers off my body, straightened my clothes and looked around the room.

The windows of this guest room were wide, letting sunlight in from all sides. The bed was a simple cot-like mattress covered in an old quilt. In the corner stood a tiny dresser with both men's and women's clothing of various sizes. Patrick had said I could pick out something to wear from it. He never explained, but I assumed the women's clothes were for when Kryssa came and visited, and the men's clothes must have been for her father. My mind peaked with curiosity, but after having spent all night thinking about the mystery and coming up with nothing I discarded the thoughts quickly.

Next to the bed was a simply carved little table with an oil lamp sitting on top. Again the feeling of living in a different century washed over me. Above the dresser was a small circular mirror; the glass was slightly distorted as though it had been hanging there for years.

Tired of trying to sleep, I hopped out of the bed. Its creak resounded in my small chamber, and I made my way over to the dresser. I picked out a white shirt and some simple shorts and put them on. Even though the clothing felt foreign, it was still nice to get out of my dirty clothes from the day before.

Without glancing in the mirror, I left the room and walked across the bridge connecting the guest room to the main cabin. I tried not to look down, because I knew the sight would only make me queasy.

Reaching the door, I bit my lip while debating on how to enter. *Knock or just walk in?* I stood there considering what to do for a moment and then decided to casually knock.

"Come on in," Patrick yelled in reply from somewhere inside. I pulled on the tough string which lifted the latch allowing the door to swing open. The smell of cooking bacon wafted over me and my eyes rested on the man standing, with his back to me, at the black wood stove.

With a glance over his shoulder his gaze swept over me. The familiar feeling of curiosity mixed with fear pinched my stomach. I placed a hand to my belly trying to ignore the uneasiness. He worked quickly, but his movements were gentler than yesterday. I felt a bit more at ease.

"I trust you slept well?" His said louder than necessary.

"Yes," I nodded while trying to hide my smile; his phrase sounded old fashioned.

"Well good," he said casually over his shoulder. "You hungry?"

Without waiting for a response, he handed me a plate laden with food and I sat down on the wooden bench. While we ate we spoke about trivial things. At times I was surprised by his sudden change in manner toward me. All harshness and caution were gone from his face. Instead he seemed excited.

Perplexed by this new side of him, I listened as he told me about which books in the library were his favorites. His vocabulary and literary knowledge was expansive and I soon found myself feeling inadequate.

After a while Patrick grew quiet. When I looked at him he seemed to be deep in thought as though debating something. I wondered where his mind was when he suddenly spoke, "Do you want to go on a walk? There's this really neat place I want to show you."

"Sure," I said, more confidently than I felt. "That sounds great."

Later, as I walked beside Patrick the grass tickled my bare feet. He led the way through the trees; this time heading farther inward to what I assumed was the center of the island. We climbed over rocks and around large trees, but there was a definite pathway we followed along the rising hills and jagged landscape. Sweat beaded along my brow, but I continued to follow Patrick—certain he was leading me somewhere interesting. If it was anywhere near as beautiful as the rest of the island then I would be satisfied. Although the cautious side of my mind couldn't help but notice that he still had the dagger tied to his forearm.

As we walked my senses were heightened and before long the sound of rushing water pervaded upon my ears. This was not the sound of waves slapping the shore in a dancing rhythm, but rather a constant thrum of rushing water. I glanced to the side to see if Patrick heard it as well, but he gave no hint as to whether the sound had yet reached him.

Climbing down a hill, the sound came closer as we broke through some trees and into a flat piece of grassland. Without stopping we pressed forward, the blades of green caressing our feet. The air was damp with moisture and the cold touch of leaves brushed against our shoulders and arms.

Up ahead through the trees, I spotted a bright shimmer reflecting the sun. With a skip in my step, I broke through the last branches that had blocked my view.

The source of the thrumming water finally stood before my eyes. A brimming blue waterfall cascaded over the edge of a rocky cliff and into a crystal pool below. The water was so clear I was able to see every rock beneath its surface. Taking in the sight, I knew my jaw had fallen open as the fantasy-like scenery danced before my eyes.

On one side of the large pool there was a massive rock that stuck out from the water and reached toward the heavens. The top then flattened out as if to serve as a perfect diving platform for the pool below. The side opposite this cliff was a steep hill of green, but near the bottom a flat rock jutted out just above the surface of the water. Canopied with shade by drooping leaves from above, it looked like a perfect place to sit and enjoy the waterfall's beauty.

I stood frozen for the moment in awe. A soft chuckle reached my ears and I looked to the side slightly embarrassed while a blush crept across my cheeks.

"Stop it," I said, lightly trying to defend myself. "It's just pretty, that's all."

"Sure," he shrugged, though he looked like he wanted to say more.

"I've just never seen anything like it." I said, and my hands flew out in front of me to demonstrate what I saw.

"Not many have," he said nonchalantly, but his words only threw my previous curiosities into my head once more.

"Come on," he said suddenly, pulling me from my reverie.

Without hesitation Patrick pulled his shirt over his head revealing a tan and well sculpted body. He was lean, yet cut, each muscle profound and obvious. His shoulders were broad and ripples of muscles moved seamlessly as he strode toward the large rock beside the waterfall. He scoured the side of it with expert skill and reached the top incredibly fast. At the top he walked to the edge; I could barely see the expression on his face from where I stood. The height of the rock was only lower than the mouth of the waterfall by a few feet.

My heart thudded heavily as I realized what he was about to do, but my fear for him quickly turned to anticipation. If he was a merman, he would now reveal himself as such when he hit the water.

For a moment he stood with his toes on the ledge, the sun glinting off his tan skin and golden brown hair. And then he jumped. He reached full height and then began to fall toward the water. He tucked into a flip and after coming full circle let go of one of his legs. One knee still wrapped in his locked hands, he tilted to the side and I realized what he was about to do. My feet steered me clear of the water as he came down with a gargantuan splash.

I held my breath as I waited to see the fins and the all too evident flash of scales, but nothing came. Instead, Patrick broke the water's surface and flicked his hair to the side. Again I was shocked by how open his gaze was. Rather than his earlier hostility, he actually looked exhilarated. But a sinking disappointment coursed through me. As unbelievable as the idea of Patrick being a merman was, it seemed the only reasonable explanation for why he was on the island. Now I didn't know what to think.

"Alright, it's your turn." Patrick's voice distracted my thoughts. I shook my head quickly in response.

What to do? I couldn't swim, if I submerged myself in the water I would transform into a mermaid. My heart rate accelerated. Just when I had begun to let my guard down I was forced to ward off danger once more. And why would Patrick ask me to swim with him? Was it possible he suspected something? Feeling more and more trapped, I tried to think of an excuse.

"Oh, come on! It's not that high." Patrick said, trying to persuade me. I shook my head, knowing my survival was on the line. I was all the more aware of how insistent he sounded. Playing his words over in my mind, I grew more suspicious. I remembered the dagger he still had on his forearm; he had been all too quick to reach for it last time when he thought I was a threat. What would he do if I suddenly changed into a mermaid?

"I can't," I said with what I hoped sounded like fear in my voice. Patrick swam toward me and stood on a submerged rock. The water slopped against his stomach as he looked at me. Something in his eyes made me want to trust him, but I refused to follow my gut. Logically, he couldn't be trusted.

"Come on, I'll do it with you," he pleaded. I shook my head quickly and didn't allow myself to think of what he had offered.

"No," I said, determined to get my point across. Then taking a deep breath, I lied. "What I mean is, I can't swim."

It was so far from the truth that I hoped the lie was not written across my face. I glanced up quickly and saw him looking at me curiously. His eyes were soft and the sun brightened his face. I felt the need to open up to him, but I shut down the urge before it had time to grow.

"I would hold onto you if you want." He shrugged like it didn't matter. "Or I could teach you how to swim." His casual response put me at ease, but I shook my head again feigning fear.

"Look, it's not like you have to go where it's deep or anything. Just stay where it's shallow," Patrick said continuing to coax me.

I bit my lip, my mind forming a lie to save my skin. "I'm still afraid of water, from the last time, and I just feel safer not in it right now." Referring to my near drowning made my voice harsher than I wanted; my eyes flickered over Patrick's face hoping he wouldn't be angry.

"Oh," Patrick said. He grew more solemn and I couldn't help noticing the puzzled expression he tried to hide. I remembered that he didn't believe my tale of how I came to be on the island. Referring to it again had caught him off guard.

Although we stood in a secluded spot, in an area more beautiful than anything I had ever seen, I couldn't help but feel the tension between us. We were in a battle of wits. I suspected he was acting friendly to get me to lower my guard. I would have to do what I could to match his level of play.

"But," I said in response, trying to play along with his little game and throw him off track, "I could go sit over on that ledge and dangle my feet in the water." As I spoke I pointed to the shaded ledge on the other side.

Patrick turned to look at the flat canopied rock and began to make his way through the water toward it. Spotting an area where I could cross to the other side without falling into the water, I hopped from rock to rock until I reached the ledge.

I took my seat in the center and as promised dangled my feet in the cool, refreshing water. Patrick swam over to where my feet touched the crystal blue liquid and looked up at me; I couldn't help but notice how the water clung to his eyelashes. Shadows from the leaves played on his young, masculine face making the situation seem all the more serious.

He broke our steady gaze to look down and find a place to stand. His feet touched the flat stones beneath him and he stood before me, chest deep in water.

A small crease developed between Patrick's eyebrows and he broke our silence. "What's your family like?"

Surprised, I wondered what his motive was. For a moment I pondered what I could tell him, but then realized I could tell the truth. Curious, I deliberated whether I should tell him the truth. If this was a game we were playing, what was the prize at the end?

"I'm sorry," he said, his eyes wide with innocence. "I didn't mean to upset you, I just wanted to know." *But why do you want to know?*

Frustrated, I watched my feet as they moved through the water, back and forth.

"You didn't upset me." I smiled calmly to reassure him. My voice matched his carefree tone perfectly. "I was thinking of something else."

He looked even more curious—the small crease reappeared between his eyebrows. For just a moment I thought I saw understanding in his eyes. He knew that I was equally playing the game too.

"I have a very big and kind of strange family," I said. Even though I was trying to be controlled, I couldn't contain the smile in my voice. "What do you want to know about them?"

"Whatever you wish to tell me." In a skilled move, Patrick pulled himself out of the water to sit beside me on the ledge. Water ran off him and his closeness made my breath catch. If I so much as moved an inch to the right, our legs would touch. I tried not to think about it as my mouth began to run. He listened, never saying a word, his eyes focused on the water running past our feet in a gentle current.

"So," I said coming to a close, "that's my family." I shrugged even though a pang of homesickness hit my heart.

For a moment he remained silent and I wondered at his expression. A deep longing was on his face, an unquenched desire. It was more genuine than any emotion he had shown since we had gotten to the waterfall.

He took a deep breath, "I have to say, you impress me, Lissie."

It was my turn to look confused.

Glancing to his side he peeked at me and laughed. The sound was deep and rolled over my ears in a gentle sort of way. I felt myself relax slightly.

"Don't look so surprised," he continued. "We both know that your story of how you got here isn't true. But," he held up a finger, "I do believe what you said about your family. That I can tell is real."

Impressed by his perceptiveness, I matched his claims. "Then you can be honest and give up the carefree act. I know you brought me here to get answers."

Again he chuckled and this time the tight air between us seemed to shatter. The tension and distrust floated away on the breeze.

"Well," he sighed. "I guess we have wasted some valuable time today."

"I guess so," I answered, my eyes squinting from the bright reflection coming off the water. And then I wondered out loud, "What about you, do you have a family?"

Again the sorrowful expression passed over his face and he looked over the water. The moment of friendly laughter was past; in its place was the serious face I had come to know. The roaring waterfall was the only sound to be heard as we sat side by side averting our gazes.

"Sorry," I said truthfully and ducked my head, not sure of how to explain myself.

"Not a problem." His statement was too matter of fact to make me feel reassured.

"I didn't mean to be rude," my words spilled out quickly "I just wanted to... you looked..." Internally cursing myself, I couldn't finish my sentence. *What could I say?*

I could feel his gaze on me, but I refused to look up. My hair had fallen in front of my face creating a barrier, and I intended to keep it that way.

"Lissie," he said more gently than I expected. Slowly I turned to look at him and met his brown gaze with my own. His chest rose as he breathed deeply. "I'm sorry. I simply forgot what it was like to have a family."

Sympathy filled my heart and I regretted prying into his past. He had just as many secrets as I did. Internally I vowed to keep my curiosity hidden from him.

Time stood still as we sat on the ledge and looked at the water. It was peaceful, yet filled with unanswered questions. The leaves on the bowed tree above us rustled in the wind, taking strands of my hair with it. A gold strand caught my attention, its unnatural movement stirring fright within me that he would notice. Without hesitation, I pulled a hairband from my wrist and secured my waves in a sloppy bun.

I realized my sudden movement had not escaped the eye of the man beside me. Why had I not pulled my hair back before leaving the cabin this morning?

Clearing his throat awkwardly, Patrick slapped his palms onto the tops of his legs. "Should we head back?" He asked, sending a very pointed look in my direction.

"But we just got here," I protested.

"Since I'm the only one swimming," His said in a mock apology, "let's go find something we can both do."

"Okay," I said and stood up to follow him.

"But," he said, turning back toward me, "we do have one thing in common."

"What's that?" I asked; my feet poised upon the wet rock.

"We are both hiding who we really are," he said and then made his way back across the rocks to the other side.

I stood frozen for a moment, knowing that what he said was true. And yet his admittance that he had a hidden past made me trust him.

Oddly, a small smile curved over my lips and I tiptoed over the rocks to the other side where Patrick stood waiting. His eyes confirmed what I felt.

Somehow we were now friends.

13. Sisters

Time passed quickly on the island—each day produced something new. The new found friendship between Patrick and I grew slowly. We found that we enjoyed one another's company and a careful routine wove its way into our lives.

Patrick took me around the island, showing me his favorite spots and the best views of the ocean from the raised hills. One day he even took me into his workshop and showed me how to carve a fish figurine out of wood. The little object he helped me make was nothing like the intricate carvings he had on shelves throughout the cabin, though.

The library quickly became one of my favorite spots and I often found myself searching the stacks and rows of books for something to read. Part of my mind knew I would need to return to reality, eventually, but for the moment I was happy to escape Morven's threats by staying on the island. I tried to attribute my reluctance to leave as fear, but deep down I knew it had to do with Patrick. He was still as mysterious as when I had first met him, but the more I learned of him the more I liked him.

We spent many afternoons in the main cabin. Patrick would sit in his wooden chair and carve all sorts of things, whether they were tools or animal figures, and I would sit on the couch and read. Sometimes we talked and it was in these times that I felt our friendship strengthen.

Finishing dinner, we sat in our usual spots by the fireplace with the last light of day coming in through the windows.

I glanced over at the still figure that sat in the wooden chair before the fire. His eyes were open and unfocused as though he was thinking. The firelight played tricks on his hair, changing it from rich chocolate brown to honey golden in the blink of an eye. His legs stretched leisurely in front of him and his muscular arms were folded across his broad chest.

The mystery of who he was and why he was on the island was no closer to being solved. I had come close to asking him twice, but in the end decided to maintain the communal silence about our pasts. Reason forced me to think I was entitled to ask since he had questioned me about my past at the waterfall. Taking a deep breath, I decided to try and ask once more.

"Patrick?" He pulled himself from his thoughts and calmly looked at me. I bit my lip and tried to gather my thoughts.

"When you asked me about my family at the waterfall," I began. He cocked his head curiously. "Well, I was wondering where your family is."

He looked away immediately and fidgeted slightly. There was silence in the cabin aside from the popping and snapping of the burning wood. It became uncomfortable and I played with my hair self-consciously, not sure of how to proceed.

"My family is no longer alive." A lonesome sadness enveloped his voice.

Why had I broken our unspoken pact to remain silent about the past? I cursed myself for prying into his business. Once again I stared into the fire trying to ignore what had just transpired. After some time I realized I could feel his eyes on me. I tried to resist the urge to look at him, but gave in quickly.

His face was composed but regret lined his eyes, and as he blinked slowly he looked away once more.

"I didn't get the chance to say goodbye to them," he said. "One day I was with them and the next I was gone. Then they were gone too and I will always be wondering... never knowing what could have been." He broke off and placed a large palm across his face, hiding his expression from me.

Leaning forward, he rested his forearms on his knees. The silence became weighted again and I was unable to speak, afraid I would say something worse. I stared at him, wishing I had never spoken, when he looked up and gazed back at me.

Patrick inhaled a shaky breath and rubbed his face again with his palm. He was tense, the muscles in his shoulders and arms seized tightly and didn't release.

Before I realized what was happening, I moved closer to him at the end of the bench. Sitting down, I hesitantly reached out and touched his back. In all the time we had spent together, we were careful to maintain a distance from each other. In one short movement I broke the physical barrier between us. My hand rubbed back and forth along the wrinkles in his shirt, concentrating on getting the tight muscles to relax. He slowly began to breathe deeper and steadier trying to calm himself. Finally the muscles in his back relaxed and he lifted his head from his hands.

I paused. My hand on his back stilled. With a slow movement, he turned to look at me. All signs of loneliness were gone from his eyes; all that remained was a deep warmth. Uncomfortable with my hand on his back, I moved it away. I was unsure of whether it should have been there in the first place.

The corners of his mouth slightly lifted and his eyes glowed powerfully. He was looking at me as though he had never seen me before, as though he really saw me for the first time. I looked back at him. I was uncertain of what it all meant. The distance between us had somehow closed without either of us moving. I could feel his gaze on me when I looked away. I knew he could feel the change too.

He moved his hand slowly and grasped my own gently. I could feel the calluses on his palms. Warmth spread through my chest and my heart pumped a little faster. Unsure of what to do, I remained still and kept my gaze averted.

I could feel him willing me to look at him. Slowly I turned my head and lifted my eyes to his. He opened his mouth to speak but then...

"I told you he'd be in!" A high shrill voice poured in through the window.

Patrick immediately dropped my hand and stood up quickly. The moment shattered.

Without a knock, the door opened and in walked a young teenage girl with bouncy red curls flowing from her ponytail. Behind her was the most beautiful woman I had ever seen, and just behind her was Kryssa. They all paused upon seeing me in the living room. I stood up from the bench to watch them as they entered.

I looked at the youngest girl. She was staring at me curiously; the hint of a smile played around her lips as her eyes darted from me to Patrick. She was beautiful, more fairy-like than Kryssa and the other woman. Her eyes held the innocence of youth, but her body was that of a young woman. I guessed her age to be around my own.

The beautiful woman beside her had the same dark hair as Kryssa, only hers fell in soft ringlets rather than in waves. Her face was serious, and her light green eyes seemed perceptive. She was the shortest of the three, but her frame was as athletic and sleek as Kryssa's. Her stance asserted her authority and the name I had heard before pervaded my mind. *Shaylee*.

There was nothing harsh in Kryssa's gaze; somehow I had earned her trust. Maybe it was because I was still here and no harm had come to Patrick. Though how I could ever hurt him when he was so much stronger than me was still beyond my understanding.

"Lissie," Kryssa said formally. "These are my sisters, Nixie," she pointed at the small red haired girl, "and Shaylee." I had guessed correctly.

Now that I looked and knew they were sisters, I could see the resemblance. The curly ringlets of Shaylee and Nixie matched perfectly, though the color was different. The three girls also shared the same shade of bright green eyes. The longer I stared the more, I could see that Nixie and Kryssa hardly looked alike; instead they both shared certain features with Shaylee. It was as though Shaylee was a mix of the two girls and they each had different parts of her.

"It's nice to finally meet you," Nixie said in a twinkly voice—the same voice that had come through the window only moments before.

"When you said you would be back, I thought it would be sooner than a week." Patrick's deep voice came as a shock and made me jump. I looked up to find him casually smiling at the three sisters.

"Yes, well, plans change." Kryssa's tone was light and comfortable, but I could tell Shaylee was not so laid back. Her hands were by her sides, her fingers spread apart making me feel threatened. Once more I felt a tingling in my own fingers in response. Before I could wonder about it, Shaylee blurted out. "How long?"

Everyone turned to look at her, wondering what she meant. When she realized no one understood, she rephrased. "How long has it been since you fell from the ship?" Her eyes bored into mine.

I swallowed hard, worried she would pull the lies from me. I may have come to an agreement with Patrick about the past but I knew this woman wouldn't be so obliging. Out of the corner of my eye, I saw Patrick glance at me.

"About a month before Patrick found me," my voice was nervous.

"And where were you between falling off the ship and then?" Her gaze was piercing.

"I already told them," I said weakly, trying to be innocent. I dropped my eyes to the floor. "I don't really remember what happened or how I got here."

"Yes, we know." It was Kryssa who spoke, her tone softer than the other day.

I felt terrible deceiving all of them, but Patrick understood. There was something in his past that made him just as keen as I was to leave old memories unstirred.

"Come on," Kryssa nudged Shaylee, forcing her to loosen her stance. "I told you all of this. She is innocent and you know it."

I gazed at Shaylee, hoping she would see something in my face. She continued to look back, but after a moment she dropped her gaze and sighed.

"I know you already told me," her hard features softened and her gaze fell upon Patrick instead. "It just causes one to wonder about—" She broke off suddenly.

I glanced over at Patrick to see what he made of the situation, but he was calm. "That's exactly how I felt when I first saw her."

The tension in the room eased between the girls, but I felt more uncertain about my situation than ever before. What was it that Patrick saw in me?

"I presume you have a reason for showing up so unexpectedly?" On the last word Patrick caught my eye and winked. His actions puzzled me. Not only was he being more friendly than normal, but his words were so carefully spoken that I felt he was trying to hide something.

"Yes, but let's sit." Shaylee's authoritative voice was once more in place. Hardly moving from where I stood, I sat down on the wooden bench as the sisters took their seats. Patrick stood beside the fireplace while he let Shaylee take his own chair.

Shaylee's eyes snapped to mine and I knew she was all business; this was not a meeting for the faint of heart. Trying to keep my wits about me, I gathered my courage and flicked my eyes to Patrick. He stood leisurely with an arm against the wood carved mantle, but the lines in his face spoke differently than his casual body language.

"Lissie, I am unsure of all my sister told you, but I gather you know we do not live here on the island?" At my subtle nod, Shaylee continued. "Where we live there are many others, who like us, would be concerned with your arrival. For that reason your whereabouts have remained a secret. We three are the only ones to know about your presence here."

Patrick exhaled softly. I glanced at him quickly and saw the relief on his face.

"What I need now from you is very important." Shaylee's words rang with truth and I held my breath in anticipation. "You have to tell me the truth of who you are and why you are here."

Alarm filled my heart and every nerve in my body stood on edge. I wanted to flee. There was nothing they could do to make me tell the truth. I would have to leave.

Feigning ignorance, I tried to maintain a calm façade. "I don't know what you mean. I have told you who I am and where I came from."

"I understand that, but it's this month period in which you claim you had amnesia that has me worried." Shaylee's eyes pierced into mine sharper than ever before. She was able to read me like a book; somehow I got the feeling she had done this numerous times before.

Fear and confusion riled inside me, making me see an approach I hadn't considered before. With more confidence than I had expected I forced myself to speak clearly.

"You are right," I said. Shaylee's eyebrows rose slightly at my words; to the side I saw Patrick straighten his posture as though on alert. "I didn't speak truthfully. I remember everything that happened during that month. But I still won't tell you."

Nixie, who was sitting beside me, inhaled sharply while I continued to focus my gaze on Shaylee. Miraculously, my mind was calm even though my heart was beating out a staccato rhythm.

Kryssa stood up from the bench, but her eyes were not on me. Instead she looked to Patrick. "If she will not tell us the truth, then we have to take her. I know you didn't want it to come to this, but she is too much of a liability to not be taken."

The words made no sense to me, but Kryssa's logic seemed to be working on Patrick. I could see it in his gaze as he lifted his eyes to my face. He nodded his head slightly, without looking at Kryssa.

"Why won't you tell them?" Patrick's voice floated through the room just above the sound of the fire.

"Because I can't." I said, my voice growing stronger. "If I tell someone the truth, I endanger their life. I won't risk your life for this."

Shaylee broke in forcefully, yet a hint of respect was threaded in her words. "It does not matter your reasoning, we need to know or you will have to come with us. It would be much easier to do things here."

For a moment I wanted to tell her, but then the vivid memory of Morven's flashing blades and incredible speed returned. He was an unimaginable threat.

"I don't mean to be rude," I said, turning my gaze back to the sharp green eyes. "But you would not be able to defend yourself in this situation. I won't tell you."

"Then we have no choice but to take you with us," Shaylee said sighing heavily. "I hoped it would not come to this."

"Do you have anything to do with the war?" Kryssa blurted out from beside Patrick. Confusion ran through my mind while my eyes widened.

"War? What war?" I asked quickly unsure of what I was being accused of.

"Kryssa!" Nixie hissed under her breath, admonishing her older sister.

"What?" Kryssa shrugged, "Shaylee wanted the truth, and by the look on Lissie's face she is innocent just like I said."

Shaylee glanced at me, her eyes registering relief. Somehow I had passed some test without even knowing it. *Who were these people?*

"I still want her to come with us," Shaylee spoke, this time more calmly.

"No," Patrick said causing all of us to look at him. "She will not be leaving here."

"As difficult as it may be for you," she said sarcastically, "she has to go. Others will find out soon enough and come here anyway. Its best we keep the situation under control and handle this now." Shaylee was standing in front of him while she spoke. I felt as though she was trying to communicate something deeper to Patrick. In return his eyes flashed and his nostrils flared in anger.

"I will go," I said quietly. Four pairs of eyes turned to me. "Kryssa, mentioned your father the other day. I will meet him if that is what you want. But, I have no idea what you're talking about and I have never heard of a war."

In the silence that followed my words, I knew I had settled the matter. There would be no further questions; my acquiescence was all they needed (though their reason for needing it still evaded me).

Shaylee was the first to regain her composure. "I will hold you to that," she said. "We will return tomorrow to take you with us. Thank you for being so cooperative."

In her last statement, a touch of a smile appeared on her lips revealing a lighter side to her personality. Without another word she walked toward the door. Nixie rose off the bench and followed her.

"Sorry," she said, smiling slightly when she passed me. She paused awkwardly. "It really was nice to meet you." Then she scurried out the door as though afraid of what she had said.

Kryssa still lingered in the room, the strange silence weighing and pressing upon us. "Well, I guess I had better go." Patrick made no move in response, so I rose from the bench instead.

"Thank you for coming." It was all I could think to say. As if the conversation had been too hostile and I needed to make it seem friendlier.

A short laugh escaped Kryssa. "That was far from being a nice visit. But don't worry, Shaylee is only harsh when she has to be." She passed by me toward the door and paused before stepping outside. "I'll see you both tomorrow."

I nodded, but Patrick once again made no response. With a sigh and apologetic look, Kryssa turned once more to leave.

"Kryssa." Patrick's voice made me jump. "Let your father know I'll be coming with her."

For a fraction of a second Kryssa's eyes widened in surprise, but she covered it well. "I'll do that. Goodbye."

The door closed behind her quietly, but the soft thud rang with finality.

The silence which had been in the room before was nothing compared to what hung thickly between Patrick and I now. I felt as though I were drowning in a cloak of dark secrets, unsure of how to escape.

"Don't worry about their father," Patrick said, his voice strained. "He'll treat you with respect, there are just... others that I'm worried about."

Again the reference to more than the sisters' father fell upon my ears, this time making me curious and uncertain of what I had done.

I nodded at his words, uncertain of how to respond and not wanting him to notice the fear beginning to build within me.

"Really, Lissie." my name rolled off his tongue. "You have nothing to fear."

"Should I be worried about the others?" I placed emphasis on the last word while biting my lip.

He stepped slowly toward me until his hands reached my shoulders. Again the distance between us was closed. I felt that we had formed some type of bond. Somehow I knew he was on my side and as much an outsider as I was.

"Won't you look at me?" His tone was lighter than before and a soft grin spread on my face as I shook my head. "Oh, come on," he said and poked me in the rib. I jumped back from him, a small squeal escaping my lips.

"Ticklish, are we?" he cocked an eyebrow as a new kind of foreboding filled me.

"Don't do it," I warned, holding up a finger.

He took a quick step toward me and I staggered backward, laughing. It seemed so long since I had felt so happy; to feel the lightness fill my heart. For just one moment I felt like myself again.

I looked back at Patrick, his smile reaching his eyes. Slowly his lips slipped at the corners, fading into the serious expression I was used to seeing. I swallowed heavily and waited, wondering what had changed.

A crease formed over his brow and he looked away from where I stood. It was as though he put up a stone wall between us. I knew it was a barrier that I could not cross.

"To answer your question, you don't have to worry about the others." His voice was deep and solemn. "Their father will keep you safe." He half smiled, but still avoided looking at me.

"Okay," I said awkwardly. "Well, goodnight then."

He nodded, but kept his gaze averted. I opened the side door and strode across the wooden walkway to my room. The night air was chilly, contrasting how warm I had felt just a moment ago.

Walking into my room, I lay down on the bed and let the loneliness reclaim me. In the darkness the shadows seemed larger and they called out to me. Speaking the dreaded name that I tried to run away from but could never leave behind.

Marina

Shivering, I slipped into sleep and images flashed within my mind. *He* was there. His dark hair floating on the wind. His blades flashing in the moonlight. The silver fins twitching back and forth beneath the pounding waves. I struggled to get away, but he snatched me into his arms. Forcing my head back, he let the rain pound on my face while the waves tossed us back and forth. And with his lips at my ear he told me to look at the shore. Through the haze I made out the form of a body, bleeding and lifeless. The familiar brown eyes stared blankly. I opened my mouth to yell Patrick's name, but Morven tightened his grip and pulled me under the oncoming waves and into the depths of the ocean.

With a choking cry I woke up and shuddered in the darkness.

14. Lathmor

The next day arrived slowly—the sisters' arrival could not have come quick enough. I had not seen Patrick all morning; I guessed he was off somewhere on the island probably trying to avoid me. Yet, his declaration that he would go with me was encouraging and helped ease the nervousness in my stomach.

I had no way of knowing when the girls would show up. In preparation I put on some clean clothes, pulled back my hair, and read a book in the main cabin. My hope was that Patrick would walk through at some point; I wanted to patch up the distance from the night before. But as the day wore on it became obvious that he would not come back to the house.

Reaching a lull in the novel, I looked up from its worn pages and sighed heavily in boredom. I avoided thinking about what lay ahead of me, since I was unsure of what the day would hold exactly. All I knew was that the sisters would take me somewhere.

Twisting my hair around my finger, I counted off the seconds, and then the minutes, until I finally heard footsteps on the stairs. Excited and not thinking, I dashed to the door and threw it open just as Kryssa was reaching the top. She froze, startled for a moment, and then relaxed.

"I guess you are ready to go," she said. The words were more of a statement than a question.

I nodded. "Yes," I replied. My voice sounded breathless even to my own ears.

"Let's go," Nixie, who I had not seen behind Kryssa, spoke up. She turned around on the stairs to walk back down. Kryssa followed, but I held back.

"Shouldn't we wait for Patrick?" I questioned.

Kryssa turned, her eyes glancing around quickly. "If we are lucky we might be able to leave without him. Come along." Her smooth hand grasped my wrist and I could do nothing but follow her. She looked different today and it took me a moment to figure out why. Both she and Nixie had their hair pulled back tightly in a bun, making them look older than they were.

The sky was just beginning to change, the blues turning to lighter shades of orange as the sun began its slow decent. Through the branches above, little stars were becoming visible.

We passed through the meadow and the wall of greenery, walking on a path that led us directly to the ocean. The closer we got, the easier it was to hear the washing of the waves upon the shore. A tight coil wound in my belly, refusing to let me relax.

Breaking through the last of the trees, the sand pushed up against my feet and I saw a small boat ahead of us. It was nothing like the large boats I was used to seeing in Coveside; instead, it looked more like a lifeboat with a small motor protruding off the back.

"Come," Nixie said in her high voice. "We must hurry." There was urgency in her voice and seriousness that I had not detected the night before.

She beckoned me forward with well-manicured fingers, a black piece of fabric wrapped around her palm.

"We have to blindfold you for security reasons," Kryssa explained as Nixie handed her the soft strip of darkness which soon settled over my eyes, leaving me to rely on my other senses.

"I hope you have two of those." Patrick's voice was like a warm blanket of security around my shoulders. The knot in my stomach uncoiled. Until that moment I had not realized how nervous and frightened I was.

"We don't," Kryssa said, her voice sounding disappointed that she hadn't managed to fool Patrick. "But you don't really need one. So get in."

My ears heightened as I listened to his feet pad past me and step into the old boat. Kryssa urged me forward, guiding me carefully across the sand toward the tiny vessel while I waited to feel a thud against my shins.

Instead, I felt my hand being lifted by the calloused grasp of the man in the boat. I let Patrick guide me into the unstable vessel, grateful that he directed me gently on where to place my feet and finally on where to sit.

All too soon he let go of my hand and I suddenly felt very lost and alone. It was as though his touch had kept me grounded.

"We're ready," Nixie spoke from behind me, near where I assumed the motor was.

"Give me a chance to push her in," Kryssa said. A moment later I felt the gentle rock of the boat as the waves rushed against it. Disoriented, I had no idea which direction we were facing.

"All right, let's go," Kryssa spoke, and Nixie cranked the motor in response. The sound of the whirring machine filled my ears with a pathetic rumble and I couldn't help but think we were never going to make it. Surprisingly, the little boat lurched forward and moved faster than I would have thought possible.

The wind whipped all around us and I was thankful my hair was pulled back tightly against my head. If it had been free, its unnatural movement would've been all too evident and would've been my undoing.

After what seemed like an eternity of no speaking, the sound of water breaking on rock told me we had arrived. The crashing of waves got closer, and I felt a change in the air as if we had entered a cave. The air was damp and the waves echoed in what I assumed was a waterway entrance to an island. Disoriented, I waited patiently until the boat scraped along the bottom and Nixie's fingers began to tug on the small knot resting on the back of my head.

The fabric fell away and a dim, dark room met my eyes. The boat had been pulled up to a small shore of rocks and pebbles where Kryssa and Patrick now stood waiting for me. Still nervous, I stepped out of the boat and onto the shore, acutely aware of Patrick's gaze upon me.

Without a word Kryssa led the way into another cave lit by torches along the walls. She picked something up off a battered, wooden bench in the corner.

"Sorry," she said. At first I thought she was speaking to me, but instead she was looking at Patrick.

He sighed. "I expected as much," he said as he extended his hands toward her. I noticed that his dagger was missing.

Kryssa hesitated, but then began to wrap the thick rope around his wrists, securing them tightly together. Alarm shot through me. "What are you doing that for?" I blurted out.

Kryssa paused in her movements and glanced up at me. "Another safety precaution," she replied. Something about her appearance was different than before, but I couldn't figure out what it was.

"But he wouldn't hurt anyone," I objected.

"Yes, I know that, but there are others who think he would." Again with the others. Who were these people?

"But I don't understand," I said, not really sure how to voice my fear of what was taking place. How could they consider Patrick a threat, and if they found out what I truly was, what would they do to me?

"It's just better for everyone if they see him secured," Nixie tried to calmly explain, but her words did nothing to ease my confusion.

Kryssa returned her attention to the tight knot around Patrick's wrists and finished it quickly, leaving his hands securely pressed together. As she peered over the knot in the dim light to check her work, a strand of hair fell from behind her shoulder. Its movement caught my attention.

"Is *he* here?" Patrick asked softly, putting emphasis on the middle word.

She straightened and shook her head from side to side. And in that moment everything clicked in my mind, a shock of surprise and trepidation ran through my veins like a bullet.

Her hair, moving like mine, flowed slowly as though it had a mind of its own. There was only one explanation I had for why her hair would move like that. I figured she *must* be a mermaid. My heart pounded rapidly as I realized what I was walking into. Had I left my home only to fall right into Morven's lap?

Then the words Patrick had just spoken ran clearly through my mind. Was the *he* Morven? Unbidden, the image from my nightmares returned to my mind and my blood pumped furiously through my veins.

Oblivious to my revelation, Nixie called for us to follow her. On legs that felt like shaky gelatin I followed her out into the night air and onto a well-worn path leading into the trees.

Kryssa and Patrick followed behind, but I was too concentrated on what I was about to face to give it any thought.

The more steps I took, the more I realized I could be nearing him. As I walked I felt his presence. I could see that evil smile he used whenever he knew I was frightened. But most of all I saw his gleaming blades, dripping with blood.

With a pang, I remembered the sharp slice of the cut on my hip. I closed my eyes and tried to concentrate on my feet. I had to keep following Nixie's, picking one foot up after the other. Right, left, right, left, right…

15. Resentment

Within a few minutes, a small structure became visible. We walked past this white-washed house without pausing, but I stared at it. Its design was similar to a home from ancient Greece, flat, white walls creating a square with a courtyard in the middle. The longer we walked the more we saw these houses.

Rounding a corner, the trees gave way to a breath-taking view. A city of white spread across a large hill. The houses began at the bottom near where we stood, and a stone pathway wove through the bleached buildings leading to the very top where a large structure rested ominously. Thick columns surrounded its sides, making it seem powerful and beautiful.

Trying not to seem too astounded, I continued to follow Nixie as she led us along the shadows of the trees. She was careful to not step into the moonlight.

Rather than walking along the stone pathway through the city, Nixie led us around to the left, keeping the houses within view on our right side. We came upon another dirt pathway which led directly up the hill to the largest structure. After swallowing a lump in my throat, I followed Nixie as we clambered up the hill. I tried not to think of how much harder this would be for Patrick who had his hands tied together.

Reaching the top, we stood before the large columns which looked even more immense and powerful up close. They seemed to reach toward the heavens while holding up a pointed white roof far above our heads. Stairs led into the open structure and we glided up them easily after the climb on dirt. The cold marble sent shivers up my spine.

We pressed forward, silently moving through an archway into what appeared to be a throne room. Gauzy, white fabric hung in the wide, low windows and blew gently into the room from the cool night breeze. Along the walls were intricately carved figures, slightly larger than life, but their faces as real as any portrait. Each statue was scantily clad, the marble carved fabric draping perfectly over the chiseled bodies. The figures were both male and female, and some were merfolk with marble tails curling about a pedestal. But every face had the same expression. Their eyes were clear, honest and real and turned toward the end of the large room.

At the end of the chamber was a small set of stairs and more columns. These columns were different from the ones we had passed upon entering; not as many and they were not as thick.

Three small columns stood on either side of the gliding stairs, further pointing the eye to focus on the exquisite marble throne which sat in the middle of the raised platform.

Somehow the sight did not fit with the picture I had concocted in my mind. When I thought of Morven, I only thought of darkness. I couldn't think of anything pure or artistically beautiful, but before my eyes was the proof. Still something nudged my mind, keeping me from believing this reality. The memory of Morven standing on the *Lady Marie* with his mermen behind him sent a round of goosebumps over my flesh. What was to become of this?

"Where is everyone?" Patrick's deep voice broke through the hushed reverence of the room and startled me.

"We aren't meeting here," Shaylee spoke from the other side of the throne room. She had just entered from a large hall. "Come," she said, as she gestured with her hand and beckoned us to follow her through the arch she had just exited a moment ago. We followed wordlessly, passing through the intricately carved pillars and into a long white corridor with a high vaulted ceiling.

My heart was still pounding out a disjointed rhythm, but the sight before my eyes made me forget it. Turning back slightly I voiced my suspicions.

"Your father is the king isn't he?" Without breaking stride, Kryssa came up beside me and nodded her head in answer.

"Yes, he is," her words confirmed. I was in the presence of three mermaid princesses. Shocked, I wondered what role

Morven would play in all of this. If there was a king, than who was he?

"You are in Lathmor," Kryssa spoke with a hint of pride in her voice. She opened her mouth to say more, but then shut it quickly. Catching my eye she smirked. "Best not to say something I'm not supposed to."

I nodded my head while turning my gaze back to Nixie who was continuing to lead the way next to Shaylee. A large wooden door painted in a faded blue, to the point of almost being turquoise, stood at the end of the hall. With trepidation I followed, unsure of what would meet me on the other side of the door.

Nixie knocked gently, and we waited until the door opened, revealing an oddly shaped room. Three sides were straight; the fourth wall, and opposite from where we stood, curved outward in a large arch. Near this wall was a massive desk with thick stump-like legs, each one intricately carved. The top of the desk was sleek black stone. Throughout the room were plush cushions, antique chairs, and wooden benches, but they were all pushed up against the walls creating a wide open space in the center of the room. Torches hung along the walls and an oil-lit chandelier hung from the middle of the ceiling. Gray marble squares created a jigsaw of lines across the floor around a large black diamond shape in the middle; directly in front of the desk.

I took all of this in in a matter of moments. It was not until we stepped into the room that I realized how many eyes were upon us. Standing and sitting along the sides of the room were men and women who all had their gazes latched on our group. The weight of their eyes bored into me while I frantically searched the room, looking for the one pair of grey stormy eyes that I knew would seal my fate.

"Daughters," a man who was standing behind the desk looking out one of the large windows, spoke calmly. His voice did little to calm my nerves as I waited for Morven to appear at any moment.

The man's hair was light red; streaks of subtle grey wove through the shoulder-length strands and gave him a sense of dignity. The wind from the open window blew his white shirt against his arms showing how powerful he really was, and the black pinstripe pants made him look more human than I knew him to be.

He turned slowly and his eyes alarmed me. They were a sharp green and seemed to convey intelligence. In some odd way I felt as though he recognized me, as if he had seen me before. Trying not to fidget, I met his gaze calmly. There was neither hostility nor friendliness in his eyes—my fate had yet to be decided upon.

"Father," Shaylee spoke up. She walked to the center of the room where the black diamond was located. With a small tap on my wrist, Nixie beckoned for me to follow her over to the center of the room. My fear increased, but the sound of Patrick's steady feet helped to soothe me. I remembered that he was an outsider like I was.

"May I present to you, Lissie," she requested. With a hand she acknowledged my presence.

Once more the king's eyes met mine. This time there was a trace of melancholy in his gaze. He closed his eyes for a moment as though planning what he should say next.

"Lissie," his voice said, strong and filled with authority. "What is the reason for your presence here in Lathmor?"

The whole room seemed to hold its breath waiting for my answer. I had the feeling my answer was important, but I had no idea what would be the appropriate thing to say.

Gathering what little nerve I had, I spoke loudly enough for everyone to hear: "I am here for the sole purpose of meeting you, sir. Your daughters kindly brought me here."

A smirk formed on the face of one of the merfolk near the king's desk. His hair was a dark curly black, his eyes jovial. He leaned toward a merman beside him to comment, but the look on his companion's face silenced him. The rest of the merfolk did not seem as amused with my response.

"Let me restate my question," the king said with a glint in his eye. "How is it you came to be on the island with Patrick?"

Upon Patrick's name being spoken, the room fell even quieter than before; this time the silence was hostile. In the faces of the merfolk I saw fury and hatred, but it was not focused on me. Their eyes were on the person just behind me. I now realized why the princesses had hoped to leave him behind—it was obvious he was an unwelcome guest. Why he was unwelcome was a mystery.

"A little over a month ago I was thrown overboard. I had been on a boat with my father and brothers. Sometime after this I happened upon the island and met Patrick there."

The king pursed his lips slightly, and I knew he did not believe me. I wouldn't believe me if I was in his position, there were just too many open holes in my story. But what was I going to do? I had already told the princesses that I remembered what happened between my accident and how I had found the island. If I lied here, they would only counter my statement. For the time being, I wanted to keep it a secret. If Morven was here then he would reveal me eventually, but I wanted to hold off the inevitable as much as possible.

"You just happened upon the island?" The king asked raising a skeptical eyebrow. He knew I was lying.

"Yes, sir." I would say nothing more.

"Father," Kryssa spoke up beside me, "she does remember everything that happened between her accident and her arrival on the island. But she has said she cannot tell us because it would risk our lives. I believe her."

Shocked by Kryssa's loyalty, I stared at her and wondered how she knew I had told the truth.

"As much as I appreciate your input," the king began, his eyes softening as he spoke to Kryssa. "I cannot take the risk."

Knowing I was playing with fire, I butted in. I had been able to convince others before, why not these merfolk? "But what if being told the truth runs more of a risk than not hearing it?"

Silence filled the room and the king's eyes focused on me once more. His approval was evident this time. Slowly he walked out from behind the desk and my heart began to hammer in my chest. His stride brought him closer to me, but still in a place where he was at the head of the room.

"We are at war, Lissie." His statement confused me. "Whether you are human as you claim to be, or something different, I need you to understand this. I will not place my people in danger only because your word tells me otherwise."

His admonishing only made me more self-conscious of where I was and who I was standing before. "Have you ever heard of the Hyven?" He asked calmly, his hands slipping into his pockets. Behind me I heard Patrick's sharp intake of breath.

"No," I said.

"Years ago," the king began, "we Lathmorians were one people. We were peaceful and there were no battles. I am presuming you understand who you are in the presence of?"

Again he raised an eyebrow, but Shaylee scoffed. "Father, she has no idea."

The king, however, did not take his eyes from mine. "Oh, she knows plenty."

At his words everyone looked at me once more; the heaviest gaze came from the eyes behind me. How much I wished I could have seen his face to know what he was thinking. With every moment the king only further revealed my betrayal to him.

"You do in fact know what we are?" the king asked.

I let my silence be his answer, and a collective gasp filled the room.

"Finish her now!" The harsh words rang in the large room coming from a man who stood with his arms threateningly at his sides. The stance was all too familiar, each one of the mermen Morven had had with him on the night of my transformation had stood in an identical manner. The speed of the now unseen blades could lash out at any moment. The very thought sent my blood racing.

"You make one move, Voon," Patrick's voice was almost unrecognizable, every word spoken with precision and malice. He never finished the threat, but instead left it hanging in the air as he stepped forward and came into my line of sight. His stance was every bit as hostile as the merfolk around us. Though his wrists were still tightly locked together, I couldn't help but think he would be able to hold his own regardless.

The merman named Voon widened his stance, ready to attack. My eyes moved over to the king, wondering what he made of it. Rather than interfere, the king was looking at Patrick with a burning curiosity.

"What are you going to do about it?" Voon spit. I couldn't help but notice that others were looking at him with approval, as though what he was saying was necessary. Turning his eyes away, Voon addressed the king.

"All I ask, King Oberon, is that we find the truth. As you said yourself we are at war. Those who withhold the truth are not welcome here and nor are those who put innocent lives in danger." His last phrase sent a shiver through my soul, but he was not looking at me. Instead he looked at Patrick with disgust.

Patrick's jaw clenched, and he shifted toward me slightly. I realized he was cutting off any approach Voon could make toward me.

"You remember what happened the last time we let something *foreign* slip into our midst." The hatred Voon had for Patrick radiated off his body.

"Yes, I remember well." The soft words spoken by King Oberon sounded ancient, revealing the lines on his face. He was older than he appeared. "Yet, he is not the reason we suffered and you know that."

Voon's mouth snapped shut in anger, but he did not speak against the king. For a moment the muscles in Patrick's shoulders loosened, no longer standing taut and ready for action.

All was silent as though no one knew what should be done next; each eye turned to the king waiting to hear what he would say. For some time he did not speak, but instead walked to the large open window behind his desk. The dark sky was cloudless and the moon shined brightly against the deep blue canvas. The king sighed heavily and ran a hand through his red flecked hair.

"Elik," he said. The dark haired merman who had smirked earlier when all others had been serious stepped forward.

"Sir," he said, his voice pleasant and excited. Even the way he stood, broad shoulders thrust back at attention, had a sort of buoyancy to it. He was serious and experienced, but optimistic.

"When will the Captain return?" *Captain?*

"He should arrive any moment."

"Very good," King Oberon said, nodding his head in approval. "You all may leave us, except you five." He drew a circle in the air with his finger that contained the group in the center of the room. But I knew that I was supposed to stay. The Captain would be back soon. And I had a hunch who this Captain might be.

16. Discovery

The patter of bare feet on marble rang through the room until everyone had exited. Left in the room were our small group, the king, the merman named Elik, and another young man with hair so blonde it was almost white. The large door shut with finality and its closing took away some of my stress. For the first time since we entered the room, I was able to really breathe.

"Take those infernal things off him," the king said gesturing with his hand toward Patrick. Elik stepped in front of Patrick, his blades breaking his forearms. With one quick motion, he sliced the ropes binding Patrick's wrists. The severed ropes fell to the floor.

"Thanks," Patrick said while rubbing his wrists.

"Don't mention it," Elik smiled. "Although from the looks of it, Kryssa must have been the one to tie the knots?"

"Of course," Patrick chuckled, surprising me with his calm. I had not expected him to be so relaxed.

"I had to make it look real," Kryssa snapped as she bent to pick up the broken pieces of rope. "Otherwise Voon would have been even more unpleasant."

"Just what we need," Elik said, shaking his head in disgust. "How are you? It's been a while." His dark eyes searched Patrick's face in concern making me warm up to him immediately.

"It has been a while," Patrick returned and clapped Elik on the shoulder. I wondered if I was the only one to notice his ignorance of answering Elik's question.

"I am sorry for the formalities, Patrick," King Oberon said. He walked forward his hand extended in greeting, and Patrick grasped it in response. The king smiled at him, his eyes holding none of the earlier abrasiveness. All too soon those eyes turned to me, and I was even more uncertain of myself in this new relaxed setting.

"And I apologize to you too, Lissie. There are certain standards I am expected to uphold here in my court."

"I understand, sir." I nodded, not really sure how to respond to his kindness.

"Well," he smiled calmly and the lines around his eyes deepened, "make yourselves comfortable for the time being."

He turned back toward his desk and beckoned to Shaylee. She followed him and bowed over what appeared to be a large map. The light-haired merman sat on one of the wooden benches, where Nixie followed suit beside him. The connection between the two was obvious.

"Hey." Somehow the one word calmed all my nerves. I looked up and Patrick's mouth quirked. He was back to being my friend. The composed features of his face mirrored my own. I knew that the previous night's events were behind us. A feeling of kinship and understanding tied a bond between us.

"Hey." I replied and nudged him with my shoulder, not sure of what else to say since so much had been revealed in the past few minutes. He now knew that I had been lying to him. Although he didn't know about me yet, I had a feeling it wouldn't be much longer before someone figured it out.

"How long have you known?" he asked. He didn't have to explain himself, I knew what he meant.

"Not long at all," I sighed, putting a hand to my forehead. "I only figured it out on our way here."

He nodded and continued, "Kryssa tried to be sly pulling us through the water. All that caution for nothing." He chuckled while I realized what he meant. I had thought the motor was too small to make us move so quickly. It's ridiculous I hadn't figured it all out then, but I pretended to agree with Patrick. If I told him how I had noticed Kryssa's hair it would only lead to more questions. For now it was best to remain ignorant.

"I have a question though," I said quickly.

"That's not a surprise," he said, folding his arms over his broad chest. Distracted for a moment, I looked at the deep golden color of his skin so different from my own. If only he knew how different we truly were. "You were saying?" He said, pulling me from my reverie.

"Well, when King Oberon was talking about the enemy, what were they called again?"

"The Hyven." Patrick said the word quickly, but I couldn't help noticing how every line in his face grew solemn at the word. His voice was deep and menacing.

"Yes, the Hyven," I said, trying to act as though I hadn't noticed his change of demeanor. "Well, umm, who is their leader?" I asked the question innocently, but all my worries and fears were riding on his answer. If it was who I now guessed it could be, I would no longer have to worry about his presence here in Lathmor.

Patrick quirked an eyebrow and his eyes narrowed slightly. I tried to look as innocent as possible. "His name is Morven."

Relief flooded me even though I had been anticipating this response. My feelings whirled as I realized I was safe here. Morven could not touch me where I was, and I did not have to worry about him coming near me. The feeling was enough to make me want to run, to scream and shout for joy, but I reined my emotions in not wanting to be suspicious. Although from the way Patrick was looking at me, I assumed I wasn't doing a very good job of it.

"I was just wondering," I said, trying to be nonchalant and failing miserably.

Patrick opened his mouth to say something, but whatever he meant to say I'll never know since at that moment Elik approached, his hand extended toward me.

"I'm sorry I didn't introduce myself earlier. I'm Elik," he said as a dimple formed in his right cheek as he smiled.

I shook his hand. "Nice to meet you," I choked out, nervous of making a bad first impression.

"Have you been enjoying yourself on the island?" The question was simple enough, but the way Elik said it was suggestive. Patrick stiffened in annoyance, but I smiled and then hated myself when my cheeks warmed.

I opened my mouth to answer, but my response was cut off by the loud creak of the door opening into the chamber. A powerful looking man stepped through the door; he was tall and broad, with well-defined muscles. His hair was cut close to his head, much shorter than any of the mermen's hair I had seen thus far. He was dressed in all black clothing, dark pants and a tight long-sleeve shirt covered his arms, enhancing the size of his chest. I couldn't help but notice the small slits in the sleeves of the shirt along the forearm, just where I knew the blades would protrude if ejected.

The man's eyes were serious and perused the group quickly. He held my gaze for only a moment, but there was something in his eyes which gave me a sense of foreboding.

"Tunder," Shaylee said. The name fit the powerful person before my eyes. The one word was an exhale of relief, but it was enough to break the tension in the room. Without another word, Shaylee crossed the open space and embraced the man whom I assumed was the Captain. Their affection for one another was evident and the moment they shared somehow seemed private even in this big room. The look upon Tunder's face transformed as he beheld Shaylee and she smiled back at him, her eyes holding more emotion than I had ever seen her show before.

"That's the Captain," Elik confirmed quietly to me. "Shaylee's husband." His statement put everything into place.

"Captain, how was your mission?" King Oberon spoke, breaking up the reunion between husband and wife.

Tunder tore his gaze away from Shaylee and she stepped aside. "It did not go as planned." His voice was deep and rough.

Kryssa sighed heavily and crossed her arms over her chest, her disgruntled look reflected in the eyes of all in the room. Beside me, Elik's shoulders slumped in slight defeat.

"How many casualties?" The king asked, showing no emotion.

"None sir, and no injuries." Tunder spoke with finality, "We were unsuccessful because we could not find Morven."

At Morven's name I tensed unintentionally. Patrick glanced my way, noting my reaction, but I pushed it aside too focused on what was being said.

"Something has changed. You were right sir, he is no longer busying himself with infiltrating Lathmor. The Hyven are not fixed upon us anymore; any time we caught sight of them they fled as though they were unconcerned with our presence. It's as though they are searching for something."

The king nodded, rubbing his chin with his hand. "It has happened then." His words were subtle, but the simple statement was like a dropping cloud of depression on every person in the room.

"You can't mean—" Patrick said and then broke off as though what he wanted to say could not be true; his grasp tightened around my hand.

"Yes," the king said, his eyes lifting to Patrick's. The compassion within them only confused me more. Patrick stiffened, his chest lifting as he tried to breathe deeply to calm himself.

"What?" Shaylee asked, wondering at the exchange. I had the sudden feeling she was not used to being left out of things. Beside her Tunder was looking at me, his eyes honest, and in that moment I realized what had happened.

They knew.

Patrick turned his eyes to mine and the thoughts running through his head were obvious: he knew what I was.

"Lissie," Tunder said slowly. I waited for his words to undo me. "Do you know who Morven is?"

For a moment I stayed still, my chest lifting in distress with each breath I tried to take. "Yes," I said, my throat clogged.

"Have you ever met him?"

"Yes," I confirmed.

"How could you?" Kryssa yelled, and I was taken aback by her sudden outburst. "I trusted you!"

Ignoring her, the king stepped forward, his eyes staring intently. "Did he mark you in some way?" he asked.

Struggling to contain myself, I nodded once more. Patrick's arms fell to his sides and he stepped away; the small space separating us felt like a large valley. I looked at him, but he refused to meet my gaze.

"Father," Kryssa beckoned from where she stood, "what are you talking about?"

Nixie and the pale-haired merman were now standing. Their eyes, like everyone else's, fixated upon me.

"Lissie is not human," the king spoke slowly. There was grief lining his eyes. "She has been changed."

"What?" Kryssa again spoke, "It can't be," she whispered.

"I think it is time you told us the truth," Tunder coaxed.

Taking a deep breath I raised my trembling chin. My greatest fear was that I would be handed over and that they would use me in this war to abate Morven and his Hyven. "The night I fell overboard, Morven found me in the water," Patrick sighed heavily, and moved to look out of one of the large windows. His shoulders were tense as he leaned against the window pane, but I tore my eyes away from him and instead looked out a window across the room. The memory took over my mind, transporting me from the confined marble walls and the watchful eyes of the merfolk to the night that changed my life forever.

"He took me back to my family and let them pull me back on board, but then he reappeared on deck." My voice grew strained but I pressed forward. "He said he *wanted* me and told my father I was no longer his concern. There were others there, more Hyven, all ready to take me away, but they didn't. Instead he cut me and placed part of his own flesh inside the wound. I didn't know what was happening. He told me I would be different, and then I blacked out."

My sentences were becoming jumbled, one running into the next. But I couldn't stop the spew of words.

"I woke up later and my father told me what I was, what I *am*. I left home so he wouldn't be able to take me. I won't sit back and let him control my life." The last words I spoke rang with defiance as I thought of the Morven who reigned in my dreams.

Silence met my speech. No one moved or spoke. The only sound was my heavy breathing.

Somehow I found the courage to look at Patrick, but he was still turned away from me. His head was hung as though defeated. Guilty, I looked away. I knew I had betrayed him. Betrayed what little friendship we had kindled. Yet, I couldn't help but hope he would forgive me.

The king cleared his throat, "Where is your mark?" He asked quietly.

In one slow, fluid movement I grasped the bottom of my shirt and the waistband of my shorts. Sliding each a few inches in opposite directions, I revealed the lavender scar on my hip. The very sight of it was a symbol of my disgrace: the marking which made me something I was never meant to be.

An exhale of resentment reached my ears and I lifted my eyes to the brown ones I knew so well. But the kindness which usually filled them had disappeared and they were instead filled with anger. His eyes were fixed on the shimmering lavender mark and he left the room without a word.

I knew there was nothing I could do to coax him back.

17. Past

Moments later I was once more being led around the palace, this time by Kryssa. We passed through rooms and corridors, but I hardly noticed my surroundings. The anger in Patrick's eyes was forever burned in my mind and I knew he would never forgive me.

I did not speak, but followed Kryssa obediently. The decisions made after Patrick's departure were all a blur. I clung to one hope though. Tunder had immediately left to go after Patrick, the worry on his face was evident.

It was then decided that I should stay in Lathmor for a few nights until they could figure out what was to be done. King Oberon granted me the privilege of staying in a guest bedroom, but I declined in favor of staying with Kryssa after she offered. Being alone in a foreign room was not something I wanted to face at the moment. Kryssa would provide the needed distraction to keep me from worrying about what I'd done to Patrick.

I was surprised with how quickly my story was accepted. As soon as I had flashed my scar, the king had declared me a victim rather than a threat; yet I was still to be kept in secret on the island. All the more reason to stay with Kryssa, because, as she said, no one would suspect it. It was obvious as we skittered around the palace that she was taking me through rarely used halls and roundabout rooms.

"Here we are," she said quietly, coming upon a white painted wooden door.

With a quick lift of the metal latch, the door opened and I followed her into the wide open space. The room was airy with pastel green rugs on the floor and matching gauzy curtains in the windows. Her bed was white with a veiled canopy cresting the top, and soft pink and yellow thread was stitched into the pillows and sheets to match the flowers growing just outside the large bedroom window.

The room was beautiful and cheerful even with the dark skies outside. I could only imagine how bright it must be during the day. In a sense the room was in contrast to what I knew of Kryssa's character—maybe there was more to her than I expected.

"It's a little girly, but I like it," Kryssa spoke softly to break the silence.

"It's lovely," I said forcing a smile. Kryssa's relieved expression made me glad I had said so.

"I'll get you some bed clothes. Feel free to look around," she called over her shoulder as she opened a door that led to a large walk-in closet.

While she was inside I perused the room, my eyes focusing on a small stack of books beside the bed on a little table. Looking at the old titles and worn covers of the works of literature, I knew they had come from Patrick's library.

Distracting myself from thinking of him, I stepped into the closet timidly. Inside was a sight I had never seen before: dresses of all different cuts, styles, and designs hung from various rows, one on top of the other. I couldn't help but notice that some of the dresses looked as though they were from different time periods, much older than the girl who was pulling clothes out of a worn dresser beside me.

"Beautiful, aren't they?" Kryssa asked once she saw me gaping at the wall of dresses, and, at a loss for words, I nodded. "You accumulate a lot of dresses when your sister is a seamstress." Kryssa laughed to herself and walked out of the closet, clothing in hand.

"Which one?" I asked, exiting the smaller enclosure.

"Hmm?" Kryssa muttered as she changed her clothes and tossed a pair of simple shorts and camisole to me.

"Who makes the dresses, Shaylee or Nixie?"

"Oh," Kryssa said, distracted as she threw her clothes across the room. I began to strip my clothes off after checking to make sure the door and curtains were firmly closed. "That's all Nixie, she's been sewing ever since she was little." Kryssa was tugging on the bed's comforter while she spoke.

"How old is she anyway?"

"She's sixteen and a half, but she acts younger most of the time." Kryssa laughed affectionately. Her behavior was more open and real than I'd ever seen before.

Once I had finished changing, I walked over to help get everything settled. Just as I was about to climb under the covers, Kryssa spoke up.

"Do you mind if I ask you some questions?" The words sounded formal, but the concern in her eyes told me she was only curious.

"Sure," I shrugged, grabbing a pillow and crossing my legs to sit on her bed.

Kryssa leaned over and flicked the lights off. For a moment we were in complete darkness, but then a small lamp clicked to life on the bedside table. The warm glow of the light cast our shadows on the walls.

"So, what do you want to know?"

Kryssa took a large breath before voicing her concerns. "How did it all happen? I mean, did he say anything? Were you afraid of him?"

Her inability to form her questions clearly gave me the comfort I needed to find my voice. That night was not easy to speak about, but I knew it would help me to get the pain of it out in the open.

"It's like I said before, he changed me by placing some of his own flesh inside the cut."

She nodded, "I know that. I guess what I meant was how come he didn't take you with him? Or do you even know?"

"He told me it was because I was too young." I plucked at the comforter, slightly self-conscious of the way she was looking at me as though I were a fascinating creature. She should look in the mirror more often.

"Wait," she said holding up a hand, "how old are you?"

Her question reminded me all too much of the way Morven had prodded me for my age. "Seventeen." I revealed.

Kryssa's mouth fell open. "Did he know how young you were?"

I nodded, "Yes, he asked me just before he cut my hip."

"Unbelievable," Kryssa muttered under her breath.

"Sorry, but what is unbelievable?" I bit my lip nervously, not really sure why she was so astonished.

Kryssa took a very large breath. "You don't have control over your fins do you?"

"What do you mean?"

"If you are submerged in water you automatically transform into a mermaid." Her words were a statement, not a question.

"Yes," I confirmed regardless. Again she sighed heavily, and I wondered what she was thinking about. "I have a lot of questions, too," I said, hoping she would answer them.

"I expected that," her lips pulled at the corners of her mouth. "It's why I told father you could stay with me. I had a feeling you knew very little about us, even though you somehow figured out we were merfolk." She quirked an eyebrow.

"It was your hair," I pointed. "I saw it in the wind as we were walking up here earlier today."

"Ahh," she nodded. "I was wondering how you knew." There was a twinkle in her eyes as though she appreciated my perception.

"Now," she clapped her hands together, "what questions do you have?"

A million thoughts flooded my mind, but there was one person whom the most questions revolved around. He was a complete mystery, something entirely unknown.

"Tell me about Patrick," I requested softly while staring at my hands. "Please."

Silence followed my words, and I looked up to see Kryssa staring toward the window, her face a mask of indecision.

"I will tell you all I can. But I don't know the whole story." I nodded calmly, though inside excitement was steadily building within my chest.

"It happened when I was very young so I don't know exactly what took place. But first, you need to know something about merfolk." Her eyes were very serious as I gazed into them. "We do not live like humans do." She shook her head when I scrunched my face in confusion. "What I mean, is we live much longer than humans."

"You're immortal," I said without thinking. Kryssa shook her head.

"No, we live our lives and we'll die eventually, but our life span is much longer." She paused for a moment and said quietly, "It will happen to you too, Lissie."

The thought hit me hard. Did it mean I would outlive my family? Would I surpass them by a lot? Genuine concern flitted across Kryssa's face.

"You'll notice a great decline in the way your body changes once you turn eighteen. You won't grow and change at such a quick rate." A solemn look passed over her face like a shadow. "What Morven did to you was wrong. The act of changing a human into a mermaid or merman without their consent is one of the cruelest acts any merperson can place upon another. What he did to you is an old art that began a long time ago." I narrowed my eyes, intrigued, and waited for her to continue. She laughed. "I can see you want answers."

I didn't even bother to bob my head in response, I just hugged the pillow closer to my chest.

"First, you need to know that some of the answers to your questions can be answered through our history; others will be through Patrick's story."

I waited in anticipation, pleased she was going to tell me the truth.

Taking a deep breath, Kryssa began to speak in a far off voice.

"Merfolk, as I said, live longer lives than humans. I was born," she hesitated for a moment, "in the year 1052." She waited, while I did all I could to control my expression. The life span she had spoken of earlier took on a whole new meaning.

"In comparison to humans, merfolk live one year to every fifty years of a human life. With that in mind, I am nine-hundred and fifty-seven years old in human years." I stared at Kryssa in the dim light, completely stunned. The silence made me aware of the vast expanse between us; we were more different than I had thought.

"Is Patrick?" I began, barely able to form the question fully with my dry lips.

Kryssa shook her head, "Before I can tell you about him, you will have to understand some Lathmorian history." I nodded. "The merfolk, like my father said earlier, have always been a peaceful species with one king ruling over the entire population. We do not multiply quickly, so Lathmor had always been a large enough island for all merfolk to live on, and no one had ever left. This all changed when my mother inherited the throne.

"Her name was Cordelia, and she was a princess like my sisters and me. Her father and mother failed to provide a male heir to the throne, and so the duty of finding a worthy husband who could rule as king fell to her. Many of the mermen grasped for her hand, but she chose my father Oberon.

"Her decision was met with approval by all except her childhood friends, Nerissa, her cousin, and a merman who was in love with my mother, Pyron. When my mother chose my father over Pyron, Pyron fell into despair and his anger toward all Lathmorians grew. Nerissa, who had been infatuated with

Pyron ever since she was a child, tried to coax him out of his depression but nothing worked. At least, not until Nerissa began to spin tales of how they could overthrow my father and rid him of the throne of Lathmor.

"Together, Pyron and Nerissa began to dabble in an art which was forbidden: the practice of transforming humans into merfolk." Kryssa paused at that moment and my heart felt as though it was lodged in my throat. "They changed many humans, hiding them in caves on the island, but they could not make them powerful enough to fight against a merman. Their plot was discovered when merfolk heard the tortured screams of humans. Pyron was trying to teach them how to fight, relentlessly using his blades on those who had no weapons of their own."

The image forming in my mind sent shivers through my spine. I could just see this Morven-like creature slicing through the innocent without a thought for their pain. The nightmare that came to me most nights flashed in my mind.

"Pyron and Nerissa were sentenced to death, but my mother banished them instead. She could not forget the friends of her youth and would not have them die by her hand.

"Years later, when I was four years old, Nerissa returned to the palace secretly. I remember when it happened. She came into the nursery where my mother was putting us to bed. Nixie was already asleep in the cradle, and my mother jumped up to protect us. But Nerissa just laughed at her and told her she was not here for revenge. She spoke of how she had succeeded, finally figured out the way in which she would dominate the human and merfolk world.

"Maybe it was because my mother had spared her life, or because she still loved my mother, I don't know. But Nerissa asked to be allowed back into Lathmor. She said her new discoveries would permit the merfolk to take over the world. My mother refused and once more Nerissa disappeared.

"After Nerissa's visit, my mother was never the same. She blamed herself for Nerissa's downfall and left Lathmor to find her and stop whatever evil she and Pyron had created. She found Nerissa and killed her. But," Kryssa's voice choked with strained emotion, "not without a price. She was fatally wounded upon her return and died a few days later. Our only clue to what happened was with the unconscious man she brought back with her." Once more, Kryssa stared out the window, wells of water floating in the bottom of her eyes.

Licking her lips she continued, "We waited for the young man to regain consciousness." My stomach knotted tightly, I knew just whose past she was speaking of.

"From the beginning, we knew there was something different about him: something dark and sinister. My father thought of executing him, but he hesitated. He knew there was a reason my mother had brought him back alive. We waited to see what the man would be, but he remained a mystery. He lacked the powers of a merman. He did not sprout fins when submerged in water, his hair was that of a human's, and he did not have blades to call his own. In the eyes of many, he was a disgrace."

A sear of pain shot through my soul as I realized how difficult *his* life must have been. To not really know who or what he was would be far more excruciating than what I had been through. At least I had been given a forewarning.

"On top of all his irregularities, Patrick never changed." It was the first time Kryssa had actually referred to the young man in the story as Patrick; somehow it made the memories more tangible, gave them a life of their own. "We noticed how his hair never grew and how he never looked older. He looks the same today as he did the day I first saw him many years ago."

Remembering how old Kryssa was, I tried to grasp what she was saying. *How old was he?*

"On second thought," Kryssa said, in an interested voice "he has changed." She locked her eyes on me. "When he first arrived, he had this awful scar on his right shoulder," she gestured, dragging a finger along the back of her shoulder blade. "It healed eventually, but then it was a dark scar that shimmered, well, a lot like yours does. Now that I think about it, his must have faded."

I thought back to the time we were at the waterfall, trying to remember a scar, but I came up with nothing. If the scar was as dark as she said, surely I would have noticed.

"I didn't see one," I admitted.

"It's got to be there though." Kryssa muttered and then spoke up. "I'll have to check. Although he doesn't really like to talk about it." She made a face and silence fell.

Outside a great whoosh of wind swept by the palace windows. The leaves in the trees churned restlessly reflecting the whirling thoughts in my mind.

"Have any of Nerissa's people ever tried to find Patrick?" I wondered why they would let him go without a fight. If he was something Nerissa had spent time creating, wasn't he worth fighting for?

"Yes," Kryssa nodded solemnly. "The Hyven has been searching for him ever since. There was a battle roughly six years ago, that's three hundred years for you, where the Hyven infiltrated Lathmor. They had never reached our island before and they came close to capturing Patrick. We were able to get him off of Lathmor in the nick of time, but it cost us many Lathmorian lives." She paused as tears filled her eyes once more. For some reason I got the feeling this hurt was deeper than the loss of her mother. She shook her head, "It's why so many merfolk, like Voon, are hostile towards him. Almost everyone lost someone they loved in that battle."

The quiet fell between us once more, but my brain was restless. Rather than finding answers, I had formulated more questions. There was too much to ask and not enough time to ask it all.

"Is there anything else that you want to know?" She asked. One person stood prominently in my mind, but I had to find the courage to speak his name.

"Where does," I gulped, "Morven come into the story? And why does it matter to him whether I'm seventeen or eighteen?"

"The main reason why Morven probably became angry when he found out how old you were is because of your abilities. Once you turn eighteen, you will become as much a mermaid as I am." The idea was too incredible to consider. How could it even be possible?

"You mean, I will be able to control my fins? I could choose to swim without them if I wanted?"

Kryssa's head nodded slowly, "That and other things as well." She perused my face and heaved a sigh. "He really didn't tell you anything, did he?" The question was rhetorical and the pity in her eyes was a comfort to my confused mind.

"There are differences between mermaids and mermen. Besides the obvious differences in appearance, each has their own abilities. Mermen can swim and run faster, and are stronger. Mermaids on the other hand, have sharper eye sight and better hearing. It makes it easier to escape when you can hear the enemy before they can hear you." She winked.

"Mermen also have the blades to contend with though," I added, catching on to her good humor.

"So do we," she said and the side of her mouth quirked as she flexed her fingers. In the dim glow of the lamp I looked at her hands. Without warning sharp blades projected from her fingertips. They were shiny, similar in texture to the blades I had seen Morven wield, and were at least five inches in length. My jaw dropped open as I looked at them. A familiar tingling sensation surged through my fingertips and I stared at them in wonder.

"As to your question about Morven," Kryssa continued, ignoring my fascination with her fingers, "he is believed to be Nerissa and Pyron's son."

Fear pulsed through my veins as I thought of what her words meant. The couple who had started the war between the merfolk bore a son—the very son who had changed me.

"It is unknown what happened to Pyron, but we believe Morven is trying to finish what his parents, or more particularly his mother, started."

I opened my mouth to question her some more, but couldn't get my thoughts in order. Everything was a question in this new world where flashing blades and black arts took precedence over peace.

"I can't think of just one question right now," I said, slightly ashamed. Kryssa laughed.

"That's to be expected." Grabbing a section of her long black hair, she began to twist it in her fingers. "I do have one more question for you, though."

"Yes?"

"Did you ever see Morven before the night he changed you?"

Immediately I began to shake my head, but then I paused. The memory of a murmur and the shimmering of fins pressed upon my mind.

"Actually yes, he did see me." Kryssa's eyes kindled with intensity. "The night before the storm I was out on deck singing to myself when I began to hear another sound. It was like a murmur and it hummed with me for a while." Just thinking of the memory caused goosebumps to rise on my flesh. "When I tried to see what the sound was, I heard a loud splash. I later saw a gray shimmer in the water a ways off. It felt like something was looking at me and I know it was him."

Kryssa's lips were pressed tightly together, her jaw taut with something I didn't understand. "Well," she said in a light tone that didn't match her expression. "I guess we had better get some rest.

Rather than argue, I acquiesced and climbed under the covers, all the while knowing there was something she wasn't telling me. The sheets felt cool and fresh against my body, and it wasn't long before I heard Kryssa's slow, steady breathing.

My exhausted mind slowed its soaring thoughts and fell into a place of relaxation. The last sight behind my eyes was the anger on Patrick's face before he walked out the door and away from me.

18. Worries

The roar of breaking waves filled my ears. Blurry images with soft patches of sunlight confounded my eyes. There was a deep desire within my body to find something, I just didn't know what. Part of my brain wondered if I was dreaming, but the other part was unsure. I tried to recall the last memories of life, but they wouldn't come. I was tired, hungry, and afraid. I needed food, shelter, and help. Gazing around at the blurry beach, I looked for what I was trying to find. Then I saw a man walking toward me. My body immediately relaxed as I realized this was what I had been looking for. The man continued toward me. His gait strong and powerful, I didn't recognize him. When he got closer, I saw who he was. It was Patrick! My heart skipped a beat as he lifted his dark eyes to mine. A brilliant smile lit his face and I smiled happily back. He reached a hand out toward me and our palms met. I turned and walked with him, continuing in the direction he had been headed. Part of my mind remembered doing this before—I couldn't recall if it had been real or in a dream. Then, all of a sudden, Patrick stopped walking. Fear tickled my insides. I was unsure of what was happening, but instinct told me it wasn't good. I gazed at Patrick, wondering if he knew what was happening. My heart squeezed in horror. His eyes were filled with terror and there was no trace of the happy smile I had seen moments earlier. He was staring into the distance as though he could see something I couldn't. His hand squeezed mine tighter as though he was terrified to let go. I held on, desperately wondering what it was that caused him to act like this. He stepped in front of me as if to shield me from some unseen enemy. And then he was gone. My hand held nothing. He had disappeared. Pain and anguish speared my heart.

I fell to my knees, sobs wracking my body.

And then it was all black.

I could remember nothing, feel nothing.

I drifted in a mindless world of the unknown.

When my eyes finally did open, it took a while for them to adjust to the bright light streaming in through the pale green curtains hanging in the massive window. My mind felt clogged and fuzzy. I glanced to my left and saw Kryssa beside me, her dark, straight hair tangled all about her shoulders. With a slow mind, reality seeped in. Clarity felt wonderful. I turned my head back to the ceiling and tried to recall my dream. It took time, but recollection slowly infiltrated my mind as a nagging dread crept into my blood.

Kryssa rolled over on the bed beside me, her sleepy face pointed in my direction. She squinted with one eye to let in some light, and swore softly. I laughed at her expression, causing the bed to jostle slightly. She raised an eyebrow and opened the same eye again.

"Sorry. I'm just not a morning person," she grumbled.

"That's okay," I said, smiling at her. She yawned loudly. I raised my hands above my head to stretch. "Do you have any idea what time it is?" I asked her.

She shook her head. "Don't know, don't care."

"Oh, come on," I said, nudging her shoulder. "You had enough sleep, look how bright it is outside!" Kryssa suddenly bolted up from the bed.

"We had better get moving!" She exclaimed and ran to the closet. I followed behind her, but was just at the entrance to the large closet when clothes were thrown at me. I caught them and changed quickly. Kryssa came out of the closet a moment later fully dressed, her tangled hair pulled back into a loose braid.

"Come on," she said urgently and I followed her out of the bedroom.

"What's the matter?"

"Nothing," she said while she walked faster than I had ever seen her move before. "We just need to tell them about when Morven first saw you." Goosebumps rose on my flesh as I realized what she was asking of me.

We whipped through deserted halls, continuing to skirt the main rooms of the palace, moving unseen within the shadows. Kryssa was serious, her eyes focused in front and her gait determined. I kept up with her easily, though the speed at which she walked surprised me and only heightened my senses.

Rounding a corner, two mermen came into our view. They called out to us as we approached.

"Daggin," Kryssa nodded toward the blonde merman who had stuck close to Nixie's side the night before. "Elik."

Both mermen nodded in return.

"Is the king in his study?" She asked quickly, wasting no time to get to the point.

"No," Daggin's voice was deeper than I had expected for such a young face. "He is speaking with the soldiers in the throne room."

Kryssa muttered under her breath and I watched as she debated what to do next.

"Tunder came back after leaving last night. He's with Shaylee." Elik said. My interest rose. If Tunder had returned, it meant Patrick was no longer angry. *Right?*

With a quick bob of her head, Kryssa made up her mind and squeezed through the two mermen.

"We'll gladly escort you there," Elik offered as he began to walk beside her.

"Lissie and I can manage, thank you," Kryssa's sharp tone made me wonder at her feelings toward Elik. She had never used such a stern voice with anyone other than him.

"All the same, Daggin and I will follow you. We have business with Tunder."

"Sure you do," the sarcasm in her tone was evident.

Puzzled, I looked to Daggin for clarification, but he just shook his head from side to side as if to tell me it was not worth explaining. We proceeded forward in silence. Kryssa's posture became even stiffer.

We sped into a thin hall that was different from the rest of the palace. Its area was closed and tightly shrouded, instead of open and bright. The hall reminded me of a medieval castle with its dark walls and shadowy corners. At the end of the passageway was a spiraling staircase that led upward. We reached the top of the ascending blocks in seconds and approached an ancient looking wooden door.

I expected Kryssa to knock, but instead she yanked on the metal latch and entered the concealed room unceremoniously. The furnishings and structure of this room matched the medieval stairwell. The room we stood in was a sitting area of sorts, antique sofas and cushions decorated the living space while large blue heavy-looking curtains covered the windows. The only light in the room came from a crack in the curtains. Elik drew back the thick fabric, letting the sunshine enter in unrestricted.

Directly across from where we stood, creating a path to the next room, was a tiny staircase beneath an intricately decorated stone archway. Matching blue curtains hung beside the opening and darkness filled the opposite side of the doorway. I had a feeling it led to a bedroom.

"Tunder? Shaylee?" Kryssa called out loudly, startling me.

Silence met her calls and I wondered at the possibility of Tunder already having left. I glanced at Kryssa nervously. I could tell our minds were in the same place, since a worried expression lined her features.

I then heard the scrape of what sounded like a large door and looked to the place where I believed the sound had come from. Peering into the darkness behind the archway, Tunder's masculine form slowly took shape and he stepped out of the shadows.

He was rubbing his eyes from the bright light, his face groggy with sleep. I couldn't help but stare at his large biceps which bulged against the sleeves of his white shirt. Taking a moment to gather his bearings, he then addressed us softly.

"Kryssa," he nodded at her, his deep voice filling the room, "And Lissie." He looked at me and nodded again. "Is there something I can do for you both?"

His face was more relaxed than it had been the night before. Something in his eyes had softened, making him appear less harsh. His posture was welcoming rather than hostile.

"Well." Kryssa paused, not really sure how to begin. Her eyes moved to Daggin and Elik as if unsure of whether they were liable to hear what she had to say. "Lissie told me something last night which I think is of great importance. I wanted to take it to my father, but he is busy at the moment."

Tunder nodded, "Why don't you tell me and I can deem whether it is worth troubling him."

Kryssa nodded and was just about to speak, when the door that must have stood somewhere behind the archway creaked loudly. Shaylee stepped into the living room, her curly hair lying in perfect waves even though her clothes suggested she had just woken up. She smiled when she saw us.

"Hi, everybody," her voice was soft and rounded, her former sharp tone no longer traceable. As if attracted to his very presence, she strode toward Tunder, fitting perfectly into the side of his body underneath his arm.

"Hey," I replied, but Kryssa remained silent.

For a while the room remained quiet, each of us waiting for the other to take the initiative. There was an unknown wondering in the air, a palpable sense of something important. My stomach tightened in agitation as I tried to figure out how to begin, how to bring up what might be my reason for being changed.

"What are you girls here for?" Shaylee asked, her question direct, but rounded perfectly by a relaxed yawn.

I looked to Kryssa, hoping she would answer. She looked frozen in place. I wondered why she was so worried about this. I also wished that she would stop looking like that because she was making it worse for me.

"Well," Kryssa paused again, as uncertain as I was about how to move on. "Lissie told me something last night which I think could be important."

"Oh," Shaylee said, her mouth circling and her brow creasing. Elik and Daggin moved closer to where we stood, not wanting to be left out.

"Yes," I said. "Umm, it's about the night I was changed." Tunder nodded his head for me to continue, and I proceeded while trying to ignore the worry running through my mind. "Morven saw me once before I was thrown overboard."

If the tension had been tangible before, it was nothing compared to now. It was a weighted physical presence in the room, as real as the people standing before me.

I continued, explaining how I had been singing on the boat alone the night before the storm. Part of my mind cursed myself for bringing everything into action by simply singing. But I had done it numerous times before, how was I supposed to have known a merman would hear me that time?

Coming to the end I let my voice fall silent. Shaylee was twirling a strand of hair around her fingers while she looked at Tunder, who had moved to one of the couches to sit. He leaned on his knees, his eyes boring into the floor, but his mind was obviously elsewhere.

"Is it important?" Daggin's deep voice surprised me again.

Tunder nodded, "Yes, it's very important." He fell silent and it seemed as though he would not elaborate further. Frustrated, I tried to wait patiently, knowing he knew more about this than anyone else in the room.

Tunder was the first to break the silence with a loud exhale. I thought I heard him swear softly under his breath as he rubbed his hands over his face. He looked stressed when he finally pulled his hands away.

Shaylee walked over and touched his arm gently. His unfocused eyes snapped back to reality.

"What is it, sweetheart?" Shaylee brushed a hand along the side of his face.

"He's going to use her," Tunder revealed. The sensation of feeling trapped wrapped around my body, pressing upon me as though it was trying to suffocate me. I struggled not to panic.

"What do you mean?" Kryssa asked abruptly from where she stood by my side.

"Our worst fear has been realized," Tunder said disbelievingly. By the looks on everyone's faces, they were all as confused as I was.

"What fear?" Elik voiced.

"Morven is going to use Lissie to overtake us. He will use her power"

Power? What power? This wasn't what I had been expecting.

My heart pounded sporadically, waiting desperately for what he would say next and feeling more and more like a piece in a game of wills.

"Somehow Nerissa figured out how to transform a human into a creature that could contend with the strength and of a merman or mermaid. She said these beings could be controlled to do her bidding." A chill ran through my spine, I remembered what it was like the night he came to Coveside. I recalled how I felt like an object of his choice that he could control.

Tunder looked directly at me, speaking quickly to further explain. "The whole reason we avoid humans is because they are inferior. In ancient times, some mermaids used to watch sailors. Seeing how lonely they were at sea, they would sing to them. But their efforts only crazed the humans. The men would become so obsessed with what they heard, and sometimes saw, that they would die or drown trying to find merfolk. For this reason it was decreed that all merfolk would avoid human contact and thus we have remained a mystery to the human world.

"Yet, some continued to pursue humans since it gave them a sense of control. They would prey upon ships or coastal villages, revealing themselves only enough to make humans curious or transfixed with seeing them again. These are the merfolk which gave rise to the human myth of sirens."

The term was familiar to me, one I had heard in one of my high school English classes. Immediately an image of a ship rolling on the sea and beautiful half-human women singing and gesturing sinuously to ragged sailors popped into my mind. Was this really the foundation for such myths?

"But," Tunder continued for my benefit, "The practice of tempting humans died out when it became punishable by death. It wasn't until Nerissa that humans *really* had any contact with our world."

"That still doesn't answer what power you think Lissie has," Shaylee pointed out to her husband.

Tunder looked at each of us as though we were dense for not having connected the dots. "Her singing," he said. "Morven is transforming her into something he can control and in turn use to control others."

"So he wants to use her to hypnotize fishermen?" Elik asked with a laugh in his voice. His words declared how ridiculous he thought Tunder's hypothesis was; I couldn't help but agree with him.

"No," Tunder shook his head slowly from side to side. "I think he means to control merfolk with her voice."

The whole room froze. No one moved. I glanced around, hoping this idea would be tested and expelled quickly, but no one was arguing the point. Instead they all recognized it as a clear possibility. Panic like I had never before felt flooded into my mind.

"The power of seduction," Kryssa mumbled softly under her breath, just loud enough for us to hear. Tunder bobbed his head in agreement and stood to pace around the room.

"Yes, he will use her voice to help him take us over. When she turns eighteen, she will be more powerful than she is now."

"I'm sorry, what?" I blurted out, no longer able to contain myself. All eyes turned toward me. "You speak as if I already have this power. I haven't been able to seduce *anyone*." I hated saying the word—it made me feel like a sexual object trying to entice someone into lust.

"But you have," Tunder said. His eyes kindled in a sort of frenzy, finally realizing what was happening. "You were able to make all of us believe that you were a human. You may not know this, but it's *very* difficult to lie to merfolk—we have a keen sense for falsehoods. The fact that you were able to fool us and persuade us to trust you only shows the power that you have."

Shaylee spoke softly, as if trying to break the news to me gently. "Was there ever a time you can remember making someone do what you wanted by simply suggesting it?"

I started to shake my head no, but then a particular memory popped into my mind. The night Morven had visited me in Coveside, I had asked him why he had listened to me singing. I remembered watching his eyes go blank, if only for a fraction of a second, and then it had all cleared. But that was not what stood out in my mind. What sent confirming proof was the look he had given me just after it had happened. He had been satisfied. He knew then and there that I would fulfill his purpose.

I let my silence be my confirmation. What I had just realized was too much for me to put into words.

Kryssa's cold fingers touched my arm gently, her expression pitying when I looked at her. I shrugged, not really sure how to respond.

Everyone was uncertain of how to proceed, as though a trance had come over each of us. Daggin broke the spell by clearing his throat.

"In that case, sir, do you wish for me to seek out the king?"

Tunder nodded, but then changed his mind. "Actually no, tell him I will meet with him in his study. Shaylee, get dressed. We need to strategize." Shaylee nodded and returned to her bedroom without hesitation. "Elik, go to Patrick and tell him of the new developments. Maybe it will help him to remember something. And Kryssa, keep Lissie with you. She can return to the island tomorrow."

His words were decrees for all to follow. Elik left the room quickly and we followed him out the door. Reaching the bottom of the stairs, we split to walk down different halls. I could still hear the tread of Elik's feet on the other stone pathway. All I could think of was how each step only made me feel like more of an object than ever before. The haunting memory of that terrible name prodded my mind.

For all I knew I was turning into her.

I was becoming *Marina.*

19. Returning

I awoke to darker skies than the morning before. Glancing around, it took me a moment or two before I realized where I was. Kryssa lay beside me on her large soft mattress and over on one of the small settees beside the wall was Nixie. She was curled into a tight ball beneath a thin blanket. I feared she might be cold, but her face was completely relaxed.

The previous night had actually turned out better than predicted. Pitying me, Kryssa had done her best to cheer me up. Her efforts had worked and were only further successful when Nixie showed up.

We spent most of the night talking and both girls were all too happy to answer my questions about their childhood. Their upbringing and lifestyle fascinated me. They told me how humans were kept away from Lathmor; merfolk often had to either dislodge parts of the motor or steer the boats away without being seen. I found out that Lathmor was always being watched, guards constantly on the alert for any sign of trouble.

They also told me that there was a system of mirrors surrounding the island. The reflection of the water hid the island from rare passing planes.

While I found all of this fascinating, what was amusing was their equal interest in my normal human life. They wanted to know about everything: my family, school, the restaurant. Their questions were endless. It wasn't until we could hardly keep our eyes open that we settled down and slowly drifted off to sleep.

Like the sunshine creeping into the perky room, so did my worries from the night before return. In the morning light they were more direct and focused, though. What I was to Morven was inevitable, but what worried me most were the thoughts and anger I had seen in Patrick's eyes. I craved for his presence though I wondered why I craved it so much.

The way he had stood by my side, ready to protect me, was something I couldn't forget. I wondered if he would do the same thing now that he knew the truth of what I was.

Rolling to my side I watched the slanted square of morning sunshine on the wall slowly ascend in the room. I dreaded what I would face in the coming hours.

Later that day when it was time to leave, Kryssa and I exited the palace through a back door on the bottom floor. It was obvious I was still being kept out of sight from the other Lathmorians, but that was fine by me. The hostility Voon had sent my way was enough to keep me from mingling with the general crowd. In reality, I craved the quiet solitude of the island.

We trudged along the dirt path toward the caves neither of us speaking. Rounding the curve which brought the caves into view, we saw Elik walking toward us. His head hung lower than usual and bobbed with each step he took. The moment I saw him, all I could think about was where he had come from. My heart raced in anticipation of what he could tell me.

He saw us from a distance and made an effort to look more dignified, but his attempts were obvious. Upon reaching us, I could see the solemnity in his eyes and gulped while my stomach tightened.

As I looked at him, I saw how weary he was. His shoulders were slightly slouched and there were bags under his eyes. When he blinked, it was rather slow as though he was having a hard time getting his eyes to readjust.

"Kryssa, do you mind if I speak to Lissie alone for a moment?" He raised a tired eyebrow at her and she passed him to enter the cave. Before she was out of sight he called to her, "Do be careful when you leave, they just switched the watch but still be on your guard."

I thought Kryssa would snap at him in response as she usually did when he cautioned her, but this time she didn't. Instead, she nodded her head in acceptance just before stepping into the shadows of the cave. For a moment Elik looked after her, his face betraying his raw emotions clearly. I looked away, not wanting him to know what I saw in his eyes.

"Lissie," he said calmly and I turned back to him. "Patrick and I are very good friends. In fact we all are, Tunder, Patrick and I." The information only confirmed what I believed, but made me wonder why the princesses so often visited the island while Elik and Tunder didn't.

"When I left yesterday, I told him everything." Elik seemed to want my approval of his actions, even though I knew he was only following Tunder's orders. "Tunder and I didn't want you to be the only one there when he found out everything. This is very particular to him and we weren't sure how he would react." I had seen the burning rage when Patrick had found out what I really was. I was glad I wasn't there when Elik told him of why Morven had changed me.

"You see, Patrick is different than what you think. He is, well, he's—" Elik was beginning to speak quickly, fumbling for words.

"It's okay," I butted in, touching his arm with my hand. His lowered eyes reached mine. "I already know what happened to him. Kryssa told me." He nodded.

"He just needed to know," he said softly.

"Well, thank you," I said, knowing the gratitude could be heard within my voice. "I really do appreciate it." Elik smiled partly.

"I'm sorry this happened to you," he offered.

"Don't be," I said, swallowing difficultly, "who knows? Maybe this was just meant to happen." I shrugged and spoke with more optimism than I felt.

"Maybe." The wind picked up while we stood in the silence for a moment. My hair floated gently in the breeze.

"I guess I had better be going then," I said awkwardly. Elik nodded, and when he spoke his voice was thick with concern.

"You take care of yourself now." I nodded immediately. "Most likely I will see you soon, but stay on the island. I will try and visit if I get the chance." He smiled in a brotherly way.

"You do that. Come along with Kryssa sometime." His smile broadened at my suggestion.

We parted ways and I entered the cave. Kryssa was waiting on a bench, her face solemn.

"You ready?" Her forced light tone caused me to answer in the same manner.

"Yes," I confirmed.

"Here," she extended a small black pack with a strap towards me. "It's a waterproof pack, for your clothes."

"Oh," I said while looking for somewhere I could change out of my clothes without having to prance around naked in the cave. "Uh…" I said, looking around uncomfortably until Kryssa burst out laughing.

"What?" I said, feeling both self-conscious and amused.

"Your face," she laughed and pointed. Her outright laughter was new to me and I realized the sound was nice to hear; she was much too serious most of the time. "You change quickly in the air as you jump in."

My brow creased, "How do you do that?"

"I don't know," she shrugged. "You just do. Here, I'll show you."

She stood at the edge, her toes just touching the tips of the lapping water. In her hand was a similar black pack to the one she had given me. Then, with expert skill, she jumped into the air twisting and wiggling as she went. She hit the water with a delicate splash. She resurfaced immediately, her head and shoulders out of the water. She was fully transformed, the black pack flat and buckled around her stomach and tightly secured. A silvery-blue strip covered her chest, and her hair spanned out around her as she waited in expectation.

"How'd you do that?" I asked, my eyes wide.

She laughed again. "Just jump and pull off your clothes. You'll be surprised how quickly you can change."

Gulping nervously, I stepped up to the water's edge just like she had done moments before. I checked to make sure the pack was unzipped and prepared myself for what I knew would be failure.

With as much strength as I could, I leapt into the air and everything seemed to move in slow motion. I pulled at my shirt, then my shorts and underclothes. They came off quickly as if in a blur and I was able to push them into the bag and zip it without trouble. Reaching the top of my arch, I hurtled down towards the water while fumbling to get the pack around my body. I crashed into the water ungracefully. My fins sprouted immediately. The pack was securely fastened about my waist. It was similar to the one I had fashioned at home, but sleeker and flatter against my skin as though there was nothing inside in.

Breaching the surface, heat flooded my face as the sounds of Kryssa's hysterical laughter reached my ears. She was slightly bent over in the water, clutching at her stomach as she laughed. It was contagious and I couldn't help but giggle at myself.

"That was. The-funniest-thing-I've-ever-seen!" she said between spurts while trying to get air. I splashed water her way and she shrieked playfully.

"Hey, it was my first try," I laughed.

"I know, I know," she said sobering, but still smiling. "Merlings, merfolk children, do better than that. But you'll get better with practice." Her eyes still held all the mirth she felt.

"I better." I shook my head and she burst into laughter again. "Shouldn't we be going?"

She nodded, "Yes, if you can manage that?"

There was a spark in her eyes I had never seen before and I found myself liking this Kryssa more than the one I knew before. She was more carefree and not so rigid or sharp around the edges.

"I'll try and manage," I concluded with a smile.

In one giant kick Kryssa leapt over the water like a dolphin, her blue tail flicking into the air. When she re-entered she took off like a rocket through the shadowy water. I took a large breath and then gave into the desires of my body. The ocean had been calling to me ever since I had stepped onto Patrick's island. My body ached to feel the water moving swiftly past me again.

Mimicking Kryssa's jump, I arched over the water and reentered with a dignified splash and sped toward the light at the end of the cave.

I caught up to her quickly and we moved in synchronization, our fins lifting and pushing the water with powerful strokes as we propelled through the salt water. The tension which had been residing in my gut ever since reaching Lathmor finally released, and I gave myself over to the distinct inbred joy of swimming.

We moved effortlessly, but my senses alerted me to another presence in the water. Kryssa jerked her head to the side and made a sort of high pitched sound that came from her throat. Somehow, I easily understood her meaning.

That's just another Lathmorian up ahead. Wondering if I could respond, I let my body control my movement. My throat contracted and the words I was thinking became a guttural mumble, telling her that I understood.

All right. The sound made perfect sense and my whole body jerked in stunned surprise. Shocked, I lifted my hand to my throat not sure of how I was able to speak merlanguage. Kryssa smiled, obviously amused.

This must be a first, she said and giggled.

Who's there? Kryssa and I whipped around at the deep throaty call of a merman who floated a ways off. His posture was tense and I realized merfolk looked even more daunting and powerful in the water than on land. He wore a black shirt with slits on the forearms. The fabric looked tough under the water, as though it was some sort of armor. I shivered to think about an underwater battle, tails and blades flashing.

Upon recognizing Kryssa, the merman relaxed his position. *Lady Kryssa. Lissie.* He nodded in greeting as he spoke each of our names. We nodded back. *Do you need an escort?*
No, Kryssa responded quickly, *we will be fine.*

All the same, do be careful, princess, the guard spoke firmly and swam away without further acknowledgement. I looked to Kryssa for an explanation.

The Guard has tightened severely in the past few months. Not to mention your presence has stirred things up once more. Everyone is on edge. I nodded, but Kryssa did not seem to notice. Her eyes were staring out into the distance. *Come on,* she said, apparently ready to go.

We continued to move forward, streaking past the ocean floor with great speed. The rises and falls of the ocean floor dazzled the eye with its sandy waves and slippery pits that lead to deep caverns and black holes. I shuddered to think of what might live down there.

Onward we went and I knew it was all going to come to an end soon. It had been so long since I had last been able to spring free from the tight confines of a human body and allow the mermaid within me to take control. My spirit was soaring and I couldn't help but smile as I launched ahead of Kryssa, too caught up in the adrenaline pumping through my veins.

With a laugh, Kryssa suddenly shot past me. Her shimmery blue fins flashed as she dipped toward the bottom and then arched back toward the surface, twisting and turning her body. Reaching the surface, she broke through the clear sheet of rippled glass and disappeared momentarily. Reentering with tremendous speed and precision, she came to a rest by my side, breathing heavily. Her cheeks were filled with a kind of excitement and her eyes lit with a spark of anticipation.

Go ahead, try it.

Taking a deep breath of water, I felt my lungs refresh and then plunged forward, mimicking Kryssa's movements. It was like a self-controlled rollercoaster where I could do whatever I wanted. I twisted, turned, flipped, and then dashed toward the surface where I let my body arch out of the water. For one instant I became human, but then changed back immediately, hardly enough time to even realize my legs had returned before my head plunged back into the crisp ocean water.

Eventually we collapsed on the ocean floor, exhausted and exhilarated at the same time. I found it strange that no noise came from my mouth and bubbles didn't exit my lips. The laughter between us was more of a high-pitched woven whisper that came from our throats.

I don't think that counted as being careful, Kryssa giggled to herself.

That's true, but it was too good to pass up. I smiled and Kryssa rolled over onto her side to look at me.

I think that's one thing we have forgotten in this war: how to be happy. It's what I miss more than anything. That, and—never mind. She broke off abruptly and floated up to look around us. I sat up, wrapping my arms around my fins and wondered what it was she missed the most.

Do you ever worry about sharks? I asked, trying to diffuse the awkward moment.

It worked. Kryssa broke into laughter, the merriment in her eyes doing my heart some good. Too often she looked so sad. *No. We are faster and stronger than any shark in the ocean. They are afraid of us actually.* I recalled the shark I had seen upon leaving Coveside and how it had swum away so quickly.

Kryssa continued, *Their teeth are no match for these.*

Her blades shot out of her fingers and I stared at them in astonishment. It was only the second time I had seen mermaid blades, but underwater they had a much more eerie appearance and the very sight of them made my own fingers tingle.

Looking around again, Kryssa retracted her blades and extended her hand toward me, pulling me up beside her. I laughed to myself thinking how human her actions were.

We better move on.

This time we swam with a purpose and a few minutes later I could see the ocean floor rising in the distance.

You should know where to go now. Kryssa's voice sounded calm, but her eyes continued to dart around as she tested our surroundings. *You best be quick about it.*

All right, I agreed.

I guess I'll see you later, she said awkwardly. Surprising me, she leaned over to give me a quick hug.

Thank you, I said while noticing how disconcertingly quiet it was under the surface. *For everything*, I added softly.

It was fun.

We both took deep breaths and I turned to look at the rising ocean floor. Nerves tightened within my stomach. What would Patrick be like when I got back? I bit my lip, unsure of what would happen.

I'll be back for a visit, she said. I nodded in agreement to her words and twisted to look at her again.

I look forward to it, I said. She smiled and turned to leave. I watched her streak away in a shimmery blur of blue and silver ripples, then took a deep breath and repositioned myself with the island directly in front of me.

This is it, I mumbled to myself and kicked off toward the rising ocean floor.

Reaching the island, I hunkered low so the waves crashed just above my head. I fingered the zipper of the small pack around my waist and waited for the courage I needed to proceed forward.

With another deep breath I shot forward, arching perfectly out of the water while zipping open the pack and pulling on the clothes before my feet hit the sandy shore. Without pausing, I broke into a stride heading for the shadows of the large leafy trees. My stomach was in knots over what would be waiting for me.

Not knowing where to look for Patrick, I decided it would be best if he came to me. Thinking ahead, I trudged on toward the house while plans formed in my mind. Maybe a little dinner would help soothe his anger. A myriad of recipes flew through my mind as I tried to figure out which one he would like the most.

Having a plan and something to do seemed to ease the nervous pangs I was feeling. But they were still there, nagging at my insides.

20. Truth

The delicious smell of lobster chowder wafted throughout the cabin, filling my nostrils and making my stomach grumble in hunger. I laughed nervously to myself. It had been almost five hours since I had returned to the island, and still there was no sign of Patrick. In fact, nothing looked different. It was as if he had yet to set foot in the house since we left for Lathmor. I stood next to the hot kettle of lobster chowder biting my nails nervously.

Where was he? The thought ran through my head for the millionth time. His absence was making me uneasy.

After all ten of my nails were practically gone, I made up my mind. I had a right to know what he was thinking. If he was angry with me, then he should tell me to my face. A small part of me worried about what would happen when he surely rejected me. Somehow this friend had crept deeper into my heart than I thought.

Marching out the front door and down the spiral staircase, I began my search though still unsure of where to look for him. The sun was just sinking below the trees and I knew my time was limited; though my eye sight was impeccable underwater, it was still the same on land.

I followed the trail that led to the waterfall, thinking I might find him there. But all I found was the cascading waters. In the orange light, the water took on a mournful glow as though it was lonely and I couldn't help but feel connected to it in some strange way.

Pressing on, my search led me to other areas around the house, circling wider and wider, but I was too afraid to call out his name. In the back of my mind I knew I was going to have to give up soon. I dreaded having to try and go to sleep without knowing where he was. I tried to fight the pang of remorse churning within, but it threatened to take control.

Was he really so angry with me? Had I been wrong in hiding my true identity? Did he think our friendship was false?

My feet carried me without my knowledge. Branches brushed against my face, but I didn't care. I was miserable and determined at the same time. My heart was on a mission, refusing to give up and afraid of the end result.

Dim light from the sunset peeped through the trees as I neared the outer edges of the island. The familiar sound of the waves caressing the shore met my ears, but I paid it no mind. I all of a sudden knew where he would be. The cliff, the very rock edifice on which I had found refuge on the first day I arrived on the island, lay ahead. My heart began to pound heavily, the sound of it ringing in my ears. I knew he had to be there.

Keeping the cliff in my sights constantly, I pushed forward and finally broke through the last few branches to a clear view of the rock. Without looking at the top, I began to climb. I reached the summit quickly, knowing what I would find.

Shards of ginger clouds and a pastel orange sky created a dome above my head, but my eyes zeroed in on the person I was most anxious and dreading to see. Patrick sat in the exact spot where he had found me; his legs were bent with his arms resting lightly on top of his knees. He didn't turn, but I knew he was aware of my presence. I waited for what seemed like hours.

Patrick sighed heavily and untangled his ankles, rising to his feet. My breath caught in my throat. He seemed larger, more determined, as though his defiance of Voon's threats to my well-being had awakened something within him.

His hair blew gently in the breeze as he turned to meet my gaze. The small corner of my heart opened. I cared for him more than I had thought. I knew in that moment that walking away from him would cause me a great deal of pain. How close that moment could be was something I didn't want to think about.

Just seeing him now, after knowing what Kryssa had told me of his past, was enough to transform my view of him. I remembered how Kryssa had said he was old, and for the first time I could see the years in his eyes. He seemed wise and knowledgeable, and yet wary of me.

He did not speak, but continued to look at me calmly. I gulped nervously, wondering what he would say. I knew I wouldn't be the first to speak; I couldn't, there were too many emotions churning inside to form coherent thoughts. But he didn't speak either. Instead, he walked toward me carefully. Nerves gripped my stomach. Part of me wanted to run away, but the stronger part won. I would face the rejection that was surely coming.

With one slow but deliberate movement, Patrick extended his hand and placed his palm in mine. Again, I tried to swallow and the sound was rather loud. I hoped that he didn't hear it. Then, without looking at me, he turned and softly pulled me along behind him, his very touch sending shots of electricity along my flesh.

I followed him with my head held high, but dreading every step. *Why couldn't he just get it over with?*

I didn't know where I would go once he turned his back on me. Lathmor was a possible haven, but there was only impending capture for me there. The island was where I wanted to be; it was the only place I felt safe with a future that didn't involve the threat of Morven.

Patrick led me down the steep hill. We approached and entered a cave hidden within the crevices of the cliff. I remembered seeing the opening on my first day exploring the island. Curiosity pushed the threatening fears aside and I blinked rapidly to adjust to the dim light of the stone walls dripping with salty water.

His grip never loosened, and he continued forward with a determination I had never seen in him before. The light from the outside behind us grew smaller and just before it disappeared from sight we broke off to the left into a small hole in the rocky wall. If I had been alone, I never would have seen it.

Patrick came to a sudden stop and dropped my hand. I immediately felt separated from him, as though mere contact had given me insight into what he was feeling.

The room we stood in was large, but not any wider than the first floor of Patrick's cabin. The circular chamber was entirely empty aside from various unlit torches that hung along the walls. Softly packed dirt covered the floor and kicked up in little puffs as Patrick walked around the room, lighting each of the torches in order. I scrunched my toes in the dirt as though it could provide me some security for what was about to come.

He lit the last torch and I swallowed heavily, preparing myself.

He turned slowly from across the room to face me. My earlier confidence fled and I couldn't bring myself to meet his gaze. I stared at his chest, too afraid of what I would see in his eyes.

"I'm sorry."

Of all the words, I had conjured in my mind, these two were the least I was expecting him to say. "I'm sorry that this happened to you." Patrick's deep warm voice caressed the silence. It was not angry, and for this I was thankful. Although I knew it would still end the same, at least he wouldn't be furious with me. At least I would never again have to see the anger he had flashed at me in Lathmor.

Finally I met his gaze. His eyes were somber, and yet frustrated as though he couldn't put his feelings into words. I waited while trying to think of some solution to give him an easy way out.

He broke our gaze and looked away, his finely carved face casting dancing shadows on the damp cave walls.

"Lissie," he said as he turned his face back toward mine. "Please say something." He sounded desperate.

"What do you want me to say?" I asked softly, my voice barely above a whisper. He sighed heavily and, obviously exasperated, laughed slightly.

The tension was so strong in the air that I could taste it on my tongue. But it was a strange tension—it didn't cause blood to boil and fear to spread. Instead, it forced all emotions to coil into a tight ball and wait silently for the moment when it could explode into lurid fireworks. I knew that moment was coming soon. I knew it would come when he told me to leave.

"I don't know." Patrick's voice was like mine, hardly audible. Again the silence cloaked us. "Why don't I tell you my story so you can understand?"

He looked up to see if I accepted his request, but I simply stared back unsure of what he was talking about.

"I'll start at the beginning." Again he looked to see if I had any thoughts on the matter, but my mind was frozen, refusing to allow my thought to move quick enough to react to his words.

He inhaled deeply and his eyes became distant, looking back at memories that were hundreds of years in the past.

"I was born in England in 1257, the son of Lord Kenton Walsh and one of four children. I was the oldest boy in my family and had a younger brother and two younger sisters. We lived in the west near the shores of a beach where I would often go on long walks after arguing with my father. It was after such an occasion that I met Nerissa."

A shiver ran down my back as he spoke her name. He said it like a curse, a fowl word that poisoned the mouth.

"It was early evening when I saw her for the first time. My dog, Hector, was with me and I think he knew she wasn't human the instant he spotted her. She was sitting on a rock looking out over the ocean. I remember being amazed by her beauty and knowing that there was something different about her. Little did I know then what she would do to me," Patrick said, shaking his head slowly.

"She spoke smoothly to me. She wove a tale of trouble in which she was stuck and asked for me to help her. I was obliged to, not only out of chivalry, but because I wanted to. She had lied to gain my confidence and it worked. I had known nothing of her true nature and the power she possessed." Patrick grew frustrated, obviously angry with himself for being so gullible.

"She left me that night, but told me to be ready for her to come back someday. She spoke of wanting to be with me forever and at the time the idea sounded wonderful. She spun stories of ruling the world together and I dreamt about the day when she would come back. Being the eldest son of a Lord was not enough for me anymore.

"It was not until the summer of my twentieth year that I saw her again. It happened almost the exact same as before: I was once again walking with Hector, and she was sitting on the same rock as I had seen her last time. Her beauty was just as stunning as it had been, but I hinted a sense of urgency within her. This time my instincts told me to not trust her.

"I remember how she looked at me," Patrick said, his eyes narrowing as he remembered. "It was as though I was a possession, not a person. I was something to be owned." I knew this look well and could see it in my mind's eye. How many times had Morven looked at me that same way?

"She said it was time to leave, time to conquer. But her urgency scared me and I told her to go away. I was angry with her. For two years I had waited patiently, and now that my life was finally heading in the right direction she had returned. But she only laughed at my threats and gave me a choice. I could either go willingly or be forced. I refused her again, this time foolishly telling her off. Then everything changed."

The lines on Patrick's face deepened as he remembered. Part of me wanted to cover my ears. I didn't want to hear the horror I knew was to come. My own nightmares ran through my mind.

"She laughed again and a little boy stepped out from behind the rock she was sitting on. He glared at me and there was something about him that made me want to run away, but being the son of a Lord I simply drew my sword in response." I knew immediately just who the young boy was. In my mind, I could not think of him as a child.

"The boy did not speak," Patrick said, "but looked at my sword as though it was useless. He walked close to me, circling Hector and me slowly, and then without warning he pulled my hunting dagger from my belt and plunged it into Hector's chest." I gasped and raised a hand to my mouth, but Patrick continued to speak as though he had not heard me.

"Hector didn't have a chance of surviving, but before I could react the boy pulled the dagger from Hector's limp body and sliced my leg open." Unconsciously, Patrick grazed a hand over his right thigh while my eyes widened in horror. "The next thing I remember was flying across the top of the water in Nerissa's arms, the boy beside us."

"When we reached land, I had a fever and later awoke in a large bed in a stone room. Nerissa tried to nurse me back to health, but I refused to eat. It was only when she threatened the wellbeing of my family that I gave in to her ministrations. Over the next few weeks while I began to heal, I tried to figure out a way to escape. My only weapon was the dagger which the boy had used to kill Hector and wound me. Why they had left it in the room I'll never know.

"Nerissa and the boy entered my room one night while I feigned sleep. I remember trying to be as relaxed as possible, when they suddenly tied me down to the bed. Nerissa, with the help of the boy, lifted my right shoulder and drew her blades across my skin." My mind flashed back to what Kryssa had told me about Patrick; again I wondered about the scar that supposedly traced the back of his shoulder.

"She shoved something sharp into my flesh, and when she pulled away from me her hand was bleeding. One of her blades was missing." Horror washed through my gut, making me nauseated.

"I blacked out for a moment, but when I came around I was no longer restrained and a woman I had never seen before was in the room. She spoke to me quickly, but all I understood was that she was there to rescue me." Thinking of Kryssa's mother Cordelia, I waited in wonder to know what happened. "Just as I got to my feet, Nerissa and the boy entered the room and the women began to fight." Patrick's eyes were wide and his breath had escalated without his knowledge. He was physically present in the cave, but his mind was transported far away from the island.

"The woman who had come to save me began to lose. She was hesitant, as if she didn't want to hurt Nerissa. But Nerissa gave her no mercy while the boy stood by and watched. Without thinking, I picked up my hunting knife and threw it at Nerissa, killing her. The boy came toward me, vowing to avenge his mother."

"But he didn't get far. My rescuer stopped him—she gagged and tied him to the bed post. We escaped, and with what little strength she had left, Cordelia brought me to the safety of Lathmor." Patrick sighed heavily and turned his palms open as if there was nothing else he could say to explain himself. "And when I awoke days later, my life was changed forever. Of course, at the time I didn't realize just how much."

21. Confession

The only sounds in the cave were our soft exhalations of breath as we stared at one another. The silence was heavy, it felt like a physical presence in the room. I could feel it closing in on me, pressing into my flesh powerfully.

We stood in this dreaded silence for a long moment, my heart thundering within my chest. Patrick's eyes slowly refocused and he looked at me calmly without anger or frustration.

"I believe you know the rest of the story?"

"Yes," I said, my voice shaky.

He nodded awkwardly and the quiet shrouded us again. I could tell he wanted to say something, so I waited for him to do so.

"Lissie, I've accepted what's happened to me because I've had plenty of time to come to terms with it." Again his voice was calm and steady. "But the other day when I found out about you," he raised a hand to his head as if it hurt to think about it,

"I've never been so angry in all my life." I winced knowing what was about to happen. Helplessly, I waited.

"What Morven," he said the name as if it were a curse, "did to you makes me so infuriated that I don't, I don't…" He broke off, his hands shaking by his sides and the dark anger which he had shown in Lathmor reappearing. I wanted to reassure him, calm him, do anything to make the anger he felt disappear.

"It's okay. At least, I think I'm okay with it." My feeble voice tried to reassure him.

"No, it's not okay." His voice was sharp; making me flinch. "From the very beginning of this, Morven has been there. He murdered Hector, kidnapped me from my family, helped his mother transform me into whatever it is that I am. He prevents me from living near anyone. He searches for me constantly, never relenting. And now he's trying to take you from me." His words ran together leaving me stunned. I had never heard him speak so quickly before.

"I don't know what you mean," I said, shivering. Somehow the distance between us felt smaller even though neither of us had moved.

"I have been alive for seven hundred and fifty-two years, and I have never met someone like you. The moment I saw you on the cliff I fell for you. I've been falling for you ever since that day and I won't ever be able to give you up." His words caught me off guard and my mind whirled in the reality of what he was saying. "I have nothing to offer you. I don't know what I am, and I can't protect you from Mor—"

"Patrick, I ran away from Morven out of fear," I butted in. Frustration and anger was reeling off of him, his chest heaving with pent up emotion. "It's you that I want to be with."

My words hung in the air while I stood, stunned that I was bold enough to say them aloud. Patrick closed his eyes for a moment, but when he reopened them they were alive with a kind of fire.

"He's taken everything I've ever had," Patrick's deep voice said, filled with an emotion I couldn't name. "But I'll be damned if he takes you from me."

In four long determined strides, Patrick closed the space between us and before I knew what was happening, his lips were on mine, raining tingling sensations throughout my body. His lips were warm and perfect, and his hands gently caressed the sides of my face. He kissed me fiercely for a moment and then his lips became softer. They moved against mine flawlessly, gracefully.

His hands that adorned my face brushed my cheeks softly. Goosebumps crawled all over my legs and arms, while those same large hands slid off my face to my back. I inhaled deeply, and found myself crushed into his body, his strong arms swallowing me.

Cautiously, I lifted my hands to his face, placing them on either side just like he had done. I traced his eyelids and cheeks with my fingertips, my heart pounding with the disbelief that I was actually touching him, kissing him. Slowly, my hands made their way into his hair. It was soft, like gliding my fingers across the surface of water, until they became tangled in his wavy locks. I wrapped my hands around the back of his head, holding onto the kiss wishing, hoping it would never end.

Patrick pulled his lips from mine and exhaled softly. I leaned my head back slightly to see his eyes. His face was so beautiful up this close, eyes kindled with an excitement and joy which matched my own. Small lines crinkled around the edges of his perfect lips in an impish grin.

"You have no idea how long I've wanted to do that," he whispered, partially breathless against my face, as he nudged my forehead with his.

"Really?" I asked, smiling.

"Really," He confirmed, and laughed gently. My heart soared and I laughed with him. This was my friend, the one I laughed with, and shared ideas with. Smiling to myself, I leaned into his chest and reveled in the safety and warmth of his protective embrace.

"This is a large cave," I said, my mind slightly distracted. Patrick looked down at me, obviously amused. "I've just never been inside one this big," I explained further while he gazed around the torch lit chamber, his brown eyes a melting chocolate in the fiery light.

"Yes, I guess it is rather large," he shrugged. "As you can see this was one of my favorite places back in the day." He snickered to himself.

"What do you mean?"

"Huh?" He was distracted and looking at the cave walls.

"What do you mean by 'as you can see'?" I asked again, looking up at his handsome face. He peered down at me curiously as though I was missing the obvious.

"I'm talking about the scratch marks on the walls. They're evidence of how often I was here." I tried to make out the so-called scratch marks, but couldn't see anything. Narrowing my eyes, I still couldn't see them.

"I don't see anything," my voice said dully. *Were my eyes really that bad?*

"You don't?" he asked surprised. "Well, here."

He took his arms from around me and pulled me toward the wall by my hand. As we got closer, I could finally see what he was talking about. Millions of little scratches ran over the walls like tally marks.

"What are they?" I asked, reaching out to brush my finger over one.

"When they first put me on the island, I decided to keep track of the number of days I would be here." There was a sarcastic incredulity to his voice, as though he couldn't believe he had been so foolish. "It gave me something to do, a reason to get up each morning."

His words made me wonder how he had found the will to keep going after so many years. The millions upon millions of scratches were a part of his history, and yet here he stood before me looking no older than the day he made the first scratch.

"Do you still do it?" I asked.

"No, I stopped a hundred years or so ago. There just wasn't really a point anymore."

We stared at the wall for a moment longer while my mind explored the incredibility of it all. Each mark was a day to him, more days than I could ever imagine, but days which I now knew my transformation would allow me to see. The very thought of living so long was daunting and really just impossible to grasp. It was difficult to think that I was holding hands with someone who had been living for centuries.

Off to the side, a small archway in the cave wall caught my attention. It was not the same hole through which we had entered earlier.

"Where does that lead?" For some reason, I whispered in a hushed voice and pointed. Patrick's eyes followed my finger.

"Oh," he hesitated, "That... that's just another room." He sounded a little nervous.

"What's in it?" I prodded.

"Well, it's a," he laughed and cleared his throat. "It's actually my armory." He smiled, embarrassed.

"Really?" I said louder than I intended. "I want to see!"

I walked quickly toward the opening, tugging Patrick along behind me. His fingers suddenly let go of mine. I stopped abruptly and turned to look at him. He smiled.

"Just getting us some light." His voice was reassuring. I waited patiently for him to pull the torch free from its holster and walk back to me. A pool of golden firelight surrounded our feet as Patrick reached for my hand. Somehow, it felt so right to have our hands joined. It was routine, like breathing.

We stepped into the so-called armory, a small room filled with crafted wooden shelves. All were loaded with assortments of weapons. I grew conscious of my wide mouth as I stared at it all. Swords, daggers, whips, spears, bows, tomahawks, and many other weapons that I didn't even know the names of adorned the shelves. Some of the objects looked very medieval, while others more modern. I recognized the Scottish claymore, and right beside it was the whip called the cat-o-nine-tails. Just looking at some of the weapons made my skin crawl in fear. I shuddered to think of the damage they could do to a human body.

"Wh—why," I stumbled on my words, "Do you have all of these?"

"Just because I don't have blades like a merman, doesn't mean I won't be able to fight one." Patrick spoke seriously, as though he had recited these words many a time before. I realized I was not the first to voice my concerns over his safety, but pressed forward anyway.

"You don't intend to fight Morven, do you?"

"Of course I do."

"Patrick!" My reaction was immediate. "You can't! He'll kill you!"

"I don't intend to seek him out," he said. His face never turned toward me as his eyes roved over each of the weapons. It was as though he was selecting which would be best to fight

Morven with. "As wonderful as it would be to hunt him down, I know it would be foolish." His voice was calm, too calm, as though he was keeping it in check.

"I just," I broke off not really sure how to put my feelings into words. "Have you actually seen Morven now that he's, he's," I swallowed hard, annoyed at my stuttering, "now that he's big."

Patrick shook his head. "I haven't, but that's beside the point." There was a finality in his voice that sent fear into my gut. He was serious and somehow I knew it would all come to pass and there was nothing I could do to stop it. "And if you are near me when I next see him, he is a fool if he thinks he can touch you without taking me out first."

"Please don't," I hung my head and shook it slowly from side to side. How could he not see the danger?

"Do you honestly think I am going to let that monster take you from me?" His voice was harsh, but I knew it wasn't because of me but who he was talking about. "You have completely changed everything for me." I knew what he meant. My world was changed because of him too. He was like me, and yet unlike me. We were the same, and yet different. Somehow intertwined with what plans Morven had, and fated to be together.

"Just remember," I said as I brushed my thumb against the back of his hand, "if he kills you then I don't have anything either." I meant it too. Losing him would be losing not only a friend, but the one person in my world who understood. Together we were the misfits of the world.

I glanced at his handsome face to see if he took me seriously. His smile was brilliant as he leaned in to brush his perfect lips softly against mine.

"Believe me, I know," he whispered softly. I smiled and he straightened back up, the light creating a silhouette of his head. "I believe you made dinner earlier and I'm hungry." He tugged gently on my hand, "shall we?" I hesitated.

"How did you know?" I asked curiously. Dinner was going to be a surprise, but now he had ruined it. A devilish half-grin appeared on his face.

"It was easier to think when I was able to watch you and not worry about what you thought of me." I smiled to myself, thinking of how worried I had been about the same things.

"I didn't think you would understand how different I am." He spoke softly, admitting his earlier doubts.

"I guess those feelings were mutual then." A soft smile played around my lips and I tried not to blush as I confessed my same doubts.

"That makes things easier," he said, partially to himself and partially to me. I nodded, unsure of whether he wanted a response.

"Dinner?" It was my turn to give his hand a small tug. He smiled.

"Dinner."

22. Reason

The lobster chowder disappeared quicker than I had anticipated; Patrick's appetite polished off the meal in an honorable fashion.

I was enjoying myself, sitting in my usual spot on the bench finishing up my meal. The simple conversation we carried cheered my soul and I relished in the feeling of belonging. We were together, and yet the idea did not seem foreign.

I studied him in the firelight, his golden head tilted slightly down while shadows flickered across his face. With a satisfied sigh, he polished off his bowl of soup and set it on the side table beside the bench I rested on.

We sat in silence for a moment. I stared at the crackling fire, aware of the eyes looking at me. Try as I might, I couldn't resist them. I looked at him and smiled, without a word he stood and moved over to sit on my right side. His heavy arm reached over the bench and around my shoulders, hugging me to his side.

Leaning down I placed my head on his shoulder sliding, fitting perfectly under his arm.

"Are you ever going to return home?" Patrick's voice vibrated in his chest and thrummed against my ear. I tilted my chin to look at him, pondering his question. He gazed back down at me with honest curiosity.

"I don't know," I said as I bit my lip and looked back into the fire. "I'd like to go back and see them, but if it's safer for me to be gone then I'll stay away."

"I see," he said, but I got the feeling he wanted to say more. I waited, but he didn't speak.

"Do you know what happened to your family?" I asked, looking up toward his face again.

He inhaled deeply, the breath making me move with him. When he exhaled I accidently slid a little closer into his side but before I could move back his arm tightened pinning me where I was.

"For a long time I didn't know what happened to them," he said as he gazed into the fire while he spoke. "When I had regained consciousness in Lathmor, I was confused. I knew what my name was, but it took a long time for me to put the whole story together in my mind."

I nodded, remembering how confused I had been the day I woke up and spoke with my father after my transformation. I couldn't imagine how much harder it would have been to wake up to complete strangers.

"But I can remember everything now as though it happened yesterday." He shrugged, falling silent.

"And your family?" I asked, still looking at him. He looked down at me and smiled softly.

"Guess I didn't answer that, did I?" My head rubbed against his shoulder as I shook it back and forth in response. "Well, like I said, it took me a while to realize who I was and then it took even longer for me to accept that I wouldn't be going home." Patrick sighed heavily. "But that wasn't to be. Although, Tunder was nice enough to go and spy on them for me every now and then when he wasn't busy. He was able to get away with it back then since he was only a boy."

I tried to think of Tunder as a child, but the thought was impossible. The dominating and commanding air with which he held himself could not be placed in a young boy.

"Every year or so, he would sneak into my family's house and live there for a few days, usually helping the servants. Each time he had a different disguise so no one would recognize him. He always told me everything he heard when he got back, and in some way it gave me a connection to them." Patrick broke off and I let his words hang in the air.

"My mother was the first to die." He squinted into the firelight avoiding my gaze.

"Tunder thinks she died of grief over my disappearance—it happened about a year and half after I was taken. My father passed away some ten years later in a hunting accident, leaving the inheritance to my younger brother who actually became a rather influential lord. He died when he was about fifty-three. My sisters both grew up and married into very wealthy families. They had fifteen children between the two of them. Tunder said they seemed happy and died of old age. And that's all I know."

The fire seemed to roar in the quiet after his voice ended.

"I'm sorry," I said softly to offer him some comfort. He turned to me and shrugged.

"It's been around seven hundred years since they died. I'm used to the idea." His mouth quirked at his jest, but the lines around his eyes showed his solemnity.

"What were their names?" I asked, hoping it wouldn't be too much to wonder.

"My younger brother's name was Bryon, the older of my sisters was Elspeth, and the younger was Gwendolyn." I nodded to acknowledge that I had heard.

For some reason I wanted to know more; to know these siblings who had been Patrick's companions so many years ago.

"How old were they?" I asked, I added, "If you don't mind telling me?" He laughed softly and ducked his head closer to mine.

"I'll tell you anything you want to hear." His lips pressed against my forehead softly and I sighed.

"When I was taken away, Bryon was eighteen, Elspeth was seventeen, and Gwendolyn was twelve. My mother had lost two babies in between my sisters."

I pondered those words and realized just how much I missed my family. I could see their faces in my mind. Aaron's mischievous eyes; Caitlin's missing teeth; Sara's dimples; Justin's bouncy curls; Kaleb's chubby cheeks; and Emly's sleeping face. But the two identical faces that I treasured the most in my heart were the clearest of all, and I missed them the most. It was all easy to remember, yet distant as if they didn't belong in the world I now lived in.

I sighed softly, and Patrick's hand reached under my chin. Slowly, he lifted my face so he could look at me. His eyes were filled with a pity that only made my insides hurt more. I wanted to look away, but his gaze held me captive.

"You'll see them again," he said tenderly. Somehow he had known what I was thinking.

"Okay," I said, my clogged throat sounding funny.

In a gentle gesture, he leaned my head back down onto his shoulder and I began to relax in the warmth of his closeness. Falling into the steady rhythm of his breathing, I closed my eyes. I felt completely content with where I was. A sudden thought entered my mind and I voiced it almost immediately.

"How have you lived alone this long?" I bit my lip, thinking I had spoken rashly.

"Do you mean how have I not gotten bored with life?" I nodded, his wording making more sense. He cleared his throat in a business-like manner. "At first it was difficult. I was depressed most of the time and seriously considered suicide. But after a while I grew used to the idea and decided to wait for Morven to find me." Patrick gave a short irritable laugh and looked down into my eyes. "I'm ashamed to admit that Morven was the only thing that kept me alive back then; I vowed to kill him before I died. I *still* hold onto that vow." The last words were spoken fiercely.

"It was then that I began to train myself in weaponry." The thought of him fighting Morven still scared me more than I wanted to admit. But I did not voice my thoughts, knowing it would do nothing to change his mind.

"Haven't you gotten even a little bit bored?"

"Of course," he said nodding his head. "But what you have to understand is time moves quicker once you are changed. Everything seems to blur together. There are periods of years I can hardly remember because they were so uneventful."

"I'm sorry, but that sounds terrible." How could he go on, each day being the same as the one before it, never knowing when it was all going to end?

"It's not so bad," he shrugged. "After a while you get used to it. Living any other way would be strange for me at this point."

"So is that all you do to pass the time? Just practice with your weapons?"

"No," he replied and a humorous smile played around his lips. "I taught myself other skills."

When he grew silent, I prodded, "Such as?"

"My carving," he explained, and I wondered why I hadn't thought of it before. "When I lived in England, I was unskilled with my hands and I was never taught how to use them. Everything I know now I taught myself." Patrick smiled to himself. "It was a rather large shock when the Lathmorians left me on the island—being the son of a Lord I had never taken care of myself before." He laughed, his eyes far away remembering what must have been amusing memories of his struggles. "You have no idea how long it took me to build my first little hut, and it was hardly even worth living in. Not nearly as nice as this one." He glanced around the room.

He piqued my curiosity. "How many houses have you built?"

"I usually try and build one every fifty years or so. This one is four years old, and it's a little more over the top than the others. But I couldn't resist when Elik and Daggin asked how many supplies I would need." My brow furrowed and he explained. "Whenever I need things the island can't provide, I get them from Lathmor or someone will go and meet up with Hugard."

"Who's that?"

"He's a merman who lives among humans. He maintains a façade, moving often to not cause suspicion when he doesn't age, but we use him to get certain goods. For the most part, though, the Lathmorians are self-sufficient."

I nodded my understanding while wondering where Hugard lived. To think of having to hide your true self from others for so long made me cringe. I had barely managed with a little over a month.

"It's a hassle, but without all the supplies this would've never been possible." Patrick's approving eyes swept the floor and ceiling.

"I like it," I confirmed.

"I'm glad you do," he said and pulled me closer. "There is something I want to apologize to you for."

I raised my head quickly to meet his gaze. What would he need to apologize for?

"The way I left you in Lathmor" He took a frustrated breath as I remembered the anger in his eyes. "I was angry, not at you, just Morven. I couldn't believe that the one person I had come to care about was in the same situation I was. It was hard enough wondering how I was ever going to tell you about my past, but to find out that you were a victim of his as well made me much angrier than it should have." Reaching up, I touched his cheek softly with my fingertips. He turned his gaze back to me.

"I'm sorry," he said. "I saw how you were afraid of me that day. I never want you to feel like that around me again."

"You don't have to be sorry," my soft voice filled the space between us. "I'm as strange as you now. An outcast from Lathmor." We laughed in the quiet night.

"Yes. We are rather odd, aren't we?" His dark eyes glowed in the firelight. "I'm sure you have never met anyone like me, and stayed around, huh?" He tried to sound nonchalant, but I knew what he was really asking.

"No," I said. "I used to meet transformed mermen, but now this one I recently met is becoming a bit of a hassle." He laughed heartily. "And to answer what you are really asking me, no, I have never dated anyone." His eyebrows rose, and he shrugged his shoulders as though he was innocent. I couldn't help but notice the self-satisfied expression on his face.

"No I will challenge you," I said and poked him in the rib. "Has there ever been another girl?" Patrick sighed heavily, looked away, and nodded.

"It was before I was changed." His eyes were far off, but not happy. "I was betrothed to her, actually. One of those arranged marriages from birth." He waved his hand and fell silent.

"Was she pretty?"

"She was... decent looking." He fidgeted obviously, uncomfortable. I laughed, and he looked down at me curiously.

"Hey, you started this whole thing." I pointed at him, and he smiled.

"I guess that's true." He inhaled, "well, I never really actually talked to her. At the time I was refusing to accept my father's wishes."

"You wouldn't marry her? Why?" I asked.

"I was in love with someone else." He cleared his throat and smiled. "She was a servant in our household. It was all quite scandalous, actually. The only reason I did it was to annoy my father."

Patrick laughed shortly and turned his gaze back to mine. My heart still fluttered at his look but I felt a small surge of jealousy towards this woman. Trying to purge my soul of the unwarranted feeling I looked away. Warm gentle fingers lifted my chin, but I kept my eyes downcast as long as possible. When I finally did look up, Patrick's gaze was patient.

"She's nothing compared to you." My heart thundered at the words. "Besides I hardly remember her. I used her and I'm not proud of it. But with you, I know I have someone who understands. You are my friend, which is more than I could have ever hoped for."

Shifting slightly, Patrick wrapped his other arm around my body, tucking me beneath his chin. His woodsy smell filled my nostrils and I found myself content and protected in his arms. His chest rose and fell, gently rocking me to sleep. Slowly, like a water droplet falling off a leaf, I drifted into the world of peaceful dreams.

23. Love

The morning sun peeked shyly through my windows. I could see it beneath my eyelids, and knew it was time to get up, but my body resisted. Instead, I lay back thinking of last night. My heart fluttered and a smile crept across my face. Pressing a finger to my lips, I remembered what it felt like to kiss Patrick in the cave. The mere thought made my heart beat rapidly inside my chest.

Slowly, I opened my eyes to the morning light in the guest bedroom. I heard footsteps from outside that were coming closer. Acting quickly, I brushed my fingers through my tangled hair knowing there wasn't enough time to fix it completely.

The door to the room opened carefully, slowly revealing Patrick as he poked his head in and looked directly at me. My chest tightened and I smiled. Something had changed last night. We had come together in the cave in a moment of passion, but the memory was not what made my heart skip a beat. Instead it was him; all of him, his past, his fears, his courage, and his kindness. That was what made me look at him the way I did. How could I ever tell him what he meant to me as a person?

Pushing the door open with his bare foot, his hands revealed a tray laden with food. As he walked toward the bed I sat up in order to make room for him and the tray on the end of my mattress.

He set the platter of food on the bed and without a moment's hesitation handed me a plate. Our fingers brushed slightly and a surge of something I had never felt before ran through my skin. The connection I felt around him frightened me. I was alive and scared and excited all at the same time, and uncertain of what to do.

With a moment of clarity the kiss we had shared in the cave flew through my mind. I remembered what it was like to touch his face and run my fingers through his hair. Warmth flushed over my cheeks and I ducked my head in the hopes that he would not notice.

"Thanks," I said and picked up a fork to begin eating. Each bite sounded impossibly loud.

"Yep," he said casually, and picked up his own plate. "How'd you sleep?"

I kept my head down. I still was uncertain of what was going on in my mind. "Fine," I said thinking it sounded casual enough.

My eyes stayed focused on the plate of scrambled eggs, wedged potatoes, and bacon. Glancing up, I caught site of

Patrick devouring his own food with rigor. A small laugh escaped my mouth.

"What?" He looked up, his lips quirking. The awkward embarrassment between us shattered.

"You look like you haven't eaten food for days." I laughed again and he smiled sheepishly.

"Well, I wasn't when I first woke up, but since you slept in so long I got hungry."

Looking outside I tried to see where the sun was in the sky. "What time is it?"

"Just after nine."

"That's not even late," I pointed out.

"Yes it is, I usually get up at five," he bobbed his head up and down. He looked out the window and sighed dramatically, his demeanor changing in an instant from serious to silly. "I don't know I guess all that kissing really had an effect on you. We will just have to be more careful next—"

But he didn't get to finish, because I swung a pillow at him and hit him square in the shoulder. He laughed so hard at his joke that I couldn't help but laugh with him.

"So, what's on the agenda for today?" I asked, trying to distract him. He pursed his lips for a moment.

"I don't know," he said as he ran a hand through his golden-brown hair. "We could go for a swim if you would like to. Might as well make the most of our freedom for now."

Somehow his words made the situation we were in seem trivial. We were both outcasts, stuck on an island while the

Lathmorians decided what to do with us. And Morven was a threat to our very existence, but the way Patrick referred to it so casually made it seem comical. Slightly giddy, I grew excited about what the day would hold.

"That sounds like a good idea to me," I agreed.

"Are you sure?" He quirked his eyebrow. "I know you don't know how to swim so it's not very much fun for you to just sit there." A mischievous glint trilled through his eyes.

"You are so full of it this morning," I said, shaking my head pityingly.

"Hey, that's just me babe," he said and shrugged his broad shoulders. "Are you finished?" I nodded and handed it back to him.

"Let's go now," I said excitedly. There was a tingling in my legs telling me that my body was ready to transform.

"All right," he smiled, "as long as you won't drown. I don't want your death on my hands."

"Oh, come on!" I exclaimed as I jumped out of bed and headed for the door.

"You know what?" He said behind me. "I just might have some water wings or a raft somewhere around here for you. Maybe we should take a look around."

Gritting my teeth I turned back around to face him with my hands on my hips. "You aren't going to give this up are you?"

"Why would I?" He asked and walked toward me. His eyes gleamed with a light I had never seen before. He walked forward and passed me by the door and whispered, "You are just too

«276»

easy to aggravate." Laughing he stepped out the door and I followed him.

The sky was completely different from the day before. It was bold and beautiful without a cloud in sight, and its electric blue hue lit harmonious colors on the island. When we reached the waterfall it was as beautiful as I remembered on the first day Patrick had taken me to it.

The water beckoned to me, calling to my inner creature in a desperate voice. My instincts strained toward the edge until my toes grazed the surface. A feeling of home coming enveloped me; I would forever be attached to the water.

"Ready?" Patrick asked and I nodded my head.

I fingered the black pack which Kryssa had given me that lay flat against my stomach. Anticipation surged while I watched Patrick hit the water. I moved quickly, arching slightly over the water, stripping off my clothes and slipping through the surface into the cool blue liquid. I was a blur to the human eye, my movements taking no more than a split second. Immediately my legs locked together and my shimmering lavender fins appeared, sending sparks of light throughout the pool

Returning to the surface, I tossed the water-tight case onto the grass beside the water and turned back to Patrick. His brown eyes found mine and there was an expression of astonishment on his face. I blushed instantly, wrapping my arms around my shoulders while my hair pooled around me. He was seeing me in my true form for the first time.

"What?" I asked, afraid of the answer.

Slowly he shook his head from side to side, the silence surrounding us on all sides while I waited for him to speak.

"I'm just... you are..." He broke off.

"What?" I prodded again.

"Beautiful." He sighed the word as though it was a struggle to get it through his lips. He blinked rapidly, making me all the more aware of my appearance and how I must look to him.

"Stop it," I said and I splashed water in his direction, trying to diffuse the awkward moment.

"I mean it," he said, his face completely serious. "You really are." A flicker of a smile passed over his mouth and then like a wave washing over the shore something changed. One moment his eyes swerved over me, taking in everything in one continuous glance, and the next it stopped. His eyes ceased to melt and instead hardened like congealed lava, though they still burned. I shrunk back as the fiery anger he had revealed in Lathmor returned.

Moving away, closer to the waterfall, I kept my eyes on him. I wondered what was happening, but didn't know what or how to stop it. His eyes were glazed over, the pupils dark and masked with something I couldn't name.

I dove under the water thinking it would be safer to pull myself away from him, yet still unsure of what it was I had done. Reaching the bottom, I glanced around at the little nooks and crannies in the rock walls. A current from the thundering waterfall up above pushed me down to the bottom of the pool. Lying on the sand I glanced around.

My lavender tail glowed radiantly in the sunshine, patterns of interlocking light dancing on the rock walls. A surge of movement in the water caught my attention and I looked up. Patrick was slowly moving himself over to the submerged rock where he could stand. Knowing I needed to speak with him, I took a deep breath. The water satisfied my lungs.

I broke through the surface, my hair drying quickly and beginning to ripple in the wind. Moving cautiously, I glided forward with as little disturbance as possible. His back was to me, and in the sunlight I was able to see the scar on his shoulder. It was long and coarsely cut, beginning at the base of his neck and angling sharply until it reached under his right arm. There was something translucent about the wound that reminded me of my own. The gray scar was not raised, instead it was a smooth and faded shimmer of misty gray that contrasted against his tanned skin. Remembering that Nerissa had placed a blade inside the wound, I flinched.

He turned around on the ledge, obviously having heard my quiet approach. His eyes were once again his own, no longer hardened by the anger that was so prevalent before.

"Hey, you." His voice matched the quiet rumble of the waterfall.

"Hey," I said, relieved the Patrick I knew was back. "You okay?"

"Yeah," he shifted, slightly uncomfortable. "I sometimes have issues with my anger."

I nodded as though I understood even though I didn't. He sighed.

"King Oberon thinks it has to do with the blade Nerissa put inside me." His voice was sincere, slightly abashed. "I get caught up in the past to easily if I think about it. In particular, I have a hard time when anything reminds me of Morven."

I moved closer to him, almost within reach. "It's fine," I said, my lips slightly curving at the corners.

The side of his mouth pulled up in response. "You are too forgiving."

"I don't think so," I said and lifted a hand to shield my eyes from the sun.

"Come on," he said. "Let me show you this underwater cave."

Intrigued, I dove over the water and waited at the bottom for him to catch up. Moving with strong kicks, he came up beside me and rolled his eyes. I laughed and shrugged as if to say it wasn't my fault that he was so slow, but he ignored me and instead pointed at a dark spot in the rock wall. Without a second glance I shot toward it and heard him moving behind me as I began to explore the depths of the cave.

We spent the rest of the day swimming at the waterfall and enjoying the moments we had with each other.

When dusk crept over the water and shades of purple colored the sky, we left the waterfall side by side. We chatted while walking, the moments from the night before had changed our connection. We no longer remained distant and respectful. Now that the truth of who we really were was out in the open we could talk freely and without hesitation. There were no secrets now. He knew me I knew him.

"I don't understand how you do that."

"It was really quite simple," he said as he waved a hand in front of us. "I just continued to practice breath control until I could hold my breath longer and longer."

Earlier he had amazed me with his ability to hold his breath for minutes at a time as we swam below the surface.

"Just admit it," he nudged my shoulder with his own. "You think I'm a fascinating creature." I shook my head but couldn't help smiling as we stepped into the clearing that led to the cabin. Glancing up, my eyes widened. Light was pouring from the windows and I immediately froze. Fear seeped into my veins.

"Lissie?" Patrick asked, but his voice sounded far off, there was a rushing in my ears as I tried to maintain control. *How had he found us?* "Seriously, are you all right?"

I tried to find my voice but couldn't. Lifting my hand, I pointed at the cabin and waited for his anger to return. I hoped he wouldn't pursue him.

"*He's* here," I said so softly he had to lean forward to hear me.

I shivered, thinking of what could happen once he realized who was up there. A shooting jolt of trepidation ran through my blood.

Slowly, comprehension passed over his face and I waited for the dark eyes to return, but they didn't. He was calm.

"He's not up there," he said, shaking his head. "It's probably Kryssa, or maybe even Tunder."

Doubt surged, but reason prodded my mind. They had said they would come, why hadn't I thought of that before? Why was my immediate reaction to think it was Morven? Would my fear of him always reign in my mind? Was it really Morven that I was afraid of? Or was it the Morven in my nightmares, the one who destroyed the man by my side, that scared me the most?

Like a soothing balm, Patrick continued to waylay my fears. "Morven has no way of knowing I'm here. He hasn't found me for seven hundred years, and I don't think that's going to change anytime soon." I nodded, letting his words surround me while I pressed a hand to my heart to try and still its throbbing pulse.

"You can even hear Nixie talking. Well, rather loudly if you listen," he said jokingly.

I smiled feebly in response. "Oh." It was all I could say.

"He's really scared you hasn't he?" Patrick's tone was comforting.

I appreciated his concern and I nodded my head while looking at the ground. In a moment he wrapped his arms around me. The feeling from the night before enveloped me. I felt safe and secure in his arms, as though they were a barrier from the rest of the world.

"Come on, we had better get up there before they go looking for us." Again I nodded and we walked toward the house and up the spiral staircase, all the while Patrick held my hand.

Stepping inside, the warm light from the fireplace enveloped us and cast a golden light on the people inside. Kryssa, Shaylee, and Tunder were situated on the couch. Nixie stood next to Daggin on the other side of the room, her hands gesturing while she spoke so quickly her sentences ran together. Elik sat in the chair Patrick usually occupied. Upon our arrival, they all turned to greet us. I suddenly became very aware of Patrick's hand around my own, and warmth filled my cheeks.

"There you are!" Tunder approached, a smile on his face. The change was amazing; the serious authoritative demeanor was replaced by a man worthy of winning Shaylee's affection.

Patrick and Tunder embraced in greeting, and without hesitation Tunder held out his hand to me. Slipping my hand from Patrick's, I reached out to accept. A feeling of approval and ease washed over me and I relaxed.

The rest of the group greeted us kindly and Patrick immediately began to speak with Tunder. There was a light in his eyes like I had never seen before. Something about his excitement made my heart warm knowing he was enjoying himself. To even think of how many years he spent alone on this island made me shudder; he deserved these visits and I didn't want to intrude.

Realizing dinner was not yet made, and seeing it as an excuse to depart from the long-term friends, I moved into the kitchen and began to prepare a recipe from the family restaurant back home.

"Hey," Kryssa said, coming up behind me as I placed the noodles in the water.

"Hey," I said back and smiled up at her.

"What are you making?" she asked curiously, and I wondered if merfolk would even eat shrimp scampi.

"It's a recipe from back home. We call it shrimp scampi. It's noodles covered in a creamy sauce with shrimp. One of my favorites," I shrugged. Kryssa looked very interested.

"Sounds yummy," she said with some enthusiasm that put my worries aside. "Can I help?" she asked sounding like a child who was interested in learning something new. I realized it was my turn to introduce her to a new skill.

We worked side by side. She listened to my instructions and asked a myriad of questions that I answered easily. Her eyes were excited as though we were embarking on a fascinating adventure; I laughed to myself, in wonderment that she enjoyed it so much.

As the noodles cooked, I began to make the sauce. I added the ingredients efficiently until the aroma filled the room and reminded me of home. Kryssa glanced into the saucepan and nodded in approval. She then returned to her job of cutting the bread right next to where I stood at the stove.

Well, cutting was an understatement. She was carving the bread with a vengeance and chunks of it were falling off in different oddly shaped sizes and crumbling onto the floor. Each time one fell off the cutting board, she tried to grab it in midair but always missed. With no regard for the sharp knife she wielded, she would dive to the ground and pick up the mutilated piece and continue her desecration of the loaf of bread. I had to look away to keep from laughing.

"So," Kryssa said, still carving like a madwoman, "How'd it go with Patrick?" I knew what she meant.

"Pretty well, actually," I said, thinking back to when I had first seen Patrick after returning from Lathmor. "I admit I was scared to death though. But it turned out fine."

"I knew it would." Kryssa paused for a moment and then asked in a soft whisper, "Have you kissed yet?"

My blush that followed was enough of an answer for her and she laughed out loud. I hushed her quickly while peeking over my shoulder to make sure we had not attracted attention. The last person who needed to know that right now was Nixie. If she knew, then all of Lathmor would know all too quickly—not that the other merfolk would care. Patrick glanced up and caught my gaze. He flashed me a quick smile, and I warmed under his gaze. That feeling of connection once again filled me as I turned back around to the bubbling sauce.

"You love him, don't you?" Kryssa's assured voice pulled me from my thoughts.

"What?"

"I can see it in your face when you look at him," she observed without a hint of doubt.

"No," I said shaking my head quickly. "I don't. We haven't said anything... I can't be...." I broke off, uncertain of how to explain to her what it was I felt.

Silence fell after my words and I glanced up to see if she had heard me. The smile on her face told me she had. She looked as though she was trying to control some deep emotion and then all of a sudden she hugged me.

"I'm so happy for you!" She exclaimed rather loudly in my ear.

"But I haven't said anything," I tried to explain. She let go and stepped back.

"Yes you have," she said, throwing back her head and laughing. Her hair rippled gently. "You just gave everything away!"

"No," I said again. "I'm not in love with him. It's just... he is... important to me." I spoke simply, but the recollection of the cave flickered before my eyes. That was not what you did with someone who was only important to you, but I threw the thought aside.

"Sure," she said skeptically.

"It's like it's easier to be alive when I'm around him. He makes me comfortable. And in some way he understands me, because we are both similar. Does that make any sense?" I asked and glanced at Kryssa.

She didn't respond, but was staring out the window, her eyes blank as though seeing something from a long time ago. Her wet eyes shined as though she held back tears. A twinge spiked my heart as I wondered who it was she grieved for.

The crackling bubble of the sauce grabbed my attention and I returned to the stove to finish preparing dinner. Eventually, Kryssa restored to her normal self and continued the demolition of the bread. She was silent, her mind far away from the cabin in some long lost memory.

"Okay," I said, breaking the silence between us. "Dinner is ready. Are you done cutting the bread?" I glanced over and saw that the previously pretty loaf was now a crumbled mess.

"Yeah, I'm done," Kryssa said and handed me the basket of disfigured chunks.

"Good, thanks." I turned around and called everyone to dinner. They all lined up, got their plates, and formed a sort of lunch line while I distributed the warm noodles and shrimp.

"This looks and smells delicious, Lissie," Shaylee complimented once we had all taken our places in chairs around the fire.

"Thanks," I said. "I hope it tastes just as good."

"Here's the bread," Kryssa said as she passed the basket around.

No one seemed surprised by the uneven chunks; in fact, they all looked like they expected it. Patrick didn't though—when the basket reached him he glanced at me with a smile and winked knowingly. A choked gargle of a laugh escaped my throat, but I turned it into a cough. The others were unaware and expressed concern, but Patrick was smiling brightly in my peripheral trying just as hard as I was to not laugh. I avoided his gaze in order to compose myself, but it was quite a few minutes before I was even able to look up from my plate.

"So, Lissie," Nixie said, sounding very formal. "I have something very important to ask you."

"Okay," I said, hoping it was simple. I glanced around trying to get a hint from her sisters, but they gave away nothing.

"I don't think anyone has told you..." she glanced at her sisters to see if they had and they shook their heads, "but Daggin and I are engaged!" I blinked, taking in the information for a moment.

"Really?!" I asked, incredibly loud. "Congratulations! When did it happen?"

Nixie laughed, "Oh this?" she held up her hand to show a very bright and large turquoise ring on her left hand. "This happened a long time ago, but the wedding is in two weeks. I know the last time you came to Lathmor you were not welcomed in the best manner."

Welcomed? I was severely criticized. "But I have gained father's permission and so," she placed her hands on her lap in a respective manner, "I would like to ask you and Patrick to be guests at our wedding."

My eyes flickered to Patrick questioning him. "I would love to go." He addressed Nixie.

"Me, too," I smiled.

She clapped her hands together excitedly. "Wonderful! The ceremony won't be extravagant because of the war, but it's a blessing to even have one!" Her eyes filled with tears and she wiped at her eyes. Daggin nuzzled her with his nose whispering into her ear and she giggled.

"I do have one question," I said leaning toward Patrick. He cocked his ear to hear me better. "Isn't she a little young to be getting married?"

He shook his head and laughed. "No, not at all."

Nixie overheard our whispers. "It's true! Most mermaids are married by my age. Shaylee was my age when she married Tunder, and Kryssa was—" She broke off suddenly clapping a hand over her mouth, her eyes wide with horror. A jolt of awkwardness sprang into the room, everyone unsure of what to say or do. Tunder and Shaylee looked at their intertwined hands, Daggin rubbed Nixie's arm, Elik's face grew somber and he stood up and walked to the other side of the room. The tension in his body was evident. Out of the small group Kryssa was the only one to remain calm. She spoke, but when she did there was a throaty tone to it as though slightly clogged from emotion.

"You don't have to worry about finding anything to wear," she beckoned with her hand toward Patrick and I. "Nixie already has clothes for you."

I remembered the beautiful clothing in Kryssa's closet and wondered what sort of dress Nixie had prepared for me.

"Sounds wonderful," I said, trying to lighten the mood.

"So you really will come?" Nixie pleaded. "Both of you?"

"Yes," I smiled and stood up to give her a hug. She pranced into my embrace, her red curls bouncing with energy.

She pulled me down beside her on the bench and began to explain all the details of the wedding. Shaylee and Kryssa joined in, adding little details here and there and making sure nothing was left out. Every now and then I glanced over at the men. They were standing in the kitchen, their faces serious but their tones light. Tunder and Patrick carried most of the conversation while Daggin joined in every now and then. I couldn't help but notice how dejected and separated Elik appeared; the smile that usually adorned his face was nowhere to be seen.

"...And Daggin and I have been hoping that we will get the first light snow of the year on our wedding night. It should be right about that time and—"

"Snow!" I exclaimed, butting in. "It's been so warm out, is it really going to get that cold?" Shaylee and Kryssa laughed heartily.

"It's been colder than you think Lissie," Shaylee explained. "It's been in the low thirties for the past few days. You just don't realize it because of your new body."

"Really?" I asked, astonished and wondered how I could have miscalculated so poorly.

"It is mid-November," Kryssa clarified while I tried to wrap my mind around the idea. How had I lost track of time so badly? So much had changed in such a short span of my life.

"Then what day is the wedding?" I questioned.

"December first," Nixie said as she smiled with anticipation.

The rest of the night concluded with every detail of the wedding being described to me. Their excitement for the occasion was contagious—mentally I calculated how many more days until the wedding.

Eventually our visitors decided it was time to return to Lathmor, but not before Nixie explained that she would be visiting soon so I could be fitted into my dress. Shaylee and Tunder held back as the rest of the group filled the cabin with their goodbyes. A sudden silence followed the click of the door shutting. Patrick turned back from the wooden barrier, his eyes roving over these old friends.

"What's all this about?" Patrick asked, the happy moments of before long forgotten in an instant. A seriousness fell between us as we all sat down once more around the fireplace.

Needing comfort, I reached for Patrick's hand. He took mine within his own gently and rubbed it with his thumb. Tunder cleared his throat, the sound echoing within the cabin.

"Shaylee has remembered something we think is important to Morven's intentions for both of you." Patrick's grip tightened on my hand at the mention of Morven's name. I held my breath, waiting for Tunder to continue, but Shaylee spoke instead.

"I remember the day Nerissa returned to Lathmor and came to my mother." Her voice was solemn. "She came into the nursery and spoke to mother of the powers she had seen in humans who were transformed into merfolk. But most importantly, she told mother of how she was going to create two ultimate weapons. She had said 'The one to enslave, the other to maintain.' Until now I had never known what it meant."

"As we told you before," Tunder took over, "we believe Morven expects you to be some sort of siren, conquering the human and merfolk world." My grip tightened as the threatening phobia of being trapped wrapped around me. Patrick squeezed gently back and rubbed my hand even more, trying to relax the tension within.

"In regards to you," Shaylee nodded her head toward Patrick, "Nerissa mentioned the creation of a warrior."

Patrick's chest rose and fell heavily. "The one to enslave," he muttered softly and the depth of his words lay heavily upon us.

"We believe that together, you both make the ultimate weapon for winning this war. Together, you could conquer both humans and merfolk." The Captain's words rang true as if I had known this all along, but had never acknowledged it until now.

"How?" Patrick raised his head. "How would we be used?"

"We don't know." Shaylee's eyes were filled with regret. "The best I can guess is that in some way you would not be yourselves."

Her words hung in the air, allowing us to decipher what she meant. The horrible haunting name Morven had given me prodded the back of my mind. I knew what he wanted me to be and what I would be called.

Patrick leaned over, his forearms resting on his knees, still holding my hand. His eyes were closed and he looked so solemn that my heart, which I didn't think could feel any worse, ached.

"Does anyone else know of this?" Patrick's voice was rough, returning to the darkness I had only seen in him twice before.

Deep anger and hatred was buried in his words. A shiver ran down my spine.

"Only the king." Patrick nodded at Tunder's response. "It's not the end of the world." Patrick let out a short gust of incredulous air.

"How do you know that? What if I am changing? We have no idea what she did to me." Patrick was frightening while he glared at Tunder. I leaned away from him, even though my hand was still within his grasp. "For all we know I could wake up one day and not remember who I am."

Patrick's voice broke at the end. I realized now that the anger was a cover for the frustration, the fear, and the vulnerability he felt.

"I wish I knew, too," Tunder said gravely. I nodded in agreement.

"We just thought you both deserved to know," Shaylee explained. "It's not right, what they've done to you. We are going to try and help you any way we can."

"We know," I said and gave her a small smile. Patrick did not respond, his eyes were closed shut and he pinched the bridge of his nose.

"We'll give you some time alone," Tunder said. I nodded, slipping my hand from Patrick's so I could lead them to the door.

"I'm sorry," Shaylee said, her eyes wet with tears.

"It'll be all right," I said, giving her a hug. "We needed to know." Tunder awkwardly hugged me, grasped his wife's hand,

and they left together after saying goodbye to an unresponsive Patrick.

When the door shut, I stood facing it until I could no longer hear Tunder and Shaylee's footsteps. Turning back around, I faced Patrick. He sat in the same position as before, but his eyes were fixed on the floor and his jaw tight with fury.

Maybe it was my own fear, or the threat of what was to come, but I grew annoyed with his uncomfortable silence. "You could've at least said goodbye."

Patrick didn't move; it was like he was completely possessed. His mind was so far gone and the deep emotions that were playing across his face had nothing to do with present actions. The emotions were responding to memories, memories I could only imagine.

"Patrick," I tried again to get his attention, but he didn't move.

Annoyed, I walked over and sat down on the bench. Maybe I could just wait out this little spell of anger, or whatever it was. Time passed slowly while I waited, and I began to get sleepy. My eyes kept drifting closed, but I would pry them open like there was something important that needed to be done.

"Lissie?" Patrick's calm voice sounded so beautiful breaking through the quiet of the room. I turned to face him. His eyes were soft and the Patrick I knew was back. My heart jumped as his deep brown eyes scanned my face.

"I don't like to dwell on the past, but too often it creeps up on me. More frequently this past month. I just get so frustrated and angry when I think of what he has done to you, and why you were changed. It makes me so, so—" Patrick broke off looking into the fire. His hands were twisting together while the muscles in his arms twitched. My hand trembled as I reached out to touch him.

"I think if we face this together we'll be fine." I surprised myself with how truthful I was. Patrick turned his eyes to mine, his expression lost and hopeless.

"I don't know if I can protect you from him," he said, his voice desperately solemn. "If he comes for you, I'll fight him, but I don't know how it'll end."

"Don't talk like that," I berated him. "He doesn't know where we are and hopefully we will never see him again." The way that Patrick turned away from me shot alarm throughout my body.

"Wouldn't that be a good thing?" I asked, hoping the answer wouldn't be what I was thinking.

"No," he said. His voice caused my insides to cripple. "I want him dead. I want to know that you'll be safe from him for the rest of your life."

"And you're willing to kill him?"

"To protect you? Yes." His words felt like the proclamation of his own execution.

"Then I hope he never finds us," I said, trying to sound more cheerful than I felt. Patrick didn't respond.

He turned to look at me, his eyes kindled with deep emotion. Without a word, he moved over to sit next to me on the bench. Pulling me into his chest, I curled up tightly, my eyes focused on the flickering fire. Something about the ever changing light prodded my mind, reminding me of the man beside me; his anger flickering in and out. But with his arms around me, I couldn't conclude the thought and fell into a blissful sleep, only slightly aware of the strong arms that lifted and carried me to my soft bed where he left me to sleep.

24. Wedding

The day of the wedding arrived quicker than I could've thought possible. Nixie had visited the island to fit the already made dress to my body. She only had to alter it slightly and then it fit like a glove.

The ceremony was beautiful. Nixie chose to be married outside in a large meadow on Lathmor surrounded by thick trees. Green grass covered the open area, creating a soft carpet for all the barefoot guests. Tables with milky white cloths and light orange napkins rested on the tables and a long strip of white rose petals cut the meadow in half, serving as an aisle for the bride. White twinkling lights were creatively strung throughout all of the surrounding trees and gave the whole wedding ceremony a fanciful, romantic effect.

The actual wedding ceremony was over. Nixie had looked gorgeous in her white wedding gown that shown brilliantly against her red curls. The empire waste showed off her slim figure and flowed to the ground in a lustrous cascade of white fabric. Her hair was ornamented with white flowers and beads. Her smile was stunning and left my heart throbbing with happiness for her.

Shaylee and Kryssa, wore matching dresses of pale auburn, and had stood beside their younger sister as the wedding vows were spoken. Everyone at the wedding was dressed elegantly. Patrick and I stood toward the back where we ignored the harsh glares sent our way every now and then. As the ceremony continued, the stares lessened and we began to enjoy ourselves.

The wedding reception was in the open meadow, a rather large affair considering there was a war going on. But Nixie had done her best to put together a wedding that would satiate her desires and yet be appropriate for wartime. Even now she laughed gaily as Daggin swung her around to the soft rhythm of the three violinists playing in the night air. I smiled watching them spin around.

A squeeze on my hand brought my attention back to the moment. Patrick smirked at me, knowing I had been lost in my thoughts.

"Sorry, what?" I asked, raising my eyebrows politely.

"I asked if you wanted to dance," Patrick said, amused. No doubt he was laughing at my lack of concentration. My smile was enough of a reply for him and he got up from his chair to lead me onto the crowded dance floor.

The dress Nixie had made for me brushed along the grassy floor with a soft whispering sound, its light lavender color running in a gentle ripple up my body where it hugged my waist. The gauzy straps crossed over my shoulders and dipped low to reveal most of my back. As we walked forward, Patrick guided me with his hand. I shivered when his skin pressed against mine.

Spinning around in his arms, I marveled up at him. His hair was rustled, much better than when it had been perfectly combed for the ceremony. He had seemed too uptight in his suit and tie, but he now looked more like himself since removing the jacket and leaving the black tie on the table. His rolled up sleeves revealed the tan skin that I was so used to seeing. He spun me around and my eyes took in the decorations up close. Bodies passed us without glancing and I reveled in the solitude of not being looked at.

Across the meadow, Kryssa danced with Elik; their movements were stiff as though it was too awkward for them. I couldn't help noticing that Kryssa was refusing to look at him. Shaylee, as always, was by Tunder's side, their hands intertwined. But of all the people in the meadow, those who shined the most were Nixie and Daggin. They danced with no regard to those around them, lost in each other's eyes. Their love seemed effortless and perfect. It was as if they would both be completely lost if the other was gone.

"You're very distracted tonight," Patrick observed with a chuckle.

"Just thinking," I said, trying to sound casual. I let my feet flow in rhythm as Patrick waltzed us around the meadow. This was the first dance that I actually knew how to do. The merfolk apparently liked all styles and periods of dance. Sitting on the sidelines I had watched various eras performed through dancing, from medieval to the roaring twenties, the merfolk knew them all.

"Kryssa is dancing with Elik again," I noted, nodding my head in their direction.

"Hmm," Patrick mumbled, acknowledging my statement.

"I think he likes her and she just doesn't see it yet." I hadn't voiced my opinion on the matter to anyone yet.

"Yes, he does," Patrick clarified, surprising me. "But it will be a while before anything happens between them."

His words made me curious and I gazed up at him confused. He took my breath away, his hair gently floating in the breeze as we waltzed around the meadow, our feet brushing through the soft grass and the lights in the trees blurring behind his head. My heart stirred with the emotion I had been feeling for a long time. For days I had struggled with whether or not I should express them, but I could never let the words leave my mouth. I decided to stay on the safe side and maintain our conversation.

"Why is that?" I asked, steering the conversation away from what I was feeling. Patrick looked back down at me suddenly and for a moment he looked confused too.

"Has Kryssa not told you what happened?" He raised one eyebrow.

"About what?" I asked innocently.

"Hmm," he said, again frustrating me. After a moment he spoke, "She must not be ready to tell you yet, but she will eventually."

"Tell me what? Is this about what Nixie said the other night? She had said—"

Patrick butted in, "That's for Kryssa to tell you when she's ready. It's not something I would want to talk about anyway." His voice was serious, but I heard a hint of pity. Again I looked over at her dancing across the way, wondering what had happened to her.

The music transitioned into a more relaxed waltz and neither of us spoke. Leaning forward, I rested my head on Patrick's chest. He slowed our pace and I sighed softly against his chest. It was all so companionable and felt right. He was comfort, friendship, and belonging. Somehow he had made his way into my heart. Contentment rolled over me in waves as I leaned deeper into his body. I knew that I could go on forever with him just holding me and gently leading me around the dance floor.

Closing my eyes, I listened to his breathing that came in time with the music. I could hear the violinists stringing softly on their instruments, I hummed along. All of a sudden I realized the music seemed to be getting farther and farther away.

I opened my eyes, surprised to see we were within the cover of the trees. Looking up, I saw Patrick's familiar smirk. He winked at me, the playfulness giving way to his waltzing faster and faster until my dress was flaring around us in a wide circle of lavender.

We came to a stop and when he gazed down at me the spark in my chest kindled. The music was barely audible through the night and soft light broke through the trees from the moon high up above us.

"I just wanted some time alone with you," he said. His voice ran over me like melted chocolate.

For that one moment everything froze. I knew what I felt, and I knew how he felt. It was there in his eyes. The way he gazed down at me with unashamed emotion. My heart swelled and the smile on my face broadened.

With more courage than I felt, I placed my hand behind his neck and pulled his face closer to mine. My lips parted and waited. Patrick's eyes caressed my face as he placed his hands around my back. The space between us closed and my breath hitched. Then with a crooked grin, he lowered his head until his lips touched mine.

The world around us melted. He was all that mattered and I kissed him with all that I felt. This kiss was different than the one we had shared in the cave. There was passion, but more importantly there was connection. I understood him, and he understood me. We were together, joined by something beyond our control.

He moved gently at first. His lips were tight, still stretched in a smile, but slowly they released. His lips moved more forcefully and embraced my own. With his arms, he cradled me while my other hand reached behind his neck to lock fingers with its twin. Our bodies pressed together tightly in the cool night air, his warmth was everything I needed and I fell into him, giving way to what my heart felt. Slowly and gently he drew away, leaving me wanting more.

"I have something for you," he said slightly breathless.

Reaching into his pocket, he pulled out something but kept his fist closed. Curious, I leaned forward, tucking my hair behind my ears as I tried to discern what it was. Placing my hands on his forearms, I waited for his tight fist to open. Slowly his fingers fell apart and I gasped.

Sitting on his now flat palm was a beautiful bracelet made of perfectly rounded pearls that shimmered in the moonlight. The stones were white, but cast pale colors of blue, purple, and green onto his hand.

"Where did you... How did you...?" I broke off, completely perplexed by the bracelet.

"I made it," he said as he smiled impishly and clasped the bracelet around my wrist.

"You made this?" I asked, stunned, while watching the shiny stones slide up and down my wrist as I moved.

"Yes." He shrugged as though it was a simple matter. All of a sudden I hugged him tightly, taking him off guard. Words couldn't express my gratitude. He wrapped his arms around me, his warm skin brushing against my exposed back.

"Thank you," I whispered. "It's so beautiful. I don't even know what else to say."

"You are most welcome," he said so softly against my hair that shivers ran down my spine. I pulled back to look at him.

"I'm going to wear this always. You won't ever see it off me." He smiled brightly in response.

"Is that a promise?" he asked, his tone joking but his eyes serious. I nodded.

"Someone would have to kill me before they could get it off." I half laughed at my dramatic claim and Patrick did too, yet somehow we both knew I was serious.

"Lissie," he said my name in a whisper and I closed my eyes. The sound of my name on his lips brought me comfort. "There is something I want to tell you."

"What's that?" I cocked my head to the side, knowing just what he was going to say. He smiled and wrapped his arms around my back once more. I looked into his unblinking eyes and memorized them.

"I love you," he said confidently. I smiled and bit my lip, shaking my head from side to side.

"I love you too," I said and he leaned in to kiss me once more.

Just when I was beginning to feel as though my heart would burst from my chest, an earsplitting scream tore through the quiet night. Patrick's head shot up and he looked directly back to the meadow. We stood stationary for a moment, watching and waiting, but I was unsure what to expect.

The sounds of commotion and shouting reached our ears and Patrick released me from his arms. Grabbing my hand, and taking me along, he ran toward the muffled sounds. The decorated lights in the trees reappeared up ahead and Patrick charged forward, pulling me along behind him awkwardly.

He stopped suddenly and I smacked into his solid back. Groaning softly, I lifted a hand to my forehead.

"Shh," he hushed me. His hand was held up as a sign of silence while he listened intently trying to hear something.

My pulse escalated as we waited; I didn't know what we were listening for, but I could hardly hear above the pounding of my heart. More angry voices from the meadow resounded through the trees. I tightened my grip on Patrick's hand, but he didn't seem to notice.

A deep authoritative voice urged desperately, but there was no response. It took me a moment to realize that it was the king speaking. All the more worried, I waited anxiously, watching Patrick's face for any sign of comfort.

Looking down, his eyes were filled with the same worry and made me more nervous. Signaling his intent, he pointed toward the meadow and then placed a finger to his lips. I nodded silently to let him know I understood. He grasped my hand tighter and moved forward stealthily, closer to the meadow. I followed him, one hand in his, and the other holding my dress up. I was scarcely breathing, worried that I would make too much noise.

"Let her go now!" Daggin's frantic voice pierced the night.

"Daggin, please!" Nixie's voice pleaded, filled with fright.

I panicked, wanting to move faster. Patrick hurried forward as silence fell over the meadow. *What was happening?*

Crouching down behind some bushes on the edge of the meadow, we were able to see the scene before us. I placed a hand over my mouth to silence the gasp that escaped my lips.

Tables had been knocked over and pushed aside. All the merfolk stood huddled together, the mermaids behind the mermen. A few of the mermen stood out from the group. I quickly noticed Daggin standing the farthest away, out on his own. Tunder was near his side and the king a little farther back.

Everyone's eyes were trained on two figures at the end of the meadow. I bit my lip to keep from crying out as I recognized the small body clothed in white trapped inside the arms of a bulky and powerful merman dressed in all black. Something about him seemed familiar, but the tears that ran down Nixie's face as she gasped for breath distracted my attention. Her red curls fell from the pins in her hair.

"Just let her go," Daggin pleaded. Tunder was motionless, at a complete loss of what to do.

"You know my conditions," the raspy voice of the large man snapped across the clearing full of hatred and disgust. "I came here for a purpose and if what I came for is not provided soon, then this pretty young thing will be dead before either of you can move."

As he spoke, blades came out of his forearm and he rested them right against Nixie's neck. I let out a small shriek and tried to stand, but Patrick's hand clamped down on my mouth and pulled me against his chest withholding me. I turned my head to look at him, my eyes filled with horror. He slid his hand off my mouth and placed it around my shoulders, holding me close to his body.

Nixie's tears continued to fall, dripping to the front of her dress. She struggled to breathe as her emotions got the better of her. The sheer panic in her eyes reflected the danger she was in.

"Nixie, you can't," Daggin begged. "You can't leave me, just for—" his voice broke and he had to pause to try and compose himself. I wondered why Tunder didn't do something. What was it that this man wanted? Why didn't he just give it to him?

"I know," Nixie said solemnly as though she was accepting death. My eyes widened as I waited for what she would say. "But I can't give her up…"

She said something else, but I didn't hear it because Patrick gasped sharply. His arm that was around my waist yanked me backward. I followed, confused. We walked fast in a crouched position for a few steps and then Patrick straightened up.

"Run," he said. It was a command not to be questioned.

My legs obeyed immediately, and I realized the danger suddenly. The face of that merman in the meadow was one of the Hyven. I recognized him from the night I had been changed. They had come for me.

Holding my dress in a bundle above my knees I ran, my feet pounding across the earthen floor and Patrick beside me. He was glaring intensely around us, searching for some sign of danger. Eventually the sound of pounding feet rang through the night behind us, hot on our trail. Patrick swore under his breath and dropped behind me slightly.

I pushed my legs to go faster even though they were tiring rapidly. My muscles strained and blood pumped furiously though my veins. I could hear my heavy breathing, and knew it wouldn't be long before I would have to slow down, but the fear of what was to come kept me going. I knew that this creature behind us had an advantage. I worried just who this creature might be, but pushed the thought aside. It couldn't be *him*. Fear shot through me in a new wave of desperation. My body strained to move faster, but my legs slowed slightly. Patrick groaned.

"Come on, Lissie, come on," he said, breathlessly, egging me to keep going.

I pushed myself, trying as hard as I could. I closed my eyes for a fraction of a second to gather my strength so I could burst into speed. With my eyes open again, I pushed off my right leg with more power than I had used before. It wasn't as painful as I had thought it would be. This gave me courage and I continued to dash forward with more power in each push. Patrick kept up with me, but the heavy footfalls behind us were getting louder.

All of a sudden I tripped over a root and fell flat on the ground, my chest hitting the earth with a reverberating thud. Patrick shot past me and the merman behind us thundered ever closer. I could see his long legs and remembered him from the night I was changed, he had been the tallest in the group of mermen that night. A momentary feeling of relief filled me when I realized it wasn't Morven, but when the merman's blades flashed from his arms I scrambled backward on the ground away from him. His eyes gleamed with a fiery expectation and achievement when a furious yell resounded behind me; the voice was one I knew and adored, but the tone was so malevolent that it frightened me.

There was a whoosh of wind as Patrick flew past me, running directly at the merman. A loud thump echoed when he crashed into the surprised merman and tackled him to the ground. I watched in horror as the two men wrestled for a moment and then they were both on their feet.

The merman's blades shined in the moonlight. In panic, I looked at Patrick to see what he would do. He held his dagger before him, no longer than five inches. Crouching low, he shifted his weight lithely from foot to foot waiting patiently. I noticed he never let the merman get a free run at me, from where I was still splayed on the ground motionless. I didn't care if Patrick had a machine gun in his hand, I didn't want him to fight this vile creature.

The merman moved slightly, teasing, and testing Patrick's defenses. Then he attacked. I screamed as he ran forward, his blades brandished violently. My eyes were wide with horror as Patrick and the merman wrestled, blades flashing. I saw blood, and there were groans of pain, but I didn't know who had been hurt. They wrestled a moment more and then broke away.

Patrick was breathing heavily. His left arm revealed a bleeding gash, but he didn't seem to notice. The merman was now limping, however. A cut ran along his thigh, oozing blood into the dark pants he wore. As they stood, their bodies heaving from exertion, they both became aware of another sound. There were others running our way.

Excitement and relief built within me. There was no doubt in my mind that those feet belonged to someone who could help us. Just then the merman smiled at Patrick in such a spiteful manner that my hopes were crushed. The consuming fear again seeped in my veins. My mind wheeled, unsure of what to do.

"Go, Lissie!" Patrick growled over his shoulder at me. His voice was angry, but there was also panic.

"What?!" I yelled at him, my mind moving so slowly I could hardly think of what he meant.

"Run!" he yelled, never taking his eyes from the merman, who was looking more and more confident.

Somehow the word "run" triggered an instinct in my legs. I scrambled to my feet and again picked up my dress, running as fast as I could away from Patrick and the merman. The dreaded sounds of chasing feet filled my ears. Whoever was chasing me was faster than the other merman. Their footfalls were quicker and more sure-footed.

I put on another burst of speed, but they still came closer. My only thought was to get to the ocean; maybe I would have some chance of escape if I reached the water. *Patrick*. His name repeated in my mind as I thundered through the branches and jumped over roots.

The feet behind me slowed, but only slightly. I dashed this way and that, trying to shake them off, but my lungs were heaving, my throat dry. Sweat trickled down my neck but I kept pushing, thinking I could get away.

Then all of a sudden my chaser picked up speed. I tried desperately to go faster, but my legs were exhausted. A cold hand reached out and grabbed me by the shoulder. A blood curdling scream fell through my lips. I hoped desperately that someone would hear and come help me, yet knew there was no hope.

The hand pushed me and I fell to the ground, skidding in the dirt and wrestling with my captor. I scratched and clawed wherever I could, still not getting a good view of who had attacked me. Then I was suddenly pinned on my back with my arms held tight at the wrists. A sharp hand smacked me hard against the cheek. It stung while I blinked back the annoying tears that rose into my eyes.

Looking up, I was astonished to see that my chaser was a mermaid. She was beautiful in a provocative, evil way. Her eyes were a deep gold color that scorched into mine. She stared, daring me to make another move. I didn't. This woman frightened me more than the merman that was fighting Patrick somewhere behind us in the woods. The mermaid looked away from my eyes so she could tie my wrists together in front of me. When she had completed her task, she glared at me again.

"Get up," her high voice ordered, and I obeyed.

She stood taller than me by a whole head. Her body was thin, almost too thin. She was a vision in black with her dark curly hair pulled into a messy bun and her pale skin contrasting against the tight black shirt and pants she wore. Everything about her radiated hostility. I gulped, trying to find courage somewhere but coming up short.

The mermaid grabbed me under my left arm and started to walk. I had no choice but to follow her wherever she was taking me. Part of my mind started to think about whom she might lead me to, but I shoved those thoughts aside.

As we walked I stared at the ground, but I knew we were headed for the meadow as the muffled sound of voices grew louder. Approaching the edge of the meadow, we stepped into a pool of soft light. The scene before my eyes was drastically different than before.

The Lathmorians were in regimented sections, the blades of the mermen shining. The mermaids behind them flashed their own blades in a hostile manner, trying to send a message to the group of darkly clad figures surrounding the merman who still held Nixie within his grasp.

They were the Hyven. Goosebumps rose on my flesh and I scanned the scene until my eyes landed on Patrick. His hands were tied behind his back and there was a small cut on his face. A merman stood slightly in front of him, but then Nixie gasped and drew attention to my presence.

Everyone turned to stare at me, but all I could do was look at Patrick. His eyes were filled with a fear I had never seen before, but it wasn't for himself but rather for me. He strained against the men who held him. There was true apprehension and horror in his face, and his eyes flickered from mine to a merman who had his back turned to me. I moved my gaze too, and watched as the merman slowly turned around, knowing who it was.

A fear and dread as I had never felt before consumed me and I halted where I stood, drawing back from the mermaid who held my arm and ignoring the pain of her nails digging into my flesh. My insides crippled as I watched his familiar, evil smile spread across his face. A whooshing roared past my ears and my hands turned cold. It was as if I was trying to maintain consciousness.

"How nice of you to join us," he began, his voice filling the meadow. "*Marina.*"

25. Hyvar

The dreaded name washed over my ears sending fresh waves of fear coursing through my body. This was the voice I had kept at bay for so long, the voice that made me cripple in terror if I thought of it. The memory of him. The memory of my nightmares. Before my eyes flashed the recurring nightmare of Patrick dying on the beach while Morven pulled me away.

I breathed loudly as the sounds and images around me faded. My captor pushed me forward, but all I could see was Morven. He was all that existed. His dark clothing blended with the rest of his followers, making him look bold and powerful. A soft shudder crept to the top of my spine, but I forced it away. I wouldn't let him see me cringe; I wouldn't surrender to his will. To let him see my fear would be accepting my fate without a fight.

The mermaid that roughly held my arm came to a sudden stop. I stood next to her, glaring at Morven with all the fury and hatred I could muster. If he wanted to take me, then so be it. But he wasn't going to obtain the power that he wanted easily—I was going to resist him every chance I got.

We were now standing in the open space between the two groups of merfolk. The Hyven stood to the left and the Lathmorians to the right. Patrick was directly across from us, his eyes flickering from me to Morven and back again. There were two of the Hyven standing with him, one on each side. I noticed that neither of them was the tall merman that Patrick had fought in the woods.

"Thank you, Verna," Morven said curtly to the creature holding me. "You have proved your worth again." The mermaid straightened her posture proudly.

Morven waved his hand in dismissal and she stepped away from me, clearly disappointed. Her absence left me feeling even smaller, alone with no one to separate me from the monster.

Morven looked away from me for the first time, his gaze landing on Nixie who stood like a statue in her captor's arms.

"Release her," he said. His voice was a command that was not to be questioned.

The merman dropped his arms and Nixie almost collapsed to the ground. Slowly, she steadied herself and began to walk cautiously across the gap to her new husband. Morven's eyes followed her. As she got closer to Morven, he moved toward her. I held my breath, frozen where I stood. She cringed as he reached a hand toward her and stopped when he blocked her way.

There was a low grunt to the right as Daggin was being held back by Tunder. His eyes were alive with anger but Tunder held him fast, his large arms bulging beneath the white dress shirt. Daggin's jaw was taut while he strained against Tunder's restraint, his eyes intent on Morven's back.

With two fingers, Morven brushed Nixie's cheek gently. She closed her eyes while her chest heaved and a tear slipped from her eyes. I remembered all too well how his touch felt and I cringed as I watched.

His hand came to a stop on her throat. The long fingers wrapped around her slender neck easily. Nixie's eyes flashed open, the horror clearly written in her face. The king moved forward, his hand outstretched, but was uncertain of what to do or say. Everyone waited for what seemed like hours and then Morven withdrew his hand, obviously pleased with himself. In a manner of flare he stepped out of Nixie's way, motioning with his hand that she could proceed forward. The amusement in his eyes made the anger I felt toward him even more passionate. His only goal was to control.

Nixie stepped forward cautiously, passing Morven carefully, and then darted quickly into her new husband's waiting embrace. Daggin scooped her into his arms and retreated behind the other Lathmorians as her muffled sobs slowly disappeared into the night.

Morven shook his head and laughed loudly. The sound was so deep and horrifying that it quivered my soul. He continued to laugh for a moment and then stopped with that evil smile still spread across his face. He glowered at King Oberon who had slightly separated himself from his people.

"May I congratulate the father of the bride. She *is* a pretty thing." The Lathmorians all shifted, each one ready to move in to attack. The king stood still; his calm face gave me an explanation of why he was the leader of these merfolk. He looked down on Morven as though he was a small child. I slowly gained the courage I needed to face him. "But she is not as beautiful as my Marina."

Morven turned back to me and I dreaded what was coming. The steps that brought him closer seemed like they were in slow motion, each one a proclamation for the looming future.

"You see," Morven's voice was loud and clear as he spoke, "Marina is a beautiful creature. The type that I find attractive." Morven smoldered me with his eyes. My heart plummeted—he was going to humiliate me in front of everyone. He had reached me by now and spoke even louder and clearer to make sure everyone heard.

"She has sinful eyes, her locks of hair are tempting." At these words, Morven ran a hand through my hair. My muscles locked up. I forced them to stay put and not to fight the disgusting hand that touched me. "And her body is just—"

"Take your hands off her!" Patrick's command sliced the air like a knife. My nerves almost gave out at the sound of his voice. I panicked, not sure of what to do next.

Morven slowly turned to look at Patrick. I couldn't see his face, but I could imagine the dark look that came from his eyes.

I had seen it too many times to not know what it would look like. Morven stepped to the side, giving me a clear view of Patrick.

"And why not? Why can't I touch this lovely shaped specimen? She is mine, so why can't I touch her?"

Patrick did not answer, but instead looked at me, his eyes confirming the same feelings I felt. He was as scared for me as I was for him; he was frightened that we would not be together, that this was the end for us. The recent revelations of who Morven wanted us to be throbbed through my mind as I desperately tried to let him know I would be alright.

Tears filled my eyes and I blinked to keep them at bay, but they broke through and blurred my vision. Glancing at Morven, I saw him looking back and forth between us. A huge smile split across his face. He began to chuckle again and shook his head.

"This is just too good." He turned back to me. There was a loud grunt and the sounds of a scuffle. Morven whipped around and I stared in horror at the sight before me. Patrick had broken free of his bonds and one of the merman that had been holding him was pinned to the ground. He straddled the merman's stomach and had both of the man's arms held to the ground with his knees. His hands were wrapped around the merman's throat. The other guard who was standing by himself looked lost and frightened that he had not reacted sooner.

"You let her go, or I kill him." Patrick's threat filled the air. Morven stared back at him, clearly unperturbed. When he didn't respond, Patrick tried again. "I'll go with you freely if you let her go." His voice was serious, with no hint of fear or regret. My heart thundered in my chest. "I already killed one of your men tonight, let's not make it two."

Light whispers spread throughout the meadow. Both sides seemed surprised by this information—Patrick's skill with a knife was apparently better than anyone had predicted. I glanced at Morven and saw that this was new knowledge for him, too. Even though he tried not to show his surprise, the slight falter of his smile gave him away. With a very controlled face Morven looked back at Patrick and pursed his lips.

"Tell you what," he said, glaring malevolently. With one quick move he grabbed me by the waist and pulled me in front of him. I inhaled sharply as his strong arm grasped my waist. "You go ahead and kill him. When you do, I'll slit her throat. And don't think I'll hesitate, there are plenty of others who are just as useful and pretty as she is." Patrick waited, the threat hanging in the air. He seemed unsure of whether Morven spoke the truth or not. I breathed in short gasps as Morven's grip tightened around my stomach. His right arm lifted toward my neck and I cringed away from it, knowing his blades could appear at any moment.

Patrick stood slowly and moved away from the merman he had pinned to the ground. Two more of the Hyven came forward and quickly tied his hands behind his back.

"Well," Morven said, as his arm beside my neck dropped to his side, "I thank you all for the lovely visit. It turned out even more successful than we could have hoped." While Morven spoke he looked at Tunder, but just at the end he glanced at Patrick. The way he looked at him sent terror through my veins.

We left the clearing without hesitation, Morven holding tight to my arm and pulling me behind him. The bonds around my wrists constrained me tightly. The two members of the Hyven holding Patrick followed, but the rest remained in the meadow.

As soon as we entered the cover of the trees, shouts rang in the meadow. Glancing over my shoulder I saw a swarm of Lathmorians surge like a wave toward the Hyven, their blades flashing. Morven began to run and pulled me behind him.

We reached the edge of the island and halted, standing on a precipice high above the water. Morven dragged me forward, but I resisted with all the strength I could muster. Irritated, he tugged on my arm and enclosed me in his embrace. I squirmed as Patrick cried out.

"Now listen to me," Morven said, only for my ears. Spit flew as he spoke. "I will kill him if you make this any harder than it has to be."

Defiance like I had never felt before rose within my body. "You wouldn't kill him. You've spent too many years searching for him."

Surprised, he narrowed his eyes at me. "But I can make him suffer more than necessary." His threat hung in the air as the wind whipped my hair and dress about us. He knew he had the upper hand. "Now let's move," he said as he tugged me closer to the edge.

Looking over my shoulder, I watched in fear as Patrick was blindfolded. His arms strained against the man who held him, but he couldn't break free. One of the men nodded to Morven when the job was complete and Patrick was shoved closer to the edge beside us. I desperately wanted to reach out and touch him, to let him know I was there, but the space was a chasm of darkness impossible to cross.

In a lithe move, Morven leaned over the edge pulling me with him, and we hurdled toward the water with tremendous speed. I withheld the scream in my throat, and we crashed through the salty water and into the darkness of the ocean. My fins sprouted, extending out the end of the dress I wore. All the lavender was almost too much to look at.

Morven pulled me up toward the surface and I watched as the two mermen yanked Patrick forward off the precipice and into the water beside us. He came up choking and gasping for air, the only one having to use legs to stay above water. The blindfold had fallen from his eyes and the wet cloth hung around his neck. One of the Hyven soldiers moved to retie it, but Morven called him off.

"Leave it," he commanded. "It doesn't matter."

The merman nodded and with his partner grabbed one of Patrick's arms. Together they forced Patrick to lay back and float in the water. Morven nodded and tightened his grip on me. Without a word we proceeded forward, flying through the water. Morven pulled me behind him just below the surface. The mermen allowed for Patrick's head to stay above the water as they followed right behind us. My heart thundered as I tried desperately to think of something, *anything*, that could help us.

The sound of approaching fins reached my ears, but Morven made no recognition of arrival. Suddenly the mermaid Verna appeared. Her fins were a dull, deep red that reminded me of blood.

They are following, she reported quickly, waiting for instructions.

Good, keep them busy, Morven commanded and she fled off into the darkness.

We pressed forward and my eyes darted around as I tried to see. The sounds of blades and shrieking filled the water behind us, and my whole body tensed in terror at the thought of what might be happening. The sounds were horrible, but even more terrible when I could no longer hear them. The silence only confirmed what I felt in my heart.

Approaching fins roared around us and together a group of the Hyven pressed onward in the ocean. My only thoughts were for those we left behind and for the man on the surface, as we shot through the water like a bolt in the night sky.

———————————

Hours passed and I grew tired, trying desperately to keep up with the harsh pace Morven set. His hand was present on my wrists, his grasp pulling into my flesh as I was dragged behind him.

The water was like ice, even though my body was able to balance out the cold liquid, I still felt a great chill inside. What worried me was what the water might do to Patrick. Every now and then I tried to look up above us and catch a glimpse, but each time I did Morven jerked me forward even harder. I could hear their presence; the two mermen were kicking ferociously above their leader as they heaved Patrick's weight between them.

All of a sudden Morven pulled up, relaxing his grasp upon my wrist. I tried to slide out of the closed fingers, but they would not budge. The Hyven soldiers up above stopped in response and with one easy kick Morven took us up to the surface. My head broke through the water to cloudy, stormy skies and waves threatening to toss us from where we floated. The water was no competition for our natural fins, however.

Thunder rumbled in the bubbling clouds, but my eyes focused on Patrick. His lips were purple and his skin pale. He shivered uncontrollably, but the Hyven soldiers beside him seemed not to notice. Nor did they loosen their tight grips on his arms. Unlike the rest of us, Patrick's hair was plastered to his forehead. The golden locks were dark in the water, making him look all the more deathly pale.

I tried to inch closer, but Morven's icy grasp once more laced around my wrists and I gasped. Patrick noticed and shot a glare in Morven's direction, but the large body beside me didn't react.

"Are we waiting, my lord?" one of the Hyven asked as they paused for instructions from their leader. Morven didn't glance their way, but instead his eyes searched the horizon even though there was nothing to see.

"Blindfold him." Morven spoke so quietly that I almost didn't hear him over the churning water. A large wave lifted us upward in its arch, but we came down with it gracefully. Patrick, however, was dunked under the water and came up sputtering and choking. It pained me to hear his wracking cough. The two Hyven soldiers ignored his coughs and retied the wet black cloth over his eyes. He held still, but couldn't quite control the violent shiver of cold that surged down his body from the wet rag pressed against his face.

"Morven," I said, and the two Hyven stopped in their tracks, staring at me as though I had just committed a crime. The black cloth slipped from Patrick's eyes.

Morven turned toward me. "You would do well to call me Lord."

"Or what?" I asked, challenging him. My eyes met his, and trying to force him to realize I was not going to be taken easily.

"Drop him," Morven said not even turning his head. Before I could react, Patrick disappeared beneath the surface and into the churning waves. I gasped loudly and strained with all my might to go after him. The lavender dress flared around me, brushing against Morven's grey fins as he held me tight within his grasp.

"No. Let me go!" I yelled loudly. "Don't do this to him!"

A slight nod of Morven's head was enough of a signal for one of the soldiers and he disappeared into the wet blackness. I held my breath, tears filling my eyes, until two heads reappeared above the surface. Patrick's chest heaved with exhaustion, his cold shivering body not allowing him to hold his breath as long as he had trained for.

Brown eyes met my own and I revealed the fear, the wonder, the horror, and the love I felt for him. Somehow, even in the cold his eyes, were able to melt and I felt a warm throbbing in my heart that had nothing to do with the desperate situation we were in.

"I haven't got all night," Morven snapped quickly and the two mermen returned to tying the rag around Patrick's head. Just before his eyes were covered, Patrick nodded to me, his eyes burning into my own. He mouthed the words, *I love you.*

One of the soldiers approached us and I shrank back. Morven held me still as my vision was compromised by an identical black rag tied around my own head. The ocean seemed louder and the waves more violent now that I couldn't see.

"Let's move," Morven said and once more we pressed forward, this time moving a little slower than before and staying on the surface.

I lost track of time as we sped along. The wind smashed into my cheeks making them raw, but all I had to do was let the water hit my face and it was once more refreshed. Patrick was not so lucky; I feared for him. The longer we went, the louder the chattering of his teeth became. Thinking of how hard he must be trying to not show weakness only made me fear more for him.

The crashing of waves upon a shore reached my ears and I rejoiced for Patrick's sake, but dreaded the sound. Hyvar was up ahead.

Slowing our speed, Morven pulled me forward and the wind and sound of the rushing water disappeared. The darkness behind the blindfold became even darker and the lapping of rippled water against stone walls pressed upon my ears. Aside from the chattering of Patrick's teeth, there was no other sound.

My fins soon nicked the bottom of the cave floor and for a half a second Morven's hands disappeared, though they quickly reappeared. His footsteps were loud as we moved in water up to our waists. In my mind's eye I imagined him already transformed and dressed in his black clothing.

Suddenly my legs reappeared and my feet slipped along the slimy bottom of the cave. The lavender dress dragged behind me and clung tightly to my skin.

"Stand up," one of the Hyven guards spoke harshly and I heard a subtle splash. I tried not to think of how stiff Patrick's body was from the cold and how painful walking would be.

Morven pulled me forward and I stumbled into his chest, but I pushed back not wanting him to think I needed his assistance. He chuckled. I tried following him, but my feet slipped once more on the rocks as I tripped over the wet fabric of my dress. Morven's strong hands quickly caught me and swung me into his arms. Surprised, I squealed.

"Lissie?" Patrick's voice was full of alarm, his breath shaky but still strong. My heart thundered, heavily feeling more trapped than ever before with Morven's arms wrapped around my body.

"Put me down," I said. I tried to sound confident, but my voice was weak even to my own ears. Morven obliged for some reason, but I had the feeling he was only humoring me for the moment.

"Take him, and I'll be down in a moment without her." Morven's voice again sent shivers down my spine. I feared him, but then as I processed his words I feared something else even more; he meant to separate us. All this time I had been expecting Patrick and I to be near each other. I had been expecting to go through whatever was facing us together.

Morven gave me a sharp tug and I dug my heels into the ground. My mind concluded that this might be it, this could be the last time that I would ever hear Patrick's voice.

"Lissie?!" Patrick was furious now. He yelled from the other side of the cave, his voice echoing.

"Patrick," I said with a sob in my throat, the tears soaking into my already wet blindfold. There was another sharp tug on my arm and I whimpered. "Patrick," I cried again, desperately wanting him to hold me even though I knew it was impossible.

There were sounds of a struggle and then the sickening thud of a punch. Patrick groaned, and my senses heightened as I tried to figure out what was happening. I was being dragged at arm's length by my secured wrists. My feet dug into the ground, using all of my strength to stay as close to Patrick as possible. Sharp rocks cut into the heels of my flesh, but I didn't care.

Again Morven reached for my waist and this time he picked me up and threw me over his shoulder like a sack of flour. I cried out through my thick throat, my heart feeling like it was shattering into pieces.

"Lissie!" Patrick's desperate voice came from far away. I sobbed, thinking of him all alone with the soldiers. There was another loud grunt. "LISSIE!" The call was louder, but just as far away. Lacking all hope, my heart sank.

Morven walked on, ignoring what had just transpired. His strut was uncomfortable and my stomach jostled painfully against his shoulder with my pressing weight.

In the corridor, Morven's feet thundered on stone and the sound echoed against solid walls. A musty smell of moldy stone filled my nostrils and I tried to keep my bearings, but was soon lost as Morven turned down numerous passages and walked up and down staircases. Forcing myself to concentrate on the matters at hand, I realized he was trying to confuse me so I couldn't go looking for Patrick. In despair I concluded that it didn't matter. I was so turned around I would never be able to find my way back. Not to mention that Patrick was being taken somewhere too. Like a beckoning cry, my heart surged. I wanted to ask where he was even though I knew the response would never come.

Soft mumbles lifted to my ears every now and again, but each time the voices would come to a halt in our presence. These Hyven would murmur their submission by addressing him as

Lord Morven when we passed by. Their lord gave no sign, however, or at least movement, to acknowledge their presence.

Turning down yet another passage, the sound of heavy feet on stone came toward us.

"Ah! Lord Morven, you have returned." The voice was low and scratchy.

As I hung over Morven's back, I pictured an old decrepit man in my head, but for some reason the agility of the man left me wondering whether I was incorrect. From the sound of his footsteps, he moved too quickly to be an elderly person. His feet paused for a moment and then began to walk in the same direction Morven was headed.

"I see that you were successful," he rasped. I blushed, knowing that he was looking at my backside that was high in the air. I tried to adjust, but Morven lifted his shoulder into my gut and restricted my movement momentarily.

"Yes." Morven's voice never failed to chill me to the bone. I could feel the vibrations of his deep voice next to my body. "We were more successful than we could have ever dreamed." There was wicked joy in his words, and I feared dearly for Patrick.

"What do you mean?" The scratchy voice asked.

"We found *him*." Morven's words made the man gasp and stop walking. A moment later he took some quick strides to catch up.

"How? And where?" The man was so astonished his voice was almost inaudible.

"He was with them," Morven explained casually, "at that wench princess's wedding."

Frustration built within me by his degrading term for Nixie. He was so vile it disgusted me, but there was nothing I could do at the moment. My time with him would come, but not tonight.

"Do you think he's been there all these years?" the man who walked with us asked, curious. Morven fidgeted his shoulders in what I guessed to be annoyance.

"No, he's lived somewhere else. I just don't know where." Security filled my mind with the knowledge that the island was still untouched.

Both men were quiet for a moment. The pounding of their strong booted feet echoed throughout the corridors while I waited for the men to speak once more. I wanted the man to ask more about Patrick, to ask a question that might give me a hint as to where he was and what would happen to him, but he didn't.

"Is it ready?" Morven asked breaking into my thoughts.

"Wha-what? Oh! Yes, the mermaids finished it this afternoon."

"Good," Morven said, his voice still distant. "Take her there. I have some unfinished business to deal with." I quivered at his words, wondering what he meant by them.

The large hands I dreaded lifted me off his shoulder. I huffed loudly, glad that my belly was no longer pressing into my spine. Morven placed me on the ground effortlessly and I marveled at the idea of my weight being next to nothing for him. His overpowering strength made me feel smaller than usual around him.

With wobbly legs, my bare feet touched the cold hard stones. I winced when my weight pressed against the scratches in my heels, but was sure to keep silent. I swayed as the blood rushed to my head, and Morven steadied me with his hands on my shoulders. He reached for my still-restrained wrists and lifted my arms out in front of me.

"Here," he said, offering my bound flesh to the stranger merman.

"She's not unconscious?" the scratchy voice asked, surprised and a little angry. I wondered why it bothered him.

"I grow tired of your questions, Gell. Just take her and go," Morven snapped. I shuddered as his loud voice sent a shiver down my spine. For the moment I was thankful to be blindfolded so I didn't have to see the malicious anger in his eyes that I knew was there.

"Yes, my Lord," Gell said quietly as he took my wrists obediently. His hand was surprisingly firm and smooth, confirming my original thoughts about him being younger than he sounded.

Morven's feet retreated and my fear returned. Even though I hated Morven's presence, it made it so I was able to predict his actions. Without sight, I was left dependent upon this merman Gell. Maybe he would be gentler than Morven, but a sharp tug issued on my wrists jerked my whole body forward. *Then again, maybe not.*

After being blindly led and pulled down different halls, Gell stopped me and opened a door that sounded heavy as the hinges squealed loudly in the silent corridor. A strong musty smell reached my nose as I was pulled into the room. My senses heightened taking in the crackling of a fire and the wafting of food. Saliva built within my mouth, but I ignored my hunger.

Gell dropped my bound wrists and I wobbled stupidly while trying to gather my bearings. To my surprise, I felt a sharp tug on the blindfold behind my head and the tightly secured knot soon fell away. I blinked fiercely and tears tried to lessen the sting of the fire lit chamber. Closing my eyes and squinting slowly, I was able to adjust to the light and I eventually gained a clear picture of my surroundings.

A large bed stood against the wall with an ancient hand carved headboard. An ugly dark green quilt rested on the top of the thin mattress and matching green drapes hung beside the bed. Huge pieces of wooden furniture stood at attention against the walls throughout the room. Next to the bed was a large wardrobe that looked as though it could fit ten people inside, and on the opposite side of the room was a mirror that stretched from floor to ceiling.

As I looked at the barren walls, I felt trapped. With only one tiny window in the room, high up near the ceiling and barred with crisscrossing metal, an overpowering sense of being confined in a secluded place overwhelmed me.

With the sound of movement behind me, I turned to see Gell for the first time. His back was to me, but I could tell from his stature that he was as young as I had presumed. He was shorter than any of the other Hyven soldiers I had seen, but his body was still muscular. His legs were thick and solid and he had a wide strong chest. His head was buzzed to very little hair and a small scar adorned the back of his scalp. Dressed in all black like the other Hyven he moved without regard for my presence. When he turned around, he caught me staring and I looked down at the table he stood beside.

On the table that sat before the fire was a plate of food. There was a large chunk of brown meat and a hunk of what looked to be dry bread. Gell gestured to the plate, beckoning me forward. I moved cautiously while eyeing him. He stared back just as carefully, his eyes mirroring my own fear. I froze for a moment, realizing he found me dangerous. Deciding to test the theory, I raised my head with confidence and strode past him to the table. My heart was thundering inside my chest, but I refused to let him know my fear.

Taking my seat with a dignified air, I began to work whatever advantage I could gain from his hesitance. He fidgeted under my gaze, concluding my observations, and a bubble of hope built within my chest. Falling into my new role I waved a hand in dismissal and to my pleasure Gell turned around immediately and headed for the door.

Hope was building within me when I saw the massive wooden door swing to a close. Plans for escape were thrashing through my mind until I heard the telltale scrape of a key within the lock. With a loud click the door shut firmly, locking me inside.

Everything shattered in that one instant. All the tears, the anger, the fear, the desperate love, the pain. It all fell into a crumbling mess, into wracking sobs that shook my body while the still wet dress clung to my dry skin.

Shoving the plate of food forward on the table, I rested my head on my arms. My shoulders shook with each gasp of breath as I realized what had become of us. I feared for Patrick, yearned for him.

Still trembling with tears and emotion, I rolled my head to look into the fire. Wet drops rolled down the side of my face and onto the table. Something cold and hard pressed into my scalp. Curious, I lifted my heavy head to locate the cause of my discomfort.

There on my wrist was the bracelet Patrick had given me. Sweet tears trickled down my cheeks as I remembered his face as he gave it to me. Smiling, I touched the delicate stones and rolled them against my skin. The soft pearly white circles tickled my flesh and flickered pink in the light of the fire.

As I gazed at the bracelet, something strong returned to my soul. Hope. I had to hang on to the love that had given me this token. The love that was the only thing worth living for. The love that I felt for Patrick, love that I would rather die for than live without would pull me through.

With determination, I rested my head once more against my arms and closed my eyes. No more tears were shed.

26. Trapped

A week slowly inched by leaving me crazed as I paced the room back and forth, never stopping and always wondering what was happening in the rest of the stone castle. I never saw anyone other than Gell. Every day he entered the room and placed food on the table and then left without so much as looking at me. I tried to get him to speak, but every time I asked him something he ignored me and only hurried out of the room quicker.

The frustration I felt at being trapped, never knowing when this monotonous string of days would end, was like nothing I had ever experienced before. The lack of knowledge about what was going on outside my four stone walls made me anxious and I bit my lip until it cracked and bled.

A soft knock sounded on the wooden door.

"Come in," I said quietly, and the door opened with its usual loud whine. Not caring to look back, I continued to face the fireplace from where I stood with my arms crossed over my chest.

The familiar sounds of a platter being placed on the table clattered behind me. I could smell the freshly cooked meat and bread, and hear the water slosh into the crude wooden cup and a thud when the pitcher was placed once more on the table. Immediately the soft retreat of footsteps began.

"Gell?" I asked, a sudden thought reaching me. The footsteps stopped and I turned to look at the stocky young man. "How long will I be here?" I had asked the same question before and had never received an answer. It didn't surprise me when he turned to leave again.

"Wait," I called quickly and once again he paused. His face was uncertain as though he had been given orders not to speak to me. *That's it*, I thought. Morven must have warned him against conversing with me. Inside me, the anger which was growing gradually every day increased even more.

"Gell," I said slowly, trying to get him to respond. Trying a different tactic I continued, "Since it seems that I will be here for some time, could I get water for a bath and some clothes?" I motioned toward the now filthy lavender gown that I was still wearing. Over the past week and a half, he had provided a pitcher of water and rag for me to wash myself. I thought that asking for more might get him to open up. But Gell looked at my dirty dress for a moment and then turned and left quickly, leaving me more hopeless than before.

Disgruntled, I sat in the hard wooden chair. Was I going to be driven mad by this room? *Probably*. I had paced for hours the night before, unable to sleep. The fears of what Morven was doing continued to control my mind. Not knowing what his plan was or what was happening was more fearful than being in his presence.

Rapping my fingers against the wooden table, I chewed my lip once more and winced as I reopened the crack in the raw skin. Every part of my body ached for something to do, something to occupy my mind other than the constant pressures and worries of the situation I was in. The lack of action by Morven made me all the more stressed.

My gaze landed on the wardrobe standing in the corner of the room. Its presence annoyed me, every day I had tried to open it but the lock was rusted shut. With a loud huff, I crossed the room ready to retry my feeble attempts. This time I carried the dull bread knife from the table in my hand.

Reaching out, I touched the brass handle and jerked on the rusted lock. The familiar sound of grinding metal filled my ears. Frustrated, I stabbed the bread knife into the crease and pulled down hard trying to jostle the lock. It wouldn't budge.

With a cry of anger, I grabbed both knobs and placed my foot against the stubborn wood and yanked with all my strength. The doors creaked and moaned loudly, but broke with a shattering clang and I stumbled backwards to the floor.

The hinges on both doors squeaked as they swung back and forth. Through the dim lighting I peered into the wardrobe, trying to make out the shapes inside. Leaning forward, my face met the musty smell of ancient air. I scrunched my nose, but stood up to touch the clothing hanging inside.

The fabric was softer than I expected, and the dark pieces of wear appeared to be from the middle ages, like costumes out of a movie. Grabbing one hanger, I strained to lift the heavy article of clothing out of the wardrobe. In the firelight my eyes rested upon the dark cloak, taking in the size and intricate design. Swinging it over my shoulders, I found it to be too long, but very warm as it encased my entire body. Looking into the large mirror across the room I lifted the hood of the cloak, surprised to see how well the dark fabric covered my appearance and made me look more like a man than a woman.

Looking back into the wardrobe, I scoured through the other articles of clothing, but didn't find anything interesting. Everything in the wardrobe was for a male and all much too big for my use.

Squatting down, I turned my attention to the two drawers at the bottom of the wardrobe. Using the same amount of strength as before, I tugged hard on the top drawer and it grudgingly opened to reveal more old clothing. Riffling through the perfectly folded fabric, I found nothing interesting and turned my attention to the next drawer. This one was even stiffer than the first and after many jabs from the butter knife and pulling as hard as I could, it relented. As soon as I saw what was inside, I froze.

There was only one piece of fabric in the drawer, and as I pushed it aside my hand touched something hard. Moving what appeared to be an old shirt or tunic of sorts, I spotted something heavy on the bottom of the drawer. Squinting in the dim light, I reached in and picked up the object. It was no longer than my forearm and very light in my hand. Curious, I carried it over to the fire to gain a better look.

As the light revealed the object in my hand, I gasped and almost dropped it. My fingers were wrapped around the handle of a dagger that was in its sheath. Shaking, I pulled the blade from its sheath, revealing a glinting blade with a sharp pointed edge. I pondered at the presence of the knife in the wardrobe. Why would it be here? Wouldn't they have gotten rid of all weapons? All of a sudden certain words came back to me.

I found it strange that she had kept the knife in the room and within my reach. I gasped when I thought of the words and how Patrick had related them to me. My mind whirled. This couldn't be the same room. I spun around, hoping that this was not the place where his life had turned into such a nightmare. As I looked, only more things pointed toward the conclusion; the bed, the roughly furnished room, the medieval clothes, the dagger, and the window that was too high to reach all seemed to agree.

I flew to the wardrobe, hoping to find something in the drawer that would prove me wrong. I pulled the ruffled shirts and pants out. To my great horror I found the one piece of clothing that concluded my fears. It was a white billowy shirt and on the right shoulder there was a huge gash and bloodstain. I thought of Patrick's terrifying tale and the tears began to flow, filling my eyes and pouring down my cheeks where they hit the stone floor.

Hanging onto the shirt, I rocked back and forth. It was as close to Patrick as I could get, but the foreign smell of the shirt only reminded me of how far away I currently was from him. The feeling of doom as though I would never see him again crept over me and I tried to remember when I last saw his face. Just before the blindfold was placed over my eyes he had looked at me, more confidently and lovingly than ever before. Yet that was so long ago, and the sounds of the Hyven beating him in the cave were still ingrained in my mind.

Breathing deeply, I tried to regain my confidence and hope, but it seemed that the old bloody shirt had taken everything from me. I now knew where Morven was. He was turning Patrick into a warrior so he could have the power that he desired. He was finishing what his mother had started.

My mind conjured up pictures of Morven beating Patrick and I shuddered, still rocking back and forth while hugging his shirt.

With a shaky breath I pulled myself together. I was going to have to fight for what I wanted, and what I wanted was Patrick. I wanted him in front of me safe and sound. I wanted to see him smile when I told him that I loved him.

These thoughts replaced my courage. I was going to do all that I could to make it so, even if it meant standing up to Morven.

Looking down at the handsome dagger in my hand, I put it away. I couldn't let them know I had a weapon. The possibility that it could give me an advantage was enough of an incentive to put it back where I had found it.

Carefully, I placed the shirt and hunting knife back in the drawer and rehung the cloak in the wardrobe. The doors snapped shut with a click of finality and I returned to my spot near the fire, watching the embers fall as my mind ran rampant with the new information I had acquired.

Once more a soft knock rang through the room and I jumped. Usually Gell only came once a day. My heart sputtered, unsure of how to proceed.

"Come in," I called, hoping I sounded confident and not weak like I felt.

Gell entered the room, his eyes looking at the floor as always. In his hands he carried something dark and bulky. I was immediately curious, and then shock absorbed me when two mermen I had never seen before entered the room. They carried a large marble tub between them and hot water with rising steam sloshed within its confines. The mere sight of the water caused an immediate reaction within me. I wanted to slip into its warmth so badly. It had been twelve days since I had last washed and the idea was most inviting.

The two mermen set the heavy tub on the floor and the water slopped loudly. Without a glance toward me, the mermen left, shutting the wooden door noisily behind them. Gell, still looking at the floor, walked over to the bed and placed whatever was in his arms upon it. He moved it around and pulled out two bottles from inside the bundle.

Keeping his face downcast, he walked closer to me and offered with outstretched arms the bottles. I took them cautiously and his arms dropped to his sides. In one quick glance I realized that the little glass vials contained soap for my hair and body.

"Thank you," I said genuinely.

Gell glanced up at me, his youthful face confused. Never having had the chance to look directly at him, I was surprised to see a long scar along his throat. Remembering his scratchy voice, I concluded this scar was the reason for it.

"What happened?" I nodded toward his throat and Gell became self-conscious. He dipped his head back down. "Did someone fight you? Did Morven do that to you?"

My voice grew harsh as I spoke the last question, my anger building inside. Gell flinched in reaction. Slowly, he lifted his head once more and stared back at me.

"What happened, Gell?" I asked, surprised by my reaction to his past pain. Looking nervously from side to side, Gell opened his mouth to speak.

"I got in a fight a long time ago," he said, his raspy voice harsh and causing the hairs on the back of my neck to stand up. "I was foolish and paid dearly for it."

I nodded, not really sure what to say. He still looked very young to me. Then again, he most likely wasn't much older than me.

"I almost died, but the mermaids saved me." Gell half-smiled.

"Who did it?" I asked, certain it was Morven.

"The Lathmorian prince." Shocked, I stared at him in surprise. I couldn't believe Tunder was capable of something like this, but then again it was war. Gell's eyes were kindled with the fire of hatred, a look that I had seen in Morven's eyes too many times. My hopes fell: Gell was just like the rest of the Hyven—he was power hungry and wanted revenge.

"Oh," I said, not sure of what else to say.

Gell nodded again and then looked at me curiously. He unexpectedly turned around and headed for the door. The loud click of the key resounded in the chamber and I was once again alone. With a heavy sigh I looked toward the bath and began to undress.

The warm water rose over my body and a cry of relief passed through my lips. The water provided comfort and the luxury enveloped me. I remained in the tub until the water turned lukewarm. Regretting the end of my comfort, I hopped out of the old tub and shivered, looking around for something to cover myself with while my body quickly dried. A pool of water formed beneath my feet.

My eyes rested on the tattered and dirtied dress I had worn at the wedding. The color was no longer a vibrant lavender, but had faded to a dull ugly pink—bland and dank like the walls surrounding me. Looking at it off my person made me realize how much damage the trip to Hyvar had had upon it.

Beside the dress was the dark bundle Gell had carried in earlier. Reaching out to the large bundle of cloth, I unfolded a long, dark corseted dress. Lifting it up off the bed by the shoulders, the heavy draping skirt grazed the floor in a curtain of iridescent black. Knowing it was meant for me, I struggled my way into the gown, closing up the front of the corset bodice with a thick black string which wove between the two pieces at the front. The hard boning structure ended just above my chest and left me in want for more fabric. Black cotton rose from beneath the corset and stretched around the tops of my arms, leaving my shoulders bare.

Out of the corner of my eye, I caught my reflection and stared at it openly. The sight was odd and unfamiliar. The midnight black of the dress enveloped my body, and the hem grazed the floor while the bodice pinched in my waist and emphasized my chest. Once more uncomfortable, I shifted in the gown, wanting it to reach higher up in the front. Tugging at it did nothing, and I sighed heavily, knowing I must get back into the worn out lavender dress.

Looking down, I reached for the strings to untie the bodice. But just then the lock in the door clanged open and I whipped around to watch as the door swung wide, revealing the one creature I dreaded seeing.

His feet pounded heavily toward me, but his face was livid with anger and his eyes cold and harsh. I was frozen where I stood, blood pumping through my veins rapidly and my heart throbbing in my chest as though reminding me it was working.

Resting his gaze upon me, I shrank as far as I could into the dress. He looked at me as though I were something for his own pleasure. A blush like I had never felt before crept over my cheeks, warming my face while an embarrassment and anger of what he was thinking filled my mind.

"Trying to tempt Gell, are we?" he sneered, his lip curling up over his teeth in a quick movement. My eyes widened in fear. Shaking my head, I backed away like a scared and trapped kitten.

Morven surprised me by being the first to look away. His hand twitched while he pursed his lips and his skin was greatly contrasted by the all black garb. From the black boots to the black jacket, all of his clothing was richly made and perfectly cut. I could not help but realize how similar it was to the dress I now wore.

His hair hung loosely, as it always did. The dark locks were both beautiful and somehow terrifying in their pristine perfect color. An unintentional shiver rippled through my spine, but I kept my eyes on him and waited for his next move.

He snapped his attention back to me suddenly, but the hatred and malice which was in his face before was replaced. Instead he was calculating, pondering, wondering, looking at me with judgment. I got the feeling that he was waiting for me to react, but didn't know what it was he wanted me to react to. Again I waited, unsure of where to move or how to get away from him.

Slowly, like watching a droplet grow into a ripple, a tight crooked grin spread across his small lips. Their color was a deep red in the firelight while odd shadows flickered over his face. With careful steps he moved forward, and I braced myself for what was to come.

With each move my eyes flicked toward his dark boots that clacked on the stone floor. Gathering all my courage and gritting my teeth, I waited as he moved ever closer, his steps becoming quicker until he was before me. His mere presence caused me to fight the urge to run.

Cold, vice-like hands snatched my wrists and I bit my tongue to keep from screaming. I jerked back in response when he pulled me toward him, and he chuckled softly.

"You cannot run from me." His chilling words crawled upon my flesh. I tugged from his grasp again.

"Don't touch me," I said. My voice was weak even to my ears. Morven snickered at my feeble threat, a wicked sneer on his malicious face.

"What will you do about it, Marina?" He taunted and pulled me against his body.

I lurched back and pushed against him with all my might, but it was no use. His grip was firm and unbreakable. No matter how I struggled he held me fast, I continued to try and pull away.

His head came closer and the hard, tight red lips smashed into my own forcefully, nearly knocking me off my feet. Panicking in his tight arms, I squirmed and then, desiring escape more than anything, I took his lip between my teeth and bit down ferociously, surprising myself.

A muffled cry of pain reached my ears and the strong arms released me. I stumbled back, but regained my balance quickly and took my chance toward the door. Darting around him, I made it a few steps before his long fingers once more locked around my wrists. Reaching around, I scratched and clawed at his flesh, trying to pull his hand from my own. But once more he jerked me forward. This time I was ready, and I cocked my hand into a fist. With all the power I could muster, I threw my balled up hand at his jaw.

His head snapped to the side while a stabbing pain surged up my arm, but he recovered too quickly and grasped both my shoulders tightly. I could feel his hot breath on my face as his thumbs pressed painfully into my collarbone.

Meeting his eyes with a fiery glare of my own, I realized what damage I had just done. The malice upon his face was like nothing I had ever seen before; this was a whole new creature.

For a moment he stood there, his eyes boring into mine. But I gazed back just as ferociously. The feelings of fear were gone. At that moment I had no more fear for him. I knew that at some point the feelings would return, but right now I was too angry to feel anything but hatred for him. It was as though my body could only contain one powerful emotion at a time, and at the moment it was a scorching desire for Morven to be hurt. And hurt badly.

With a quick motion that caught me by surprise, Morven grabbed one of my arms and tugged me toward the door. My shoulder was thrust up at an awkward angle as he pulled me roughly behind him. His large hand reached for the door handle and it opened when he gave it a massive tug, finally revealing what lay outside of the room.

As soon as we stepped out the door, the anger I had felt inside dissolved and was replaced by a consuming dread of what was to come; somehow I just knew he was taking me somewhere very different than the room we had just left.

27. Dungeon

Through the door and down dark corridors I followed Morven's angry footsteps. My mind whirled over what I had just done. I had no idea where I was headed, but all I did know was that I would rather die than have him ever touch me like that again.

His footsteps thundered on the stone pathways. I stumbled along behind him trying to keep up. I knew that if I lost my footing, he would not hesitate to pull me across the ground. Concentrating as best I could, I made my shaky weak legs follow him and avoided slipping on the grimy stones.

We flew down staircases in a whirl of dark fabric. The skirt of the black dress flowed behind me and whipped out in a large circle every time Morven flew around a corner. As we plunged deeper into the castle, I could feel the air growing colder and thinner. Smells of dirty flesh and unclean clothing reached my nostrils. I gagged at the putrid stench and tried to breathe more through my mouth.

A dim light became visible at the end of the corridor we were descending. Morven strode toward it even faster while I tried to maintain my balance. The stones in this corridor were slippery, the walls oozing with salty, briny drips.

We reached the end of the hallway where a spiral staircase lit by torches plummeted steeply even deeper into the castle. I shuddered to think of stepping down the steps with bare feet once I saw the grime blanketing each step.

Ignoring the gush between my toes, I followed the creature who still held my arm tightly and pulled me behind him. My arm throbbed, but I would not give him the pleasure of knowing I was in pain.

The repulsive smell of rotting bodies and human sweat filled my nostrils. Bile built in my throat and I almost emptied my stomach on the floor.

We stepped down onto the landing and Morven jerked me forward violently, making sure I lost my footing. Without pause, he led us into a dimly lit, skinny pathway.

Rounding a corner, before my eyes, was a dungeon, a place of human desolation that I had only seen pictures of in a history book. Two overly large mermen stood guard at the gated entrance. I found myself wondering how their appearance did not match the fowl stench; they were well groomed, their clothing spotless and clean.

They expressed shock at our appearance, but straightened to attention and bowed slightly at the waist. "Lord Morven," they both muttered.

One of the men, who had pale blonde hair just long enough to reach his eyes, stared at me with disgusting desire. I recognized him immediately as one of the mermen who had been on the *Lady Maria* the night I was changed. His fierce grey eyes roved over my body, and I silently hated myself for ever having put on the black dress. Ignoring him, I turned my head defiantly and watched as the other merman unlocked the iron gate. Morven waited impatiently and strode past both guards once the gate had opened with a long and loud squeal.

He pulled me forward past many different cells that lined both sides of an aisle. Flashing glimpses of the insides of the cells revealed their emptiness. Some were spacious while others were cramped, but all were empty. The reality of being alone in such a place hit me like a punch to my stomach.

The aisle between the cells was like a horseshoe, curving inward to the right with large cells on our left. Thinking back to where we entered, I realized there had been two entrances. The other must have been for the other side of the loop.

Halfway through the horseshoe, in the middle of the bow, Morven came to a halt. I slammed into his side and slipped on the floor. He pulled me upright with a jerk while I bit my lip to keep from crying out.

Reaching into his pocket, he produced a key and squeezed it into the lock. He fumbled with the catch momentarily until it clicked loudly. The sound echoed against the bare, dripping walls. He opened the grinding gate and thrust me inside, throwing me to the floor.

I caught myself just in time as I hit the dirty stone floor. A groan escaped my lips, but I whipped back around to look up into Morven's face.

A flicker of a smile on his lips was visible through the flat steel, grid-like bars of my cell. But he stepped away wordlessly and stormed back the way we had just come. His strong pounding footsteps retreated and the iron gate that was the entrance to the dungeon creaked and then slammed with finality.

Tears threatened my eyes—whether from relief or fear I did not know. Sitting up, I tucked my chin against my knees and one tear fell down my cheek. A torrent of water followed, the one tear causing an avalanche of emotions to pour from my soul. I cried silently, letting the tears stream down my face on my slippery skin to where they hit the dirty dress with soft patters.

Taking a deep breath to relax, I shuddered and gagged once more on the awful smell. Choking on my own saliva, I spit it onto the stone floor.

Pressing a fist into my stomach, I refused to give in to the contractions in my gut. Feeling shaky, and my palms and head sweaty, I tried to stand, but fell down once more with a small cry. I regained my breath gradually, even though each inhalation almost overturned my stomach.

Just then I heard a soft movement and froze, holding my breath. Images of rats and mice that nibbled on flesh entered my mind and my heart thundered loudly.

The sound repeated and again I stayed still. It was a heavy drawn out brush, the dragging of something heavy across the floor. Goosebumps rose on my flesh, and my body began to shake as I tried to figure out where the sound was coming from.

I inhaled shakily, no longer caring about the disgusting stench. Frozen where I sat, my ears picked up every sound. And still the dragging came closer, but it was muffled as if blocked by something. I looked at the walls to make sure that there were no holes large enough for anything to sneak through.

"Hey." A low almost-grunt reached my ears, shocking me so much I nearly screamed out of fear. The dragging scratch filled the dungeon once more and I trembled.

"Hey." The word was spoken again, this time a little closer. The voice was low, scratchy, weary, and yet familiar. I conjured up a picture of a tired old man in my head; maybe he was in the cell next to mine.

"Hello," I said, my voice shaky and thick from tears.

"Lissie?" The scratchy voice asked, shocking me even further. The voice was worried and desperate, but something inside me recognized it. My mind whirled as I realized with horror who had spoken.

"Patrick?" I called just as desperately, and I crawled to the end of my cell up against the bars. I tried as best as I could to see into his, but could just barely make out the gridded steel.

"I'm here," he rasped earnestly. His voice was so foreign that it caused tears to fill my eyes. Thinking of what he had been through worried me even more.

"Are you okay?" I asked, knowing the answer.

"Fine," he rasped and then coughed loudly, his throat dry and cracked. The sound rattled in his chest. He hacked for a moment. "You're here now. I'm fine."

"Oh, Patrick," I said, and reached my hand through the bars toward his cell. "Can you reach my hand?" There was a low grunt and the sound of a body sliding across the ground. I closed my eyes and a tear ran down my cheek as I tried not to think of him painfully crawling on the floor.

I pressed the side of my face against the bars to try and see him, but I couldn't. A hand came into view and I grasped it quickly. His hand fell limply into my own and I struggled to hold up its surprising weight. We could only touch up to our wrists, but I was so thankful to be given even this much of him.

Rubbing his hand with my thumb, I reveled in touching him. I remembered the words he had spoken to me on the night of Nixie's wedding. The conviction of his love rang true, and more than ever before I believed him. I knew I could never love someone as much as I loved him.

"Patrick, your hand is freezing," I said softly and the worry increased, but I tried to keep it from my voice. His icy fingers held me tighter as a scratchy laugh poured from his lips before turning into a dry, cracking cough.

I cringed and brushed his hand even more gently, but something wet and slimy was on my fingers. Leaning forward, with my cheek pressed against the stone wall, I was able to reach more of him. The farther I went up his arm, the more damp skin and bumps I felt.

"Are you okay?" He asked. His voice was filled with so much love that I nodded at first, unable to speak. Then, I stupidly realized he couldn't see me.

"Yes, I'm fine." I heard him sigh.

"Where've you been? I was really worried about you." His voice grew terribly cracked at the end and I realized the effort that it took to speak was difficult for him.

"He put me in a room." I would not say Morven's name. "I've been locked in there this whole time." I paused and decided to carry on, giving him something to entertain his mind. He had been down here all this time alone; it was amazing that he hadn't gone crazy yet.

"I was actually in the room that Nerissa put you in." I paused, wondering if he would comment, but he didn't. "I figured it out from what you had told me. I don't think they've changed anything about that room."

"How so?" he asked, his scratchy voice sounding interested and slightly relaxed. I smiled softly to myself. If I could give him comfort by talking, then I would talk all night and day for him.

"The room still looked like a man's room and I found a bunch of your clothes in it." I broke off not wanting to tell him about the bloody shirt that I had seen. "Your old hunting knife, I found that, too."

"Really?" his voice was amused, yet still weary.

"Yes," I said, trying to sound casual. I stopped talking since I didn't know what to say anymore. The silence spread and I continued to rub his hand gently with my fingers. I wasn't sure, but I had the notion that this movement was making him relaxed.

"Why did he bring you down here?" his voice was hoarse and concerned. I hesitated before I answered.

"Well," I said sort of stuttering, "He forced me to kiss him and then I punched him." The silence grew long and then Patrick groaned angrily.

"What?" I asked, worried.

"Why did you punch him? You should've just let him kiss you! You cannot realize what—" He broke off with a loud cough that rattled in his chest. He was angry with me, that I could tell, but I didn't know what he would've me do instead.

"What was I supposed to do Patrick?" My voice came out more desperate than I had wanted it to. "Was I supposed to let him take advantage of me? To let him have me?" Cold silence met my questions and Patrick heaved a frustrated sigh.

"No, not that. Anything but that. I'm sorry," he said and I could tell that he was exhausted. We sat in the quiet just holding hands. I tried to think of something to say, but couldn't. He broke the silence first.

"Lissie?" he asked softly, his creaky voice splitting the silence. "Can you tell me some stories from when you were younger?" I smiled to myself, knowing I could finally give him something to soothe his mind.

"What do you want to hear about?" I asked, wondering what would interest him most.

"Anything that you want to tell me," he rasped and I grasped his hand a little tighter, afraid that he would leave me.

My mind sorted through different stories and memories that came back so easily. It was incredible to think that I was still on the same planet, in the same time period as the rest of my family.

After a moment I settled on a Christmas memory. It was the Christmas when I got my first pair of ice skates. It was one of my earliest memories, one of the few I had of my mother. Warmth filling my heart, I remembered Derek and Sean as they were when they were little. Still protective, but excited for me to learn how to skate.

My voice filled the silence, explaining everything in detail. The snow, the ice, the visit to see Santa Claus, my first attempt where I fell flat on my face. Each moment was precious in its own way, and without pausing I moved into other memories. No matter what I said, Patrick listened, never interrupting, but continuing to let me speak. I didn't know if he was even awake, all I knew was that if I stopped talking his breathing got louder and his hand twitched for me to continue.

At the end of one such story, I paused and waited for the twitch while I thought of something else to tell him.

"Thank you," he said. His voice filled with gratitude and affection I didn't deserve. In response I rubbed his hand. Once again silence filled the dungeon and I assumed he had fallen asleep.

"Lissie?" His voice made me jump with its abruptness.

"Yes?"

"Can you promise me something?" His words were weighted and serious.

"Promise what?" I asked tentatively, not sure where he was going with this.

"Promise me that you will save yourself if you have the chance." His voice was commanding, the request clearly sincere. "Promise me that if there comes a point when you think you can escape, then do it. I don't want you to even pause and think about me. I want you to get out of here."

My chest fell up and down as the reality of his words hit me like a blow to the gut. I realized what he wanted me to do, but couldn't think of actually doing it. Would I really be able to escape without him if I got the chance? I shook my head at the absurdity of it all. It wasn't going to happen, why would I need to answer him?

"Promise me. Please," Patrick spoke, his voice urgent.

"I don't think I can," I choked out, deciding to tell him what I really thought. He exhaled loudly as though frustrated.

"Look," he said, his voice sounding fiercer in its raspy tone, "I love you more than anything I've loved in all the years that I've been alive. You're the most important thing that has ever happened to me. Please promise me." His croaked plea plucked at my heart and water filled my eyes.

"I know," I said, the emotion overflowing in my voice. "But I can't leave you, I just can't." A sob escaped my lips and I reined in my strength to hold back the other sobs creeping up my throat.

"Lissie." He was frustrated and there was pain in his voice. "I'm not going to get the chance to escape. Even if I had the chance to I wouldn't have the strength to take it." He heaved a large irritated sigh. "Please let me have this one comfort. Let me know that you'll try to save yourself if you get the chance."

The sobs I was trying to hold back broke through my thin layer of strength. I gasped for air as my whole body shuddered over and over again. I nodded my head to agree to his request before remembering that I actually had to speak.

"I will, Patrick," my tear-clogged voice spoke in the silent dungeon. "But I'm going to promise you something: if I get out of here and make it back to Lathmor, I'm coming back for you. I promise you that. We will come and rescue you."

My voice had grown fierce at the end of my little speech, and a plan began to form in my mind. I could escape, somehow, someway, and if I got to Lathmor, Tunder would know what to do.

Hope, which had been abandoned, crept back into my veins. It felt like the sun might yet rise again; that Patrick and I just might be together. Determination came with this hope and I realized that I was going to do this, that it had to be done.

"Thank you," Patrick said for the second time tonight.

"I love you," I said, hoping it was enough to comfort him, and he sighed happily.

"I love you," he said dreamily and then added, "more than you know." I was going to reject that and say it wasn't any more than I loved him, but stopped myself. He was too tired to argue and needed to rest. I let my thumb continue to rub his hand and he gave a contented sigh.

Figuring that I would be sitting like this for a while, I moved to a more comfortable position. My back pressed against the flat, cold iron bars, with my hand still holding Patrick's. I rested my head against the stone wall and softly hummed a tune, lulling us both into the peaceful bliss of unconsciousness.

28. Taken

Slowly I came to my senses, the grogginess leaving me and replacing me with awareness of how cold and stiff my body was. Shivering slightly, I looked around. It was darker in the dungeon now; the torches that lit the aisle the night before, had burned down and were emitting very little light.

With a yawn, I moved slightly and stopped. My hand was still holding Patrick's, and I didn't want my movement to wake him. I could feel how icy our fingers were. I couldn't help but notice that his hand was colder than mine.

Biting my lip, I tried not to worry about him, but the rattling sound of his breathing only made me more fearful.

I let go of his hand carefully. I had no blood left in my fingers and had to shake them to get some warmth. Our hands separated and I felt a stickiness on my palm and fingers. Curious, I pulled my hand back through the square bars and gazed at it. Horror filled me as I realized what was all over my hand.

The dried red substance caused my stomach to turn and I began to see why Patrick was so tired. Desperate to know if the rest of him was so, I got to my feet with the help of the bars. My legs were wobbly as I stood and walked to the far end of my cell.

Worried about what I might see, I took a deep breath before I squatted down. I hoped that with the curve of the cells I might get a glimpse of Patrick's back or at least his arm.

Through the dim light I tried to see him, and it took a long time for my eyes to adjust. After a while, my peering paid off. But what I saw didn't help my stomach, but rather made it worse. I was able to see his arm, from his hand to just below his shoulder. Every area of skin was covered in some kind of bruise or cut.

Tears spilled over my eyes as I realized the pain that he had been suffering. Part of me knew that I should have expected this, but I had been too stubborn to really believe it before. The tears flowed down my cheeks and I crumpled to the cold hard floor. I sat there silently crying, thinking of how he might die.

Just then my promise returned to me; I was going to escape, I had to. If he was going to stay alive then I had to leave, and soon. Taking him with me was not plausible at all anymore. I had to get help immediately.

A new sound filled the dungeon. There were voices in the direction of the entrance. They were mumbles and I couldn't make out what they were saying. It was not until I heard the loud clacking and grinding of a lock that I realized someone was coming; whether for me or for Patrick I didn't know.

I quickly crawled back to the edge of my cell and reached for his hand.

"Patrick," I whispered and shook his arm. He didn't stir. "Patrick!" I said, louder through gritted teeth, and jerked his hand. He awoke with a groan. I felt bad for hurting him, but couldn't worry about that now. If I saved him from being beaten for talking to me, then that was enough for now.

"Listen, Patrick." I hoped he was able to understand me. "Someone's coming." The pounding feet were headed our way. "You have to move."

Silence followed my words and I was just about to berate him again when I heard a very soft moan and knew that he was moving. His body slid against the ground as he pulled himself across the floor. I sighed with relief and skittered to the back wall of my cell. If I was the only one with strength then I could play the part of innocence. I could lie and say that I hadn't spoken to him.

The sound of thumping boots came closer and closer and I realized that there was more than one pair of feet. My heart beat began to pound in time with the footsteps and my breathing accelerated.

Morven came into view first. Behind him were two other mermen but, not the ones who were the guards to the dungeon the night before. All three of the men stopped in front of my cell and stared at me. I glared back, hoping that I looked furious and not nearly as frightened as I felt.

"There she is," Morven said, the awful cold smile that he liked to wear present on his face. I just glared at him even more. I was shaking inside with fear, but refused to show it. Morven took a few steps back and glanced into Patrick's cell. I couldn't see his head as he tilted around the wall to look at Patrick.

"Good morning," I heard him say in a voice that made me furious. How could he still taunt Patrick after all he had already done to him?

Morven's head reappeared again after a moment and he looked at me. There was a burning glow in his eyes that I could not define. I realized that something big was going to happen in the next few moments, and that whatever it was it did not bode well for me nor Patrick. I hardened my expression and waited for what was to come.

Morven kept his eyes on me, but cocked his head toward the mermen next to him. The look in his eyes reminded me of my nightmare. I could feel the chill in my spine as I watched Patrick dying on the open shore. I could feel the touch of Morven's powerful arms around me, pulling me away from him. I swallowed hard, and forced myself back into the present.

"Take her," he said, and I impulsively pressed my back harder against the wall, wishing it would swallow me whole.

The mermen unlocked my cell and marched toward me. I didn't have time to think, my mind was all in a whirlwind. I sat there, breathing heavily, my chest rising and falling with each foreboding step they took.

The guard reached down and grabbed me under the arm near my armpit, just like Morven had done. I winced as he touched the area that Morven had made tender the day before.

I was yanked to my feet. My hair swished in front of my face and the black fabric of the dress got caught between my legs. My wobbly ankles felt like they couldn't support my weight, and for a moment I was happy to have the merman holding me.

The second merman walked behind me with a rope in his hands, and it was only a moment before my arms were wrenched backward and tied together tightly. All the while I glared at Morven, hoping that my stare would kill him. He looked back at me, unaffected, the grid pattern of the bars shadowed his face, making him appear more mysterious.

Something black closed my sight of him and the tight knot of the blindfold was secured over my eyes. My heart began to pound heavier. It was one thing to be handicapped without your hands, but without vision I felt completely dependent on those around me. My other senses heightened in response.

The merman who still held my arm shoved me forward. I stumbled, and for a second thought I would hit the ground, but his powerful hand jerked me back to my feet. He led me toward the open cell door.

Once through the door, the merman surprised me by tugging me toward the left. I had assumed that we were going to leave the dungeon, but apparently not. We took a few steps and then I heard Patrick's raspy voice.

"Morven, no." His voice was so full of pain that I had to bite the inside of my cheek to keep from crying. We stopped walking. I heard Morven sigh heavily as though this was all so troublesome to him.

"You know what?" Morven's voice was dead and spiteful, the hatred clear in every sound he made. "You have been less than helpful lately so you've left me no choice."

"No," Patrick said, his scratchy dry voice filling my ears. "You can't. Please, I'll do anything." He was pleading, but I was confused and knew that I had missed something.

"No," Morven replied, his voice as cold as ever. "You've had your chance and this *thing* is just a distraction to you."

There was the sound of sudden movement like someone turning around, and then Morven's powerful steps could be heard echoing off the dungeon walls. The merman jerked my arm painfully again and we took a few steps in what seemed to be the same direction as Morven. There was a loud groan to the side of us that I knew came from Patrick. Water filled my eyes at the thought of being separated from him again.

"Morven!" Patrick's loud yell reverberated through the silence and surprised me. I was not the only one who was jostled by the voice—the merman beside me paused momentarily.

"Morven!" Again the dry, cracked voice yelled angrily.

It was a frightening sound. I knew that it came from Patrick, but the voice was so foreign and full of anger that it terrified me to the core. There was a definite challenge in the voice; Patrick was furious. It brought to mind the few times I had seen the anger take over, when his eyes went blank and he became secluded. It was a fury that ran deeper than my understanding, anger that had been imbedded in him for the past seven hundred years.

We started walking again. The merman beside me seemed cautious, but I was too distraught to think about it. My heart was left behind me.

I heard a soft moan and wished that we could get out of this dungeon as soon as possible. I couldn't stand to hear anymore of his pain. It was ripping away at my heart piece by little piece.

"Lissie." I heard my name being moaned and tried not to listen to what else he had to say, but my ears strained over the pounding boots anyway. "I'm sorry."

The tears were flowing fast now. The desperation and defeat had been so evident in his voice. I stumbled even more and relied completely on the merman's strength. My weight didn't seem to bother him.

I heard the sound of a squealing door up ahead. It made the hairs on the back of my neck stand up, and my fingers became icicles. My senses were on complete alert. Something was definitely about to happen and I wanted to know what. The sounds around me became muffled and I realized that we were in a more enclosed pathway. And then a hand grabbed my head and bent me forward.

"Watch your step," the gruff voice of the merman beside me said.

I put my foot out tentatively and tried to find the floor. I leaned down a bit and realized that we were supposed to go down some stairs.

After about five steps we reached the bottom. I felt the merman straighten beside me and I followed his lead. We walked forward, and then all of a sudden he let go of me. I wavered in fear, feeling like the world was tipping and turning. A sharp blade cut my bonds, my wrists sprung free, and I heard footsteps retreat quickly and head back up the stairs. I waited for the loud squeal of the door closing, but it didn't come.

I reached cautiously for my blindfold and pulled it off my eyes. The darkness that met my pupils was almost as bad as the blindfold. I blinked, trying to find some point of reference or object I could focus on. I could see nothing before me and turned to see if there was anything behind.

A small sliver of light appeared in the darkness, I assumed that this was where we had entered. My mind was confused. Could I just go? What was happening? I stood there, frozen, unsure of what to do.

A soft rustle brushed upon the floor. My breath caught.

"Hello?" I asked, frightened. My voice was barely above a whisper.

Nothing happened. I waited in the silence, not sure of what to do. Looking back, I found the sliver of light and took a quiet step backward toward it.

Again the soft movement revealed itself. I froze, my blood rushing through my veins like never before.

Everything happened so fast. I heard the fast sound of a step and almost instantly something grabbed me from behind. A blood curdling scream escaped my throat.

Then, in the silence, a soft chuckle belonging to the creature I hated most filled the darkness.

"Perfect," he said under his breath.

I turned to look at him, but something hit me hard on the back of the head.

Everything went black.

29. Flight

A loud pounding thud throbbed inside my head. Trying to press it out, I squeezed my eyelids tighter but it only grew louder in resistance. Slowly, my mind grappled with what surrounded me. A familiar pain to my midsection brought back the previous moments in a flash and I opened my eyes quickly.

The sight was exactly what I expected. Morven's shiny black boots rang against the stone floor and my heart accelerated as I remembered the darkness, the fear, the sorrow, and, most of all, the cries of Patrick as I was led away.

Slung over Morven's shoulder like a rag doll, I watched as his feet ascended a staircase easily. For only a moment I hung in despair as I let the emotions of the torture Patrick had been through and the pain in his voice wash over me. But once Morven stepped into a dimly lit hallway, the floors cleaner than those down in the dungeon, I realized the advantage I had.

Lifting my head slightly, without shifting my weight on his shoulder, I took in our surroundings. Thinking I could keep track, I began to count the turns and pathways in my head, but they all looked so similar I began to lose track. Tears of frustration welled inside my eyes and rolled quickly into my hair as I hung upside down.

With each step of Morven's boots I could hear Patrick's last words to me. It was like an echo of desperation from his soul to mine. *I'm sorry, I'm sorry, I'm sorry, I'm sorry....*

Just as the despair almost consumed me, a sudden ghostly light flicked over us. I lifted my head, hope spurning in my chest. There was a window, a window filled with the most beautiful light I had ever seen. A doorway to freedom.

The window was small, and lonely, but it's very presence rekindled my desire to save Patrick's life. The ghostly light poured in, its direct source the moon, and my heart soared with joy.

With more concentration than before, I began to count the turns Morven made. With each turn I repeated the entire list in my mind and found that I could remember them all. Satisfaction throbbed through my pounding temples.

Morven mumbled as he walked, his movements agitated, but I was too concerned with the moves he made to worry about what he might be saying. His feet began to slow suddenly and then I heard the dreaded sound of a familiar creaking door.

The hope I had recently felt plummeted. Why had I been so stupid? I should have known he would bring me back here.

Pushing the door all the way open, Morven thundered into the stone bed chamber which had been my prison for the last eleven days. Lifting me off his shoulder unceremoniously, he threw me onto the overly large bed. I crashed into the mattress with a jolt, and a sharp pain shot through my head, but I remained limp, wanting him to think I was unconscious still.

He stood over me, his breathing heavy and violent. With all the control I could muster, I forced myself to remain still and not give myself away. Then he suddenly disappeared. His boots retreated and the door slammed with finality, confirming my returned state as prisoner. The loud crack of the heavy wood made my head throb in pain and I pressed a hand to my temples.

With a choking sigh I lay back on the mattress, careful to keep the huge knot on the back of my head out of contact with the bed. A sigh of frustration broke through my lips. Knowing the way out and not being able to obtain it was only more distressing. As I lay there, I thought of a plan, but everything relied on the door not being locked and there was no such way for me to get out.

Piercing through my thoughts was a mumbled voice. Sitting up with a jolt, my hair swung around my face, but my ears perked to hear more. I grimaced from sitting up so quickly, but hastened to listen for the voice again. I had never been able to hear voices inside the room before.

There it was again, muffled, but clearly a voice.

Slowly hopping off the bed, I crept forward toward the door. The closer I got, the wider my eyes became in disbelief.

Between the door and the wall was a small crack, a sliver of torchlight from the chamber outside.

With my breath caught in my throat, I wondered how it had opened. Thinking back I thought of the way Morven had slammed it shut, of the way he had been mumbling to himself. His distracted mind seemed to be on my side. A sly smile, like I had never had before, spread over my lips; I had the chance to do what must be done.

"It's all rather strange." I crouched down next to the door to listen, as though it would keep me more hidden from the voices that were coming closer. "Do you have any idea what he's doing?" Gell's voice was familiar to me, and his curiosity was blatant.

"Not really," a woman said, her voice soft and honeyed, smooth like slippery silk.

The footsteps stopped just outside my door. They began to speak in hushed tones now that their voices were the only thing in the corridor. I strained further to hear what they said.

"All I know is what Bolrock told me." There was a long silence while Gell and I waited for the woman to continue. "Marina was taken from her room the other night and put in a cell right next to Patrick." The way she said his name made the hairs on the back of my neck stand at attention. Something about the way she spoke of him made me fear for his life even more.

"Bolrock was standing guard when it happened," she said to confirm her story, but then a hard laugh escaped her mouth. "Do you know what he said? He told me that, like the old legends, he could actually feel her power." She laughed harshly again in disbelief. I bit my lip from where I crouched in the shadows.

"Then what happened?" Gell prodded anxiously.

"Nothing *has* happened yet, but I will tell you the plans." The woman baited Gell with her voice and I could picture him in my mind, so eager to hear her words. "Morven told Bolrock what he's planning. He's going to take Marina out of her cell, as though she is condemned. He wants Patrick to see her being led to her death."

My heart thundered, wondering just what motive Morven had behind all of this.

"But why?" Gell asked, clearly as confused as I was.

"Look," the woman began, sounding irritated as though Gell was wasting her time, "Bolrock has been at every single one of the human's beatings." I winced, remembering the bruises and cuts along Patrick's arm. "He said that no matter how hard they beat him, he wasn't giving in. That's why Morven has been so irritated lately."

"But what do the human's beatings have to do with Marina?"

"It's rumored that Marina and the human are in love." The woman whispered the words, her voice slicing through the dank hallway like a knife. My heart pounded heavily in response. "I was there to see it all in Lathmor. I was the one who caught her actually." The memory of the dark-haired, thin woman popped into my mind and shivers ran through my spine. Her name was Verna.

"Bolrock believes that Morven is trying to blind Patrick with pain. He wants to take away everything he has."

My breathing accelerated as I realized what had happened. Verna and Gell might be unaware that these events had already occurred, but I knew. *I knew.*

I had seen it unfold. I realized now that all of it had been a plan, a well-crafted plan. Morven had kissed me only to give him a reason to take me to the dungeon. It was a way for me to think him angry enough with me that I would not find it suspicious. Somehow he had known I would hit him.

My hands shook as I further realized what had just occurred. The reason I was put beside Patrick, the reason I was led away like a criminal, and the reason he had made me scream in the dark chamber was all for one reason.

He wanted Patrick to think I was dead.

Anger coursed through my veins as the treachery and awful horror of what Morven had done crashed into my mind with clarity. My plans immediately changed. I couldn't escape, not now. Patrick had to see me alive, he had to know I was still living.

I had to get down there, somehow, some way. I must.

Waiting in the darkness, Verna and Gell finally retreated. As soon as I could no longer hear their footsteps, I bounded to the dark wardrobe and grasped the heavy brass handles. Moving quickly, I pulled out the heavy dark cloak and secured it over my shoulders.

Reaching forward, I pulled on the wooden drawer and it slid toward me silently. Snatching up the solid hunting knife still resting in its sheath, I drew the hood of the cloak over my golden hair and slipped like a ghost over to the ominous door. Needing my hands to be free, I slid the knife into my corset. It was enclosed in a secure spot, but close enough so I could quickly grasp it if needed. Thinking of the blades I would be up against was almost enough to keep me from walking out the door.

I pulled the door open slightly, thankful that the small movement didn't force a loud squeal from the creaky bolts. When the space was just big enough to fit through, I took a deep breath and slithered into the flickering hallway.

Glancing both ways, I saw no one, but drew the cloak closer about my person for protection. I moved as quietly as possible, but my feet pattered loudly on the stones. Aches and sores from the night before protested, but I ignored them—the pounding and fear in my heart was of more concern.

Counting the passages carefully and whipping around corners with the black dress and cloak billowing about my person like a shrouding shadow, I finally reached the moonlit corridor. The very sight of the natural light sent a pang through my soul again. *Oh, to see outside these walls.*

Breaking into my reverie were the sounds of approaching boots. My heart rate escalated as I dashed to the first door I saw, hoping it would be unlocked. It let me pass through easily, and although I wanted to shut the door completely I was afraid the click would alert the intruder to my whereabouts. Grasping onto the handle with a shaky hand, I held the door as securely as I could. A small sliver of moonlight filtered into the closet and I could make out a thin glimpse of the hallway. With my heart hammering in my chest, I waited.

The feet approached and as their faces passed I saw who they were. I had never seen the mermaid before, but the blonde merman was the one guard who had looked at me so disgustingly the night before. He was the one I recognized from the night I was changed. Could this be Bolrock?

Their conversation was low and of no importance. I pressed a hand to my mouth to keep my breathing from being heard. In the shadows, I waited patiently for them to move along. A loud yell of alarm came suddenly from above us.

Bolrock and the mermaid stopped in their tracks right in front of my door. They turned to face the way they had come, their expressions as cautious as I was worried.

Pounding down the halls came the scurrying of heavy boots and through my small crack I saw Gell come flying into view around the corner of the hallway. He ran at full speed, almost knocking into Bolrock and the mermaid. With one strong snatch, Bolrock grasped Gell by the arm and brought him to a halt.

"Whoa! Slow down there, Gell," his voice boomed loudly.

"Let go!" Gell yelled frantically as he tried to tug free of the merman's sturdy grip. The tiny blonde mermaid laughed. Gell looked like a child between the two of them.

"Did I not just tell you to attend to Marina?" Bolrock asked harshly. My eyes widened.

Gell knew. My window of opportunity was gone. He knew I had escaped.

"But she's gone!" Gell's voice was loud and echoed in the empty hallway. Both merfolk stared at him as though he had gone mad. "Check for yourself if you need to," he said, shrugging off Bolrock's hand, "But believe me there's no one in that room. She is gone. She escaped somehow!"

"Go and tell Lord Morven. Now!" Bolrock pointed toward the end of the hall I had been heading to only moments ago. My pathway to the dungeons was cut off.

Without a word, Gell sprinted forward as fast as his stocky legs could carry him.

"LORD MORVEN!" he yelled, his cry echoing against the walls.

"Ressa," Bolrock spoke quickly, his words flowing in a stream of commands. "Alert everyone of Marina's disappearance. I will go and warn the guards. I don't think she's made it outside yet, but she is clearly more cunning than we realized. Shut this down before she makes it to the ocean. We don't want her reaching Tunder and his soldiers." A bubble of hope threatened my soul; were the Lathmorians just outside these walls?

"Yes, brother," Ressa said formally as she turned to run back the way she had come. Bolrock stood for a moment longer and then followed his sister out the corridor.

I would have thought that my heart would relax when they left, but it was thundering louder than ever before. I was on a precipice, a moment of decision in which I could fall one way or the other.

I could try and make it to the dungeon to let Patrick see me, but what were the chances that I would make it?

Or I could flee. Frozen where I stood, I tried to decide. It was impossible to think of letting him suffer my apparent death. What would he do? What could he be thinking?

Then his beautiful and yet achingly sick voice rose in my memory.

Promise me that you will save yourself if you have the chance, the memory said, pulling at my heart. *Promise me that if there comes a point when you think you can escape, then do it. I don't want you to even pause and think about me. I want you to get out of here.*

Nodding my head to myself, I knew what I had to do. Taking a moment to control myself and put my emotions aside, I wiped my eyes with an edge of the heavy cloak. One last deep breath filled my lungs and I threw open the door without caution.

Dashing to the window, my fingers worked furiously at the rusted latch trying to pry it open. But it wouldn't move. I pulled the hunting knife from my bodice and hooked it under the latch. With a resounding click it opened and I pushed the pane as far as it could go. Hopping onto the ledge, I didn't even glance at how far the drop would be before I jumped. Desperation pumped through my veins like never before, spurring me toward the freedom that lay in the churning ocean waters.

After a short drop, my feet hit the ground. I tumbled ungracefully to the packed earth with a thud, the cloak twisting about my legs. Getting up as quickly as I could, I threw the hood once more over my light hair and dashed to the shadows of a nearby tree.

The clouds were moving quickly in the sky, creating dancing patches of light on the wide open lawn. From where I stood there was a great distance to be covered without any cover from the moonlight. Throwing caution to the wind, and steeling my heart against churning fear, I dashed forward, intent to reach the shadows of the dark trees.

With each bounding step the same words resounded in my head over and over again. *Get to Tunder. Get to Tunder. Get to Tunder.* He would know what to do.

I reached the shadowy cover, but didn't slow my pace. Every moment I expected to hear approaching feet, the dreaded sound of someone chasing me. But nothing came. It was quiet. Almost too quiet.

Minutes passed and the sound of waves reached my ears. My nerves yearned for the water, but I slowed to a sudden halt at the trees' edge. The shadows still hid me from view. Glancing to both sides I waited, searching for any movement. Nothing pervaded my sight. Just as I was about to step out onto the rocky shoreline, a sound seared into my brain. Like a moaning roar, similar to the groan and rumble of an elephant, the sound grew to a deafening level. Squeezing my eyes shut, I covered my ears with my hands, waiting for the sound to stop.

The eerie silence that followed sent my fears soaring once more. The sound had come from close by, and it was all I could do to not give myself up in panic. Gazing along the shore, my eyes made out a form, a human form, standing waist deep in the water. His hands, which had been cupping his mouth, fell to his sides. He remained where he was, waiting.

His long hair reached his hips, just touching the top of the water. It blew in the wind as he continued to scan the horizon, moving his head from left to right and back again. His head snapped suddenly as his eyes focused on something in the distance.

Quicker than I could comprehend, other mermen and mermaids emerged from the waters and were standing with him. They all leaned in closely as he spoke, his hands gesturing in wide arcs as he pointed back toward the castle repeatedly. Their numbers were great; I lost count after fifteen and instead focused on what I would have to do.

I had to flee before they reentered the ocean, my chances were limited. How quickly they would be able to catch up with me was not something I wanted to take into account. Counting to ten, I breathed deeply and loosened the cloak. It fell into a puddle around my ankles and I took comfort in its warmth for one more second.

Squeezing my eyes shut, a silent cry spilled from my heart. *I love you, Patrick.*

Running as fast as I could I pounded down the rocky shore, the waves coming ever closer. Shouting reached my ears, but I didn't turn toward the sound. My focus was on the ocean. Small chance though it was, it was my only chance.

The water touched my toes. Ten feet away from me a body shot out of the water, and the shimmering flash of fins changed to clothed legs in a split second. Too horrified to scream, I froze, coming to a halt, but the person zoomed past without a further glance. To either side of me, the rising bodies of transforming mermaids and mermen shot past in gusts of short wind.

I watched them run forward, swarming upon the group of Hyven soldiers who had gathered only moments before. The bodies smashed together, blades shining in the moonlight. Both sides wore black. The fight was like a violent dance, where the partakers spun and sliced whenever there was an open chance.

Horror struck, I forced myself to move forward, to tear my eyes away from the ghastly sight. The water slapped against my ankles and then my knees, the dress tugged against me, catching into the current. With all the strength I could muster I pushed forward, knowing safety was somewhere up ahead.

"Lissie!" The voice was familiar yet more forceful than I remembered. "Get down!" Elik yelled over the waves and shouts along the beach. I tripped and slammed into the water with a loud splash. Water hit my face, but I knew I was not yet deep enough to transform.

Behind me came the sounds of running feet, and in one quick look I saw the long-haired merman approaching quickly. A scream gathered in my throat and I helplessly crawled backward.

From over my head, Elik shot from the water and transformed easily. His bare chest and back gleamed from sea water as he collided with the Hyven soldier. Their blades sliced at one another as they ducked and dealt each other blows. I stood and moved farther back in the water. The waves pounded against my back but I continued to move, cautiously now, making sure no one was following me.

A hand reached out and grabbed my shoulder; the scream I had built in my throat almost escaped my lips until a strong hand covered my mouth. I struggled desperately, but the arms were like a vice. A voice tried to reach me, but I could hear nothing. My only thought was to break free.

"Lissie, stop!" The voice whispered loudly in my ear, "It's me, Tunder."

I relaxed immediately and he let me go momentarily, only to grasp my hand in a tighter grip. "We have to go," he said and pulled me forward into the breaking waves.

Chest deep, we ducked under the water and my legs sucked together to form my fins. The thick dress billowed around me, but I reached quickly into my bodice and pulled the knife from its confines. Slicing through the corset, I shredded the disgusting article until I was able to break free. Tunder helped pull it off and he let it go into the water. Grasping my hand once more, he pulled me forward.

The dreadful sounds of fighting were not silenced under the water; instead the sounds were louder than above the surface. In the murky shadows I saw the twisting bodies of merfolk fighting one another. Their fins chased each other and swatted their opponents, while their blades worked expertly to cut and dice flesh.

Bile rose in my mouth, but I held it back and pressed forward, hoping Tunder would be able to protect me. The dagger in my hand gave me small encouragement for safety.

Shooting like a rocket in the night sky, a merman smashed into Tunder powerfully, pushing the three of us to the ocean floor. The surface was now thirty feet above. The growl of the merman made the hairs on my neck stand up, but Tunder pushed back against him, slicing his chest.

The merman backed away with a swift kick and sized up his opponent. His face was familiar. I realized it was Bolrock. A bubbling fury laced through my blood and I moved closer, my own lavender fins looking dismal and gloomy in the dark depths of the ocean.

With a grimace, Bolrock raised his arms in what could only be a fighting stance. His hands were held up so his blades pointed directly at us. Swallowing hard, I noticed that Tunder's arms were outspread. He was leaving himself open for attack in order to protect me.

In an instant, Bolrock rushed forward and Tunder grasped him about the middle. The two men struggled, groaning as they clawed for the upper hand, but they were evenly matched.

Go now! Tunder yelled, his merfolk cry making sense to my ears. I backed away, my fear too great, but the thought of what this Hyven soldier had done to Patrick made me halt. With a cry from my lips, I surged forward. With all the strength I could muster brought the blunt handle end of the dagger down upon Bolrock's head.

The thud shocked both mermen and they parted from one another. Lifting a hand to his head, Bolrock looked around blearily, unsure of where we were. Blood billowed into a cloud and he stared at it as though amused.

Not wasting time, Tunder reached for me once more and pulled me along behind him. I wondered why he didn't finish him when he had the chance, but I soon realized that Tunder was also bleeding, and bleeding badly. His shoulders were littered with cuts and gashes. He noticed my gaze.

Don't, he said when I stopped moving. *We have to keep going.*

I nodded, wanting to say something more but not knowing what.

Pulling up short, Tunder tugged us to the surface. I scanned the horizon looking for Hyvar; the distance we were from the island was amazing. I tried to comprehend how we had made it so far so quickly.

Arching his back, Tunder called into the night air. His voice was like the rumble of the long-haired Hyven I had heard earlier, yet somehow his voice sounded more powerful. Looking down at me, he jerked his head backward.

"Come on, we need to leave."

"But the others?" I asked, thinking of Elik.

"They are retreating."

"Won't they follow us? How will we get away? They will catch us, and they will kill us and then *he* will be left alone, *he* is all alone, and... and... I need to go back for him. I have to, he needs me, and, and—"

"Shh," Tunder soothed as he pulled me tightly up against his chest. "We can't save him now. You know that."

"But I can't leave him," I sobbed.

"Lissie, I need you to be strong right now." He separated us and held me at arm's length. He waited until I finally looked him in the eye. "If not for me, then be strong for him," he said solemnly.

His last sentence was like a question, asking me if I would be able to make it. I nodded and let him take me forward through the water. For one moment we turned back to Hyvar and then plunged under the surface and shot off into the darkness in the opposite direction.

The image of the thick sturdy fortress remained forever before my eyes; inside those stone walls was the man I loved.

I knew I would be back here. I would come back to save him, no matter what it would take. Tightening my grip on the dagger in my hand, I surged forward and followed Tunder's lead.

Epilogue

Two weeks had passed since our escape from Hyvar and every moment I was away from Patrick was like the scraping of nails on a chalkboard. The worry I felt was constant; I knew what he had suffered and was still suffering.

The days following our arrival on Lathmor were filled with a flurry of planning and scheming. Shaylee and Tunder led the organization of numerous attacks on Hyvar that failed. I learned that they had actually tried to infiltrate the castle four times while I was secluded in the old stone room. Their last attempt, the one in which I escaped, was only successful because of my sudden appearance.

Every time they left I waited in hope, but the result was always the same. Morven had the castle heavily guarded, more securely than before I had left. In the back of my mind I knew it was because he didn't want anyone to mess with his plans again. My hope of saving Patrick was growing smaller and smaller.

Just what Morven was doing to him was yet to be fully determined.

Biting my lip, I continued to stare out the Lathmor palace widow, waiting for the moment when the soldiers would return. My heart thudded heavily, hoping they would have Patrick with them this time. The last three attempts in the past two weeks had failed, but maybe something would go right this time.

A soft knock tapped on the other side of Kryssa's bedroom door. Spinning around, I watched the door open to reveal Shaylee.

"Are they..." She shook her head, ending my question abruptly.

Her worry was equal to mine; I knew her husband would be out on the front lines of the battle. His wounds healed quickly when we returned to the safe haven of Lathmor, and rather than wait to fully recover, he had continued to lead the Lathmorian soldiers to Hyvar.

"I just came to tell you that dinner is ready." Disgusted, I turned back to the window. How could I even think of food at a time like this? At a time when Patrick was probably starving to death no less. The image of his scarred arm passed before my eyes and I fought to dispel it.

"You need to eat," Shaylee prodded. "Trust me, it helps more than you would think."

Knowing she was right, I decided to appease her and walked out of the bedroom and headed toward the dining area. We stepped into the spacious room adorned with long tables.

Lathmorians lined the benches and many of them looked up as we entered. Some even nodded in our direction. Their hostility toward me had changed upon my return to Lathmor with Tunder. Somehow I had proved to them which side I was on.

Inching forward and ducking my head, I approached the long line of Lathmorians waiting to eat. The table of food was laden with all types of seafood. The sight should have been welcoming, but there was nothing within me to react to it.

Just as I stepped up to the table a door slammed open. "Princess!" A mermaid called from the entryway. Shaylee and I both spun around in response.

"They are back," she breathed heavily, her eyes flickering to my face. She quickly averted my gaze and I knew.

My heart plummeted, further tearing into pieces. Each time I hoped for his return and was disappointed, the gap in my heart only grew wider. Closing my eyes I tuned out the rest of the report, not wanting to hear the casualties or the number of injured soldiers.

Not reacting to anyone or anything, I left the room while I could still maintain control. My feet moved of their own accord and took me away from anyone, anything that tried to cheer me up. And yet, even though my soul had been ripped apart once more, there was still the hope I constantly felt inside. Somehow I just knew Patrick would be okay. He had to be. That part of me would never give up.

Gliding into a jog, I padded my way down a dirt path toward the cliffs that overlooked the ocean. Off to my right a voice called my name, but I barely heard it over the sea air.

Peering off in the distance I saw the large form of Tunder approach, his shoulders slumped forward in defeat. The awkward remembrance that I was not the only one mourning for Patrick's safety pervaded my mind. Too often I believed I was the only one who cared for him. Yet, before my very eyes, was a group of mermen who had risked their lives more than once to save him. My gratitude was poorly shown and the feeling of unworthiness swept over me.

Within the group of exhausted soldiers were Elik and Daggin. Both nodded in greeting, but didn't show more emotion than that. Their solemnity only further proved the seriousness of the situation.

"I'm sorry, Lissie," Tunder said upon approach as he met my eyes. The circles beneath his own shocked me. He was pushing himself to the limits—yet another sign of his loyalty to Patrick.

"Don't be," I said, shaking my head. "I know you're doing everything you can. I just wish there was some way I could help." The forbidden subject once more arose. At the beginning I had fought to help the rescue party, but my lack of defensive skills shot down my position immediately.

Tunder gazed off into the distance, his eyes shimmering in the orange sunset. "I'm afraid," he admitted in a soft whisper and I gawked at him. How was he capable of fear? "Morven has had so much time with him. I'm afraid of what he's doing to him." He knew everything: I had told them all that had happened—our separation, the night in the dungeon, and, most importantly, my faked death. All of it was enough to worry even the strongest of leaders.

I nodded as Tunder's voice choked. Reaching out my hand, I patted his shoulder and tried to comfort him in some way. Seeing his own pain was almost as hard as knowing Patrick was in danger. It made the reality of what was happening in the dungeons of Hyvar all the more real.

"I am, too," I admitted.

Tunder sighed heavily and turned back to face me. "We need a new strategy. I want you to be trained and ready. Next mission, you are coming with us."

The sudden weight of responsibility fell upon my shoulders, but I held it up gladly. Finally. I would be able to do something to help Patrick. The guilt I felt for leaving Hyvar without letting Patrick see me was growing larger every day. If I could only do something to withhold it, even for a moment, I would feel so much better.

"I'll be expecting you to help Shaylee and I plan the next attack. I know we asked you for information about Hyvar, but I am going to need you to go over it with us again. Every detail could be important."

I nodded, my posture immediately straightening. His standard of expectations was rising and I would meet them with everything I had in me.

He turned to leave, his strong gait loping forward with determination. I looked away, back over the ocean.

"Oh, and Lissie." I turned back to face him. "You did the right thing by leaving Hyvar. If you were both still there all hope would be lost. Now we at least have a chance." Not saying another word, he continued up the hill toward the palace.

I wondered at his words, knowing he was right. Part of me warmed at his heartfelt concern; in some way he had become a dear friend. They all had.

Continuing my trudge toward the ocean, the wind pulled at my loose, unruly hair. There was a chill in the air that would discomfort some people, but I found it pleasant in my jeans and sweatshirt and bare feet.

Reaching the shore, I found a large flat rock to sit on up on a cliff. The sandy beach spread out beneath my dangling toes, while the waves made a harmonic rhythm as they crashed upon the shore.

Looking down solemnly, I clasped my hands together. My eyes rested on the naked skin about my wrists. The bracelet Patrick had given me was gone. I had noticed its disappearance upon our desperate arrival in Lathmor. The sign was a bad omen for things to come, but I tried not to think of it in that way.

I sighed heavily at the loss of the gorgeous bracelet, the only gift Patrick had given me. Rubbing the place where it was supposed to reside, I looked back out over the sea.

I don't know how long I sat there staring at the waves, watching them as they crashed, rushed forward against the sand,

and then fell back again into the lapping waters, but after a while I noticed someone was beside me. I startled slightly.

"Sorry, I didn't mean to scare you," Kryssa apologized softly, her eyes squinting out over the ocean. The wind rippled her long dark hair while tugging harshly at the sweater she wore. It made her hair look as though it was moving in slow motion while the rest of her stood in real time.

"You're fine," I said, reassuring her that it didn't bother me.

"I saw Tunder. He told me about the new plan." I nodded at her statement and bit my lip. "I think it'll all turn out fine. So lighten up and look forward to the day when you'll see him again." Kryssa nudged my shoulder positively and gave me a tentative smile.

Shaking my head, I squinted into the wind once more. "I'm scared," I admitted, the emotions making my throat thick. "I'm afraid for him. For what is happening to him. But most of all I am afraid he's gone. What will I do if he is?" The very thought of living in a world where he was not also breathing sent a shard of ice through my heart, physically painful to the point of having to concentrate on breathing in order to regain my composure.

Kryssa didn't speak. Instead she picked at the weeds growing beside us. Her fingers tugged them up from the ground, exposing their weak little roots as she ground them between her fingers.

"You'll learn to go on by yourself," she said softly and I gaped at her, shocked she would say something like that to me. How could she say that to me after I had just confessed how forlorn and afraid I was without Patrick?

"I know what you're feeling, Lissie." Her eyes softened and she closed them for a moment. "It's a pain that starts in your heart and spreads to every part of your body. It makes you feel hopeless and doomed, and the world holds no more joy."

I stared at her, wondering how she knew. How could she so easily describe every feeling I felt?

Suddenly it all fell into place. The reasons for her being so alone, for her behavior toward Elik all made sense.

Seeing my understanding, she nodded and once more turned back toward the ocean.

"His name was Wyeth." A small smile crept across her face as she said his name. "We grew up together and fell in love as we got older. He was my whole world." Tears pushed into my eyes. I knew where the story ended, and didn't want to hear it. "After we were engaged, the Hyven attacked. And he was severely injured in the battle." A tear slipped quickly off her cheek and I bit upon my shaky lip as I listened to her words.

"He died slowly in my arms a couple of nights after they brought him home." Kryssa's tone changed; it was stronger and more confident. "He was so wonderful to me and not a day has gone by that I haven't thought of him."

She breathed a heavy sigh and turned to look at me, her eyes still showing the signs of pain and emotion.

"All I'm saying is that you need to hope." Her voice was convincing. "Every shallow breath that Wyeth took when he was dying was like a blessing. As soon as they brought him back they told me that he wasn't going to live. Once I accepted that fact, I was able to spend the last few moments with him, reassuring him of my love.

"But you have the chance to see Patrick again, you just need to hope for the best. Whether or not you'll see him again, you know he loves you and that he's doing everything he can to stay alive for you." Her words had a profound effect upon my outlook.

"Think of what you can do to get to him again," she concluded. "Rather than what you would do without him."

"I will," I said, my words drifting off into the breeze. She smiled and wrapped her arm gently around my shoulders to give me a light squeeze.

"What do you say we start practicing your defensive skills?" She quirked an eyebrow and got to her feet without saying another word.

Knowing I would follow her, I took a moment to gather my breath. The road I was headed down was unlike anything I had ever done before. Yet, for the first time since leaving Hyvar, real hope filled my veins. I could see the future and Patrick was still in it.

Rising to my feet I adjusted the hunting dagger that hung on a belt beside my hip and began to move back up the hill toward the castle.

Reaching the crest of the hill I glanced over my shoulder, taking in the bright warm colors spreading across the horizon. Looking upon them a feeling of hope swelled within my chest.

But just as I turned to finish my walk, I noticed a cloud gathering speed.

A storm cloud surged forward to turn the bright warmth into darkness.

COMING SUMMER 2015

The second installment of the DROPLETS trilogy

Ripples

MEAGHAN RAUSCHER

Prologue

It felt wonderful for the first time in days he was able to relax. The contact was exactly what he needed. For too long he had been worried. His every thought was now focused on her. For her, only for her, was he able to endure.

He listened to her voice; it rose and fell in a perfect rhythm as she told her stories. Images formed in his mind as he tried to comprehend the pictures she painted. This was what he'd wanted all along.

Her thumb rubbed the back of his hand. He knew that she could feel the stickiness, the blood that had crusted and dried over his flesh. And yet, she didn't comment. She was selfless, comforting him in his time of need and not asking him what he'd been through.

Leaning heavily, he rested his head against the stone wall. His arm, the one she touched, was bent at an odd angle. Painful, but nothing like the cracks of the whips that still rang in his ears. Just knowing she was safe, knowing she was alive, was enough to give him the strength to endure; this was relief in his greatest moment of need.

Her voice came to a stop. He knew that she was waiting for his hand to twitch, his signal for her to continue, but he didn't move. Instead, he thanked her. There was something he must tell her, he needed to tell her. She *had* to understand.

He said her name and she jumped. Her involuntary movement jostled his hand. He adjusted slightly, the metal bars of his cell cutting into the wounds on his back. The thin, shredded fabric of his shirt did little to protect his skin from irritation.

She replied, beckoning him to speak.

His dry lips cracked when he asked, "Can you promise me something?" His voice sounded wrong to his ears. It sounded deeper, crustier, older—nothing at all like how he used to sound.

"Promise what?" she asked. Her voice was cautious, it seemed and he knew she would resist what he was asking her to do. He himself would never be able to do it. But she was stronger.

Gathering himself, he spoke clearly. "Promise me that you will save yourself if you have the chance. Promise me that if there comes a point when you think you can escape," his voice broke, "—then do it. I don't want you to even pause and think about me. I want you to get out of here."

She was silent. Her thumb no longer moved over his skin and the loss of it left a hollow feeling in his stomach. But he wanted her to understand. He always knew that something like this was going to happen to him. Ever since that day, hundreds of years ago, on the beaches of England. This was his purpose, but it didn't have to be hers.

"Promise me. Please," he felt as though he was begging.

"I don't think I can," she said slowly and his heart sunk. She had to know that this was the only way he could keep going. He exhaled, visibly frustrated and desperate.

"Look, I love you more than anything I've loved in all the years that I've been alive." He knew he sounded weak, croaking through his dry throat, but he didn't care. All he worried about was her. "You're the most important thing that has ever happened to me. Please promise me."

"I know. But I can't leave you, I just can't," she said with a sob. He hated to be the cause of her sorrow. It hurt him, almost as much as the whips that battered his flesh daily.

"Lissie," he said softly, quietly pleading for her to understand. "I'm not going to get the chance to escape. Even if I had the chance, I wouldn't have the strength to take it." He inhaled deeply. "Please let me have this one comfort. Let me know that you'll try to save yourself if you get the chance."

"I will, Patrick," she said through tears. He could hear the deep emotion in her voice. "But I'm going to promise you something: if I get out of here and make it back to Lathmor, I'm coming back for you. I promise you that. We will come and rescue you."

There was a passion in her voice that lifted his heart. She still cared for him so much, even though at times he wondered why. Here she was saying that she would come back and even though he so desperately wanted to accept it, he fought against the hope trying to grow in his chest. He wasn't getting out of here, but he would endure. Knowing that she would keep herself safe, knowing that she was going to try and escape, made him feel more at ease than he had felt in weeks.

"Thank you," he said.

"I love you," she said softly, and in that moment he recalled that image of the first time he saw her. The roundness of her face, her bright eyes, and her blonde hair rippling in the wind tore through his mind. There she was again. That memory of the first time he had seen her, sitting on the hill with the sunset, was what he could hold onto. She was exactly what would get him through this.

He sighed again, contently this time. "I love you," he said as he leaned his head against the wall more heavily. "More than you know," he added.

His swollen eyes closed, feeling as though they were sealed together, but he didn't mind. For the first time since he had been separated from her he felt as though he could go on. It was the knowledge of her even being alive that brought him this comfort.

As long as she was breathing, he could keep going.

As long as she was safe, he would find the strength to carry on.

As long as she was alive and his, he could endure…

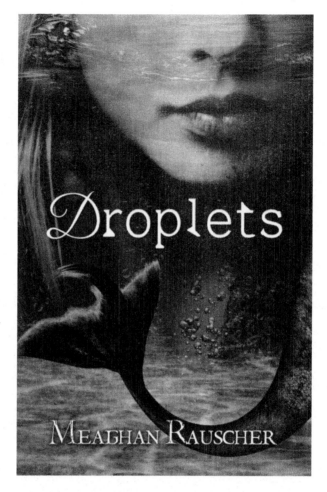

For all the latest DROPLETS information follow:
•Twitter @DropletsSeries and @MeaghanRauscher
•Facebook: facebook.com/dropletsseries
Official Author Website:
•discoverexplore.wix.com/meaghanrauscher

Meaghan Rauscher graduated from the University of Georgia with a Bachelor of Arts degree in English. She currently lives in Augusta, GA with her family where she continues to write. DROPLETS is her debut novel and will be followed by two sequels to complete the series.

Find Meaghan on twitter at @MeaghanRauscher to get all the latest information on DROPLETS and the release of DROPLETS sequel, RIPPLES in the summer of 2015.

Author website: discoverexplore.wix.com/meaghanrauscher

CPSIA information can be obtained at www.ICGtesting.com
Printed in the USA
LVOW05s2257180815

450690LV00011B/281/P